THE DEVIL TAKES HALF

THE DEVIL TAKES HALF

LETA SERAFIM

Coffeetown Press
PO Box 70515
Seattle, WA 98127

For more information go to: www.coffeetownpress.com
www.letaserafim.com

Cover design by Sabrina Sun

The Devil Takes Half

ISBN: 978-1-60381-965-7 (Trade Paper)
ISBN: 978-1-60381-966-4 (eBook)

Library of Congress Control Number: 2014935756

Printed in the United States of America

For Philip

Acknowledgments

The following people contributed to the writing of *The Devil Takes Half*: first and foremost, my husband, Philip Evangelos Serafim, and my children, Amalia Serafim, David Hartnagel and Annie and Yiannis Baltopoulos. Also my parents, John and Ethel Naugle. Without their encouragement and tireless support, this book never could have been written.

Thanks also to my first readers: Artemis Gyftopoulos, Nancy-Nickles Dawson, Flora Kondylis, Linda Rosenberg Brown.

My thanks to my agent, Jeannie Loiacono, and my wonderful friends at Coffeetown Press: Emily Hollingsworth, Jennifer McCord, and Catherine Treadgold.

CHAPTER 1

Under every stone, a scorpion sleeps.
—Greek proverb

THE DAY WAS hot and the mules were stubborn. The trail ahead rose in a series of sharp curves up the scarred face of the hill. Sitting sidesaddle on the wooden frame, the American shifted his weight and looked down. He could see the village of Campos receding in the distance and beyond it, the narrow strait that separated the island of Chios from Turkey. The mule slipped on the gravel and the American grabbed the edge of the saddle and hung on. The saddle appeared to be built of orange crates and had proven to be a tortuous ride. A swallow dipped and soared over the empty expanse of rock. The sky was pale blue, slowly whitening as the sun rose higher. The American wiped his brow with his sleeve.

"How much farther?" he asked Vassilis, the Greek in the lead. The man shrugged. "Half a kilometer. Maybe more."

As they neared the crest of the hill, the ground underneath shifted, the gravel littered with pieces of broken clay that crunched under the hooves of the mules. The American studied the ground as closely as he dared without losing his mount. "Shards," he said. "She was right." *Though not about the mules*, he thought ruefully. *No, the mules had been a mistake.*

"You have to arrive on horseback," she'd told him. "To get a sense of the site. How protected it is. The view's amazing, you'll see." But there'd been no horses, only mules. Weary, irritable mules that drew clouds of flies that bit. He saw now that he could have driven most of the way and walked the rest. But driving was not Eleni's way. She believed in total immersion. Live as the ancients had. She'd probably frolic with the Minotaur if a Minotaur was to be had.

He and Vassilis climbed steadily upward. A few moments later, the Greek shouted at the mules and drove them hard across the silent terrain and up the far side of the hill. The path rose steeply here, traversing a narrow ridge that served as a bridge to another, more isolated crag. It was dominated by the massive walls of an old monastery. As they neared the entrance to the citadel, his mule whinnied and pawed the ground. The shards were heavier here, forming a thick layer that shifted uncertainly as they made their way forward. Towering above them, the gray basalt walls cast a long shadow over the landscape. "A fortress fast," the American muttered, turning in his saddle to get a better look. The base of the monastery was made up of blocks of chiseled stone, two to three meters in length, of finer quality and workmanship than the upper reaches. It appeared to be built on a shaft of lava, part of the eroded crest of the mountain. The builders of the monastery had incorporated the lava into the construction of their citadel, outlining the jagged edges of the stone in white and dotting them with crosses. Another blackened wave of lava formed the ramp up to the entrance. The door was original—bronze, from the look of it—studded with intricate carvings and disintegrating metalwork made of copper. A round porthole was cut high in the metal near the top of the door.

Holding the reins while the American slid off, the Greek climbed down from his mule and led the animals into a grove of eucalyptus trees, where he tethered them. Dusting himself off and quickly making his way to the door, the American ducked his head in the wind. It wasn't locked, and they entered a stone passageway about four meters long.

Beyond it was a vast courtyard, paved with black and white pebbles. The pebbles were arranged in crude patterns: dolphins and fish, boats and anchors. A small chapel stood at the center of the courtyard next to an ornate marble well. The frieze above the door of the church was unlike any the American had ever seen. Instead of Byzantine saints in postures of piety and devotion, this one was painted with crude images of demons setting humans aflame with burning torches. The well, too, was unusual. A low marble pool, it had a row of columns chiseled around the base. Each of these columns was surrounded with images of writhing snakes, their carved heads emerging from the rock, poised with their fangs bared as if to strike. Interspersed between the columns were hammered metal plates, etched with what looked like waves. On closer inspection, the American realized it wasn't water he was seeing, but flames—flames consuming masses of naked men and women.

The Greek removed the cover of the well and splashed some water on his face. Snakes and flames. *Odd motifs for a monastery*, the American told himself. Suffering without redemption. Hieronymus Bosch.

"What's the name of this place?" he asked.

"Profitis Ilias. In Greece, they always build for him on the highest place."

"Profitis Ilias," he repeated, remembering a conversation he'd had with Eleni Argentis. "Elias. Helios. The Greek word for sun." Chances were good this place had once been a shrine to Apollo. In fact, Eleni had told him some of the older churches still had icons of the prophet driving a blazing chariot across the sky. It was her theory that what had been sacred ground in ancient times remained so, well into the Christian era. He'd argued with her, saying she had no proof.

"It says in the Bible that Elijah rose to heaven in a flaming chariot. Perhaps the early Christians just copied that," he'd said.

"You don't understand," she'd replied. "They always built for him on mountaintops, exactly as they did for Apollo. It's a continuation, a living link with the past. They exist all over Greece. Villages in the eastern islands have carnival celebrations that echo pagan Dionysian reveries. The funeral dirges the old women sing in Mani, the *miralogia*, predate Homer. They still hang blue stones on infants to ward off the *matia*, the evil eye, a custom that's one of the oldest on the planet. It's like your writer William Faulkner says: 'The past is always with us. In fact, it isn't even past'. Nowhere is this more true than in Greece."

The American smiled at the memory. "That's what you think," he'd answered. "You've never been in Mississippi." But she had been right. In fact, they'd recently sent teams out to interview villagers in Crete to record their stories and legends in hopes of gaining new insight into the world of Theseus and the Minotaur.

There was no sound.

He looked around. "Where is she?"

"Down in the fields," the Greek said. "Beyond the walls."

"Show me," the American said.

Vassilis shook his head. "First, we see the priest, Papa Michalis."

A group of buildings were constructed around the perimeter of the courtyard. The one behind the chapel had a cross carved on the stone lintel above the door. The Greek knocked twice there. "Papa Michalis?" he called.

"Enter."

After the brightness of day, it took the American a few minutes to adjust to the darkness. A long stone table dominated the space, surrounded by benches hewn from the same pale limestone. Frescoes illustrating the life of Christ, the miracles of the loaves and the fishes, the raising of Lazarus, were painted on the walls. "An old refectory," the American said to himself. "The monks' dining hall." The pale blue ceiling was very high and had gold stars painted across it. The walls were crumbling from age and water damage, and the air in the room smelled of mildew. An elderly priest was sitting at the far end of the table.

He rose to greet them. "Vassilis," he said, clasping the Greek on the shoulder. "How is your family?"

"Praise God, we are well."

"Your journey was uneventful?"

Vassilis gave a rueful laugh. "A mule is a mule, Father."

The priest motioned for them to join him at the table. "Well, you're here now. Sit. Sit." He was a small man, birdlike in his motions, neat and self-contained. His hair was white and looked to have been recently trimmed, his beard clipped to a point, like a Spaniard's in the time of Goya. He was wearing a blue cassock and heavy orthopedic shoes. A ring of keys dangled from a ring on his leather belt and jangled as he moved. His watch was modern as was the Palm Pilot he'd been consulting when they came in. He shook hands with the American, his brown eyes watchful, wary even, and he gave the impression of total alertness, like a gazelle that had caught the scent of a predator.

"How do you do," he said in careful English. "Welcome to Profitis Ilias."

"Thank you, Father," the American replied.

"I believe you are our first American."

"I'm not surprised. This place is pretty well hidden." He guessed the monk was well over 75 and foreign-educated. Strange to find such a man here, on a mountaintop within a stone's throw of Turkey.

The priest in turn studied his companion. The American was deeply tanned with a loud, avuncular manner. Athletic probably, judging by the muscles in his calves and forearms. American, yes, the perfection of his teeth and the faintly condescending manner were unmistakable. One of those who fancied himself an explorer, who'd climbed Mount Kilimanjaro and visited Patagonia. *If they're so worried about terrorists*, these people, the priest thought, *they need to lower their voices and lose this habit of theirs of taking everything they need with them and thinking they need so many things*. Yes, only an American would think he needed mirrored wraparound sunglasses and khaki shorts with pockets inside pockets and a cellphone attached at the waist. Or a hat like an Australian soldier's, pinned up on one side, a hat this man had yet to remove. The priest shook his head. *An old man who thinks he's boy.*

"Profitis Ilias is well disguised," he said. "The mountains hide its secrets well." He bowed slightly. "I am Papa Michalis, Professor Alcott. I am pleased to finally make your acquaintance."

The man gave him a sharp look. "How do you know my name?"

"Eleni Argentis has talked of nothing but your visit for weeks." He unhooked his ring of keys and gave them to Vassilis. "You will take him down to the site. She and Petros are usually there at this time of day. Go the back way."

Vassilis nodded. He opened the door and stepped back out into the sunlight. "Come," he told the American.

"Kyria Papoulis is here and she will prepare dinner for us," the priest called after them. "Take as long as you need. You can eat whenever you like."

Vassilis led the American across the courtyard and down a set of stairs near the back wall of the monastery. He unlocked an iron gate and pushed it open. The door groaned eerily in the silence. "Shorter this way," he said.

The American followed him through a short tunnel cut in the rock. "When was this built?" he asked.

"Eighteen twenty-two," the Greek replied and drew a line across his throat.

The American swore under his breath. Was there no place on this island the Turks hadn't bloodied? In every church he'd visited, some old crone had paused in her sweeping to point out the scarred patches on the floor, claiming they were bloodstains, talking about the massacre as if it had happened yesterday. He'd heard the story on four separate occasions so far and he'd only been on the island two days. Thousands slaughtered or sold into slavery by marauding Turks in the spring of 1822. Stirred by the tragedy, Delacroix had even painted it. There was a reproduction at his hotel. It was a gruesome work. Genocide clothed in nineteenth-century dress, the Turks prancing around in velvet slippers and fezzes, the dead Chiots piled up at their feet. In spite of the stories, the American remained skeptical. Still, the evidence of the skulls stacked up in the corners of the churches was hard to deny, especially the small ones, the children's, as were the ruined villages, abandoned on the hillsides.

He touched the wall of the tunnel. The workmanship was impeccable. The square stones fit together seamlessly. Narrow openings at the top let in light, and the air was surprisingly fresh. Alcott doubted it had been built in the nineteenth century. More likely by the Romans, who'd used it as an aqueduct. Eleni had been right to look here. He hurried after Vassilis. They walked for a few minutes in silence. There was no door at the end of the tunnel, only a rough opening in the rock. The American looked back. The tunnel was well hidden, the entrance just a shadowy cleft in the lava.

"Over there, they are digging." The Greek pointed to a small plateau in the distance. The American could see the plastic tenting strung up over a grid of trenches dug in the earth. The Greek stood and watched from above as Alcott made his way down to the dig site. It was a treacherous climb. The loose gravel and debris made the ground slippery, and by the time he'd reached the clearing, a red powdery dust caked his shoes and hands. Cicadas buzzed in a forgotten olive tree and the air was hot and still.

The view was astounding. From where he stood he could see deep into the interior of Turkey. Far below, boats crisscrossed the channel that divided the two countries, their wakes white in the dark water. Whoever had selected the site in ancient times had feared their neighbors and wanted to keep an eye on them. Bordered on all sides by a series of skeletal peaks, it was as well-hidden as Machu Picchu.

He walked toward the plastic tenting, moving carefully between the trenches dug in the ground. He paused, fingering one or two of the shards left out in an open box. "Old, old," he muttered. "Damn her."

"Eleni," he called.

There seemed to be a surprising number of flies everywhere, whining in the heat. "Eleni," he called again.

Where was her assistant, the village boy who was helping with the excavation? He jumped down and inspected the dirt on either side of one of the trenches. Layers of white material were interspersed throughout the clay. He pried out a piece. It appeared to be part of an amphora, the handle still in place. He ran his fingers over it tenderly before placing it back where he'd found it and climbing out of the trench. He looked around him again, disturbed now. About ten feet off, he could see the beginnings of a third trench and walked toward it. There were more flies there, and tubes of polymer filler and archeological equipment were scattered everywhere. "Eleni?"

As he peered into the trench, he dropped to his knees. "Oh, God."

Choking, the American tried to rise and stumbled backward. "Vassilis," he screamed. "Oh, God. Vassilis."

CHAPTER 2

What man went to the Land of the Dead with more than one coin obolos?
—Greek Drinking Song

NIGHT WAS FALLING as Yiannis Patronas, the chief officer of the police, climbed into his old Citroen and set off for Profitis Ilias, the distant hills purple in the fading light. He cursed as he drove, honking and beating the steering wheel with his hand when the car in front of him stalled. He dreaded the trip up the mountain to that wasteland of a monastery, especially at this hour. The path would be treacherous in the dark, the wind threatening to pull him off the peak. Normally he would have ignored the call, but there had been something in the old man's voice. The priest had sounded badly frightened.

He could smell smoke billowing from the exhaust pipe of the Citroen, the engine burning oil by the bucketful. He desperately needed a new car and had repeatedly petitioned the authorities in Athens for one, but his supervisor had denied his request. "Don't you read the papers? The Germans have bled us dry." Two weeks later he'd received notice that his salary had been cut in half because of the crisis. Now, in addition to having no car, he was going to starve to death.

He parked at the bottom of the hill and started up the path. Ahead the monastery was a menacing presence on the hill. The huge eucalyptus trees that surrounded it were bending in the wind, the leaves roaring like the sea. He kept one hand on the wall as he made his way to the summit. The path was built along the edge of a sharp precipice. Horses overburdened with supplies had plunged to their deaths on the rocks below, and he had no wish to join them.

A cable strung with naked electric bulbs crisscrossed the courtyard of the monastery. Providing scant light, it made the space appear even more desolate, like a deserted carnival. The priest was standing in front of an open door. He had summoned Patronas by phone after the American had come stumbling back from the trench.

"Thank God you're here," he said.

The American had vomited outside on the steps, he told him, and twice inside the room. Two other people were with him now, Marina Papoulis and Vassilis Korres. Patronas knew them both. He and Marina had gone to school together and Korres was the son of local farmer. The woman was clearing away the remnants of lunch, spread out on the table. The smell of the heavy food, the stewed lamb in *avgolemono* sauce, was overwhelming in the heat. The American was sitting on a chair. His face was ashen, his shirt flecked with vomit and blood. The others avoided looking at him.

"After he showed up," Papa Michalis said in a low voice, "I went down to see for myself." He stopped for a moment, unable to continue. "Chief Officer, there was a great deal of blood, a pool of it at the bottom of one of the trenches. I thought perhaps an animal … but there was too much blood for a sheep or a goat." He took off his glasses and rubbed his eyes. "Also, I saw part of hand, nearly whole it was, mixed up in it."

"Are you sure?"

The old man nodded. "I'm afraid for her. I called and called, but she didn't answer."

He fetched a propane lantern and handed it to him, then led him out through the tunnel in the back. He pointed to the plastic sheeting, glimmering in the deepening twilight. "Go, see for yourself," he said. The trenches were darker than the land around them. They looked like wounds in the earth.

Patronas made his way down to the dig site. Bats were flitting across the sky, and he could see the moon rising out over the sea. A large tarp covered most of the area, a pair of folding tables pushed together beneath it. On top of the tables were three or four wooden boxes. The priest had said the trench farthest away from the monastery was where he'd seen the blood.

The trench was about as wide as a coffin and nearly three meters long. A breeze had come up and the air was surprisingly cool. Aside from the blood, there were no other signs of violence, only scattered pieces of whitened material that crunched underfoot like shells on a beach. Crouching down, Patronas moved the lantern back and forth over the trench, studying the ground below. The pool of blood was there, just as the priest had described it. Congealed now, it looked to be about three centimeters deep. The palm of a hand was evident, too, mixed in with the blood.

"She had an assistant, you know."

Startled, Patronas spun around. He relaxed when he saw the cloaked form of the priest. The old man must have crept down here after him.

"He's a local boy, her assistant," the priest continued. "Petros Athanassiou.

He's been working here since school got out." The priest looked out over the dusky hills. "He's only sixteen years old."

"Was he up here this afternoon?"

"I didn't see him today. But he usually is."

"Perhaps he left before this happened. Perhaps he's back in Chora."

"Perhaps," the priest said without conviction. He waved feebly at the blood in the trench. "I didn't believe the American at first. Such things don't happen here. In Rwanda maybe, but not here, not on Chios. In New York, too, they happen." Papa Michalis nodded to himself. He knew about the mayhem in America from the police shows he watched, rebroadcast from the states on Greek TV.

Grunting, the chief officer stood up. He wanted to get on with the job and be rid of this garrulous old fool. "Could we talk about this another day, Father?"

But the priest was not to be put off. "Do you think it's hers? The hand, I mean?"

Patronas looked down. The ground was sodden with blood. He doubted that either Eleni Argentis or the boy had ever been fingerprinted, and DNA analysis was not available on Chios. "I don't know whose it is," he said gruffly.

He climbed into the trench. Reluctant to go farther, he stopped near to where the pool of blood lapped at the dirt walls. Watching him, the priest was surprised by this. He himself was not squeamish, having served in the army during World War II more than sixty years before. He had been forced to bury more dead than he cared to remember, German and Greek alike. *In the army of the dead, there are no nations, no flags.*

After a long moment, Patronas knelt down and carefully gathered up the hand and dropped it in a plastic bag; then he swabbed the blood and put it in a second bag, thinking that he'd send both pieces of evidence on to the crime laboratory in Athens. He raised the lantern and took a final look around. Aside from the blood, there was little else, no discernible trace elements. "Eleni Argentis is in charge here, isn't she?"

The priest nodded.

"What's she like?" He took care to use the present tense. No need to start rumors in town before he knew what had transpired here, whose blood this was.

"Generous. Hard-working."

"Rich, too?"

"Exceedingly so. She bought everything you see, all the equipment, even a laptop computer for Petros, a Toshiba, to use for his schoolwork and to track their findings."

Patronas began to bag the dirt and shards next to the bloody pool. "So she's not like the rest of them, her stepmother and that son of hers?"

"Oh, no. Eleni's simple in her pleasures. Archeology is all she cares about. She sleeps here sometimes in a little pup tent she brought from the United States. Camps out to save time. A young woman like that. She bought a generator to light the site so she could work at night."

"Where's the generator now?" Patronas asked, thinking the light might help him now.

"It quit about a month after she got it. We could never figure out why. Vandalism would have been my guess. It's in the monastery if you want to take a look at it."

"What did she tell you about the American? The one who found the blood?" He passed him the lantern and climbed out of the trench. It was too dark now. He'd have to do the rest tomorrow.

"Alcott? She knew him from Harvard. Jonathan Alcott. Supposedly he's a great scholar, an authority on Bronze Age Greece. She was thrilled when he agreed to come to Chios. She said he'd validate her findings."

"Father, what exactly did she think she'd found here?"

He hesitated. "A Minoan site or perhaps the remnants of some more ancient, unknown race."

Together they walked up the hill, the lantern making a circle of light at their feet.

"She was sure she'd found it?"

"Yes," the priest said. "And for that they killed her."

CHAPTER 3

Where many roosters crow, dawn is slow in coming.
—Greek proverb

"It's late," the priest told Patronas. "Why don't you sleep in one of the rooms here? You can stow the evidence in the refectory, use it as your murder room."

"Murder room?" Patronas raised his eyebrows. He was proving to be a strange one, this Papa Michalis, full of police lore he'd apparently gleaned from American detective shows like *Law and Order* and *CSI*. He'd spoken knowledgeably of serial killers, and as they'd walked back up the hill from the dig site, named a few—Charlie Manson and that cannibal from Milwaukee, Jeffrey Dahmer, citing the specifics of their misdeeds, all the grisly details. He'd evidently made a study of these men, knew that John Gacy liked to dress up as a clown and Ted Bundy had used a fake broken arm to lure victims. He even went so far as to ask how many killers like Bundy Patronas had 'busted,' using the American term.

"None," Patronas had replied.

"Really? How long have you been a policeman?"

"Over twenty years."

"And no homicides?" The priest was obviously disappointed.

"That's right." He'd regretted sharing this, as the priest had gone into overdrive afterwards, sharing what he knew of American crime detection and instructing Patronas on how best to proceed. Most priests quoted the Bible, cited proverbs to explain human behavior, the Old Testament to depict God's wrath. With Papa Michalis, it had been chapter and verse of *Murder She Wrote* and *Colombo*.

"I mean no disrespect, but Colombo and the other detectives, they always use a murder room in their homicide investigations. It's the place where they keep the evidence. It's rudimentary in crime detection, fundamental. As a policeman, you simply have to have one."

He led Patronas up a wooden staircase and out along a creaking balcony. Opening off the balcony were a series of cell-like rooms. The priest unlocked the door of one and turned on the light. It was a cramped space, narrow and long, with an iron cot and makeshift closet, set off from the rest of the room by a cloth curtain. A monk had probably occupied the space at one time. The window was open and Patronas could see the lights of the town in the distance.

The priest handed him a ragged towel and a bar of soap. "Bathroom's at the other end of the balcony. A bit primitive, but at least there's running water and a toilet."

"What happened to the American?"

"Kyria Papoulis took him back to his hotel in her car. Vassilis went with them. His uncle's mules are still here."

"Mules?"

"Yes. The American rode up here the traditional way, on a mule with a wooden saddle."

"But he was wearing shorts."

"Indeed." There was a ghost of a smile on the old man's face.

Patronas shook his head. Another tourist trying for the Greek experience. They always got it wrong, the tourists. "So, in addition to all his other problems, he now has an assful of splinters."

"Fly bites, too," the priest said. "I saw him scratching."

❧

YIANNIS PATRONAS CALLED his wife on his cellphone to tell her he would be spending the night at Profitis Ilias. "It's serious," he said. "I'll probably be here a few days."

"What do you mean 'serious'?"

"A murder."

"On Chios? You're joking."

She had him there. The last murder on Chios had taken place during the German occupation. And in Patronas' view, it hadn't really been a murder. More an act of patriotism, the killing of an SS man who'd been in charge of the local Gestapo. If Greek partisans hadn't shot him, it would have been worse for everybody. His death had been a good thing. Not like this.

"Listen to me," Patronas said. "It looks like a woman was killed up at Profitis Ilias."

"What woman?"

"Eleni Argentis." There was a long silence.

"So it's true what they've been saying."

"What who's been saying?"

"Spiros and Antigone Korres. You know the ones. They live on the road to the monastery. They say she found some kind of treasure, better than the gold in the National Museum."

"When did you hear this?"

"At the open air market, the *laiki*, on Wednesday."

"Ach. Who was with you?"

"It was the *laiki*, Yiannis. Half of Chios was there. And that Spiros, he's a loud one. He doesn't whisper."

"Ach," he said again.

"That's right, Yiannis." As usual, his wife had gotten there first and was eager to point it out to him. "Your killer? It could have been anybody."

Sighing, Yiannis Patronas closed the phone. He hated it when his wife did this. As if they were playing chess and she'd yelled 'checkmate' before he'd gotten his men on the board.

⁂

Judging by the sound, the rooster was somewhere close by. Patronas fumbled for the light and opened the door of his room. The bird was perched on the railing of the balcony directly across from him, crowing raucously. When it saw him, it flapped its wings and moved to attack him. "Get out of here," Patronas yelled, backing away. "Go on, beat it."

The priest came hurrying out of a room two doors down. "Sorry," he said. "I should have warned you. He's a monster, this one. Mussolini with feathers. Very demanding and unlike his fellows. He doesn't just crow at sun-up; he crows all day long."

Waving his arms, he shooed the bird away. "I suppose I could eat him. But the truth is, it's lonely up here and he keeps me company. Come on, it'll be light soon. I'll make you breakfast."

The kitchen was a cold, dark space with battered pine cabinets and a cement floor. The counters were white marble, stained with rust in places. What looked like an immense sink was propped up against one wall. Hewn of a single block of stone, it had no pipes attached, no faucet. Water had to be drawn from the small well at the center of the room.

Patronas ran his hand across the sink. It had a Latin date carved on the front of it.

The priest noticed his interest. "Part of a sarcophagus. It's old, this place. Eleni told me it's been in continuous use since Roman times, maybe even earlier."

Pushing a stack of books aside, he motioned for Patronas to take a seat at the little table in the corner. It was covered with a printed oilskin cloth and held a pitcher full of wilting sunflowers. The priest opened the door of the refrigerator and got out a bowl of eggs, then lit the propane burner on the counter and made Patronas an omelet with feta and tomatoes. He himself ate only bread.

Patronas picked up his fork. "How long have you known Eleni Argentis?" he asked.

"Two years." The priest faltered for a moment. "When she first came here, the Bishop asked me to look out for her … and I did. Or at least I tried to. I spent a lot of time down here in those ditches, helping the two of them. She liked to show us bits of clay she collected and talk about them. As you can see, I am an old man and she took pity on me. She washed my clothes and helped me in the garden. She even made dinner for me once or twice. She was …." He ran a gnarled hand over his face. "She and Petros, we were friends."

"You *are* friends. Whether or not anyone is a victim here remains to be seen." Blood or no blood, Patronas was unwilling to concede that a death had occurred without a body, a proper *Corpus Delecti*. Be it Eleni Argentis' or someone else's. Homicide was a serious matter, a term not to be bandied about, blood and body parts notwithstanding.

The sun was up by the time he finished breakfast and returned to the dig site, the air already warm. It was going to be a hot day. Even now the cicadas were loud in the trees. A pair of goats watched him from a distance, their fur golden in the early morning light.

Uninvited, the priest had followed him and now stood at the edge of the trench, looming over him, his black cassock billowing in the wind. "Chief Officer, with your permission, I'd like to assist you in your investigation."

"Sorry, Father. You know that's impossible." Patronas was measuring the depth of the blood. He wasn't sure what had happened, if the blood was even human, and he wanted to sort it out before his men arrived, before the day got any hotter. "This is police work and the police and the church, they're at cross purposes. They don't mix."

"Hear me out. I can be of service. I'm familiar with the excavation. No one knows it better than I do. I am also familiar with crime detection. I am a fervent devotee of the mystery novel and of all manner of American detective shows. I know about trace evidence and DNA."

Patronas waved him away. "You are a man of faith, Father. You've no business in a homicide investigation."

"Faith and homicide are not incompatible. The Bible is full of homicides."

"Be that as it may, I have no need of your services."

Patronas entered his measurements in the spiral notebook he'd brought with him next to the date and time. He didn't know what had transpired here, but he suspected it was a double homicide. He had never seen so much blood. Perhaps the priest was right and he should look to the forensic specialists on television to guide him. Write things down the way they did. As to what those policemen did with it after they wrote it down, he had no clue. As he'd told the priest, he'd never investigated a crime like this before. Assault and battery, sure. Violence against one's spouse any number of times. But murder, never. As a cop, he was an amateur at best and he knew it.

"I can't stop thinking about her," the priest said. "Dead out here someplace."

"What makes you so sure she's dead?" There had been no doubt in the old man's voice, only sadness.

"No one's seen her. After I called you last night, I checked with Marina and Vassilis, people who were here yesterday. Eleni always said good-bye before she left, and yesterday she didn't. Petros either."

"Who was up here yesterday?"

"A lot of people: Petros' mother and her boyfriend. Manoulis, I think his name was. Eleni's stepmother, Marina Papoulis and Vassilis Korres, Jonathan Alcott, the American you met. Another archeologist was here, too, but earlier in the day. An Englishman."

"Do you remember his name?"

"McLean."

"Anyone else?"

"Not that I know of."

"You were here the whole time?"

"No, I got a haircut in the morning, did some errands in town. But Marina Papoulis was here, getting lunch ready in the kitchen. She'll know if anyone came by while I was away."

"Did she go down to the dig site that day?"

"No. To my knowledge, Marina has never visited the excavation."

Not a long list. He'd start on it as soon as he finished here. "It seems she was concentrating on this end." Patronas pointed to a break in the whitened matter, the broad indentation where the shards had been emptied out.

"Eleni kept a log. She told me you have to make a very precise drawing of the site with the elevations and afterwards number each fragment and pinpoint where it was found before you remove it."

Patronas climbed out of the trench. He'd leave the rest to his men. He'd been in charge of the police force on the island of Chios for over twenty years, and the novelty of violent crime had long since worn off. He'd collected his share of teeth from barroom floors, driven the combatants to the hospital to be stitched up. The sight of blood no longer stirred him. It just made him tired.

He started going through one of the boxes on the table. A stiff wind was blowing, and above him the tarp swelled with air, the ropes clanging against the metal poles like the rigging on a sailboat. The box contained pieces of clay with numbers painted on them. He guessed Eleni Argentis had been killed because of her work here, because she'd found something so valuable it had drawn the attention of a killer, a killer who'd had enough time to bleed a woman to death in the dirt. He was sure now the blood was hers. There'd been a strip of fabric, too, mixed in with the blood, the front of a shirt. Patronas had inspected it closely before placing it in the evidence bag. Though sodden with blood, he could still see the logo, an alligator. Lacoste, far too expensive to belong to a village boy like Petros. She'd found something this person wanted. It had to be.

But there was nothing. Only random bits of clay. Nothing worth killing for. He sadly noted the remnants of the archeologist's stay on the hillside—the abandoned radio, the shabby cardigan on a chair. He found a single blood-soaked leather moccasin on the ground nearby, but no journal or papers of any kind. Some of the equipment was thrown down, a second chair upended.

He got down on his hands and knees and moved the chair aside. His hand brushed up against something metallic buried deep in the grass. It was a gold necklace with a charm suspended from it. Both the chain and the charm were soaked in blood.

The priest knew it well. "It's Eleni's. It's her *galopetra*."

"What the devil is a *galopetra*?"

"They're how Evans found the ruins in Knossos. He'd been working in Peloponnese near Mycenae and noticed the strange amulets the local women wore, carved out of translucent rock. When he asked the women about them, they replied that the stones were talismans to protect them in childbirth—'milk stones'. Evans followed the stones back to their source in Crete and eventually to Knossos. The amulets, you see, were actually Minoan seals."

For an Orthodox priest, he seemed to know a surprising amount about Minoan archeology. "You're sure this is hers and not something she found here?"

"Oh, yes. She always wore it. I chided her … an Orthodox Christian wearing a pagan symbol. But she said her father had bought it for her and that she'd never take it off."

Patronas fingered the necklace. The charm was a pale blue stone, carved with the image of a woman surrounded by snakes. A superstitious man, he felt a chill as he held it. He pocketed it and returned to his inspection of the site.

⁂

PATRONAS' SECOND-IN-COMMAND, EVANGELOS Demos, arrived a little after ten a.m. with Giorgos Tembelos, a longtime veteran of the force. Alerted by a cloud of flies, Tembelos moved toward a rocky crevice some distance from the dig site and slowly worked his way down to the bottom of it. After a moment or two, he called to Patronas.

"Boss, you'd better come."

"What is it?"

"I think I found something."

Patronas climbed down the crevice after him. The rocks on either side were splattered with blood and the air was thick with flies. Tembelos was kicking gravel away from something with the toe of his shoe, unwilling to touch whatever lay buried there with his hands. The mound was covered with dead weeds and loose stones, and insects crawled over it. Brushing them away, Patronas began to dig through the debris.

"It's the kid," he yelled in a strangled voice. "It's Petros Athanassiou. Someone slit his throat."

Though the body had been covered with trash, birds had somehow found it. Patronas turned away, fighting not to be sick, when he saw what they had done to the boy's face.

"Jesus Christ," Tembelos whispered.

They quickly shifted the debris aside, taking care not to touch the body. After they finished, Patronas stood looking down at the corpse. The boy was dressed in an orange t-shirt and cotton shorts. His sandals were scuffed and caked with dust and he'd been badly in need of a haircut. The key chain in his pocket had a motorcycle insignia on it, and he had a silver baptismal cross hanging around his neck, the chain buried deep in the gaping wound in his throat. *Young and poor*, Patronas concluded after taking inventory. Both of the boy's shoes had been mended repeatedly and his watch was the kind sold in kiosks. *From his dress, he needs not fear the thief.*

"So young," Tembelos said.

After Patronas took photographs and logged the details in his notebook, he and the other two policemen hoisted the boy's body on their shoulders and carried it up the hill to the monastery. Petros Athanassiou had been small for his age and didn't weigh much. No one spoke. The cicadas had fallen still, the only sound now the relentless drone of the wind.

The priest had been watching from a distance. "Holy Mother of God," he cried when he saw their burden. He unlocked the door of the refectory and hurriedly motioned them in. He was crying openly, tears wetting his cheeks. He reached out and touched the boy's shirt as they passed. "Petros," he kept saying. "Petros."

Signaling the men to lay the body down on the table, he sank down beside it and covered his face with his hands.

Patronas could hear him weeping. After a few moments, the priest raised himself up again and left the room, returning with a handful of candles and a hymnal. He lit the candles and handed them around to the policemen, then opened the hymnal and began to chant the Orthodox prayer for the dead. His voice kept breaking, and it took him a long time to finish. Patronas and the others joined in near the end, singing in hushed voices. Rigor mortis had given way during the night and the congealed blood that covered the child had thickened and turned black. When the priest was done, he got a sheet and covered the boy with it. The candles cast long shadows against the walls and over the small, shrouded form on the table.

"Who could have done this?" the priest asked.

"I don't know," Patronas answered.

Papa Michalis wiped his eyes. "He was a wonderful boy. He helped his grandmother and worked hard in school. Tried to do his best, always."

"How well did you know him?"

"Pretty well. I tutored him a time or two last spring. He was having trouble with his ancient Greek and asked me to help him. He was a pleasure to teach. So quick, so amazingly quick. Eleni said he had the makings of a great scientist. You wouldn't believe what he'd …."

Papa Michalis had been about to say something more, but stopped in mid-sentence. "Never mind." He bent over the body, straightening the sheet that covered it. "It doesn't matter anymore."

Patronas looked around, troubled by the empty rooms, the eerie silence that hung over the place. "Are you alone up here, Father?"

The priest nodded. "Marina Papoulis comes when she can, three or four times a week. She cooks for me, sees to the sweeping up, the laundry. If there's heavy work, Vassilis Korres does it, but he never comes unless I call him on the telephone."

The chief officer asked his assistant to contact police headquarters and arrange for the removal of the body. "Have them take this, too." He pulled the necklace with the *galopetra* out of his pocket and laid it down on the table. "The chain isn't broken. They must have removed it from her neck and dropped it by mistake. That means they took their time. Whoever did this was methodical."

"And Petros got caught in the crossfire?" the priest asked.

Patronas didn't have the heart to correct him. Slitting throats did not generate crossfire. Crossfire came from guns.

CHAPTER 4

It is better that a priest, a doctor, and a policeman
not enter one's house.
—Greek proverb

PETROS ATHANASSIOU'S GRANDMOTHER lived in a small weathered house in Castro, the poorest section of Chora, the capital of Chios. The area had housed Turks and Sephardic Jews during the time of the Ottomans. Now it was a congested, filthy slum, home to immigrant workers from Africa and Bangladesh.

Patronas drove his Citroen over the garbage-choked moat that led into the quarter. Most of the old houses had been broken up into apartments, their facades heavily defaced with graffiti. A gas station had been grafted onto the first floor of one. The plasterwork on the upper stories had rotted away, exposing the timber framing beneath, in marked contrast with the shiny gasoline pumps and neon sign out front. *A perfect symbol of Greece*, Patronas thought to himself. The uneasy relationship between the past and present there on display. The modern not well mastered, too often a graceless intrusion, the past just below the surface, beneath the walls, the soil, omnipresent. Oil cans and discarded auto parts blanketed the vacant lot behind the gas station. A flock of chickens were living there and watched the car warily from their perch on a soiled mattress. He'd often been called into Castro to break up fights, usually arguments between husbands and wives that had turned violent. He knew the area well and found the house easily.

He parked and helped Papa Michalis out of the car. He'd brought the priest along, thinking, as a religious man, he might know how best to console the old woman. He himself had no words to offer her. He'd been a policeman long enough to know that. He didn't buy the bunk people told themselves when something like this happened, the crap about earthly suffering and heavenly reward. Perhaps there was some rationale for the death of a child, some divine purpose. Perhaps on the day of reckoning, it would all make sense. He didn't think so. 'Spare me the explanations,' he'd tell God when that day came.

She'd made an effort to grow a garden, he saw. The front yard was fenced in with chicken wire and planted with spindly-looking rose bushes. The whitewashed walls were dirty, splashed with mud where someone had watered the flowers. An elderly woman opened the door.

"Good morning." She looked back and forth between Patronas and the priest, confused as to why they'd come.

"Good morning, Kyria Athanassiou," Patronas said. "May we come in?"

She was wearing a blue-gray cotton housedress and had a black sweater thrown over her shoulders. Her hair was what Greek children called '*malia pisgrias,*' cotton candy hair. It had been hennaed some time ago and at least two inches of white now showed at the roots. They'd taken her by surprise and she was barefooted, not dressed for company. He recognized this as a sign of poverty. Shoes were to be hoarded and worn only when necessary.

The woman stood back to let them enter. The room was small and crowded, with furniture from another era, heavy and dark. The sofa and chairs were covered with handmade lace antimacassars, the top of the table with cheap souvenirs and painted china animals. The space smelled closed in, musky. She motioned for Patronas and the priest to sit down on the sofa. "A moment please."

She returned a few minutes later with two demitasses of coffee, glasses of water and a plate of candied nectarines. It was one of those unspoken rules that governed life. A matter of *filotimo*, pride, to be able to offer something. Even during the war, when there had been nothing and people were starving, the Greeks had saved a little food, a sweet on a plate in the kitchen, to offer visitors. The guest was expected to refuse this food the first and second time it was offered. If the host offered it a third time, that meant there was other food in the house and the guest could eat. If not, the ritual had been observed, the shame avoided. And all this was done in silence. Nothing was ever said. The tray the woman offered reminded him of those times.

"Kyria, I have bad news," Patronas said.

She clutched at her sweater. He noticed she'd slipped into her shoes in the kitchen and put on a clean apron. She closed her eyes for moment. "Tell me," she said quietly.

He guessed she was a refugee from Asia Minor, forced into exile by the genocidal rampage that had accompanied the first stirrings of Turkish nationalism at the turn of the century. From Smyrna, perhaps. Chios was full of such people. The few who'd survived the massacre, the burning of the Greek quarter of the city, had never recovered and wore their grief as if it were part of their national dress. His mother had been such a refugee and had the same sense of sorrow and darkness about her.

"I'm sorry, Kyria. We found your grandson's body up at the monastery. Someone killed him."

She didn't say anything for a long time. Just looked at him. Then, slowly, she began to keen, rocking back and forth in her chair, chanting the name of her grandson.

"I'm sorry," Patronas said again.

She cried for a long time, then wiped her eyes and stood up. "What about her? The woman?"

"You mean Eleni Argentis? We don't know. We think they might have been killed at the same time."

The woman nodded as if this pleased her. "I warned him about her. About that place. To stay away." She began to cry again. "But he liked her. He couldn't keep away."

"What do you mean, 'liked' her?"

"He was a silly boy, young. I found a poem he wrote her."

"May I see it?"

She went to a bureau and opened a drawer. On top was a piece of ruled paper. Patronas scanned it quickly. She was right. It was a silly poem, written in pencil and smudged in places, the kind an immature boy would write to a woman he was sexually attracted to. "Did he ever talk about any visitors to the site? Anything suspicious he'd noticed when he was working there?"

"No. When he first started he used to talk about what they did, but then she came by once to pick him up and I saw what kind of woman she was. Wearing the top of a bathing suit, clothes like that to go to work." The old woman made as if to spit. "She thought because she was rich she could do as she pleased, that it didn't matter. I told Petros she was a dirty woman, a *vromiara*."

Seeing Papa Michalis, she covered her mouth with her hand. For a moment, she'd forgotten the priest was there and now was embarrassed she'd let the vulgarity, the word for whore, slip in front of him. "I told him to find another job. But he wanted to buy a motorcycle and she offered him more money than any other work would bring in."

"And so he stayed on."

She nodded. "He never talked to me about her again."

"Perhaps he spoke to someone else. His mother, perhaps?"

"How do you think I know about women like that? His mother was one. That's why she lives in Athens. She had a baby, a baby and no husband. There was no place on Chios for her. She left Petros with me when he was six months old and took off. I'm the one who raised him."

"Didn't she visit him?"

"When it suited her. She's here now with her boyfriend. On *vacation*." Her tone was bitter.

"Is he the boy's Father?"

"What do you want from me?" the old woman yelled. "The boy had no father. Or he had many fathers. You pick. My daughter was a whore."

She felt her way to the back of the house as if blind-folded. "I did the best I could for him. He had a nice room, clothes." She pointed to a small, whitewashed space off the kitchen. "Go see for yourself."

Unlike the rest of the house, the furniture in this room was new, Scandinavian, as were the brightly colored curtains at the windows. The boy's clothes were copies of popular brands, clumsily reworked in cheap cotton. There was a box of new Timberlands sitting on his bed, the shoes still wrapped in paper.

"A gift from his mother," the old woman told him. "She bought them in Athens."

There was something desperate about the posters of American movie stars taped to the wall, the pictures cut out of magazines. The boy's blanket had been crocheted by his grandmother, Patronas guessed, and she'd probably made most of his clothes as well. He had a cheap stereo set up next to his bed and Greek CDs were spread out on the floor. In the armoire, Patronas found school books and winter clothing neatly stored in taped plastic bags. It held nothing else of interest, only a small box of toy cars and trucks, some photographs of his grandparents and a woman he assumed was the mother. There was also a book bag, embossed with cartoon figures, forgotten in one corner. Patronas turned the bag upside down and shook it on the bed. Inside was a small gold bull.

The priest did not seem surprised. "Minoan," he said when Patronas showed it to him. "The bull was sacred to them."

Patronas turned the bull over in his hand. "I've gone over every inch of the dig site and there's nothing like this there." Less than two centimeters long, it was a beautiful thing with tiny ivory horns and turquoise eyes. "Where did it come from?"

"Perhaps it was a gift from Eleni." The priest stood at the window, looking out. Without turning around, he added, "Eleni liked to give people expensive presents."

"She is an archeologist. She wouldn't give something like this to a kid."

"Maybe it's a copy."

"Maybe." He was sure now the priest was lying. If it were a gift from Eleni, why would Petros hide it? To keep peace with his grandmother? No, it didn't make sense. Especially if it were gold and he wanted money. Patronas carefully bagged the bull. Between the mattress and the bed frame, he found a piece of paper with a childish drawing on it, a round circle with pictures in squares. It looked familiar, but Patronas couldn't place it. The drawing was erased in places, and he thought the boy might have copied it out of a book. There was no sign of the laptop the priest said Eleni Argentis had bought him. "Where's his computer?"

"He often took it with him to the dig site. Perhaps it was there when …." The old man's voice trailed off.

Petros' grandmother came to the door. "Where is he now?" she asked.

As Chios had no morgue, they'd sent the boy's body directly to the funeral home. "Stelios."

"I must go sit with him," she said. "He shouldn't be alone."

"Do you want us to take you there?"

"No. I'm an old woman and that's one of the things you learn." She began to cry again. "You learn the way to Stelios."

"Why did she say that about her daughter, about her being a whore?" the priest asked Patronas on their way back to Profitis Ilias.

"An old wound. That's what happens with something like this. All the old wounds, they start to bleed again."

CHAPTER 5

No one envies the dead.
—Greek proverb

A FISHERMAN NAMED COSTAS Stamnas was about to push his rowboat into the sea when he heard the car. It was after midnight and the small cove was dark, the cliffs behind him hidden in the shadows. Few people used the cove. It was hard to navigate a boat around the rocks, the jagged knuckles of basalt that protruded from the water like the bones of a vast decaying animal. Veins of iron ore crisscrossed the rocks, staining them where the water touched and leaving dark, bloody puddles on the sand below. The only sign of life was a stunted olive tree, growing out of the cliff. It creaked in the wind, its twisted roots clawing at the pebbly earth like arthritic fingers.

Costas had planned on spending the night fishing. He'd shine his lantern on the water and the fish, thinking it was daybreak, would rise to the surface. He loved to work then, to cast his net and watch the fish dart back and forth in the silvery light.

A car turned onto the road that led down to the cove. Its lights off, it slowly moved across the packed sand to the water's edge. Costas wondered who it was. The cove was small and isolated, and as far as he knew, only he and a few other fishermen anchored their boats there. It was convenient for him. His farm was the only one in the area and his acreage extended to the cliff's edge. Wary, he left his boat and crouched down behind an outcropping of rock. He'd found syringes here and was sure the cove was being used as a drop off point for hashish and heroin smuggled in from Turkey. The car stopped. Costas could hear the radio playing, but the music was too faint to tell if the station was Greek or Turkish.

After a few moments a man got out of the car and walked along the beach, checking out the cove. He paused when he reached Costas' boat and ran his hand along the length of it to see if it was wet. Satisfied, he returned to the car and turned it around. He had a small boat hitched to a trailer in the back. It was a Zodiac from the looks of it, a small inflatable one. It had no registration numbers on the side, no name painted on the back or across the bow.

The man unhitched the boat and pushed it out into the water, then returned to the car. He removed a large plastic bag from the back and carefully set it down on the sand. *It must be heavy*, Costas thought, *judging by the way he carries it. Not hashish. Something else.* The man unloaded two more bags, then moved to stow them onboard. He dropped one of them and it opened, its contents slipping out onto the beach. Cursing, the man scooped up the soggy material and stuffed it back in the bag. He threw it into the Zodiac, stepped aboard, and fired up the engine.

He steered the Zodiac in the direction of the breakwater. It rode low in the water and left a sizeable wake, white in the moonlight. The boat moved quickly beyond the breakwater and out into the open sea.

As soon as the boat was gone, Costas crept forward, curious to see what the man had dropped out of the bag, hoping for something he could sell. He thought the man had been transporting guns, given his furtive manner and the heaviness, the bulky shape of the bags. He could see the outline of the boat on the sand and something dark at the edge of the water. It was a smaller plastic bag. Drawing closer, he tugged the bag loose from the sand. It was half buried. The boat must have run over it when the man pushed it into the water. He gasped when the plastic unrolled and he saw what was inside. He heard the Zodiac start up again in the distance and hurried back to his hiding place in the rocks.

When the boat reached the beach, the man jumped out and pulled it ashore, then maneuvered it onto the trailer attached to his car and made ready to leave. He paused for a moment, spying the trail of footprints Costas had left. He opened the trunk of his car and pulled out a pair of binoculars and a gun. His binoculars were bigger than any Costas had ever seen, with a headband and green lenses, and his gun looked like something out of the movies, the kind that spat fire and split people in two. The man fitted the binoculars over his head and began scanning the cliffs and surrounding rocks. Costas stayed very still.

The man stood there a long time, watching the cliffs through his headpiece. Suddenly Costas heard another boat churning in the waters off the cove. It looked to be a fishing boat, a local one. Putting down his binoculars, the man watched the boat for moment. It was turning in toward the beach. This decided the man, who threw the binoculars and gun in the backseat of his car and drove away quickly, the Zodiac swaying from side to side as he sped up the hill.

Costas stayed where he was, thinking the road home was too dangerous, that the man might be waiting up there to ambush him. Maybe he'd be lucky and the man hadn't seen his name stenciled on the side of his boat. He'd wake his wife. "Calliope," he'd say. "Gather up the children. Chios is too dangerous. We are taking the first plane to Athens." His wife, a quarrelsome woman, would protest, but even she would grow silent when he told her of the events of the night, how he'd seen a smuggler and stepped on a human leg.

"Worse than an animal he was," he'd tell her. "He would have shot me with no more feeling than a shark tearing up a fish."

PATRONAS STUDIED THE ground under the bright crime lights. He'd once seen a hawk swoop down on a flock of chickens at his father's farm. The ground beneath his feet reminded him of that. Blood, ground up earth, and a shoe, a leather moccasin, on its side at the waterline, the waves rolling it over and over.

It had been 3 a.m. when the duty officer, Evangelos Demos, had summoned him here. A fisherman, Thanos Solomos, had been returning from a night of fishing and beached his boat next to a rowboat, only to stumble across something soft there on the beach. A very shaken Costas Stamnas had emerged from his hiding place a few minutes later and embraced him and together they'd called the police.

A half hour later Patronas had arrived at the crime scene with three other men. He'd cordoned off the area and set up the portable electric lights. The coroner was there now, rolling the leg in plastic. They'd found a hand, too, a little farther down, closer to the water. There'd been traces of polish on the nails of both. Until now there'd been no need for body bags on Chios, and they'd been forced to improvise. What was left of Eleni Argentis was now being wrapped and sealed in saran wrap, and it was proving to be a slow, tedious process.

The two fishermen, Thanos Solomos and Costas Stamnas, were still there, huddled together with blankets thrown over their shoulders.

"I was worried even before I found it," Costas Stamnas was saying. "No one ever uses this cove and last night there was a man here. He drove in late with his lights off and unloaded an inflatable boat, a Zodiac it looked like. After he left, I could see there was something dark on the sand, a real thin trail of it. Sometimes happens when you fish, a little drizzle of blood on the ground like that. I saw something buried in the sand and I went to pull it out ...." He started to gag and covered his mouth with his hand.

"Go on," Patronas prodded, his voice gentle. He saw how frightened the man was.

"I thought at first maybe someone's boat had overturned and a propeller had ... that the leg had washed in from the sea. But it was too neat, the bone .... Propellers, they're messy, they rip you up, the wounds are all jagged-like, and sharks are rare in these waters. It couldn't have been a shark." He was trembling all over. "Whose leg do you think it is?"

"I don't know." Patronas motioned for his men to wall off the entire cove with crime scene tape. "Did you get a good look at the man in the Zodiac? Could you describe him for us?"

The fisherman shook his head. "It was too dark."

"If you saw him again, would you recognize him? Was he one of us?" he asked, meaning Greek.

"I don't know, Chief Officer. I swear. He was dressed all in black and had something over his head. A *drakos*, he was. A monster. That's all I can tell you."

CHAPTER 6

Outside a doll. Inside the plague.
—Greek proverb

CHILDREN WERE SELLING pottery along the road on the way to Campos. A farmer threshing wheat in his stone *aloni* waved to Patronas, the chaff making a golden cloud in the air around him. Patronas wondered how much longer the man would continue to do it that way, using a donkey and a millstone, how much longer the Greece of his youth could withstand the pressures of the modern age.

The Citroen, an elderly 2CV, protested as Patronas turned onto the cobbled road. He'd heard from Tembelos that there was a cartoon in which a Citroen such as his transforms itself into a giant robot and performs a dance routine. Personally, he'd settle for a little more horsepower. The Germans called the Citroen 2CV *Ente* or duck, and he'd always wondered if it might do better in water. It was virtually powerless on dry land.

He wanted to speak to Titina Argentis, Eleni Argentis' stepmother, before she learned of the discovery at the beach, to gauge her reaction. She lived in Campos, a verdant, well-watered valley behind the airport. The Genovese had used the area as a summer resort during the Middle Ages and their decaying villas still dotted the landscape. A few had been restored by wealthy ship owners but most remained abandoned, their grounds overtaken by vines, their windowless structures in ruins. Open to the sky, the old houses had a stark grandeur, their crumbling limestone walls blending into the landscape.

The restoration of the Argentis estate had taken four years, and the family had been widely criticized for its extravagance. An iron gate decorated with bronze griffins marked the entrance. The gate stood open and Patronas drove his Citroen in and parked. Gaslight lanterns on gilded poles lined the driveway, and he could hear water splashing somewhere.

A maid answered the door. Standing beyond her was a man of about thirty.

"I'm here about Eleni Argentis," Patronas said, introducing himself. "Chief Officer of the Chios Police."

"Mother," the man called over his shoulder. "Some policeman is here about Eleni."

Stifling a yawn, he led Patronas through the house. Although it was early afternoon, his unshaven face was still puffy with sleep. He had a heavy gold chain around his neck, but unlike the one Petros Athanassiou wore, there was no cross attached. It was purely ornamental, an indication of wealth rather than a declaration of faith. His face was handsome, yet it had an unfinished quality about it, a lack of sharpness in the nose and chin, softness like a baby's. Patronas recognized the type. Many of the Greek ship owners had sons like this, sons who went from youth to old age without ever achieving manhood. He had a glass in his hand, and Patronas could already smell liquor on his breath.

In contrast, his mother, Titina Argentis, was meticulously dressed, her black hair pinned back severely and held in place with a small bow at the nape of her neck. A gold coin belt accentuated her thinness. Her sandals were equally fancy with little heels and more gold coins along the instep. She looked a little like the Duchess of Windsor, Patronas thought, with her dark hair and narrow face. She had the same cold and precise elegance.

He introduced himself again. "Is there someplace we could talk?"

The house was expensively furnished, every surface covered with silver knickknacks and photographs of Titina, some with her son, but most of her alone, posing on ski slopes or on a beach somewhere. None of Eleni that he could see.

Titina Argentis opened a set of French doors and stepped out onto the terrace. An old Genovese water wheel, carved out of white marble, dominated the grounds, water cascading from it into the swimming pool at its base. Beyond the pool, the land dropped away, planted with thick groves of lemon and orange trees. A high stone wall enclosed the entire estate, made of the same gold and red limestone as the house. Patronas had the sense he was in a place apart, a place out of time.

Titina Argentis sat down and motioned for him to do the same. "May I get you something? A lemonade, perhaps? Coffee?"

"No, nothing, thank you."

"But it's such a hot day. You must take something. How about an orange juice?"

"Very well then."

She turned to her son. "Antonis, would you like one?"

"I'm all set." He held up his glass. "I've got water."

"Chief Officer, have you met my son, Antonis?" She said his name as if it meant something.

Antonis gave Patronas a lopsided grin. He had a wonderful smile, his teeth even and white, and when he smiled he radiated warmth and a kind of boyish sweetness. Patronas was sure he knew all too well the power of that smile and used it to get what he wanted from others. This one, *he has even the milk of the birds*. He was nursing whatever it was in his glass. Not water. Vodka or gin.

The next ten minutes were spent listening to Kyria Argentis instruct the maid on the best way to prepare Patronas' single glass of orange juice. *All quite unnecessary*, Patronas concluded after he'd tasted it. It was nothing special. His wife bought the same brand. It came in cartons at the supermarket.

He set his glass down, took a deep breath, and described the findings at Profitis Ilias. "The priest told me you were up there the day Eleni went missing."

Titina Argentis signaled to the maid to put a coaster under Patronas' glass. "Yes, I dropped off a package for her." No worry in her voice, no concern for her missing stepdaughter. From an onyx box on the table, she removed a thin cigarette and lit it with a lighter.

"Where was the package from?"

"England, I think. Antonis, do you remember?" Her voice was overly formal, stiff, as if she'd had elocution lessons.

Her son shook his head. In spite of the talk of blood and death, no worry here either.

"Did you see Eleni that day? Talk to her?"

"No. She wasn't there. I left the package on the table at the dig site and walked back to my car."

"Did you see her assistant, Petros Athanassiou?"

"No. No one."

"You're sure?"

"Yes. I saw the priest briefly when I first arrived. He was the only one."

"How did you and your stepdaughter get along?"

She concentrated on her cigarette, turning the Dunhill lighter over and over in her hand. "Eleni and I didn't see each other much after her father died. Circumstances kept us apart. I am only here on Chios two months of the year, Chief Officer. Antonis and I spend the winter season in London."

"Did Eleni stay here while you were away?"

"In this house? No. She slept in the guest house or up at Profitis Ilias, that place where she worked." Titina Argentis conveyed a great deal in the way she said 'worked,' as if whatever Eleni had been doing was unseemly, beneath the dignity of her and her son and those people with whom she spent those winter months in London. And the chief officer was sure this attitude applied to all forms of employment, that 'work' was somehow demeaning, that she considered the collection of a wage in any form to be embarrassing, even tawdry.

"Antonis, how did you get along with your sister?"

"She's not his sister," Titina Argentis interrupted. "They were siblings by marriage only."

Her hostility surprised him. Patronas turned back to Antonis Argentis. "So you didn't see her?"

Again, his mother answered for him. "Neither of us saw Eleni very much. I tried. You can ask Antonis. I invited her to join us in London countless times. But she always refused. 'Work,' she told me. 'I have to work.'"

THE GUESTHOUSE WHERE Eleni Argentis had lived was located at the back of the estate. Antonis unlocked the door and pushed it open.

"Whole place is hers. I'll be outside if you need anything."

Patronas walked quickly through the house, opening and closing doors, trying to get a sense of who Eleni Argentis was. He doubted her death was a crime of passion, but who could say at this point? She'd been a beautiful woman and rich besides. The possibilities were endless. Perhaps she'd been arguing with a lover and Petros had intervened.

There was only one bed in the house with a simple white quilt draped across it. Above it hung an icon of the Virgin framed in gold. No other decoration. It was a severe space, monastic. The clothes in the closet were neatly arranged, jeans mostly and an assortment of cotton shirts. A laptop was sitting on the table in the kitchen across from a massive antique china closet that housed dishes and table linens. Patronas removed the dishes and began tapping on the wood in the back. He could tell from the design that the chest was from the last century, maybe even earlier. Occasionally these old pieces held secret compartments that had been used to hide Greek books during the time of the Ottomans. Eleni Argentis' held a packet of letters. He opened one. Written in English, the scrawl masculine and nearly illegible.

The chief officer called Papa Michalis on his cellphone. "I'm at Eleni's house and I found some letters, written in English. Do you know who she was involved with?"

"There was someone at one time. I asked her about it once and she said, 'I'm done with all that.' When I asked her what she meant, she went and got a journal off the shelf and read a passage to me. It was black leather and looked expensive. Sometimes she wrote wrote poetry, she said. It was after dinner and she'd had a lot of wine. I don't remember the passage exactly. It wasn't a poem, something about how 'waiting defined women, waiting for love, waiting for life.' "

"What does that mean?"

"I am a man of the cloth, Chief Officer. What do I know of women?"

After Patronas found the letters, he went through the house again, emptying out the pockets of Eleni's clothes, checking the undersides of the tables and chairs. The kitchen held nothing. He carefully inspected the lone suitcase he found in the back of the closet. After he finished, he searched the shelf for the notebook of poetry the priest had mentioned. He also gathered up Colette's autobiography, a textbook on abnormal psychology, and the laptop computer. He stuffed everything in the suitcase and carried it out of the house.

Titina Argentis was standing on the lawn, talking to her son about a car he was apparently intent upon buying. "Finished, Chief Officer?" she called.

"This was just a preliminary search. A crime team will go through the house more thoroughly tomorrow."

Though this displeased her, she said nothing.

"By the way, Kyria Argentis, who inherits?"

"I suppose I do," she answered as if it were of no matter. Money, like working, was a thing she couldn't be bothered with. "And Antonis, of course. He was like a son to my husband. Themis adopted him formally when he was ten years old. He wanted Antonis to have his name, to inherit the business when he was gone. Antonis and my husband, they were very close."

"What business is that?"

"Argentis Shipping. My husband, Themis, was one of the biggest ship owners in Greece. Now Antonis manages the company." She said this with obvious pride.

How he could do that while drinking the day away in the house of his mother was a great puzzle. Perhaps he'd underestimated Antonis. "Your half-sister went to Harvard," he said to Antonis. "How about you? Where'd you go to school?"

Again, his mother rushed to answer for him. "He was unable to complete his studies. He was too busy here. Themis and I wouldn't have survived if it hadn't been for him."

But Themis hadn't survived, had he? Neither had Eleni. Patronas looked at Titina Argentis with renewed interest.

But she was done with him. Turning back to Antonis, she began speaking again about the car. "But you wrecked the last one," she said, smiling indulgently at her son, pleased by what she saw.

The son smiled back. That smile—that beguiling, disarming smile—but this time there was a hint of mischief in it, something a little disingenuous.

The smile of a boy being naughty, but only a little, and sure he was going to get away with it.

"I'll be more careful this time," he said, sipping his drink.

Chapter 7

The village is burning and the village whore is combing her hair.
—Greek proverb

THEY BURIED PETROS Athanassiou the next morning in the cemetery behind the town. The chief officer attended the funeral out of respect for the boy's grandmother, thinking she would be forced to do this alone or at best with a neighbor in attendance and that he might lend some dignity to the proceedings, perhaps furnish her with a police escort if she wanted. But she wasn't alone. Entering the chapel, he was surprised to see a woman in her forties standing beside her, holding her hand. Marina Papoulis was also there, and Papa Michalis. Women from the Castro neighborhood were crowded around her, too, talking among themselves over the priest's chanting. *They might have come out of kindness*, Patronas thought, *but more likely out of curiosity. Like those who slow down when they pass an accident. Giving voice to pity, secretly thankful they'd been spared. The great show that is death breaking up the monotony of their daily lives.*

The old woman nodded to him as he pushed his way to the front. The service was brief, the priest's chanting perfunctory. At the cemetery, the old woman led the mourners forward, throwing a handful of dirt down on the coffin. It was made of cheap pine, tricked up to look like walnut and draped with plastic flowers. As she threw the dirt, she began wailing, tearing at the front of her dress. The same woman who'd been with her in the church led her away.

Patronas waited a half hour before following them back to the house. Petros' grandmother opened the door. She was still in her funeral clothes, a black dress, kerchief and stockings, as was the custom, her face ravaged with grief.

"Come in," she said. "Meet my daughter."

The woman he'd seen at the funeral rose and came forward. Her black dress was too short and tight for both her age and the occasion. Her bleached hair was piled high, and Patronas could see the line along her jaw where her make-up ended. She had an air of spent voluptuousness about her. A*n overripe peony*, he thought, *pretty once, but now about to make a mess on the table.* Her nose and lips were too thick, too coarse, for real beauty, and her eyes were deepset and swollen, as if from dissipation.

"I'm Voula Athanassiou," the woman said. "Petros' mother." She sat down on the sofa and patted the cushion beside her, indicating for him to join her. "My mother called me and told me what had happened," she said. "Manos and I were staying at a hotel on the other side of the island. We came as soon as we heard."

She was so close, Patronas could smell the cigarettes on her breath.

"Manos Kleftis is her *boyfriend*," the old woman said by way of explanation. She laid a certain stress on the last word as if mocking her daughter.

They talked for a few more minutes. "I need to speak to Mr. Kleftis," Patronas said.

Voula got up and stretched, pulling her dress tight across her breasts. "Manos," she called in a lazy voice. "There's a policeman here. He wants to talk to you."

A man emerged from the back of the house. Although stocky, he moved with a kind of animal grace, his gait fluid and loose. His shirt was loud, Hawaiian. Decorated with sea turtles and palm trees, it hung open over his naked chest. Odd garb for a house in mourning, even in the modern age. His head was shaved and he had no eyebrows or eyelashes to speak of. His eyes were a pale green, nearly colorless, his lips thick and protruding. Though not handsome, he had an air of sensuality about him that complemented Voula Athanassiou's. He placed one hand on her thigh as he sat down and the two of them exchanged a smile. A pimp or close to it.

"How do you do?" Patronas said. "I'm Chief Officer Patronas."

"Manos Kleftis." The man crossed his legs and began fiddling with his plastic flip flop. He seemed sleepy, out of focus.

"Sorry to bother you on such a sad occasion."

"Ah, yes, little Petros."

"I heard you and Voula were up at the monastery the day it happened."

"That's right. Voula wanted to see the boy. We got there at eleven or so. Voula had arranged it. The kid was supposed to meet us in the parking lot, but he didn't show up." No sorrow in his voice, no grief.

"Did you wait for him?" Patronas was trying to establish a timeline. The coroner had said the boy was killed at least twenty-four hours before they found his body and Eleni, a bit earlier.

The man shrugged. "A few minutes maybe."

"You didn't try and find him?"

Kleftis shook his head.

"Do you remember what time you got back here?"

"Noon or thereabouts." He signaled the old woman. "Hey, Yiayia, how about getting us something to eat? I'm starving."

Without a word, the old woman got up and left the room. Patronas could hear her moving around in the kitchen, opening the refrigerator door and getting dishes out. Little more than a maid in her own house. He wondered why she put up with it.

"Tell me, Mr. Kleftis, how did you get along with Petros?"

"He was okay, I guess. Seemed nice enough." He didn't seem to hold the fact that his girlfriend had a son against her. A rare tolerance, unusual in a Greek male.

"How often did you see him?"

"Every six months or so."

"How about you?" Patronas turned back to Voula. "How often did you see your son?"

"The same. Once or twice a year. We usually came together, Manos and me. I wished it was more, but what can you do?" She flicked something off her dress. Her nails had been recently done and gleamed with coral polish. "The truth is, I was more of a sister than a mother to him. Yiayia, she's the one who raised him. I was only seventeen when he was born. Petros and I, we were children together."

Seventeen, my ass, thought Patronas. *You were twenty-five if you were a day and should have known better*. "Did you keep in touch with him? Phone him every week? Email?"

"No, nothing." She stared at him a little defiantly. "Sorry."

"When did you get here?"

"I'm not sure. July twenty-second, I think it was."

She and her boyfriend seemed well suited. *The pot, while rolling, fell in with the cover.* "How long have you and Mr. Kleftis been together?"

"Three years."

"She was in my store, buying earrings." Manos Kleftis put his hand over his heart. "I saw her and my heart stood still," these last few words in English.

"You own a store?"

He nodded. "Kleftis' Souvenirs on Mykonos."

That's probably where he learned to speak English, romancing foreign women, picking them up on one of those touristy, anything-goes beaches and spending a couple of days with them before they flew home on Lufthansa or British Airways. The chief officer had no doubt. Manos Kleftis was one of those men who make summer vacations in Greece so memorable for female tourists. He probably spoke a little Swedish, too.

A few minutes later, the grandmother came in with a plate of *tyropitas*, chopped tomatoes and feta and a sprinkling of olives. Without a word, she set it down in front of Manos Kleftis, and with an apologetic glance at the chief officer, returned to the kitchen.

Kleftis took a *tyropita* and ate it. "You're a local. Voula's been telling me how good the sweets are on Chios."

As if the boy's mother and he were still on vacation, tourists. As if sixteen-year-old Petros hadn't been buried that day. Patronas didn't know what to make of Manos Kleftis. Perhaps he was playing what they called the 'white dove,' a man who pretends to be artless, stupid even, in order to con you.

"They have *loucoumades* on Chios, Chief Officer?" Kleftis went on. "I'm crazy about *loucoumades*."

Loucoumades?! Again, Patronas couldn't believe his ears. A child had died and this man wanted honey balls. He put his notebook away. "You'll be staying on, won't you?"

He assumed Kleftis would remain on the island as long as necessary to investigate the boy's estate, to see if there was anything he and Voula could glean from the child's death. *The purse of the dead is turned inside out.* Even good people sniffed around after a family member died to make sure they got their share or—even better—more than their share. Not that people didn't grieve. He'd seen women tear clumps of their hair out at funerals, scratch their faces with their nails. But too often the children of those same women visited the family lawyer on their way home from the cemetery and fought with each other over the inheritance. Patronas was careful never to say this out loud. They'd dumped manure on Katzanzakis' grave in Crete for depicting the scavenging that had followed the death of one of his characters in *Zorba the Greek*, the picking of her poor bones. But as a policeman, he stood with Katzanzakis on this, albeit silently. Too often in Greece, death was about money.

"I'm afraid I'll have to ask you to remain here until our investigation is concluded."

"No problem. We were going to stay here anyway." Kleftis took another *tyropita*. "Help Yiayia as long as she needs us."

CHAPTER 8

The tongue serves some, the teeth others.
—Greek proverb

YIANNIS PATRONAS EMPTIED the wooden boxes out on the table in the refectory and began pawing through the shards. He didn't understand why anybody would bother collecting this stuff, let alone labeling it. To spend your life rooting around in trenches like a pig after truffles, searching for broken bits of clay, clay that when you got right down to it was nothing more than dirt, baked dirt. You'd never catch him doing it, that's for sure. He'd shared this thought with his wife, Dimitra, over breakfast.

"But you work with dirt, too." She'd waited a moment or two before delivering the *skylovrise*, the dog bite. "Adulterers and thieves, the human kind of dirt."

Marriage to Dimitra was like living in a bed of cactus. There was simply no way to get comfortable.

He looked at his watch. They were supposed to be here an hour ago. He never should have told Evangelos Demos to bring the two archeologists, Alcott and McLean, to Profitis Ilias. He should have asked Tembelos to do it.

He wasn't looking forward to interviewing the two men. He had little use for archeologists. He'd had to post a guard in Emborio, on the west side of the island, after he'd caught a pair of Dutch ones digging flints out of the dry gulley without permission from the Ministry of Culture. He hadn't thought much of what they'd collected until a colleague on Samos informed him of the worth of such items. More valuable than heroin, the man had said. Patronas had ordered the archeologists to surrender everything over and leave Greece immediately. He'd put the flints—or whatever the hell they were—in a shoe box and locked it up in the evidence room next to the contraband cigarettes and cellophane-wrapped blocks of Turkish hashish. The following summer, a

French archeologist seeking a Roman tomb had dug up the town water main by mistake. Six months it had taken to straighten that mess out. The list went on and on.

Greece would be better off, he'd long thought, if it had a less illustrious past, one that didn't draw these people from abroad, eager to relive Homer and fight the Trojan War, or worse, the ones who'd thought they'd found some kind of personal answer to life's questions in Katzanzakis and came here to drink ouzo with Zorba and dance in the moonlight. "Go home," he wanted to say to all of them. "Go back to Frankfurt and Scarsdale and live your lives." Being Greek is as much a curse as a blessing. And it is a struggle best left to the Greeks.

THERE WAS A knock on the door. Standing outside was a pale, redheaded man. He seemed not to know what to do, whether to come in or stay out, like a child uncomfortable around grown-ups.

"Good morning. I'm Dr. McLean." His Greek was flawless. "You said on the phone you needed to see me."

"That is correct." Patronas gestured to the pile of shards on the table. "I would like your professional opinion on these."

Devon McLean nodded. "Certainly."

There was something weak and defenseless about the man's pale skin and watery blue eyes. His torso was flabby and loose, his large stomach obvious beneath his clothes. He reminded Patronas of a newly hatched baby bird, had the same kind of exposed nakedness.

"I'd appreciate it if you would set aside anything of particular interest," Patronas told him.

The Englishman began going through the shards, holding them up, quickly examining them and setting them down again. "Like I told you on the phone. There's nothing here. Routine Aegean pottery of mixed provenance." His voice was high and tremulous.

Patronas opened his notebook and got out his pen. "Where are you from?"

"Oxford." McLean continued examining the shards. His fingers were unusually long, jointed like the legs of a spider. "I am one of the Senior Assistant Keepers at the Ashmoleon Museum."

"How long have you been there?"

"A little over a year. I know I'm young for such an appointment, but I have published widely in the field. As you are undoubtedly aware, I'm an archeologist. An expert on the Minoan diaspora. In addition to my position at the Museum, I am involved in two digs: the multi-period field survey at Sfakia, Crete, and the maritime archeological project off the coast of Cyprus."

He chuckled. "You can't call the latter a 'dig,' exactly, as it is under water."

"When did you arrive on Chios?"

"The twenty-fifth, I believe it was."

Patronas wrote everything down, noting that when he talked about himself and his career, McLean seemed more decisive, older. "How did you come to find out about the dig if you were busy scuba-diving off Cyprus?"

"Someone at Oxford or perhaps here in Greece mentioned it to me. I spoke to Eleni for a few minutes. Introduced myself and took a look around. Nothing much to it that I could see. I was planning to leave today, actually, to resume my underwater work in Cyprus. I was checking out of my hotel when your policeman summoned me." He hesitated for a moment. "Miserable business."

"What day was this?"

"At the site? July twenty-sixth. Eleni and I went over what she *thought* she'd found," he said, laying stress on the word 'thought.' "I left her there and returned to my hotel. I was as shocked as anyone when I learned she'd disappeared."

"How well did you know her?"

"I knew her a bit from conferences. She had the makings of a first-class archeologist." *Makings*, Patronas noted, not made. There was something here.

Thinking of the letters, he asked, "Were you involved with her?"

"You mean sexually?"

Lighting a cigarette, Patronas nodded. He tossed the match in the ashtray. "Were you sleeping with her?"

"Absolutely not. Eleni was lovely, don't get me wrong, but she was already involved with someone when I met her. And, quite honestly, I myself was very busy at the time, preparing my lectures and a show we were mounting. I really didn't have time for a serious relationship."

Mounting a show, not a woman. Ach, these English.

Patronas had been slowly reading the letters he'd found in Eleni Argentis' house, painstakingly translating each word into Greek with a dictionary. They weren't exactly love letters. There'd been long discourses on archeology mixed in with the dirty stuff. At least that's what Patronas thought the stuff was. It was hard to tell. Most of the words in those parts were missing from his dictionary. The letters were not dated and he was sure they'd been written two or three years into the relationship. Not new anymore. Both of them moving onto other things.

He slid a piece of paper over to the Englishman and asked him to write his name.

McLean quickly complied. His handwriting was spiky and narrow. It didn't match.

"So if Eleni Argentis wasn't involved with you, who was she involved with?"

McLean wouldn't meet his eyes. "What difference does it make?"

"It makes a great deal of difference, *Mr.* McLean. I'm sure a man of your erudition can understand why." *Mister.* He would not refer to this womanish man as doctor or professor.

"I did hear some things about her. Gossip mostly. Hearsay. Nothing that bears repeating …."

"I don't know if you are aware of the facts of the case, Mr. McLean, but someone slit the throat of her assistant, Petros Athanassiou, a sixteen-year-old boy. He was on a slab in what passes for a mortuary here until yesterday morning, when we buried him. As for her, we found her blood at the bottom of a trench, a couple of liters. The rest, the killer apparently dumped in the ocean. She's done. It's just a matter of time until what's left of her washes ashore."

A tremor seemed to pass over Devon McLean. "They slit the boy's throat …?"

Patronas nodded. "From ear to ear." He was enjoying this.

"You mustn't let him know I was the one who told you."

"Mustn't let who know?"

"Alcott. Eleni was involved with Jonathan Alcott."

"Are you sure?"

He nodded unhappily. "Everybody in the field knew about it. They tried to keep it quiet. It's not done, you know. One does not sleep with one's graduate students, even at Harvard. My understanding is, they were involved the whole time she was doing her thesis and she ended the affair the minute she completed it. Some in the archeological community say she used him. Others say he used her. Quite frankly, Alcott's been a bit of a bore since then, obsessing about their relationship at meetings and conferences, asking after her. When I heard he was on Chios, I was sure he'd come to try and reestablish the relationship. I told him to let it go. 'Be done with her', I said."

"Do you think he was?"

"I don't know. I don't keep up with the status of Alcott's romances."

"What do you mean 'romances'? Was there someone else?"

"That was my understanding. A lot of someone elses. A regular satyr, our Professor Alcott."

"Did you talk to Eleni's assistant when you were at the dig site?"

"Petros, of course. He was a charming boy, witty and intelligent. Quite sophisticated in his understanding of the Minoans. We had a lovely conversation. He was well grounded in the fundamentals of archeology and well aware of what Eleni was seeking to accomplish." He frowned. "It's hard to believe he's dead, that someone would kill a boy like that."

Ah, Patronas thought, hearing the rapture in his voice. *So that's the way it is*. He handed him the little bull. "I found this in his room."

Devon McLean inspected it for a few moments. "A fairly good reproduction."

"Where do you think it came from?"

"How should I know? Perhaps his mother purchased it for him in one of those tourist shops in Monasteraki."

❧

JONATHAN ALCOTT WAS standing outside, waiting to be interviewed, when McLean came out. Patronas could hear the two of them arguing.

"The shards from the dig site are valuable relics that need to be catalogued before they are lost," Alcott was saying, "catalogued by someone who understands and appreciates Minoan history."

"They are nothing, Alcott, and you know it. She found nothing."

"You can't be sure of that."

"Of course I'm sure. She didn't find it, did she? No Atlantis. No proof the Minoans were here. Nothing. Your theory is just that, a theory, at this point." He stopped when he saw Patronas, standing in the doorway, listening to them.

"Good day, Chief Inspector," McLean said, turned on his heel and left.

Patronas escorted Jonathan Alcott into the refectory. The American seemed nervous. "You said you wanted me to look at some shards, but this isn't about that, is it?" he said. "It's about Eleni. The hand in the trench."

"That's right. We're treating it as a homicide."

"What do you want from me?"

"Let's start at the beginning, Mr. Alcott." He flipped open his notebook. "When did you arrive on Chios?"

"July twenty-fourth. I flew here from Harvard."

Interesting people, these academics. Not from countries, like the rest of us, but from universities.

He noted the American's expensive athletic shoes, the spandex shirt. Judging by the tourists on Chios, Alcott's countrymen were people who liked to be comfortable and to buy things. They didn't come to places like Profitis Ilias in July, outfitted like a bicyclist on the Tour de France.

Alcott, in turn, studied Patronas. The policeman reminded him of someone, but he couldn't place who it was.

"Tell me, Mr. Alcott," Patronas asked, "what brought you to Profitis Ilias on July twenty-sixth?"

"Eleni Argentis invited me. She wanted me to help catalogue her findings."

Alcott had it now. It was Charles de Gaulle. Patronas was a dead ringer, a sort of mini version of the famous French leader. He had the same physique, heavily weighted at the center, the same high-handed manner, and certainly the same pendulous nose. Even the same grubby little moustache. And the way he spoke, slowly and carefully, braying each word as if it was graduation day and he was the one calling out the names. At this rate, they'd be here all day.

"I told you the day it happened," Alcott said impatiently. "The trench was flooded, absolutely soaked like it had been raining. All that blood, drying in the sun. Blood everywhere. And the flies, buzzing in my ears, feeding on it. It was a horror show."

Lighting a cigarette, Patronas inhaled deeply and blew smoke in the American's direction. Cigarettes were often useful in Patronas' opinion, especially with Americans. A socially acceptable form of brass knuckles.

"What happened next?"

"I ran," Alcott responded.

"You didn't hesitate? Look over the dig site? Go through her things?"

"Are you kidding? All I wanted was to get out of there."

"What was she looking for? Mr. McLean said something about Atlantis."

"There's a theory that both Eleni and I subscribe to. We believe the myth of Atlantis is actually true, that it's the story of Minoan civilization, which was lost when the volcano on Santorini erupted."

"Thera," Patronas said, correcting him. Santorini was the foreign name for the island, Thera the Greek one. They were in Greece. Hence, 'Thera.'

Alcott rattled on, oblivious. "Some scholars even go so far as to claim that the famous passage about the Red Sea in *Exodus* was actually an eyewitness account of a tsunami. And the seven plagues, the rain, the stinking river, were descriptions of volcanic activity, the eruption on Santorini."

"Thera," Patronas said, louder this time.

"It was by far the most terrifying event witnessed by ancient man," Alcott went on. "It produced huge earthquakes and tidal waves over one hundred fifty feet high. They estimate the one that hit Crete was traveling at five hundred miles per hour. Imagine the destruction. A wave of water like that, slamming into the lowlands around Knossos. It destroyed agriculture and the ash darkened sunlight all over the known world. The island itself sank beneath the sea in one cataclysmic spasm. You asked what Eleni was hoping to find. She was looking for a Minoan outpost here. To demonstrate the extent of their kingdom."

"Kingdom, huh?" Patronas motioned to the shards spread out on the stone table. "Is that what this is?" He was tired of this man telling him about Greek things.

Alcott picked up one of the shards and inspected it. He was much more thorough than the Englishman had been, comparing similar shards and trying to piece them together. "Definitely Minoan, some of them, mixed in with a great deal of later material."

"You're sure."

"Absolutely. No question."

"Devon McLean thinks they're worthless."

"I'm not surprised. He has that reputation. Unless he finds it himself, the discovery is always second-rate. He wanted to do his PhD with me, but I refused. I always thought there was something off-putting about the way he belittles the work of his colleagues, something unsavory."

Patronas handed him the bull. "I found this in Petros' room."

The American put his glasses on and studied it carefully. He turned it over and over again in his hand, running his thumb up and down its surface, caressing it.

"Gold?" Patronas asked.

Alcott nodded.

"What do you think it is worth?"

"You can't place a value on it. It's priceless. Probably the only one in existence."

"How did Petros come by it?"

"I have no idea. Eleni wouldn't have given it to him. It's too valuable."

"So where did he get it?"

The American shrugged. "Perhaps he took it from the dig site without telling her."

"How carefully would she have supervised him?"

"If she liked him, not at all."

"You sound very sure of that. Had you ever been on a dig with her? How well did you know her?" Patronas was watching him carefully.

Alcott's voice was sad. "I'm sure McLean has already told you. Eleni and I were involved with each other when she was at Harvard. At one time, she wanted me to leave my wife and marry her, but then she seemed to lose interest. There are those who allege she wouldn't have passed her PhD qualifying exams without my support and that she was 'playing me.' But I don't think so. I think she loved me in her own way. At least for a while."

"Did she threaten to tell your wife about your affair? The people at Harvard?"

"Eleni? God, no. She had lots of theories about loving and being loved. The main one being that it had to be spontaneous and voluntary. No strings, no obligations, no middle-class expectations."

"No middle-class expectations?" Patronas was incredulous. In Greece if a woman slept with you, it was only because she *had* middle class expectations, not the other way around. A man was simply the means to an end, the end being a house, children. 'The whole catastrophe,' Zorba had called it. Middle-class expectations, not hormones, were the sexual lubricant of choice in Greece.

Alcott seemed lost in his memories. "She didn't believe in free love exactly, something more poetic. The trading of souls. After we stopped seeing each other, she just took herself off to Greece. We corresponded for a couple of years, but then even that ended. I came here partly to see how she was. It's hard to explain the relationship of a professor and his PhD candidates to a layperson. When you have a student as gifted as Eleni, the relationship, the intellectual exchange, is intense; the hours are long; the commitment is all-consuming. You have a vested interest in their well being, their success. It's almost as if whoever they are, whatever they attain, is your creation. You can't let them go."

Patronas stared at Alcott for a long time. "You can't let them go?"

"No, never." The American began to weep quietly. "You don't understand. I loved Eleni Argentis. I will never forget the sight of her, hunched over her books in my office, her joy when I hooded her at her graduation. It went beyond the sexual, our relationship. She was the best student I ever had. She had such promise, such amazing promise." He began to cry in earnest now. "Forgive me, Chief Officer."

Patronas let him cry for a few minutes. "Was she the only student you were involved with?"

Alcott shook his head.

Patronas raised his eyebrows. *The old cat wants tender mice.* "How many others were there?"

"A few. Only a few." The American kept his head down, his voice low.

"Only a few." Patronas let the words sit there.

"Like I told you, the intellectual relationship between a graduate student and their adviser is intense and sometimes it spills over and, inadvertently, becomes a physical relationship as well."

"Did Eleni know about the others?"

"She might have. Someone might have told her."

Laboriously, the chief officer entered all this in his notebook. When he'd finished, he turned again to the American. "You said she was looking for the lost Atlantis." He tried to keep what he thought of this idea out of his voice. "In your opinion, had she found what she was looking for?"

"I don't know." He gently set the bull down among the shards. "Maybe."

∽∾

AFTER THE AMERICAN left, Patronas' assistant, Evangelos Demos, showed Marina Papoulis into the refectory. *She's still a handsome woman*, Patronas thought, watching her as she walked toward him. Her thick hair was streaked with gray now, pinned up at the back of her neck, but she'd kept her shape and her brown eyes were as he remembered them, the irises flecked with gold. He'd heard she'd married a farmer from Campos and had three children. After her children had entered school, she'd taken a part-time job with a travel agency in Chora to supplement her husband's income, in addition to her volunteer work at Profitis Ilias.

Vassilis Korres followed Marina Papoulis into the room. A young man, he was dressed in jeans and a polo shirt, both neatly pressed and tight. His hair was gelled and spiky, his cologne nearly overwhelming. He laid his cellphone down on the table and kept looking at it while the three of them talked.

Although Patronas questioned them at length, neither had seen anything. Marina Papoulis had been at the monastery most of the morning, cleaning the chapel and preparing lunch. She'd seen no one. No, she had not gone down to the dig site. Why would she? Her work was here. Yes, she had witnesses who could verify her whereabouts at all times.

"Why are you asking me this, Yiannis? Didn't we go to grade school together? Copy off each other's papers and walk home side by side? You've known me all my life. I'm your old friend, Marina. Remember?" She laughed as she said this, not taking him seriously. "Do want me to take a lie detector test, too?"

"That won't be necessary," he answered, embarrassed.

Even after all these years, her presence still unsettled him, made him tongue-tied and awkward.

Vassilis Korres had spent the morning leading a caravan of mules up to Profitis Ilias. The American had commissioned him to supply the mules and lead him there. It had taken them a long time, and when he arrived, he'd been tired. After taking Alcott out to the site, he returned to the refectory and spent the afternoon drinking coffee and visiting with Papa Michalis.

"Check with the priest," Korres told him. "He'll verify everything I said."

"Did you see anyone?"

Korres shook his head.

"When did you leave?"

"After you came. Kyria Papoulis took me and Alcott back to town in her car."

"What happened to the mules?"

"Papa Michalis pastured them out on the hill."

"How many were there?"

"Four. We rode two and loaded the other two with supplies. My uncle called yesterday. He wants them back, said he needs them to help with the harvest. I don't know how I'm going to do that on my own."

PATRONAS ORDERED HIS men to help Vassilis Korres take the mules back. But someone—his second in command, Evangelos Demos, would have been his guess—let the rope slip halfway down the hill and the mules broke loose and ran off in all directions. His assistant and the others went thundering after them, yelling and waving their nightsticks like the Keystone Cops.

Patronas shouted directions from the steps of the monastery. He was afraid one of his men would trip and plunge to his death, or worse, get trampled underfoot by a mule. The round-up went on for a long time. It was like watching a rodeo conducted by the Marx Brothers.

Hearing the commotion, Papa Michalis came out to watch. "No offense," he told Patronas. "But I most fervently hope the Sicilians never find out what passes for law enforcement here on Chios."

CHAPTER 9

Day sees the deeds of night and laughs.
—Greek proverb

"COME ON, CHRYSSOULA." Patronas led the horse out of the police stable, climbed into the saddle, and started up the path. Chryssoula was an elderly mare and moved like a sleepwalker, pausing now and then to snack on the bushes that lined the path. Patronas checked his watch. After learning of Alcott's affair with Eleni Argentis, he'd decided to take a closer look at him and was timing the ride, seeking to verify that it had taken as long as Alcott had said to travel from the farm to Profitis Ilias on horseback.

How do Vassilis Korres and his mother and father survive? he wondered, looking down at the farm. The soil was poor here, the rocks as brittle as bone.

When he reached the monastery, he tethered the mare to a tree outside the walls and checked his watch. Close enough. Alcott had been telling the truth. He opened the gate. Tembelos had come by car and was already waiting for him. They carefully went over the area where they'd found the boy's body, looking for clues, Patronas thinking the answer to the puzzle must lie somewhere here. But they found nothing, only a few bottle caps and a broken ballpoint pen.

"Funny thing happened while I was waiting for you," Tembelos told him. "I was walking the perimeter like you told me to and I smelled this funny smell."

"What was it like, this 'funny smell'?" Patronas asked.

"Reminded me of that corpse we exhumed. Remember? It was a year or two ago. The kids thought their stepmother had poisoned their father and we had to dig him up. Smelled the same way he did. Not so pretty."

"I remember. All for nothing, that was." He'd never gotten over those kids, willing to destroy an innocent woman for a greater share of their father's estate. He would have liked to lock them up, but there was no statute against malice, no law on the books concerning greed.

He turned back to Tembelos. "Did you notice where the smell was coming from?"

"I tried, but it was impossible. It was in the air, is all."

After sending Tembelos back to the station, Patronas rechecked the dig site. It took the rest of the day and the sun was down by the time he finished, the sky suffused with pink light. Bats were flitting over Profitis Ilias, darting in and out of the walls, seeking insects in the growing darkness. Patronas watched the bats' antics for a moment, wondering where they'd come from, remembering he'd seen them the first night he'd been here, the night after Eleni and Petros had died. The bats seemed to be coming from an isolated crag on the far side of the dig.

Patronas found a lantern, untethered Chryssoula, and rode in the direction of the crag. It was farther than he thought, the passage difficult in the dying light. Swinging the light in an arc around him, he urged the horse forward, moving beyond the dig site and on up the hill. There was little vegetation on the slope, and the rocks were riddled with fissures where the lava had folded in on itself. The soil was thin and the color of unfired clay. Patronas dismounted frequently, checking the ground beneath him. He was sure there was a cave here. The bats had to be coming from somewhere, and there were few trees, no place for them to roost in this wasteland, nothing but tortured shafts of blackened stone. Caves were worshipped in ancient times, he remembered. Zeus had been born in one, the Diktaian Cave, located on Crete, and the Minoans had sought refuge there after the volcano erupted on Thera and the resulting tidal wave engulfed their island.

"Probably had something to do with female anatomy, the cave thing," he told himself. In Athens, there was the Cave of Pan. God knows what went on there in the old days, given the lascivious nature of the god, whose image with its enormous phallus was a favorite of young tourists. Later, the Christians had taken over some of these sites. His mother had brought him to one when he was a boy, the monastery of *Panayia Spiliani*, the Madonna of the Cave, on Samos. He still remembered the total darkness, the endlessly dripping water. He wasn't looking forward to exploring a cave tonight.

He spurred Chryssoula forward. Goats were living somewhere on the hillside, and he could hear their bells jingling faintly in the darkness. So someone had been here, a shepherd perhaps. There was a rough trail leading farther up the crag, and he followed it with his horse, wondering where it led. A few minutes later, he came to the corral where the goats were housed.

It was fashioned out of twigs and brush, as was the crude lean-to in the back, shelter for the animals when it rained. A raised table of rock—broad and flat—formed the rear wall of the corral. A furrow ran along the base of this rock, but Patronas saw nothing there when he inspected it, only a thin cleft in the earth filled with spiders. For a moment he watched the goats milling around inside the corral. When he raised the lantern, their eyes reflected back at him and they shied away. Evidence of the animals was everywhere; he could see hoof marks in the trampled soil, the ground marked by droppings.

He smelled something wafting on the night air, something besides goat, but he couldn't tell where it was coming from. Patronas hoisted himself back up on the horse and rode farther. Near the top of the hill, it looked like someone had been excavating with a shovel, the dirt overturned in an orderly way. The heat of the day had broken and the stars were bright overhead. He inspected the area as carefully as he could but found no opening, nothing that led underground. He wasn't even sure it was a dig site he was looking at. It might have been some peasant's vegetable garden. Those without land often worked a borrowed plot to supplement their meager income without the owner's knowledge or consent. Whenever possible, they would lay claim to the land outright over time. Perhaps it was the Communist in him, but he was always sympathetic to these outlaw farmers. Better for those who cared for the land to possess it than some absentee landlord in Bayswater or Astoria.

He circled the area on horseback, but saw nothing and started back down, guided by the distant lights of the monastery. He was about halfway down the hill when he noticed the smell again. It was stronger here, more pungent. With a snort, Chryssoula reared up, pawing the ground and breathing heavily. Patronas patted her neck, trying to soothe her. "What is it, girl? What's the matter?"

The horse neighed loudly and jerked her head. Afraid of being thrown, he dismounted, took the reins and led the mare away on foot. He had gone about a hundred yards when he heard the noise. It was a metallic creak, the sound the monastery doors occasionally made, piercing, grating. At first he thought it was the mare's hooves clattering against the stones, but when he looked down he saw they were on soft ground. He walked in the direction of the sound but found nothing, only a stunted olive tree, creaking in the wind. A few minutes later he heard the sound again, closer this time. Raising his lantern, Patronas examined the area. All he saw were outcroppings of volcanic rock, overgrown with thistles and prickly pear. Behind him loomed the shadowy mass of the crag. It was as if the hill itself had made the sound. Patronas shivered, afraid now, in spite of himself.

CHAPTER 10

Cabbage twice over is death.
—Greek proverb

"YOU REMEMBER WHEN I asked you who Eleni was involved with?" Patronas asked. "It was Professor Alcott."

"Her adviser?" The priest put down his spoon. "You think he killed Petros?"

"Could be. I don't know."

"Eleni never said anything about him except as an archeologist. She told me many personal things. I'm surprised she didn't say something. At least give me a hint that they were …." The priest fumbled around, seeking the right word before settling on, "paramours."

"She might have been too ashamed to tell you. He's married. And if they'd gotten caught, it would have been professional suicide. It's very risky for a professor to be involved with a student. A man could lose his job over a thing like that."

The priest broke off a piece of bread. "Still, I don't think he did it. Killed them, I mean. I saw him after he found the hand. No one is that good an actor."

He ladled up some more lentils and added them to Patronas' bowl. It was two weeks before August Fifteenth, the Assumption of the Virgin Mary, and all Orthodox Christians were expected to abstain from meat, fish, cheese, eggs, and oil during this time. As a priest he must, of course, comply.

Looking down at his plate, Patronas wished he'd remembered Papa Michalis would be fasting and declined his invitation to dinner. "*A lentil boils against its will*," Patronas' mother always said. So did the eater of the lentil, in his opinion.

The priest was slurping down his meal has if it was ice cream. "The timing is also off," he said. "Petros was killed long before Alcott got here." He cut off more bread and began to mop his plate.

Patronas stirred the lentils in his bowl, disheartened by their brackish color. "Cooked these in water, did you, Father?"

Papa Michalis nodded. "I have some Lenten cake, too, if you'd like. One of my sisters sent it to me."

"The kind with raisins, sort of heavy?" His grandmother had made that same sort of cake in the weeks before Easter. It did not, if his memory served him right, deserve the title 'cake.' No matter, it had to be better than lentils.

It wasn't. "Where does your sister live, Father? Chios?"

"Oh, no. She's never left the village. She's in Mani."

That explained the terrible dryness. The cake had probably been on the road for a month.

Patronas pushed his plate away. "Tell me what you know about Eleni's family."

"The Argentis family is one of the oldest on Chios. They were originally from Genoa, or so they claim, direct descendents of the Doge. They own vast tracts of land in Campos and along the sea on the way to Vrontados. The church up there, Aghia Barbara, was donated by her grandfather as was the soccer field behind the school. They have deep ties to Chios and like to be known as benefactors here."

"Ship owners, right?"

"Yes. They are part of that group that winters in London and summers here, but who would say 'Chios' if someone asked them their place of origin. You know the ones I mean. They like to eat like the local people when they come here: a big table for twenty at a taverna, drinks for the whole village at the ouzeria, that sort of thing. I think of it as a kind of dress-up game they play. Pretending to be the same kind of people their ancestors were when, of course, they're not."

"And Eleni was one of them?"

Papa Michalis hesitated for a moment. "Yes, I suppose she was. No matter how casually she dressed or how friendly she acted, she always held herself back a little. Oh, she'd help clean up when we ate together, but you always knew she was playing at it, that what was required of others was not required of her. It was an unspoken thing, but it was always there."

"Not so different from her stepmother." Patronas picked one of the raisins out of the cake and ate it.

"No, perhaps not."

"It doesn't add up. Why would a young woman with money to burn spend her life in a God-forsaken place like Profitis Ilias, searching for Minoans?"

"I don't know. They weren't good people, the Minoans. Everyone thinks they were joyful, lighthearted seafarers, childlike and innocent. But they weren't; they were pagans and killers. They had rites of dismemberment. They practiced human sacrifice."

"A lot of the ancients did."

"Not like them. Archeologists found a little temple on Crete that had collapsed during an earthquake. Inside was the skeleton of a young man, trussed up like a bull. Eleni told me the clay bowls in the temple contained human blood, and that the priests had been bleeding him out as he died, the same as they did with the animals they sacrificed."

Patronas ate listlessly for a moment. He wished the priest would change the subject.

"That dig got a lot of publicity. It was even in *National Geographic*. It set off a firestorm, she said. Many of her colleagues in archeology refused to accept the evidence that the Minoans practiced human sacrifice, especially the Greek ones, but she was sure they had. 'That's what the snakes and the bulls were about,' she said. 'That's what makes them so interesting.' "

"So our forefathers were bloodthirsty people."

"Indeed. Greek history is full of death, ritualized death. Look at Agamemnon. He sacrificed his daughter, didn't he?"

"Iphigenia. Yes, on the eve of the Trojan War."

Patronas got up from the table. It had been a long day, and he was sick of this. "With all due respect, Father, what does this have to do with Petros' death or my murder investigation? Are you saying he was the victim of human sacrifice? That his grandmother slit his throat so she could win the war against the Spartans?"

"Interesting." Patronas climbed out of the trench. "Either Titina Argentis was lying or the killer took the package with him."

He and the priest had gone through everything but had found no trace of the package from England. Patronas looked around the dig site, struck anew by its isolation. "He had to have come up that path from the parking lot. There's no other way to get here. The rocks are too steep."

"I don't think you can assume it was a 'he,' " the priest said primly. "The killer might have been a woman."

Hercules Poirot, Patronas thought. *Or perhaps Miss Marple.*

"Greek history is full of women who kill," the priest went on. "Medea. Clytemnestra."

Patronas nodded. His mother-in-law was certainly capable of murder; his wife, too, if provoked.

"Do you have a specific woman in mind?" he asked.

"Maybe."

"Who?"

"Eleni's stepmother." He said this so softly Patronas could barely hear him.

"She came to Profitis Ilias a couple of months ago. Eleni wasn't here. She asked me to show her around. Every room she wanted to see. Eleni was furious when she found out. She said we'd all pay for it now. 'My stepmother's greed is as boundless as the sea,' Eleni said. She called her 'a cobra.' May God forgive me, but it suited Titina Argentis right down to the ground. There is something snake-like about her, reptilian. I've been thinking about it ever since. What if I opened Pandora's box that day? What if I said something I shouldn't have?"

"Like what, Father? That her stepdaughter found Atlantis?"

"You don't understand. She was after something. I'm sure of it. The way she fastened onto me with her fingers, those eyes of hers. I felt like I was gripped by a demon, that Lilith had me in tow. In the Bible it says Lilith could kill unprotected babies with her smile. I felt like Titina Argentis was the same, that everything about her was poison, evil."

"Lilith, huh?" Although he wouldn't have put it quite that way, he didn't disagree with the assessment. Titina Argentis had gotten to him, too.

Papa Michalis threw up his hands. "Oh, what's the matter with me? I shouldn't talk like this. The church teaches that all of us have souls, the capacity for goodness. We're all creatures of God."

"You ever visit a war zone, Father—a prison camp? Places where civilization wears a little thin? We're not creatures of God. We don't have the capacity for goodness. At least not all of us."

"Of course we do. It's a cornerstone of our faith."

"Your faith, Father, not mine. I'm a policeman, remember? Judging by what I've seen, human beings are the devil's own, his one true family. There's nothing divine about us. We're just a bunch of animals, greedy animals who harm their own kind, harm them to possess what they have, harm them to own. The only thing special about us is, we don't die off when we should. We adapt. We endure. That's our single greatest attribute as a species ... our staying power. In our tolerance of misery, we are quite versatile." Patronas was thinking of his marriage as he said this. "We act blindly, then ponder what we've done and find a rational or, since the advent of psychiatry, a not-so-rational reason for it."

The priest's mouth fell open. He looked like a schoolgirl who'd heard her first dirty word.

Patronas felt guilty. It was one thing to think this way, another to give voice to it in front of an elderly priest, to commit blasphemy. He hastened to change the subject.

"You said you showed Titina Argentis this place. How about giving me a tour?"

~

THE MONKS' CELLS were on the second floor of the monastery. Pilgrims used these rooms when they came for the saint's name day, the priest explained. The rest of the time, the space was empty. "They didn't have much, these pilgrims," he concluded, noting the bedroom slippers someone had left behind, the water-logged prayer books in a drawer.

The priest's room was larger and better furnished than the rest. Like the other cells, it opened off the balcony and overlooked the courtyard. A carved walnut armoire covered most of one wall. The priest pushed the door of the armoire shut and leaned against it. "Nothing to see in there. Just priestly attire and religious accouterments."

A huge leather chair and television set took up most of the remaining space. The priest sat down on the chair and demonstrated how it worked. "Eleni had it shipped here from America. They call it a 'recliner.'"

He picked up the remote and began flipping through the channels. "She said I needed to have something to do, that it was too quiet up here. 'A person can't be expected to pray twenty-four hours a day,' she said. 'Even a priest needs some entertainment.' She had a crew of men install a satellite receptor up on the roof. That's how I watch my detective shows. I get television shows from all over the world. The Bishop was furious when he found out. Said the money she spent should have gone to charity. She told him it was her money and she could do what she wanted with it. She was like that, Eleni." Tears filled his eyes. "Strong."

Thinking to distract him, Patronas asked if he could sit in the reclining chair. It was indeed palatial, padded everywhere, with room to spread out. If he upholstered the Citroen, it might look like this. "How on earth did she ever get it up here?" he asked.

The priest shrugged. "With enough money, all things are possible."

~

THE CHAPEL INSIDE Profitis Ilias dated from the fifth century, the priest told him, built to house an icon given to Chios by the Patriarch in Constantinople. A small gold-encrusted work, the icon depicted the Virgin alone on a throne and was housed in a locked glass case to the right of the altar inside the church. The earliest icons did not feature the Christ Child, the priest said. No one knew why. Perhaps it was the gradual synthesis of pagan images with the Christian that had taken place in the early years of the church. Perhaps the early painters copied Roman goddesses. Who could say?

The inside walls of the chapel were blackened from centuries of incense and candle smoke, the frescoes crude and primitive. The images looked to be from the Apocalypse—flames consuming villages, men and women running in burning clothing, the whites of their eyes bright against the sooty background. Patronas had never seen anything comparable and studied them for a long time.

"Who painted these?"

"Some Chiot, probably. The roof leaks and they've been painted over many times. I think the originals were done at the same time as the church."

"They're old, then."

"Yes. At least one thousand five hundred years old, maybe more."

At one time, the monastery had been self-sufficient, Papa Michalis explained. There'd been terraced fields, fruit and olive trees, herds of goats and sheep pastured on the surrounding hills. "I continue the tradition, but on a smaller scale," he said, pointing to chickens housed in a wire coop next to the chapel, the trellised grape arbor and the tidy rows of vegetables growing in a small plot beside it. "I make my own wine. Bread, too, sometimes." The bakery was a cold damp space next to the kitchen, the old wooden troughs as big as canoes.

Taking one of the keys from his belt, Papa Michalis unlocked an iron gate and pushed it open. "As you know, Profitis Ilias has a back entrance. They say it was built in 1822. But I think it's much older."

The blocks of stone reminded Patronas of the tunnel on Samos he'd visited on a school excursion when he was a boy. It had been carved out of a mountain in 524 B.C. to ensure a water supply in times of siege. But there was no water here. He walked back and forth, running his hands over the stones, inspecting the tunnel. Who or what had so threatened the settlers on this hillside that they had spent decades building a way to escape it?

The priest shrugged when he asked him. "Saracens. Persians. Who can say?"

"It's a strange place," Patronas said, remembering the smell on the hill, the strange clanging sound. Flowers were planted around the edge of the courtyard, but they did little to soften the harsh fortress-like feel, the gloom of the place. He pointed to the snakes carved at the base of the well. "That's hardly a Christian motif."

"No, it's not. I always had a feeling something bad had happened here."

"The Turks?"

"No. Long before that."

Patronas took a final look around. "Why did Eleni decide to excavate up here?"

"There were Minoan outposts all over the Aegean, and because of Chios' location, so close to Asia Minor, she was sure they would have come here. She said that whenever archeologists seek an ancient site, they look first at churches and monasteries. The older, the better. They found the remnants of a Minoan town near Aghios Andreas on Sifnos recently and so she thought this would be a good place start."

"Tell the truth, Father. Do you think she found something?"

"I don't know. The last time I saw her, she spoke of 'finally getting somewhere.' I don't know what she meant exactly, but I think she did find something. But be advised, an archeologist's idea of 'a find' is not like ours. She could have found an old bone or two, for all I know. Minoan skeletons are extremely rare. And believe me, that would have been enough for her."

"Bones?"

The priest nodded. "Her theory was that after the earthquakes started on Thera, the Minoans fled, not just to Crete, to Knossos and the other cities there, but to other islands. They were great seamen, she told me. They would have gotten away, certainly as far as Chios."

CHAPTER 11

He left the marriage and went for nettles.
—Greek proverb

THAT NIGHT, WHEN Patronas returned home, he checked out the computer he'd found in Eleni Argentis' house. It contained the log the priest had spoken of, the record of her work at Profitis Ilias. Her notes were comprehensive, complete with scanned photographs, drawings of the various elevations in each trench and a timetable. It was not light reading.

> Today we found what appeared to be an in situ mud brick wall about 30 centimeters down in the SW quadrant of the first trench. On June 23rd, we found crushed terra cotta tiles beneath the mud-brick in the NE quadrant of the second trench. This time the mortar was thick and pink and lay horizontally. On the morning of June 24th, we'd been working in the third trench and found three whole mud bricks in a row, roughly parallel to what looked to be the wall of a house.

Although she meticulously described everything—the location and depth where she'd been working, the times, the nature of the finds—it all boiled down to the same thing: earthen mortar, mud bricks, and terra cotta. In other words, dirt. Sometimes the dirt was sandy, sometimes pebbles or clay was mixed in with it, once or twice greenish-gray matter. She'd found patches of charcoal and two glass beads. Also animal bones, "including what appears to be the jaw of a goat and the tooth of a horse."

When Patronas read this entry in the log, he gave up. She hadn't found Pompeii or Atlantis. No. All she'd found—in addition to the various manifestations of dirt—were "the jaw of a goat and the tooth of a horse." He shut the computer. He'd have to send it on to the archeologists in Athens, along with Petros' statue of the bull, but not just yet.

The book on abnormal psychology was no better. Parts of the chapter on narcissism were underlined with her stepmother's name penciled in on the side. *So that was the person she was studying up on. No mystery there.*

He opened her journal, searching for the quote the priest had mentioned. One passage he discovered read, "There are few villains in this life. I, for one, have never met one." Yet she had, Patronas thought sadly—the man who murdered her. Farther on, in a long passage about the suffering men inflict on women, he found the quote the priest had spoken of:

> Ulysses left his wife to yearn, to wait, to grieve, fearing she would never see him again and longing for him.
>
> After a few weeks in the gilded light of summer, all men go like Ulysses, abandon their women like Penelope on the shores of a lonely sea. Hope is those women's only companion, poor hope, desperate hope. Standing there, searching the horizon for a sign that he will return, that it will be as it was. Seeking to convince themselves that there had been a point to their coming together, that it had not all been in vain.

"What the hell is this about?" the chief officer asked himself. "Gilded light. What is gilded? What is she talking about? Now 'gelded,' I could understand. Gelded would make you sit up and take notice."

Thinking this was women's business, he went downstairs and asked his wife Dimitra what the quote meant.

"Simple," his wife replied. "She thought the man she loved was one thing and found out he was another." She gave him a long look. "It happens."

"*What* happens? I don't understand."

"That part about the 'convincing themselves that it had not all been in vain'? That means that, in order to survive, she pretended their life together was better than it was, that she lied to herself in order to keep going. Like I said, it happens." His wife's voice always held a hint of martyrdom, as if there were an invisible cross on her shoulders and it was heavy. This time was no exception.

Thinking of Eleni Argentis, he asked, "Why would a woman feel this way?"

"Because men lie and deceive you. They don't really want you around. They want to be eighteen again and start all over without you."

As far as he knew, he was the only man Dimitra had ever known, so when she said 'men,' she was talking about him. *He* was the liar, the deceiver, the one who didn't want you around. Patronas sighed. So this was going to be about them. He was sorry he'd asked.

Theirs had been an arranged marriage of sorts. He'd wanted to marry Marina Papoulis, but his widowed mother wouldn't hear of it. With the face of a Raphael Madonna, Marina had been his best friend, and he'd lived for her smile most of his boyhood. A poor girl, she'd had to work as a maid in Athens to complete her education. "She's nothing," his mother had said. "A common girl from a common family." But he had loved her with all his heart and still did, truth be told, his heart quickening whenever he saw her. She'd had a pair of roller skates and used to grab onto the end of his bike, screaming with laughter as he pedaled furiously through the village, her braids flying. The memory still made him smile. Oh Marina, Marina.

But he'd done as his mother wished and courted and married the girl she had picked out for him, Dimitra Pissou. Calculating, ferret-like Dimitra, Dimitra with the face, not of the Madonna, but of a basset hound.

His mother had believed she possessed great wealth. A mirage, it turned out, this *great wealth*, though neither he nor his mother had discovered this until after the wedding, when it was too late. As for her pretenses—the way she looked down on people, her fancy manners and aristocratic way of eating, cutting her meat just so—she was simply imitating the wealthy ship owners she'd seen on Chios. Her ideas she'd gleaned from her more successful relatives, her vision of life from store displays and the gossip of neighbors.

A stolid, unwavering force of nature, his wife was rooted to the ground in every sense, with legs like tree trunks and no ankles to speak of. A perfect example of one of the older models of Greek womanhood. The kind who never laughed except at someone else and who wore black their entire adult lives. Patronas was willing to concede women like that had their uses. They were good to have around in wartime. For example, a group of them had jumped off a mountain in 1803 to avoid capture by the Turk, Ali Pasha. A victory of sorts, no matter that it killed them. It was just hard to take one on a daily basis.

He retreated to the bathroom, saying, "Enough, Dimitra. Enough." But his wife followed him upstairs, continuing their discussion in a loud voice outside the bathroom door.

"You want to know what that quote means? It means women have to put themselves back together, time and time again, after their men break them like pots."

PATRONAS HAD LONG thought that the philosopher Socrates, when condemned to death or exile, didn't drink the hemlock to avoid political exile to Larissa, a cow town north of Athens. No, he was pretty sure Socrates had downed the poison to get away from Xanthippe, his legendary, unspeakable shrew of a wife, someone Patronas fancied was very much like his Dimitra. Socrates simply couldn't face one more day at her side: Xanthippe turning up in the agora, yelling at him when he was trying to discuss something important—say, caves for instance—with Plato. Xanthippe announcing that her mother was coming for an indefinite stay. Xanthippe complaining he never took her anywhere.

Not that the chief officer thought of himself as Socrates. No, he saw himself more as a fellow traveler in the long, not so-happy, but fortunately not completely platonic dialogue that is marriage.

He thought about it as he lay in bed that night. Where had the years gone? The promise of happiness? He had to admit, he harbored little affection for his wife and none whatsoever for his mother-in-law, a gap-toothed old walrus who had iron clad opinions about everything, which she expressed in a deep, penetrating voice like a man's. Like Moses with the Ten Commandments, you could almost hear the trumpet blast in everything she said. He'd tried to overlook the gradual thickening of his wife's waist, the erosion of her face. He'd kept his hands off the Scandinavian tourists he arrested for nudity and drunkenness and came home early most nights. Well, perhaps not most nights. Some nights. A few nights.

He guessed Dimitra had had her dreams when they got married. Hell, everyone had dreams when they got married. But they hadn't come true. He was no Prince Charming. But she'd had her revenge. Yes, indeed. She was working on gelding, too, every chance she got.

The thought of growing old beside her filled him with unbearable angst. And then, to be buried side by side in the family crypt, her family crypt, which meant her momma would be there, too, for all eternity ....

CHAPTER 12

Friendships and loves are forgotten, and when they meet they talk like strangers, passers-by.
—Greek proverb

PATRONAS PUSHED BACK the cloth top of the Citroen, hoping the rush of the wind would make him feel better. He was still haunted by what the fisherman, Costas, had seen on the beach, a man throwing away pieces of a human being in trash bags. He'd ordered his staff to send the remains to Athens, along with the samples from the trench and a hairbrush he'd taken from Eleni Argentis' bedroom. With any luck, the DNA would match and he could declare her legally dead. A good defense attorney might be able to argue that a severed leg and hand did not a murder make, but it was all he had. That is, if he caught whoever did this and they went to trial. He rubbed his eyes.

The road hugged the shore. The water was so clear, he could make out individual rocks on the ocean floor. Across the bay, he could see the village of Faro and the old slag heaps where the ancients had mined gold. A pair of sailboats were tacking in the wind, slowly making their way north toward Chora.

Papa Michalis was in his garden. "Something got my rooster last night. From the way it was dismembered, I would have thought a wolf, but there haven't been wolves in these hills for centuries."

"Maybe a dog got it."

"If it was a dog, how did it get in? I always lock the doors before I go to sleep. And there was no dog in here last night."

At the priest's behest, Patronas examined what was left of the rooster. There was a narrow arc of blood splatter on the white wall above where Papa Michalis had found the bird, as if someone or something had torn open its neck. Its gizzard and guts were scattered across the pavement, the bloody feathers still stuck to the stones.

"A dog," Patronas said again. His mind was still on the scene at the beach. He didn't want to be bothered with dead roosters.

Shovel in hand, the priest scooped up the mess and gently laid it down in the hole he'd dug. "Death seems to be stalking this place."

"A coincidence, Father. Your rooster? Just one animal consuming another. Nothing more."

"That's the thing. Whatever killed it didn't eat it. It just tore it all to pieces and left it there."

"Strange."

The priest patted the little grave with his shovel. "A detective in a novel I read said, 'In homicides there are no coincidences.' "

"True enough. I'm just not sure the author was talking about roosters."

"How did Eleni get along with the archeological community?" Patronas asked Papa Michalis. He was standing on a stepladder in the arbor at Profitis Ilias, cutting grapes. The priest had asked for his help, saying he was too old and unsteady for such work.

After the fisherman's discovery, Patronas was sure Eleni Argentis was dead, but if the old man noticed his use of the past tense, he didn't let on. He still cried openly whenever he spoke of Eleni or Petros, and Patronas was afraid if he told him about the trash bags, it would set him off again. You could never tell with Papa Michalis. He was an odd duck, *loxos*. Weeping over his lost friends one minute and rambling on about crime detection the next, the most grisly aspects of crime detection, the reconstruction of burned faces out of clay or retrieval of gunshot residue from the skin of victims, terrible things. This morning he'd spoken of how difficult it was to catch serial killers like the one in Wisconsin, who'd eaten seventeen people. *Maybe that's what happens to you when you get old*, Patronas thought. *You mix it up*.

"Eleni didn't have much use for archeologists," the priest told him. "She thought they underestimated the ancients, had a bias against them. 'Because of a couple of frescoes, my colleagues think the Minoans worshipped snakes and bulls,' she said. 'That's like visiting Chartres and concluding the French worship stained glass.' "

Patronas cut a handful of grapes and dropped them in the basket. He was glad the priest had asked for his help. It was pleasant work, a welcome break from the investigation. The vine leaves provided dappled shade, a kind of green halo around him, and the grapes were so ripe they perfumed the air. "One of the archeologists said she was seeking Atlantis. Do you think he's right?"

"I don't know. She did say, 'The Minoans' relationship with the sea was the key to their civilization, and islands like Chios would have figured prominently in their cosmology.' "

"There are rumors that she found treasure up here."

Was it his imagination or did the priest flinch? "You see any treasure?" Papa Michalis asked, gesturing to the courtyard, the monastery walls. "Earthly rewards of any kind?"

WHEN PATRONAS HAD been at the police academy, his instructor had said murders were usually motivated by one of three things: greed, sexual passion and/or frustration, or blind, animal rage. He thumbed through his notes again. None of those motivations figured here. Occasionally surprising someone—a burglar, for example—would get you killed, the instructor had said, or seeing something you weren't supposed to see. He'd put the latter in the *gafa* category. No one meant for those kinds of murders to happen, but sometimes they did. Perhaps that's what this was, a mistake, a *gafa*. Perhaps Petros had surprised someone. But that didn't explain Eleni. No, he was pretty sure she had been tortured, that her hand had been severed while she was still alive.

Marina Papoulis tapped on the door to the refectory. "I saw the grapes," she said. "He's not making wine again, is he?"

Patronas looked up from his work. "That was his avowed intention."

"Don't drink it. I don't know what he does, but it's stronger than Cretan brandy, *tsipouro*, and it tastes like vinegar."

She was wearing a blue-green dress and leather sandals with tiny blue flowers on the straps. She'd been out in the sun since he'd last seen her, and there was a sprinkling of freckles across the bridge of her nose, streaks of gold in her hair.

A farm woman, she was unsentimental about the dead rooster. "Crowing all the time. I would have killed it myself. Do you know it bit me once?" Bending down, she showed him the place where the bird had pecked her ankle. Her bare legs were tan, and he could see the tiny white scar under the strap of her sandal.

"It's strange. I don't know how a dog could have gotten in," Patronas said, following her back to the kitchen. "Papa Michalis swore the gates were locked."

"There are owls here. Maybe it was an owl that killed it."

"If it was an owl, why didn't it eat it? It just left it there."

"Something might have scared it off before it had a chance to feed."

Patronas nodded. He'd noticed the volume of the priest's television when he'd visited his room. Perhaps that was it. *CSI: Miami* thundering away at 80 decibels.

She opened a cupboard, got out a plate of cookies—*kourambiedes,* covered with confectionary sugar—and urged him to take one. "They're fresh. I just made them."

The pastry made a mess of Patronas' uniform. She grabbed a towel and moved to brush him off.

Mindful of Dimitra, Patronas backed away until they had the table between them.

She pretended to chase after him, whipping the towel and laughing. "What is it, Yiannis? You scared of me?"

Not you. Never you.

"I'm just distracted, thinking about the case." He'd never spoken of his love for her, his desire to marry. She'd never known how he felt.

"That reminds me. I found something when I was cleaning up." She opened a drawer and took out a piece of ruled paper.

Patronas glanced at it quickly. It was almost identical to the sheet he'd discovered in Petros Athanassiou's bedroom. "Where'd you get this?"

"Outside Papa Michalis' room." She studied the paper for a moment. "Circles inside circles. What do you suppose it means?"

"I don't know." Carefully, Patronas folded the paper and put it in his pocket. "Did you notice anything unusual in the days prior to the murder? Someone who didn't belong? Anything out of the ordinary?" He was taking care to address her formally.

"Now that you mention it, there was a strange smell one night. Like rotting meat. I couldn't pinpoint it. I remember I was coming back from church when I first noticed it. It was very faint, the smell. I thought at first one of the chickens had died and I looked around in their cage for the carcass. But there was nothing."

"What time was this?"

"After vespers."

"What were you doing up here at that hour?"

"Keeping Papa Michalis company. I often do."

"Was it only the one time you noticed the smell or did you notice it again?"

"No, just that once, that one time. The night before Petros died."

"Have you noticed a change in Papa Michalis? The last few weeks, has he acted any differently?" *The paper.*

She turned to face him. "You can't be serious. Father would never hurt anyone."

"What about Petros? Was there a change in him?"

She returned to her work, angry now. "I don't speak ill of the dead."

"Come on, Marina. I'm just doing my job. Police work being what it is, you sometimes have to speak ill of the dead."

"Well, find someone else to do it."

"Marina." He caught himself as he said her name. "I want to find the man who did this." He described the scene on the beach, the plastic bag that had held what was left of Eleni Argentis.

That stopped her. "What can I do? I wasn't there when it happened. I was up here at the monastery."

"People around here know you. They're more apt to talk to you than to me or one of my men. I'd appreciate it if you would question them—informally, of course. Don't let them know what you're doing. Start with Vassilis' father, Spiros Korres—he owns the farm on the way here—and work your way through the neighborhood. I'll bet someone saw something. People often know more than they think they do."

"I know Spiros' wife, Antigone. I'll stop by their house on my way home."

"There's one other thing. Petros' mother told me she and her boyfriend arrived here on July twenty-second. Could you check the boat manifests at your travel agency and verify that? Same thing with the two archeologists. Jonathan Alcott supposedly arrived on July twenty-fourth, Devon McLean a day later. I need to make sure they're telling the truth."

She wiped her hands on her apron. "Let me write that down." She dug a little journal out of her purse and asked him to spell their names and give her the dates again. "Okay. I'll check it out."

He thought for a minute. "Run Antonis and Titina Argentis through your computer, too. See when they got to Chios."

"What did you do with Eleni, with her ...." She stopped and started again. "With what you found?"

"Sent it to Athens. They have better facilities there. Perhaps they'll find something."

"So there won't be a funeral."

"Not for the time being." He knew this would be the worst part for Marina, not the violent death of Eleni Argentis or the torture that might have preceded it. It would be that lack of a funeral, that denial of a final blessing.

IT WAS GROWING dark by the time Patronas left the monastery, and Papa Michalis got a lantern and walked him down to the car. Olive trees blanketed the terraced fields below, their gray-green leaves fluttering in the wind like flecks of mica. The lights were coming on in the villages below and Patronas could see the headlights of a distant car on the road to the airport. A bird left its perch in the wall and soared out over the valley.

Patronas looked back at the monastery. Silhouetted against the sky, the hulking mass was like something out of the Dark Ages. "All those empty rooms. Doesn't it bother you?"

"I'm used to it. There were never very many of us up here, only four or five."

"What happened to them?"

"They complained to the bishop about the lack of heat. They're on Psarra now."

"Psarra?!" Rocky and mountainous, Psarra was a tiny island with a sad history. The Turks had killed more than 15,000 people there in 1824 and the survivors had fled after the massacre, never to return. It was virtually uninhabited, with no electricity or telephone.

"I fear if I complain about the isolation, the same thing will happen to me. I will join my brethren on Psarra or someplace worse. Yiaros, the old penal colony, or that rock where they used to keep the lepers. Bishop Germanos is, how shall I say, a little irrational with respect to me. Given to fits. *Apolektikos*."

"Why?"

"We fell out over the poor boxes. He wanted to send the money to Athens and I thought it was best if we spent it here. I impetuously shared my opinion with a few people and the Bishop found out. He was so angry he wanted to excommunicate me, but as there were insufficient grounds, he compromised on Profitis Ilias. The thinking being I would be contained up there, like a toxic virus, and could do no harm."

The priest gave him a bleak smile. "Unfortunately, there's no Canon law against vindictiveness." He looked back at the citadel. "It's not so bad. I can come and go as I please. Visit Chora whenever I like. I am, as you policemen say, 'under house arrest.' "

"You should leave this place, Father. Two people dead. It's not safe."

"Nonsense. Profitis Ilias is secure. The doors are metal, and they bolt from the inside. No single person could get through them. They're old, but they're strong. They were designed to repel armies."

Patronas watched him walk back up the path to the monastery, the propane lantern he was carrying a small spot of light against the black hill.

CHAPTER 13

Marriage is an evil most men welcome.
—Menander

THE CHIEF OFFICER's wife was stirring something on the stove. "We'll eat in a minute, Yiannis."

Patronas studied the back of his wife. She was rooted to the earth, Dimitra, no doubt about it, the bulk of her weight concentrated in her hips and thighs as if the force of gravity was pulling her down. She'd recently started dying her hair, a reddish-brown color that reminded him of the polish he used on his shoes. It did little to enhance her appearance. A tree in autumn—that was Dimitra.

He had to admit she was not without abilities. She could supervise the mating of donkeys, the birthing of lambs. Skin a rabbit without flinching and stew the latter in a dish so tasty she'd been asked to include the recipe in a cookbook. She'd declined, of course. It was *her* recipe. Why share? She could brew a tolerable wine and spin yarn out of lamb's wool, put up supplies for the winter, lay out a body for burial.

Occasionally, she helped him with his police work, passing on gossip or asking questions in such a way that he was forced to rethink his assumptions. Her world view was a dark one. People were out to get you, Dimitra felt. Given half a chance, they'll stab you in the back and cause you suffering in thousands of different ways.

He'd never thought about what his life would be like without her. She was just there, a part of the house like the floor or the walls. No, not like that. Dimitra was more of an appliance. Not a car or a television, something that could give you a lift or entertain you. Something dull, but necessary. A clock. Yes, that was it. Dimitra was a clock. Tick, tick, ticking away the hours of his life.

After dinner, Patronas showed her the two pieces of paper. She read more than he did. Perhaps she'd recognize the drawing.

She put on her glasses to see them better. "Where'd you get these?"

"I found one at the boy's house. The other Marina Papoulis gave me."

"When was this?"

"This afternoon."

"I wondered what you were doing with her." Her face was hard to read. "The neighbor told me that she'd seen Marina, and Marina mentioned that she'd seen you, that the two of you had spent the afternoon together."

"All this has to do with the case, Dimitra. She and Papa Michalis, they're helping me."

"Yiannis," she asked in a low voice, "what are you doing to us?"

"Nothing. I'm not doing anything, Dimitra."

"Yes, you are. Your mother told me about you and Marina. She said you wanted to marry her."

He wondered why his mother had done this. Was she still upset over the lost dowry? The fact that Dimitra's father owned, not a fleet of tankers as she'd originally assumed, but a gas station, a two-pump gas station in the slums of Castro, not far from the home of Petros' grandmother. Did his mother think enough time had passed? That Dimitra would let a thing like that go? She should have known better.

"I was at your mother's house and she had some old albums out. Photographs of you when you were a boy. 'Look how happy he looks in this picture,' she said, 'standing there with Marina.' You were on a school outing. Corfu, I think."

"Come on, Dimitra. That was a long time ago."

"Why do you have to spend so much time at Profitis Ilias? Why can't you work at your office?"

"Because I'm Chief Officer and it's a crime scene. In case you've forgotten, two people were killed up there. The priest even set up a 'murder room' for me." Patronas shook his head as he said this. *Murder room. Holy Mother of God. Poor Papa Michalis.*

"So you're going to go on seeing her?"

"Yes, I suppose I am. It's a small place and she's there, so, yes, we're going to see each other. We're going have conversations, maybe even drink coffee or eat a meal together." He said this in the same voice he used at the station when his men questioned an order and he wanted to verbally slap them down.

"Stay away from her, Yiannis. You hear me! You stay away from her!"

An old-fashioned Greek male, Patronas normally wouldn't have allowed himself to be spoken to in such a way, but he had work to do tonight and didn't want to fight with her. All the signs were there—the accusatory tone, the prosecutorial mien. Dimitra had more stamina than he and could argue until morning.

"For God's sake, Dimitra, what is all this? What's the matter with you? There's nothing going on between Marina and me. You know that. I'm not doing anything wrong."

"Yes, you are. You're remembering. You think I don't know? Every time you see her, you remember when you were a boy, when it was all ahead of you, and she was the one you loved, loved in a way that only happens once."

Stung, he got up from the table. "I don't have time for this."

"Wait," she called after him.

"What is it now, Dimitra?"

She smoothed down the paper he'd given her. "I'm not sure, but I think it's the Phaistos Disc. Nobody knows what it means, but the tourists, they love it. They buy copies of it, Phaistos bracelets, Phaistos key chains. They claim it has spiritual powers."

She went into the living room and returned with a book, a tourist guide from Crete, and began flipping through the pages. "Look, here's a picture." She pointed to a photograph.

He compared the photograph to the drawings Petros had made. They looked similar, but the boy's paper had been handled so much, it was impossible to tell if the images were identical.

⁂

Patronas called Papa Michalis later that night. "When we were up at the monastery, you said that Eleni thought islands had a role in the Minoan universe. Think back. Did she ever say anything about a disc? The Phaistos Disc?"

"Funny, that. We were having dinner up at the monastery one night—the three of us, Eleni and Petros and me—and she started talking about a book she'd been reading about the Aborigines in Australia. Bruce Chatwin, I think it was. She said the Aborigines sang their universe into being, that they navigated the world using special songs and chants. It sounded like nonsense to me. But I remember she did say one thing that stuck in my mind. She said the Aboriginal drawings, the ones they'd made of Australia, reminded her of some of the Minoan stuff she'd seen. 'Maybe we need to look at the Phaistos Disc again,' she said. 'Maybe it's a map.' "

⁂

If it was a map, it was unlike any he'd ever seen. Patronas studied the image on his computer screen. The Phaistos Disc was a round clay disc stamped on both sides with hieroglyphics. Some of them were obvious—bare-breasted women were bare-breasted women the world over—but as for the rest—the boomerangs and forked sticks, the lonely humanoid-types with tails—he hadn't a clue. Searching the Web hadn't helped, as theories on the Phaistos Disc abounded. Some thought it was a board game; others claimed it was a shopping list, the fish symbol meaning simply 'buy fish.' But if it was a shopping list, why were there so many different kinds of people on it? Had the Minoans, in addition to killing their own, been buying and selling them, too?

Other theories were even more implausible. Sir Arthur Evans, who'd discovered Knossos, alleged it was a paean to victory. Another thought it was a letter to the Hittites from Lukka Land.

This surprised Patronas, who hadn't known there were Lukkas, let alone a 'Lukka Land.'

He'd been staring at the Disc for so long, he'd begun to see pornographic things in the hieroglyphics: male and female parts, dirty bits. He scrolled farther down. The other websites were worse. There was one connecting the Phaistos Disc with the stars, but no stars he'd ever heard of. Stars with quasi-mystical names, stars he suspected existed only in the mind of the site's webmaster. There was also a lot about the spirals on the Disc, spirals being the 'defining motif of the universe.' Groups of Germans were sparring over whether the Disc was stamped or incised, which would have made it the first 'typewritten' account of .... That was the problem, no one knew.

Then there were listings connecting the Disc with the lost kingdom of Atlantis, but not the historic kingdom the archeologists Alcott and McLean had spoken of. No, this was a place where the folks went for rides in UFOs and kept pet unicorns, where the cuckoo was the national bird.

One website stated the thing was a primitive computer disc, used by the Minoans as a navigational device. "Ah-ha," he said, noting the similarities between a navigational device and a map, until he got farther into the site and realized that what was being navigated was the galaxy—the mystical, spiral galaxy. He was reluctant to contact the Archeology Department in Athens, worrying he'd tip his hand, in case Eleni had been right and there was something up there. The last thing he wanted in the middle of his murder investigation was more archeologists milling around, itching to get their hands on his hillside.

He got a magnifying glass out of the drawer and studied the images again. According to something he'd read online, what he was seeing was one form of the Minoan language, Linear A, as yet undeciphered. And unlikely to be, he decided, putting his magnifying glass away and shutting the drawer. At least not by him.

CHAPTER 14

"Neighbor, your house is burning."
"Impossible, I have the keys."
—Greek proverb

When they'd first been married, Patronas had called his wife the 'electric fork,' teasing her about how fast she ate. Later it became the 'electric tongue,' for the sharpness of her speech. 'Electric' in the sense that an electric eel or an electric chair was 'electric.' That is, her tongue was a force to be reckoned with, a sort of built-in, human stun gun. Today, Dimitra ate little and said nothing.

The priest was in the church when Patronas got to Profitis Ilias, chanting the liturgy. Patronas sniffed. He could smell incense in the air, but no hint of the decay Marina had spoken of. He lit a candle and stood waiting in the semi-darkness until the priest finished.

After the priest put away his vestments, Patronas approached him. "Father, I want you and Marina Papoulis to leave Profitis Ilias."

"I can't. I explained to you."

"Then send Marina away. Replace her with one of my men."

"Your men can't cook."

"I'll bring you food from a taverna. It's important, Father. I don't want her here. It's too dangerous." With an extra policeman, the priest would be safe. Dimitra would calm down, and he, Yiannis Patronas, Chief Officer of the Police Force of Nomos Chios, could get on with his homicide investigation. It was the perfect solution.

The priest frowned. "Does she really have to go? We have fun. Sometimes she stays up here and we watch television together. Last week we watched *The Hound of the Baskervilles,* an old Sherlock Holmes movie on the BBC. You might think such an endeavor is frivolous, Sir Arthur Conan Doyle unseemly entertainment for a priest, but it isn't, Chief Officer. Oh, no, it's work. I took notes while I watched. I studied Holmes' technique. He's a genius. He'll help us crack this case."

"You think we're going solve these murders by watching television?" Patronas allowed himself a little sarcasm.

"Indeed, we are. I'm going to learn Holmes' methodology and apply it here. Inference, Chief Officer." He held up a bony finger. "Inference is the key. Holmes sees what no other sees. In *The Silver Blaze*—probably the most famous example—the clue was 'the curious incident of the dog in the night-time.' The dog did nothing in the night-time. Ergo: the dog did not bark. Only Sherlock Holmes could see that. He is a maestro when it comes to discerning such things."

"Sherlock Holmes could *see* a dog not bark."

"*Hear* then. *Hear* a dog not bark."

"How can you hear a dog *not* bark?" He was beginning to think the priest had serious problems.

"It was what wasn't there, don't you see? That was the clue: the dog should have barked, but it didn't. That's how Holmes figured it out. You should watch the show with me. You'd be amazed. Holmes is incredible. He's all-seeing."

Sort of like Dimitra. "And you think by tuning in, you'll figure out who killed Eleni and Petros?"

The priest nodded. "Undoubtedly. This panoptic reasoning, it's bound to rub off."

'Panoptic reasoning.' Put *that* on the shelf next to Atlantis and the spiral galaxies.

❧

DIMITRA HAD SOUNDED pleased when Patronas called and told her that Marina Papoulis would no longer be working at Profitis Ilias. He made it clear it had been the dead rooster, the feeling that someone had deliberately killed the bird to frighten the old man, rather than the conversation they'd had the previous evening that had decided him. It was better that way. Dimitra was like Hitler: give an inch and she'd be in Warsaw by suppertime.

"I wish I could get Papa Michalis out of there, too," he said, "but he won't budge. He claims it's because of the Bishop, but I don't think he wants to leave his television set."

His wife actually laughed when he described what the priest had said about Sherlock Holmes.

" 'Holmes could hear a dog *not* bark.' You should have heard him, Dimitra. He's obsessed. He's seen all the movies and read all the books. He thinks he can solve the crime using Holmes' techniques."

"If he's Holmes," his wife asked, "who does that make you?"

HUMMING A LITTLE tune, Evangelos Demos was laying shards out on the table in the refectory and trying to fit them together like pieces of a jigsaw puzzle. Patronas watched him from across the room, certain that if one of the other policemen were doing this it would not be in pursuit of a solution to the question of who murdered Eleni Argentis and Petros Athanassiou, but for their own obscure reasons, most probably financial. A piece of Kamares ware from the Minoan period would fetch enough money to buy a car on the black market, a fact most of the force was undoubtedly aware of. This, of course, did not apply to Evangelos Demos. Stealing from the evidence boxes would never cross his assistant's mind. His brain was too little. He'd never get that far.

"What are you doing?" Patronas asked, just to be sure.

"Trying to piece it together, to see what it was." He discarded one shard and picked up another.

Glancing down, Patronas noticed disgustedly that his assistant had grown out the nails on his little fingers, filed them to a point like a woman's. Inherited from the Turks, this was an old custom in Greece, used to distinguish those who worked in offices and shops from those who labored in fields. T*oo bad there wasn't a way to distinguish the idiots from the rest of us*, Patronas thought. *A tattoo, maybe.* When Evangelos Demos had first arrived on Chios, he'd tried to teach him police procedure and educate him about the island. All to no avail. The man was incapable of assimilating information. It had been like talking to a tree stump.

"Did you send her leg to Athens like I told you to?" he asked. His assistant had been forced on him by his superiors in Athens, and he despised him.

"Yes, Chief Officer." Evangelos pretended to study the shard in front of him, but he was really thinking about his career, how he might have to return to his village after all, that Chios for all its charm was a little too much like Belfast and the West Bank for the likes of him. That scene at the beach still haunted him. And all this talk of legs and blood spatter. He couldn't sleep. He couldn't eat. And for Evangelos Demos, that was something. He had a ferocious appetite. People said he could eat through metal.

Raised in the mountains around Sparta, he'd never really been accepted by his colleagues in Chios. They called him *xontroulis*—fatso—and *varvarus*—uncivilized. *Vlachos* was another favorite. It meant the same as *varvaros,* only with 'crude' and 'stupid' thrown in. Tembelos and the others didn't realize he knew when they were making fun of him. He'd seen them snicker. He was a detective, after all. It wasn't that hard to figure out.

Still, all in all, he'd liked being Assistant Chief Officer on Chios. His wife had been happy on Chios, and if his children ran amok, well, there wasn't that far to run here. He'd even solved the problem of his mother-in-law, a stone-faced old water buffalo named Stamatina. She distrusted boats and hadn't visited once during the first two years he'd been on the job. For that alone, he was happy to keep the job.

The work had been easy, too. Chiots didn't expect much of their policemen and that was fine with Evangelos Demos, who didn't expect much, either. He could sit drinking Turkish coffee, flicking his worry beads back and forth, from the time he came in until it was time to go home. Of course, the occasional marital eruption had to be sorted out, as did sporadic bouts of thievery. True, not much in the way of police work, but not much was far better than plenty, he'd found, when it came to police work.

Then it had all gone to hell. A year ago the Scandinavians had stolen the priceless Byzantine icon out of the cathedral in Chora and walked it out right past Evangelos Demos—this without even bothering to wrap it up—and onto a boat. Never to be seen again. And the Athens papers had gotten wind of it, not to mention the ones in Sparta. He'd had to talk to Interpol and the Ministry of Justice and innumerable representatives of both political parties. The Patriarch of the Greek Orthodox Church in Constantinople had even gotten involved. And the FBI, in case the Swedes headed to America. And the feeling of all and sundry (but most especially his mother-in-law, who finally made it to Chios on a plane following the publicity and had stayed the entire summer). Yes, the feeling of one and all was that he, Evangelos Demos, was not up to the job.

It wasn't going to help his reputation when it got around what had happened on the beach earlier this week. How, summoned by the local fisherman, he'd rushed down to the cove, and when he'd seen what was lying there, fainted dead away. And the other policemen had just left him there—the bastards—lying on the sand like a beached whale, the waves lapping at his leather shoes until the chief officer arrived.

The chief officer hadn't asked if he was feeling better. He'd threatened to disembowel him, as if there hadn't been enough of that already on the beach. *Oh, the injustice.*

Evangelos Demos moved one of the shards up next to another. He didn't understand what the fuss was about. He'd done his duty. As soon as the call had come in, he'd set about rigging up a makeshift body bag—though from the way Costas Stamnas had described the thing, they're weren't going need a very big one—and then had turned on the siren and roared to the beach. In the car, he thought he better alert the chief officer in case the two cases were related. "What do you mean *in case*?" the chief officer had shouted when he'd heard this over the walkie talkie. "Of course they are related, you imbecile.

We haven't had a violent death on Chios since 1943 and now we've had two in one week."

"It could have been smugglers."

"When was the last time smugglers generated this much blood? Use your brain, you numbskull." And so on and so forth, the chief officer continuing in this disrespectful manner for more than fifteen minutes, leading Evangelos Demos to declare to his wife when he finally got home the next day that the first thing he was going to do when he got back to Sparta was change professions. Become an accountant.

The chief officer was going through his notebook "You know what I think, Evangelos?" he asked. "I think Eleni Argentis didn't die on the beach that night. I think she died in that trench here and someone chopped her up and hid her away until he could dispose of her."

Evangelos Demos closed his eyes. And this before breakfast.

"But why? Why did Eleni Argentis end up in chunks on that beach?"

Evangelos Demos had been trying to forget that very thing. "I have no idea."

"My guess is she stumbled onto something. Something she couldn't live to talk about. Whoever did the dumping must have been in a big hurry. Didn't realize he'd dropped a piece." Patronas went on musing. "Look here." He lifted up a strip of something yellow with tweezers. "It's a piece of gold leaf I found it on her leg. I remember when they redid the iconostasis in the cathedral, the painter had sheets of it, strips of gold pounded as thin as paper. I had to post a guard there while he worked. He was very careful with it because it cost so much and well, you know, the bishop and money."

Evangelos Demos did indeed know the bishop, rather more than he liked. He'd made his acquaintance after the icon disappeared. He hadn't realized before that day that cursing was permitted of bishops, cursing and threatening people. *Oh, the shame of it. Did no one realize he had feelings?* The shards didn't match. He reached for another.

The chief officer remained fixated on the gold. "The painter applied it to the icon with a little brush, a tiny bit at a time. Static electricity helped it to adhere, smoothed it out. Perhaps this got stuck on her leg the same way."

"Are you saying she was killed by an icon painter?" Evangelos Demos was surprised. Icon painters by and large were pious men who survived off the largesse of the church and money from the more devout parishioners.

"An icon painter?" Patronas turned and looked at him. "Who said anything about an icon painter? What are you, an idiot?" His tone was the same disrespectful one he'd used on the walkie talkie.

"Perhaps she found people smuggling icons?" Evangelos Demos offered in a hopeful voice, thinking no one would blame him now for letting the Swedes walk off with the treasure of the island. Not if the Swedes were murderers and cutting people up on the beach.

"That was a year ago, Evangelos. I don't think they would have waited twelve months to move your Goddamned icon." Again, that same tone. "Holy Mother of God. Wait till I tell the Bishop that one."

In addition to switching professions, Evangelos Demos decided, he was going to have to switch religions. Become a Catholic.

CHAPTER 15

Two watermelons don't fit under one arm.
—Greek proverb

NEVER HAVING MASTERED the automobile—which, truth be told, he'd thought was a fad when it had first appeared in Greece—Papa Michalis was forced to hitch a ride with Vassilis Korres' father, Spiros, whose land adjoined that of the monastery.

"I hope this didn't inconvenience you," he said as he drew up his skirts and stepped into the farmer's weather-beaten pick-up.

"I'm heading into town anyway," Korres said. "Got a load of watermelons I want to sell."

Gunning the engine, he swung the truck back onto the highway. He was an older, sloppy looking man with a grizzled face and gold teeth on either side of his mouth. His black eyes were set deep in his face, and the glance he gave the priest was full of cunning. There was something wolfish about Spiros Korres, the priest thought, something he'd never liked. Whenever the farmer smiled, baring those flashing incisors, he found himself drawing back, feeling a bit like Little Red Riding Hood.

Korres gave him an assessing look. "Any word on the woman?"

The priest knew from his somber tone that he meant Eleni Argentis. "No, nothing."

The farmer turned on the radio to listen to the news, keeping one hand on the wheel. The truck predated the war and roared like a locomotive. Papa Michalis could feel the watermelons banging around in the back and grabbed the dashboard with his hand.

"Albanian scum!" Korres banged his fist on the steering wheel in response to something he'd heard on the radio. When all he got was static, he turned the radio up louder and cursed.

Papa Michalis wished he'd keep both hands on the wheel. "Petros' grandmother has had a bad time of it. He was her only real family …."

"Strange, a kid like that hanging around those trenches. I never understood what he was doing up there."

"Eleni was paying him to help her with the excavation. It was a job."

"Digging up shit," Korres shifted gears. "Stupid reason to die."

A typical Greek attitude, the priest thought. He remembered seeing telltale bands of shards at a construction site near the airport. Such a finding could delay a builder for years, and he wasn't surprised when the crew worked all night, burying the evidence in cement before someone could alert the Ministry of Culture.

"Something like King Tut, now that I could understand," Spiros said. "But not what she was doing. They never found anything, did they? Her and the boy. Two years and nothing. Right?"

"Not that I'm aware of."

"So, why'd they kill her?" He asked this ever so casually. "You'd know, wouldn't you? If she'd found anything?" Again, that same assessing look.

"Yes, I'd know." Papa Michalis looked out the window. "Trust me, Spiros. She found nothing. No gold. No silver. Nothing."

"Funny you should say that. I heard just the opposite. I heard that she had."

❧

Taking his time, Papa Michalis moved through the crowd at the market, inspecting the food on display. A young woman was selling home-made *bougatses*, a custard-filled pastry from Asia Minor, and he bought one.

"*Smyrneiko*," the woman said. "My grandmother's recipe."

The priest nodded. The sweets from Smyrna were legendary, the recipes brought from the million or so Greek refugees who'd come pouring out of the region after the Turks burned them out.

"You should have been here fifteen minutes ago," the woman selling the pastries told him. "Petros' grandmother and the Argentis woman had a big fight. The old woman was shouting, calling her a whoremonger."

"What did Titina Argentis do?"

"Oh, she left."

After bidding the woman 'good day,' Papa Michalis moved on. A little boy was selling painted rocks for a euro and he bought one. He could hear the voices of other children playing in the field behind the stalls, shouting as they kicked a ball around. Usually he enjoyed the open-air market, but today he just wanted to go away. Too many children about, too many boys like Petros. A stray dog with a distended belly passed him and peed on the curb.

The pavement was spotted with rotten fruit, greasy squares of wax paper. Gathering up his robes, the priest walked on, mindful of the filth.

∽∾

"THAT MAN YOU saw," Yiannis Patronas said. "Can you describe him?"

Costas Stamnas, the fisherman who'd stumbled across the remains of Eleni, shook his head. "It was too dark on the beach and I didn't want the man to see me."

"You had to have seen something. There was a full moon out." Patronas opened his notebook. "Let's start at the beginning. How tall do you think he was?"

"I don't know."

"Try."

Stamnas thought for a moment. "Like me, I guess. Medium."

"How about his weight? Thin, fat?"

"Average."

"Do you remember anything else? Anything special that could help us catch him?"

"He was dressed funny. Not in a shirt and pants. Something tight. It covered his whole body, his head, too."

"What about the car? Did you get a good look at it?"

"The muffler was shot, but he could have damaged it on the way in. The road's pretty rough. All I know is, it sounded old."

"Color, make?"

The man shrugged. "Could have been a Fiat or Ford Fiesta. Something about that size. Not too big."

"If you think of anything else, will you let me know?"

Costas Stamnas nodded and drifted out of the police station. Patronas lit another cigarette and leaned back in his chair. *What a waste of time. Average-looking and driving a Fiat or Ford Fiesta. Shit. Half the people in Chios drove those cars.*

He was leaving the station when he spied Marina Papoulis, standing in front of her car, talking to Papa Michalis. He joined them, helping Marina load her groceries into the trunk, the watermelons and bags of peaches. She had her daughter with her. Dressed in a white dress and scuffed leather shoes, the little girl had long braids and a little purse with a kitten embroidered on it.

She watched him shyly, exactly the way her mother had when the two of them had been in school together. Patronas sighed. That face, those eyes. It was as if a window had opened up and he could see himself again as a boy, wheeling around on his bike, trying to impress Marina, his precious, golden-eyed Marina.

"What's your name?" he asked the child.

"Margarita."

"How old are you?"

"Eight."

"Did you know that when your mother and I were your age, we used to hide under our desks at school and eat *svingis*?" *Svingis*, a specialty of Marina's village, Pyrgi, were rounds of fried dough. Notoriously hard to make, they were the size of dinner plates and never found in stores. Marina used to bring a bagful from home and share them with him.

"Did you get in trouble?"

He nodded.

"What did the teacher do to you?"

"Made us stay after school."

Her mother laughed. "I'd forgotten all about those *svingis*. What a mess they made! Sugar everywhere. No wonder we got in trouble."

"The teacher could have expelled me and I wouldn't care. They were worth it, those *svingis*. They were the best things I ever ate. What I'd give to taste one again."

UNABLE TO FACE another truck ride with Spiros Korres, the priest had asked Marina Papoulis to drive him back to the monastery. A careful driver, she took the slow way back to Profitis Ilias—a one-lane road that wound through the fishing villages on the eastern side of the island. Turkey so close he could see cars moving along the road on the other side of the channel. A beacon marked the border between the two countries. It had just come on and he could see the light blinking in the middle of the dark water.

There was an old map at the monastery with monsters drawn in the unknown areas of the globe. 'Terra Incognita,' the mapmaker had labeled those spots. The priest thought Turkey was the same, 'terra incognita.' In the fading light, the sloping hills seemed to ripple like the muscles of a slumbering beast. And from what his mother had told him, monsters had indeed dwelt there, the army of Kemal Ataturk, as fearsome as any mythological beast.

Kyria Papoulis parked her car and she and her daughter helped him get his bags out. "I'll bring you some stuffed tomatoes tomorrow. I won't stay. Yiannis told me I mustn't come up here anymore. I don't know why, but he wants me gone from this place."

"He has his reasons," the priest said.

Patronas had confided in him about his troubled marriage, his wife's jealousy of Marina Papoulis. "Truth is, Father, Dimitra and I have never been very happy together. *We were calling it a carnival and eating dried bread.*"

Papa Michalis hadn't known what to say. " 'A rainy day and a contentious woman are alike,' " he'd ended up telling him, quoting the Old Testament. "Contentious wives are nothing new, Chief Officer. They've been with us a long time. Like the rain, you just have to endure them."

He took the bags from Marina Papoulis. "You can come whenever you like. I'll unlock the door at first light and leave it open for you."

He reached in his pocket and took out lacquered rock he'd bought from the boy at the *laiki*. "Here, child," he said, handing it to Margarita. "A little gift for you."

Smiling, she ran her finger over the picture of a sailboat painted on the rock. "Thanks, Father."

PATRONAS HADN'T WITNESSED the fight between Titina Argentis and Petros' grandmother, but his wife had heard about it and described it to him in detail when he got home.

"I don't know what they were squabbling about, but my cousin said the old woman yelled, 'I only want what's mine, what I'm entitled to.' "

"Did she seem upset?"

"The old woman? Not really. My cousin said there was something stagy about her performance, as if she were staking a claim and wanted witnesses. She'd do anything for a euro, that one. Cut your heart out and sell it on eBay."

Patronas smiled. His wife had recently mastered the computer and had been bidding for household furniture on the Internet. He liked the concept. It made her feel as if she were shopping and yet didn't cost him money.

"Titina Argentis was having none of it. Not that she's any better. She might dress pretty, but she's a *kolopetsomeni*, a leather ass, all the same. She thinks she's something when everyone knows she's just a tricked up villager from Epirus."

Not everyone, Patronas thought wearily. It had taken him over a week to establish the origins of Titina Argentis, Eleni's evil stepmother, a week and a fortune in long distance phone calls.

"What a pair those two are. The whore's mother and that bitch from the Pindus mountains."

They ate their dinner out on the terrace. "How was Marina?" Dimitra asked, keeping her head down, picking through her food with her fork. "My cousin said she saw you talking to her at the laiki."

From the way she said it, Patronas knew that had been the real reason her cousin had called. Not to discuss Titina Argentis, but to report back to his wife on him. Dimitra must have hated that, being called by a relative about her husband. The subject of gossip.

"Fine, I guess. I only spoke with her a few minutes."

"What did the two of you talk about?"

"Not much. She was there with Papa Michalis and her daughter." *See, Dimitra?* he wanted to shout. *No reason to be alarmed. Chaperones.*

His wife got up and began to clear the table. "You should be more careful when you're around her."

"Why is that, Dimitra?" he asked impatiently. "Why should I be more careful?"

She surprised him. "Because I don't have much, Yiannis. No children. No life with you. Not much of anything when you get right down to it. You weren't in love with me the day we got married and you're not in love with me now."

"What are you talking about? I love you, Dimitra." he said, biting off the words, angry at himself for feeling guilty. "I've always loved you."

"No, you don't, Yiannis. You never have and you never will. We aren't even very good friends, you and me. That's why you should be careful. Because I have nothing and you're stealing from me."

"Come on, Dimitra. You're my wife. We love each other."

She just stood there with the dirty dishes in her hands. "You think this is what the songs are about, Yiannis?" she said. "The poems? What you and I have? You think this is love?"

CHAPTER 16

"If you play in chicken feed, chickens will eat you."
—Greek proverb

WEARY, PAPA MICHALIS set his bags down on the steps and unlocked the metal door of the monastery. The wind was up, tearing leaves off the trees, but as soon as he stepped inside, all was quiet. He used to welcome that quiet, that sense of apartness, of being removed from the world, but not now. Now it made him afraid. Bolting the doors again as he'd promised the chief officer, he hurried across the courtyard. He gathered some tomatoes from the garden then made his way to the kitchen to put his groceries away and start dinner.

He diced the tomatoes and cut two thick slices of bread, trying not to think about the meals he'd shared here. Petros or Eleni laughing at something he'd said. Gone now, both of them. The policeman who Patronas had assigned to guard Profitis Ilias was outside the walls, patrolling the dig site and fields beyond. He wasn't going to come in and watch television with him. No, tonight, he was alone.

After he'd finished eating, he tidied up, then walked over to the church and chanted the evening service, his voice echoing in the deserted chamber. For some reason, the words, instead of providing their usual solace, depressed him. "I'm just tired," he told himself.

One more task and then he'd sleep. He went upstairs to his room and opened the armoire, took out the first carton and carried it down the stairs. It took five trips to empty the armoire, and he was exhausted by the time he'd finished. It required all his strength, and he had to rest for a moment before climbing back up to his room. He thought he might do some reading and picked up his Bible, planning to read a chapter a day as part of his spiritual cleansing, his preparation for August Fifteenth.

He didn't know how long he'd been asleep when he heard the footsteps.

For a moment he thought it was the policeman Patronas had assigned to the monastery, but then he remembered the man had been posted outside and the metal doors were locked. There was no way he could have gotten in. Puzzled, he opened the door of his room and peered out; the moon was up, bathing the courtyard in light. The well was directly below him, the water so still he could see the moon's reflection on its mirror-like surface. A moment later, something set the water in motion, breaking up the image of the moon and sending waves splashing against the edge. *That's odd*, thought the priest. *There's no wind. The air is still.* He stood there for a moment, watching the water, but saw nothing more and returned to his bed. A few minutes later he heard the sound again. It sounded as if someone were walking on the balcony.

Papa Michalis opened his door again. "Who is it? Who's there?"

A cloud had passed over the moon and it was darker now. A shrouded form was standing there. When the priest saw it, he screamed and tried to back away, but the intruder was too fast for him.

It took Yiannis Patronas more than two hours to get the lock drilled and open the door of the monastery, two more to secure a helicopter to airlift the priest to Athens. Patronas wasn't sure what had happened to the old man. He'd been unconscious when they'd found him, lying in a pool of blood on the cobblestones below his room. The chief officer didn't think the priest would survive the helicopter ride.

Kyria Papoulis had found the doors locked when she came to drop off the food that morning and had called Papa Michalis on his cellphone. When he hadn't answered, she'd summoned the police.

Word of what had happened had spread quickly, and Patronas could see Evangelos Demos and Giorgos Tembelos parking their cars at the bottom of the hill. A local doctor was with them. "I can look after him until the medics arrive," he told Patronas.

Patronas ordered the two men to string special tape around the entire monastery, desperate to preserve the integrity of the crime scene. "As soon as Papa Michalis is airborne, we're going to tear this place apart," he told them.

The helicopter arrived a few minutes later, stirring up dust as it circled the monastery. Patronas waved to the pilot and he put it down inside the courtyard. A team of medics rushed out with a gurney. They quickly secured Papa Michalis' neck and spine and rolled him onto the stretcher, then stuck an IV in his arm and placed an oxygen mask over his face. Ducking their heads, they carried him into the waiting helicopter. The pilot waved once at Patronas and they were gone.

Patronas had welcomed the roar of the helicopter, the sense of action it provided. The silence after it left oppressed him. Spiros Korres had heard the sirens and followed the police cars up to Profitis Ilias, drawn no doubt by the chaos, the possibility of treasure. He tugged at the crime scene tape, trying to get past it, into the courtyard.

"Get out of here," Patronas yelled, waving him away. "This is a crime scene. You have to leave."

Korres took his time, taking a good look around before he left.

"What do you think happened?" Giorgos Tembelos asked Patronas. He nodded to the damp place on the cobblestones where he'd found the priest.

Patronas was glad Tembelos was there. A large, shambling man, he'd entered the police force the same time he had. Lacking ambition, he'd been content to remain a patrolman while Patronas moved ahead. Overweight and known for his laziness, Giorgos never moved unless he had to; no passions to speak of, save *Olympiakos*, the soccer of Athens, and the American magazine, *Penthouse*. He enjoyed the photos even though he couldn't read English. "It's not the words that matter," he'd told Patronas, wiggling his eyebrows. "It's the flesh." Patronas had always relied on him. He was the closest thing he had to a friend on the force, and he could be counted on to act intelligently in a case like this, to cover your back, unlike Evangelos Demos, who, handicapped by his innate stupidity, was apt to get confused and shoot you himself.

"I don't know, Giorgos. Someone tried to kill him."

"But who? The doors were locked. How did they get in?"

And that, of course, was the question.

~

PATRONAS LEARNED NOTHING from the young patrolman he'd assigned to guard Profitis Ilias.

"The wind came up around midnight," the young man said. "Even if the priest had yelled, I wouldn't have heard him, the way it was blowing. I don't understand how he got by me, the intruder I mean. I made a complete circuit of the place just like you told me to and checked the doors on both sides every time I went by. I didn't see anyone, Chief Officer. It was just me and the wind."

"How often did you make your rounds?"

"Every fifteen minutes or so. Once I finished one round, I'd start another. I was walking back and forth all night."

Patronas had summoned every available man to the monastery. "I want you to go over this place with a fine toothed comb," he ordered them. "Get down on your hands and knees. Move furniture. Open windows. Dust everything for fingerprints. Everything, you hear me? Leave nothing to chance. Evangelos, you start with the refectory. Haris, you check the tunnel.

See if the lock on the gate there has been tampered with and dust it for prints even if it doesn't look like it has been."

"What if I can't get the lock open?"

"Shoot it. Giorgos, you work the outside perimeter. Check the weeds, the rocks, everything, for trace. He got in here somehow, either through the tunnel or some entrance we don't know about. The bushes are high in the back. He might have snagged his clothes, so be on the lookout for threads, fabric. You, Panos Liaos, go through the monks' cells on the second floor. Most of them are empty, so it shouldn't take long. After you finish, help the others. I'll take the priest's room and the chapel. Now get moving."

Patronas worked his way up the stairs and out along the balcony. He found a tiny strip of cloth caught in the splintered railing in front of the priest's room. Papa Michalis was old. Perhaps he had lost his balance, maybe had a stroke, and crashed to the ground below. Patronas gathered up the threads with his tweezers and put them in a plastic bag, closing his eyes against the memory of Papa Michalis and his talk of forensics. "I like those American shows," the old man had said, "where they swab things with Q-tips and use DNA to catch criminals."

Patronas put the fragments of wood from the balcony in another bag and carefully inspected the priest's room. There was nothing there that hadn't been there before. The television was where the priest had left it, the remote laying on the worn lap of the chair. He rubbed his hand along the padded arm of the recliner. "Don't die," he whispered.

After he finished with the room, he moved slowly across the cobblestones until he reached the spot where he'd found Papa Michalis, the priest's silhouette outlined now in white chalk. He noticed there was a new smell about the place, a smell of damp earth and decay, deep and penetrating. Marina was wrong, he decided, remembering what she'd said about the strange odor that had permeated the air the night Petros and Eleni were killed. This was not the smell of death, at least not recent death. No, a smell like this came only after the passage of time. It reminded him of the tomb where they'd placed his grandmother after she'd died, newly opened after fifty years. "Strange," he said to himself.

He found a trail of bloody footprints near the well. So it hadn't been a stroke or an accident. Someone had thrown Papa Michalis off the balcony and then come down to check on his handiwork, bloodying his shoes without realizing it. Patronas followed the footprints until they disappeared on the far side of the well. Judging by the size of the footprints, it had been a man. Had someone like Spiros Korres come to rob this place? Been surprised by the priest while searching for treasure? Or was it personal?

He called for one of his men and showed him the footprints, then entered the church. Sometimes these old churches had a crypt under the altar. Patronas carefully inspected the marble pavement. The entrance to the crypt was on the left side of the iconostasis, hidden beneath a copper baptismal font. It was a small space, chiseled out of limestone and sealed with a metal door. The door looked original. The shiny padlock securing it did not. Patronas cracked the lock open with the butt of his gun. He'd expected to find bones, remains of saints, reliquaries, as befitted a church as old as this one. Instead, he found artifacts of a different kind—intricately worked gold beads and hammered masks, an ivory statuette of a woman encircled with snakes, everything neatly set inside orange crates lined with newspaper.

Patronas lifted out the statuette. No more than eight inches tall, it was beautifully carved—the artistry far superior to similar ones he'd seen in Athens and Heraklion. Bare breasted, the woman was dressed in a flounced skirt, a snake in each hand. Their scales were delicately etched, their forked tongues and tiny jeweled eyes pulsing with life. On her head was a tiny gold diadem with symbols he didn't recognize, and she had another snake, larger and thicker, draped around her waist like a belt. Patronas touched her painted hair. Four thousand years old and she was still Greek to the core.

In a second box, he found a pair of double axes, both of them gold. Beneath the axes was a random assortment of jewelry: pendants of rock crystal and carnelian, gold chains and earrings, heavy rings set with crude squares of amber or lapis, polished green stones he thought might be emeralds. Altogether there were five boxes. One held primitive votive offerings: fat, violin-shaped women and crude phalluses. Two clay jars occupied whatever space remained in the crypt. He raised the lid of one of the jars. It was full of human bones. Sighing, the chief officer carefully set the lid back down. "Sleep well, my brothers," he said.

He wrote down everything he'd found and drew a sketch as to where each piece had been located. "Father, Father what have you done," he said out loud when he'd finished. There were more than eighty items on his list. Save for the two jars, most were small. Easy to hide in a pocket or the palm of a hand. At least a third of it was gold. There had been treasure after all.

He refastened the broken lock as best he could. His men weren't paid much and they all had families. This would tempt them. He hid the door to the crypt as well as he could and left the church.

Giorgos Tembelos and Evangelos Demos were in the refectory. "Find anything?" Tembelos asked.

"No, nothing. It's a mess in there."

"This whole place is a mess. And that smell? It makes my skin crawl and I'm a cop."

CHAPTER 17

Seize the blind and take from him his eyes.
—Greek proverb

LOOKING OUT THE window of the cab as it drove through Athens, Patronas reflected that driving through this city was like swimming in a sea of cement—automobiles providing the motion, the eddying pools of current. The priest was in KAT, the national trauma center of Greece. The complex was located in Kifissia, a suburb north of Athens, and the ride from the airport had taken a long time. Built on a plain between three mountains, Athens was home to nearly four million people. Traffic was at a standstill, the air heavy with auto exhaust.

In the distance, he could see freighters moving out of the harbor of Piraeus into the steel-colored waters of the Saronic Gulf. He'd been forced to spend an Easter in Athens when he was a student, and he still remembered the sight of people grilling lamb outside on the pavement. *Why live here?* he'd wondered at the time. But he'd known the answer. *Sparta has been your lot. Sparta you praise.* It was easier to survive in Athens, especially after the war. You didn't go hungry. You and your family were safe.

Patronas remembered Kifissia fondly as a place with towering plane trees and tourists riding in horse drawn carriages. There'd been water everywhere in those days, running along the road in little canals. It was an oasis in the sun washed plains of Attica. Now Kifissia was an overbuilt, expensive suburb with cars parked everywhere and stores selling designer goods, Gucci and the like. Patronas paid the cab driver and pushed open the glass door of the hospital. The doctor had said Papa Michalis was housed in the new wing. A modern, seven story building, this portion of KAT had been built as part of the preparations for the Olympic Games. Thousands worked here now, and it was a confusing labyrinth, the biggest medical facility Patronas had ever seen.

"The man from Chios is in the Intensive Care Unit," a Filipino nurse told Patronas. "He's very weak. You can't stay long."

Papa Michalis was lying in a hospital bed, apparently asleep. He had wires hooked up to the side of his neck, IVs attached to both of his hands, and a bag of yellowish solution dripping into one arm. His head was swathed with bandages and his skin was mottled, covered with purple bruises. Patronas couldn't tell if the bruises were the result of the attack or of the doctors' efforts to save him.

"Papa Michalis?"

The priest stirred when he heard his name and opened his eyes. He tried to sit up, but the effort cost him and he fell back on the bed. He looked a hundred years old.

Patronas kept his eyes focused on the old man's face, trying to block out the machines, the bag of blood hanging up next to the bed, the bag of blood draining beneath it. "Did you see the man who did this to you?"

The curtains were drawn, and it was too dark to read the priest's expression, the only light in the room the green readings of the monitors. Patronas felt as if he were underwater. As if there was no air. He longed for a cigarette. He hated hospitals.

"We found footprints leading away from where you fell. Whoever did it walked through your blood without realizing it."

"Did you take an impression?" Forensics again. Even though he was broken in two, the priest wanted to play detective. Patronas found this unbearably sad.

"No. The cobblestones were too uneven. There was one interesting thing, though. They didn't lead anywhere. They just stopped."

"A ghost, you think?" The smile was feeble, but it was there.

"No, Papa Michalis, I don't think it was a ghost. I think it was a grave robber. That's what you've been doing, isn't it? You and whoever did this to you. You've been looting the site. That's why Eleni and Petros were killed. They were involved in it, too, which makes you an accessory to murder."

The priest turned away. "It's not my fault what happened to them."

"What I don't understand is how you, a priest, could hide something like that and go on hiding it after what happened." Patronas fought to keep his voice down, surprised at how angry he was. "How you, a man of God, could shield a murderer."

"It wasn't like that," the priest whimpered. "You don't understand."

"I found everything, Father, everything. In a *church* of all places—the gold, the jewelry. Museum quality, all of it." The monitors were flickering. Patronas thought he probably had another minute before the nurse appeared.

"Question is: how did it get there? How did it find its way into the crypt, behind a padlocked door?"

"I don't know what you're talking about."

"As soon as I get back to Chios, I'm going to bring in the experts and we're going to dust everything in that room for prints, and I'll bet money we won't just find yours, Father. No, my guess is we'll find Eleni's or Petros'. One of them was smuggling and you were helping them. Now I want to know which one it was."

"What difference does it make now?" The priest fidgeted with his blanket. "They're both dead. You can donate everything to a university."

"Father, tell me."

He shook his head. "It is better to lose an eye than one's good name."

"Father, whoever killed them isn't done. He'll keep killing until he gets what he wants. Until he finds that crypt and empties it."

" 'Him' again. It's always 'him' with you. I told you before: You have no evidence it's a he." His voice grew faint and he began slurring his words as he drifted in and out of consciousness.

Patronas spent the night in a plastic chair outside the priest's room, sharing the space with the family of a car accident victim. The women in the group cried for hours.

Periodically, he'd get up and check on the priest. Papa Michalis slept fitfully, crying out in his sleep. Though Patronas tried, he couldn't make out what the priest was saying. He was too drugged, whatever he was shouting impossible to understand.

He seemed better the next morning, sitting up in bed while a young aide washed his face. The bandage on his head was smaller and he was breathing without oxygen.

He still refused to cooperate.

"Don't you want us to catch him, the person who did this to you?" Patronas asked. "Don't you want him punished?"

"I wouldn't dream of it. I am a Christian priest, and one of the tenets of Christianity is that when a wrong is done to you, even a great wrong, you turn the other cheek. That's what I intend to do. To turn the other cheek."

"Father, if you don't start cooperating, I'm going to lock you up. I swear it. I'll throw you in jail, IVs, heart monitors and all."

"Go ahead. The newspapers will have a field day. You'll lose your job. They'll talk about you on television."

The story came out in fits and starts. "They were Petros' things," the priest finally admitted. "I was holding them for him in my room in that armoire you saw, the one against the wall. I didn't know what to do with them after he died. I was afraid to leave them. Suppose you or one of your men stumbled across them? I would have been—how do the Americans say?—'busted.' So I bought a padlock and moved it all into the crypt. I thought it was a good place. I hadn't shown the crypt to you and nobody else knew about it. These days no one goes to church. Soon, my brethren and I, we will be obsolete."

"You moved everything yourself?"

The priest nodded. "It wasn't easy. I had to take the bones out and move them separately. It took me most of the night."

"When was this?"

"The night I was attacked. I'd just finished."

"You were in town during the day. Do you think someone followed you into the monastery?" That would solve the puzzle of the locked door.

"No. I was nervous. I bolted the door as soon as I got there. I kept looking over my shoulder. It was still light then. I would have seen. There was no one in the courtyard. No one anywhere near me."

"Are you sure?"

"I had a feeling someone was watching me at the laiki, but only for a moment. At the time, I thought it was God, angry at me for desecrating his house." He closed his eyes, leaned back on the pillow. "Now, of course, I know better."

"How about the tunnel? Are you sure it was locked?"

"Yes. I was afraid. It was getting dark and I'm an old man."

"When you were moving the artifacts, did you hear anything?"

"Mice. Perhaps an owl. Creatures of the night."

Patronas was taking everything down in his notebook. "You yourself didn't take the artifacts from the dig site. Petros was the thief."

"Petros was a boy who wanted a motorcycle. A poor boy, who wanted to ride through town with a pretty girl, to rev his engine and make a big noise. When he found those things ...." The priest hesitated. "Of course he was tempted. The truth is, I never knew exactly what he was storing in the armoire. He came and went as he pleased. Once or twice I saw him bring in gold. Other times, pottery, a scrap of metal. He kept it to himself. We agreed it was better that way."

"When did all this start?"

"Around the end of June, I think it was. He told me there was so much down there, no one would miss it. A little pilfering, that's all. A little selling off of the less significant items."

"Father, there's enough there for a museum. That ivory statue? That's hardly a 'less significant item.' What else had he dug up? The Nike of Samothrace? The Rosetta Stone?"

"I don't know. He never said. He said it would be dangerous for me, that I shouldn't get involved. So I left him alone. I didn't know what was in there and I was happy in my ignorance. I was as surprised as anyone when I saw what he'd collected."

"You knew what he was doing was illegal."

"Petros said he'd use the money to help his grandmother. But the truth was, all he cared about was motorcycles, the bigger the better. He was a boy. That was his dream. So he stole a little. He meant no harm."

"Who did he sell the artifacts to?"

"I don't know. I was just a stop on the underground railroad, as it were, a way station."

"The loot couldn't have come from the dig site. There's nothing there. So where did he get it?"

The machines began to flicker and an alarm bell sounded. The nurse came in and checked the priest's vital signs. "You have to leave," she told the chief officer. "He needs to rest."

"Yes," he told her, "just one moment." To the priest, he said, "Petros had to be digging somewhere else. Tell me where."

"I wish I knew," the priest said. The nurse gave him an injection and his head lolled back. He muttered something before he slept. "The voice of the Lord is upon the waters; the Lord is upon many waters."

⁂

Patronas visited the priest once more before returning to Chios. Papa Michalis had said something important the last time they'd been together, but he couldn't pin down what it was. He was surprised to find the priest chatting with a young nurse, who was spoon feeding him pistachio ice cream. Some color had returned to his cheeks, and he gave a little wave when he saw Patronas.

"Chief Officer!"

Perhaps he'd been wrong, Patronas thought, and the priest would survive after all. His heart was beating, steadily if erratically. As for the rest, the concussion, the stitched up skull, it probably wouldn't have any long-term effects. God knows, he was *arteriosklirotikos,* hard-headed enough.

"You've been here for almost a week," Papa Michalis said. "Your wife will be glad to see you when you get home."

"Sure she will. She'll greet me with open arms the way a hawk does a field mouse."

"Come, come. I've met your wife. She's not as bad as all that." He winked at the nurse. "Show her a little kindness and she'll come around. That woman of yours, she'll bloom like a rose." He motioned for the nurse to give him more ice cream.

"A rose? My Dimitra?" Patronas looked at the IVs with interest, wondering what they were pumping into the old man besides ice cream. *Opiates? No, impossible. It must be hallucinogenics.* "No offense, Father, but you're a priest. What do you know of women?"

"I know women. I had a mother."

"Trust me, Father. Wives and mothers, they're not the same."

As weak as he was, Papa Michalis was unwilling to concede the point. "St. Paul said, 'I understand all mysteries and all knowledge and I can move mountains, yet without love I am nothing ....'"

"St. Paul was celibate, Father. He had no wife." He patted his pockets for his cigarettes. "I've got to go. If you need anything, call me. I left the number of my cellphone at the nursing station."

"Wait. Before you go, there's something I must tell you." Papa Michalis reached for Patronas and pulled him closer. "Those questions you asked me? The truth is, I don't know. I don't know where Petros was digging or who he was selling to. I thought what he was doing, what *we* were doing, was harmless. I'm a stupid old man. You were right. I should have come to you in the beginning. If I'd come to you, the two of them, they'd still be alive."

There were tears in the old man's eyes. Patronas got a tissue and gently wiped Papa Michalis' wrinkled face. "Let it go, Father. What's done is done. For God's sake, let it go."

CHAPTER 18

From the devil's farm, neither kids, nor lambs.
—Greek proverb

SURROUNDED BY A barbed wire fence, the Chios airport consisted of a single runway in a field of grass. The winds of August had started, and dust stung Patronas' eyes as he crossed the tarmac. A crowd of Greek-Americans were in the terminal, talking to their relatives from Chios while they waited for their suitcases. The two groups were uncomfortable with one another, the kissing of the cheeks perfunctory, the ritualized greetings stiff. "*Geia sou, paidi mou,*" the natives said as they looked the new arrivals over, taking in the tight jeans on a middle-aged woman, the tattoo on the arm of her son.

The Chinese called those who lived abroad 'overseas Chinese' and mocked them. They were not considered real Chinese, but rather an unfortunate hybrid, damaged by their association with the outside world and the strange ideas and customs they picked up there. Judging by the interplay between the Chiots and the Greek-Americans, there were 'overseas Greeks' as well, and they, too, were considered inferior by the native-born. The new arrivals were Greeks … but not quite. Greeks … well, sort of. Watching them, Patronas felt sorry for the new arrivals. Their need to belong, so obvious it was almost palpable.

A restless people since the dawn of time, Greeks had journeyed forth to seek their fortunes. Once it had been Troy, now it was the United States. These voyages had become a cornerstone of the Greek experience, the agony of leaving and joy of return, a theme in the culture since the time of Homer. There was even a song about it, "*Paloma,*" they played in Piareaus for the immigrants on the big boats bound for America. Whatever they'd been seeking, they hadn't found it, those itinerant Greeks, judging by the ones who returned summer after summer, seeking the remembered paradise of their childhoods, a way of life that had long since vanished. For them, life was a constant journey home. Like Lot's wife, they were incapable of going forward, of fully living anywhere else, because they were so busy looking back, grieving for what they'd left behind.

Giorgos Tembelos met him at the airport. "How is the priest?"

"Holding steady."

"He say anything about who did it?"

"He didn't remember much. Only that when he tried to grab him, he couldn't get a grip, that he was 'slippery.' "

"Slippery, eh?" Tembelos started the car and backed out of the parking lot.

"Did you interview Titina Argentis and Petros' grandmother, find out what they were fighting about?"

Tembelos nodded. "Seems Eleni Argentis had a box of stuff that belonged to Petros. A wristwatch he'd broken at the dig, some CDs, that kind of thing. Grandma wanted it back."

"Anything of value in the box?"

"No. Kid had nothing."

"How about Manos Kleftis? Did you check him out with the police on Mykonos?"

"Yes. No police record."

"How about the boy's mother?"

"Voula? Has stayed at her mother's side since you left. Boyfriend, on the other hand, he's been busy, took a day trip to Turkey and came back with a trunk full of cheap jewelry. Spent time at the beach, too. Swimming and talking to the foreign women. Partial to Swedes, that one—blondes."

"I ran the archeologists' passports, too. They're who they say they are. I would have called England and the United States, to run background checks, but my English ...." He shrugged.

"Ach," Patronas muttered. That meant he'd have to do it.

ACCORDING TO THE police logbook, there'd been a second altercation between Titina Argentis and Petros' grandmother, in addition to the one at the laiki. The police had been summoned and asked to escort the old woman off the Argentis' estate.

Thinking that Titina Argentis' son, Antonis, might be more forthcoming than his mother, Patronas drove to the shipyard to see him.

It was a busy place. A vast oil tanker was tied up at the dock—rainbows of petroleum glinting on the oily surface of the water—and a second tanker was waiting to enter.

Argentis was standing outside, deep in conversation with a female employee. She was the kind Patronas thought all too common now in Greece—common being the operative word—tottering around on shoes with three and a half inch heels. They must be to give her extra height, the shoes, Patronas decided, inspecting her. It was difficult to look as if you came off a catwalk when you were five feet tall and had an ass like hers, the ass of a mare.

"Ah, Chief Officer," Argentis said, hailing Patronas. "What can I do for you?"

Patronas dispensed with the usual pleasantries. "I just wanted to tell you that I've started the process to declare your stepsister legally dead. Based on our findings, she was murdered within the same 24-hour period as her assistant, Petros Athanassiou." He described the discovery of the hand, the lacerated thigh on the beach.

Antonis Argentis closed his eyes. "What happened? Was it a robbery? Is that why they were killed?"

"My guess is, one of them found something at Profitis Ilias."

"Eleni would have told me. We talked nearly every day."

"Your mother said you never saw her."

"My mother didn't know."

Patronas got out his notebook. He hadn't expected this.

"I communicated with Eleni every day, either by cellphone or email. I visited her at the dig site. Harvard, too, when she was there." He shook his head, the youth gone from his face. "Eleni, she meant the world to me."

He watched the activity in the harbor for few minutes, fighting to control himself. "My mother … suffice to say, it was difficult being a child in my mother's house. I had no one to play with, no one to talk to. Oh, we had staff, of course. But they were there to be ordered about and do my mother's bidding, not to entertain me. Everything changed when my mother married Eleni's father and she came to live with us. I finally had someone to play with, a friend." His eyes filled with tears. "I loved her, Chief Officer," he said. "I loved my sister."

"Your mother …."

"In a word, my mother despised her."

"Why?"

"Mirror, mirror on the wall. Because Eleni was young. Because she had no use for my mother and made fun of her pretenses. Because she was well educated and led a productive life. My mother had any number of reasons. Take your pick. I know my mother resented the hold Eleni had over her father, my stepfather. Hated the spell she cast over me. My mother excels at hating people."

"Your mother never realized the two of you had a relationship?"

He made a gesture of hopelessness. "It was a matter of survival. You have no idea what my mother would have said, the hell she would have put me through, if she'd known. Let alone what she would have done to Eleni."

"Killed her?"

"Murder's not my mother's style, Chief Officer. She may be a bitch, but she's also a snob. She's far too fastidious to kill someone herself. As for hiring a murderer, well, it's just not done in the circles she travels in. It would also be expensive, and my mother values money above all else. She wouldn't have been willing to pay the price."

Patronas made a note. "You said you visited Eleni at Profitis Ilias?"

"Yes, many times. I must admit I didn't share her enthusiasm for all things Minoan. But I enjoyed being up there, discussing the shards with her, watching her and that boy, Petros, work. I brought them lunch when I came …." He looked away, his eyes wet.

"What was your impression of Petros?"

"That his childhood wasn't so different from mine. That he was lost the same way I had been. You should have seen how desperately he sought Eleni's approval. He thought it was a big deal, what they were doing, that the work was going to change his life. Poor kid."

"You didn't come to his funeral."

"Again, my mother. She would have found it intolerable for me to attend the funeral of an employee, especially an employee of Eleni's."

"I heard your mother got into a fight with the boy's grandmother, that she came to your house and your mother had her thrown off the property."

"The woman probably dared to speak in the familiar to her." The smile he gave Patronas was joyless. "A mortal sin in my mother's book, using the familiar rather than the formal when addressing her."

"I think it was about some property the old woman wanted back."

"Perhaps Eleni owed Petros a paycheck, and his grandmother came to collect it. They're poor people, Petros' family. If that's the case, let me know and I'll take care of it."

"Could it have been anything else?" Patronas kept his tone casual, his voice light.

"Not that I'm aware of."

Argentis accompanied Patronas back to his car when he left. "Please keep me abreast of your investigation, Chief Officer," he said. "I very much want to know who killed my sister."

"I'll do that."

As they walked through the yard, Argentis called out to the secretaries passing by, the workmen on their lunch break. Slowly, the man Patronas had been talking to—the serious man who had loved and grieved for his dead stepsister—disappeared, and the young fool who'd been flirting with his secretary took his place, the one whose only positive attribute was his smile. A true chameleon, Patronas thought, watching him. Antonis Argentis, the master of disguise.

He sat in the Citroen, reading over his notes, thinking about what Argentis had said, disturbed by the young man's antipathy toward his mother. Unusual, that, especially in Greece. Could Argentis have been trying to mislead him? To cast aspersions on her when he himself was the guilty party? Maybe this wasn't a *gafa* after all.

Chapter 19

The crab has not learned to keep his legs straight.
—Greek proverb

Professor Alcott was sitting at the bar in the Villa Hotel, drinking beer from a bottle. He waved Patronas over. "Chief Officer."

Patronas looked around. The room was full of tourists. Aside from the staff, he was the only Greek. Holding up his hand, he signaled the bartender and ordered an ouzo. It arrived on a silver tray and the bartender made a big production out of serving it, first putting the ice cubes in his glass with a pair of tongs, then pouring out the ouzo from a little glass beaker. In the ouzeria across the street, when you ordered ouzo you got a plate of food, olives and feta, fresh bread. Even fried squid on occasion. Something. Patronas peered into his glass. At the Villa you got tongs and ice cubes the size of dice.

"I need to go over a few things," he told Alcott.

"Sure. Fire away."

"You said you and Eleni Argentis had a relationship. When did it begin?"

"When she arrived at Harvard. She initiated it." His voice was petulant. "Hanging around after class, turning up at my office to request books."

"Did your wife know?"

Picking his beer up and setting it down again, he made overlapping rings on the marble counter. "Maybe. I don't know."

"How long did the affair last?"

"Three years. Didn't stop until she finished her PhD." He took a deep breath. "I wanted to continue, but she was done. God, was she done. Done with me. Done with us. Oh, I know what you think, that I took advantage of my position and seduced her. But it wasn't like that. No, she was the one who sought me out. Looking back, I think I might have been the means to an end for her. Brilliant as she was, she hadn't quite mastered English and speaking it was hard for her."

Her and me both, Patronas thought to himself. Sometimes when he drank, he thought he spoke English more fluently than he actually did, his syntax and vocabulary not so labored. Sitting in the bar with the American, he realized that this was an illusion, one of those happy pictures alcohol sometimes paints.

Alcott went on talking. "I think she thought I might be of some use to her, that my help would guarantee her success. After she graduated, she told me she didn't want to see me again. That 'there was no need for us to continue.' " He took a big swig of his beer. "*Finito. Terma.* Done."

"If that was the case, why'd you come to Chios?"

"I thought when she invited me here, it was because she wanted to get back together again, that the dig was just an excuse. But no, the reason she wanted me here was the reason stated in her letter: to get my professional opinion of what she'd found, the provenance of the shards and so forth. Nothing else. She made that abundantly clear the night I arrived."

"When was that?"

"A day or two before she was killed. July twenty-fifth, I think it was. She met my plane and we had dinner together in Chora. I pleaded with her to take me back. I even offered to marry her, but she just laughed at me. 'You?' she said. 'You have a wife. Or have you forgotten?' We were in a taverna by the water. I'm sure there were witnesses." He ran his thumb along the side of the bottle, tearing into the label. "I got drunk after she left. Whoever was there, they'll remember."

He drank more beer. "I would have done anything to have her back in my life, Chief Officer. Anything. I thought if I helped her with the excavation at Profitis Ilias … if we wrote a paper on it or put together an exhibit …. I wanted to keep her in my life somehow." He made a desperate, bleating sound. "I loved her."

"One last question. Did you remove anything from the dig site?"

"That day?" Alcott shook his head. "When I first got to the excavation, I was too excited about seeing her to be mindful of shards, and afterwards, I was too traumatized."

"How about Devon McLean? Could he have taken something from the site?"

"He might have. There was a lot of confusion after I found the hand. I thought he'd already come and gone, but I might have been wrong. He might have been around. If he took anything, he'll tell you he only did so in 'the interest of science.' Devon's big on 'the interest of science.' He has asked me repeatedly to petition you to let us process the dig site. He even went so far as to claim it might further Eleni's professional reputation posthumously." His voice was sarcastic. "And ours, of course. That was in the mix, too."

"A little callous."

"Oh, it was. You have to remember, Chief Officer, the ego of an academic never sleeps. Especially one as ambitious as Devon McLean."

He hesitated for a moment. "He's right, though. Someone should go through the dig site. That bull you showed me, the one that was mixed in with the shards, it's unique. Its value is inestimable, absolutely inestimable. Perhaps if we resumed the excavation, we would find more." There was something shining in his eyes. Greed? Grief? Patronas wasn't sure.

"After we've laid the little matter of murder to rest, you and your colleagues are welcome to the hillside. Bring bulldozers if you like. Dig up everything."

AFTER HE LEFT the Villa Hotel, Patronas drove to the police station and placed a long distance call to the Dean of the Archeology Department at Harvard University. He wanted to question him about Jonathan Alcott. Self-conscious about his English, Patronas would have preferred to have conducted this conversation in private, somewhere away from the front desk, the ringing phones. But given the layout of police headquarters, this was impossible. One large room, it was subdivided into grubby little cubicles separated from one another by metal dividers less than four feet high. The metal desks, the walls and dividers, all were painted gray—the same flat gray the military used, the color of aircraft carriers and transport planes—and at work Patronas often felt like he was back in the Navy, back in the bowels of the battleship where he'd done his tour of duty.

The space allotted to him as Chief Officer was a little bigger than where his men were housed, but equally public. Everyone could hear everything. He knew that, because whenever he had fights with Dimitra on the phone, Tembelos and the others made fun of him, repeating word for word what he'd said to his wife. He'd have to remember to keep his voice down. A fax machine in the corner rattled continuously, spewing photos of criminals wanted by Interpol. He added them to the others taped to the wall by his desk. Once posted, he never removed them. "I need to clean this place up," he muttered, looking around as he took a seat. Some of the mug shots looked like they dated from the seventies, the wanted men sporting Beatles haircuts and platform shoes. They must be dead by now. If not dead, then getting around with walkers and canes. As felons, surely retired.

The dean at Harvard answered on the third ring. Though Patronas knew rudimentary English, he was forced to scribble down half the words the man used and look them up in his *Divry's English-Greek, Greek-English Dictionary* after he hung up the phone in a desperate effort to understand what the dean had been saying. Alcott's reputation was "stellar," which meant star, according to Divry's. Now was this a good thing, to be a star? Probably. *Ach, these academics and the way they talked.*

In addition, the Dean had claimed Alcott's reputation was "unblemished," "his teaching literate and cohesive," "his research well-reasoned, his conclusions unimpeachable."

In the Dean's experience, "Alcott's academic integrity was without parallel." He was "a credit to the department and to his field." This last bit had given Patronas the most trouble. "Credit" had to do with money in his experience. What did "credit" have to do with being a professor?

"Do you think he kills people?" he'd wanted to scream into the phone, just to hear the man's reaction, but thought better of it. Alcott, after all, might be innocent and just what he said he was—a love-sick, middle-aged fool, seeking some kind of sexual Holy Grail in the form of Eleni Argentis. These things happened. Not to Greek men, as a general rule, who saw all women as pretty much the same. One gives you trouble, get another. That was the motto of the Greek male. Your mother, now she was different. A mother you enshrined in your heart, loved beyond reason. But as for the rest? *Vrasta.* Boil them. But in other cultures, yes, he'd been told these things happened. Men made fools of themselves over women.

CHAPTER 20

The potter puts the handles wherever he wishes.
—Greek proverb

"Ah, Chief Officer," Devon McLean opened the door of his room. "Come in, come in."

Patronas couldn't face another round with the *Divry's Greek-English Dictionary*, so he'd put off calling Oxford University to discuss Devon McLean. He thought he'd return to the Villa Hotel and speak with the Englishman first and then compare what he said with what his colleagues had to say about him.

"Sorry to bother you again." Patronas waved his notebook in the air. "I have a few more questions."

He inspected the hotel room, taking in the books, the furniture. The suite was immaculate, the man's notes neatly stacked beside his laptop, his books alphabetized on a make-shift shelf. There were no shards or artifacts of any kind that Patronas could see.

"I'm sorry if you've been inconvenienced by our investigation. Hopefully, you'll be able to return to Cyprus soon."

"Perfectly all right. I haven't been idle. I've been emailing my colleagues and editing a paper. Taking advantage of the hiatus in my summer schedule, as it were, to do some work." As in previous conversations, the man's Greek was flawless.

"What's the paper about?"

"The dating of Akrotiri, those ruins on Santorini."

"Minoan, aren't they?"

"Of course, but are they Middle Minoan or Late Minoan? I think archeologists underestimate the length of time Akrotiri had been inhabited. I think it was settled far earlier, perhaps even proto-Minoan. Are you familiar with the dating of Minoan artifacts, Chief Officer?"

"Somewhat."

"Well, I think Akrotiri is Early Minoan. It might have even housed a Neolithic settlement, though that is harder to prove, given that the pumice is so heavy everywhere. It'll take a century to get down to the level of the eruption. In some places the ash is over fifty feet high."

"How can you date Akrotiri from here?"

"Oh, I've done all my research. It was just a matter of organizing everything and getting my thoughts down on paper." He said 'my thoughts' in a reverential way, like a priest in church when he reads the gospel.

"I'm working on a dateline, too. Who was at Profitis Ilias and when they were there. Could you tell me again when you visited the excavation?"

"Certainly. July twenty-seventh."

"Did you visit Profitis Ilias before July twenty-seventh?"

The Englishman's face became somber. "No. I had just arrived from abroad and hadn't yet figured out how to get up to the monastery. I didn't know how far it was from the road at that point and was reluctant to try walking the distance. Bum leg, I'm afraid. Nothing serious. Just an old court tennis injury that precludes lengthy hikes. And, though my Greek is good, I didn't really know how to go about chartering a mule."

"Tell me again when you arrived?"

"The day before she was killed. I flew into Athens from Egypt and caught a flight here."

"You and Professor Alcott are both staying in this hotel. Do you see much of him?"

"At first I did. For example, I was with him the night he found the hand in the trench. He was in wretched shape. Kept talking about what 'they'd done to her.' The blood. You've heard him. Blaming himself."

"Blaming himself?"

McLean nodded. "I must say, Jon had had a great deal to drink, a *very* great deal, and he was more than a little incoherent. I had to get a porter to help me get him back to his room. He kept saying if only he'd gotten here sooner, he could have saved her, that kind of thing. It didn't make much sense." He hesitated for a moment. "You know, Chief Officer, Alcott's a decent man. He was an even better one before he met Eleni. You should have seen him when he was in his prime. I went on a dig with him in Cyprus." The archeologist smiled at the memory. "It was amazing. Jon was unstoppable. A force of nature."

The chief officer frowned. There was something in his voice, he thought, watching McLean closely. Something off. The way he said 'Jon' caressed Alcott's name.

McLean continued talking. "When he got entangled with her, he lost something—his edge, his focus. He was like an animal with its leg caught in a vise: he just couldn't get free. You know, he risked everything, not just his marriage but his tenure, his reputation, with that affair. It was a terrible thing to see. We, members of the archeological community, all talked about it. At every conference people discussed the situation. I'm hoping once this unhappy episode has passed, he'll be able to resume his life. Get on with it, as it were."

"I know you said you visited the site. You didn't think much of it."

"Second rate, if you want the truth. I thought it was pathetic, actually, the way she'd made such a fuss about those miserable shards. Interrupting our summer schedules and bringing us here for nothing. Half of Greece is covered with better relics than the ones she and that boy, Petros, found. I'm not sure even half of it is Minoan. I think much of it dates from a much later time. Roman, perhaps, or even the early Christian era."

"I thought you came on your own. I didn't realize Eleni had summoned you here."

"It was strictly voluntary on my part, don't get me wrong. Curiosity killing the cat and all that. She spoke to a colleague of mine in Athens, who in turn spoke to me. I was intrigued by what I'd heard. I won't deny it. I thought she'd found a second Knossos. What a disappointment it all was, however. What a waste of time."

"So you don't think she was killed because of the excavation?"

"Not by anyone knowledgeable. A local might think those bits had value, but anyone in the field could tell instantly they were virtually worthless."

THE YOUNG WOMAN at reception ran a manicured finger down the ledger. "It says here Devon McLean checked in on July twenty-fifth. But he arrived on Chios long before that."

"How do you know?"

"A waiter at the hotel saw him. 'That white skin,' he said. He was sure it was him."

"Where did he see him?"

"Volissos."

"He and the other archeologist, the American, had a big fight the night he arrived. Out on the terrace. Something about a woman. The American was drunk. The Englishman was trying to calm him down." She drummed her nails on the counter impatiently. The phones were ringing and she needed to get back to work. "I wish I could tell you more. All the people you asked me about? They've all been here at one time or another. Petros' mother and her boyfriend. What a pair: the *porne* and the *porno*, the he-slut and the she-slut.

Made a nuisance of themselves, ordered drinks and ran up a big tab, then when the waiter brought the bill, they argued with him and refused to pay. *So cheap, they could get milk from a ram."*

"Anyone else?"

"Titina Argentis."

"What did she want?"

"I'm not sure. She came in late at night like she didn't want anyone to see her. It was after my shift, but I heard she was sitting in the lounge with the Englishman. It was the middle of July; I don't know the exact date. Like I said, I didn't see them myself. The night manager told me."

Patronas turned toward the dining room, where the waiters were setting up for dinner. "Which one saw McLean in Volissos?"

"Him." The girl pointed to a short man on the far side of the room. "Takis."

"Sure, I saw him," the waiter said when questioned by Patronas. "It was late June, about three weeks before he checked in here."

"Are you sure it was him?"

"Hard to miss a man like that. All pale and delicate, he was, smearing cream on his face like a woman. He's not your usual here. Men like that, you see them on Mykonos. He was on a boat. It was anchored far off, so I couldn't really see it. But I could tell it was big. Not a yacht, but a good-sized cabin cruiser or maybe a cigarette boat. Looked sleek from where I stood. Fast."

Chapter 21

He spins the rope of Ocnus.
—Greek proverb

Patronas thought of Ocnus as he drove. Ocnus was a ropemaker whose ropes were eaten by an ass as fast as he could make them. In other words, everything he did was a waste of time. Patronas felt much the same. Weeks of effort and nothing to show for it. He could almost hear the ass chewing.

Patronas took Giorgos Tembelos with him when he went to Volissos. There'd been some trouble in the village over cigarette smuggling, and he thought Tembelos, who had relatives there, might have better luck talking to the locals. When he'd arrested the ringleader, the man had taken a swing at him, claiming everyone with a boat supplemented their income with Turkish cigarettes and that he had been unfairly singled out. The bonds of family ran deep in Volissos and Patronas was afraid he was in for a long afternoon.

The ride took them through the backstreets and up over Mount Aipos. The limestone peak rose sharply, the second highest point of land on Chios after Profitis Ilias, and Patronas hated the narrow road that traversed it. A dented guard rail ran along the side, and he tried not to look down as he drove. Not so Giorgos, who was enthralled by the view and kept pointing out landmarks—the bell tower of the cathedral, the three old windmills outside Chora—and getting progressively more excited the higher up they went.

Beyond the crest of Mount Aipos was a lifeless plateau of pockmarked limestone that extended for miles. As a boy, Patronas had been fascinated by the area, home to nothing, not even insects. He'd believed that if he visited the moon, its surface would be like this, all gray rock and dust. Now, as an adult, he thought the desolation probably dated from the massacre of 1822 when the Turks had burned the villages along the coast. He guessed the flames had overtaken the woods on the mountain, and they, like the rest of Chios, had never recovered. A ship owner from the United States was trying to reestablish a forest in the area. The green of the tiny saplings made the land around them seem still more barren.

The landscape began to change as they neared the sea on the west of the island, the lunar plateau giving way to gently sloping hills, heavily forested with dense thickets of pines. Patronas loved the sight of the wind-bent pines, the grass yellow beneath them, the great wash of the Aegean in the distance, sparkling in the sunlight.

"You ever catch who did it?" Tembelos pointed to a swatch of land that had been burned the previous summer, the singed ground and blackened trees.

Patronas shook his head. He'd found a pile of discarded metal cans still reeking of gasoline and a mattress that had been soaked in it and set ablaze, but he'd never caught the arsonist. It still galled him. Greek law was very strict, forbidding construction in areas that were forested. In recent years the solution had been to burn the trees down, but then the law had been amended, forbidding construction indefinitely in areas where there had been fires. Patronas was counting on the culprit not knowing that the law had changed and filing for a permit to build. Then he'd have him.

As they rounded the curve, the village of Volissos came into view. It had grown in recent years, the cement breakwater expanded to accommodate tourist boats from abroad. He could smell fish frying in the small taverna on the quay and see people eating outside at tables under umbrellas.

He dropped Tembelos off and drove back to where the road curved high above the village. Getting out his binoculars, he scanned the harbor, searching for a fast boat, but saw nothing, only fishing boats and a flotilla of rented sailboats, making their way east.

He raised the binoculars higher and looked farther out to sea. There was a boat that looked like the one the waiter described, laying at anchor about 500 meters offshore. The Coast Guard said the boat was registered in Libya, a practice not unusual in Greece. Boats were often registered there to avoid paying taxes. The owner had filed no additional papers since anchoring. Although the boat had been there for weeks, they'd been unable to catch up with whoever owned it. Too many boats, too many people. Patronas asked them to keep an eye on it and let him know when it left and which direction it went in. "Follow it if you have to. Keep it in view."

Tembelos had heard from the owner of the local grocery store that a man had been living on the boat in question—well, perhaps not *living*, but staying there occasionally. He'd bought food from the grocer and gone back and forth a few times. He'd been a foreigner, *xenii*, with red hair and white skin and had always been alone—a curiosity in and of itself during the summer when the village was full of couples on holiday. His solitude was probably the only reason the grocer remembered him.

"Did he make a positive ID when you showed him the photo of McLean?" Not experts, they'd gone to great lengths to secure a candid photo of the Englishman, sitting at the pool at his hotel.

Tembelos shook his head. "He wouldn't swear to it. He did say he saw a woman onboard once or twice. Not with him. Alone. Looked local, he said. Not a girlfriend. A maid or housekeeper, judging by the way she was dressed."

"Boat isn't that big. What'd he need a maid for?"

"Maybe she's his accomplice."

"If that's the boat, it'd have a Zodiac tied to it."

"Maybe he let the air out, hid it in the trunk of his car."

"No car, either. I checked. No one named McLean or fitting his description has rented a car from anyone on Chios, on or off the books." Patronas lit a cigarette and looked out at the beach. He wished he was swimming, tossing a ball to children in the water, not chasing phantoms. "We got nothing, Giorgos. Nothing linking McLean to a boat or a car. No firm evidence he was even in Volissos, let alone onboard that vessel out there. The man the grocer saw? Maybe he was a guest on that boat and the woman, the so-called maid, is the rightful owner."

Tembelos persisted. "I still think he's involved."

"We have no proof. This case is like a magic trick, Giorgos. One minute, you think you're getting somewhere and then," he flung his hands in the air, Houdini releasing a bird, "poof, you got nothing."

On the way home they stopped in Lampi, a small village on a gritty beach. A rough breakwater had been built to create a harbor, and Patronas could see three good-sized fishing boats tied up there. Far out to sea, a cigarette boat caught his eye, riding low in the water.

He called to the waiter. "Whose boat is that?"

"Don't know. It's been there for a couple of weeks now, never a person to be seen. No flags flying. Nothing to identify it. My mother has been keeping an eye on it. She thinks the Turks might own it. Drugs."

Patronas nodded. "How far is it from here to the cove where Costas Stamnas found the remains?"

"About a kilometer. You passed it on your way here. There are some rocks jutting out of the sea. The beach is right in front of them."

"Was that boat here when it happened?"

The man shrugged. "Who can say? It's summer. A lot of boats come through here now. Yachts. Cruise ships. That boat might have been here. I don't remember."

Patronas drove south. They were deep in mastica country, a bush that only grew on the southeastern coast of Chios. Its cultivation had given the islanders special privileges during the time of the Ottomans; its resin was much prized by the women in the harem, who chewed it to sweeten their breath. These privileges had been revoked when the Pasha sent troops to punish the population for supporting the rebels during the Greek War of Independence. During the two-week maelstrom, Turkish Janissaries had slaughtered over 25,000 people and enslaved 60,000 more. Chios had never recovered. The houses in this area had a desolate air, the town squares and churches, a sense of abandonment. Only the elderly lived here now. People still grew mastica, but only for local consumption. The Ottomans were gone. There were no harems anymore.

"We're like the Jews in Germany," Patronas said, gesturing to one of the villages. "They were the most assimilated in Europe, had the best lives, the most money and then … boom, look what happened to them. Just like us."

"It was worse what happened to the Jews," Tembelos said, remembering a trip he'd taken to Munich to see his brother, who worked in a Volkswagen factory. They'd visited Dachau and he'd never forgotten it. The science experiments with the Russians in the icy water, the open skull and exposed brains of other men. Had the men been dead when they'd done it, he'd wondered? An air of hopelessness still hung over the place. It had been like catching a glimpse of hell.

The mastica bushes were still well cared for, the ground beneath them spread with white cloths or aluminum foil to catch the resin. The majority of the villages along this route had been built in the Middle Ages, the first floors opening out onto the street and used as stables.

Patronas decided this practice must still be in use, judging by the piles of manure and clouds of flies, the smell. The priest in the local church was hard of hearing and had no news of value, nor did Patronas or Tembelos discover much talking to the old women in the villages they visited. They wanted to complain about the deficiencies of their daughters-in-law, not catch murderers.

Their final stop was a boutique hotel near the Argentis mansion in Campos. Too expensive for locals, it was patronized largely by foreign tourists and Greek ship owners who lived abroad.

The clerk at the reception desk led Patronas into the kitchen, and he spent an hour talking to the staff—all local people. They discussed the families of Chiots who lived in England and came to the hotel—the bankruptcy of one, brought low by the prolific spending of the heir. No one had seen any artifacts pass hands or heard rumors of smuggling. They were all appalled by the death of Petros, less so the death of the Argentis woman.

"*Trelli,*" one man said. "Crazy." A woman that rich, working with men, sifting dirt for a living. They despised her stepmother, even going so far as to call her a gorgon, a legendary female monster of ancient Greece whose glance could turn a man to stone. They called her Medusa, too. There was no end of insults. Eleni's half-brother they liked better. He left generous tips and remembered the waiters' names. Not too familiar, the proper blend of warmth and distance. He would never be one of them, but for a rich person, he was okay. They loathed Petros' family, but for different reasons. Voula had brought shame on the island. Her boyfriend, they'd seen frequently in town, drinking and making friendly with the locals, but too often he let others buy and pinched cigarettes when they weren't looking. They called the American archeologist 'Indiana Jones,' the British one 'Brideshead,' after the BBC production of the same name that had recently aired on local television. The latter they suspected was a *poustis*, a homosexual. However, when Patronas questioned them about it, they admitted there'd been no sightings of McLean with a man, no Greek lover boys they knew of.

Patronas had been hoping to discover signs of new wealth as he drove around the island—an expensive car where there shouldn't have been one, a home built by someone who'd previously had nothing. Everything the waiters told him, he already knew. As police work, it had been a waste of time. Nothing. "*We spoke of winds and water,*" he muttered, recalling the old saying.

CHAPTER 22

Either the shore is crooked or our boat's going the wrong way.
—Greek proverb

THE NEXT MORNING Patronas reluctantly returned to Profitis Ilias and ordered his men to search the site again. The answer had to lie here; it could be no place else. Although he and the others walked four abreast over the entire area, they found nothing. Someone had been there, Tembelos reported back to him. A shepherd, probably, as the goats were no longer in the corral, but spread out on the slopes below, hobbling around on three legs, the fourth leg fettered to keep them from wandering too far off.

The disturbed earth near the summit was exactly what Patronas had thought—some peasant's secret garden. In daylight, the tomatoes were clearly evident in the dirt, fenced with chicken wire to keep the goats out. No, this was just another empty Greek hill. Torn shafts of lichen covered the rocks, the soil poor, gravel mostly interspersed with patches of clay. Brambles and thorns grew between the rocks, the only vegetation the goats had spared.

When the sun went down, Patronas handed Evangelos Demos a can of paint and ordered him to watch for the bats. "It's almost dark. They should be out any minute now. The paint glows in the dark. Mark the place where they come from."

His assistant nodded, not liking any of this. "But, sir, they might be rabid."

"If they attack you, shoot them."

"How long do I have to stay up here?"

"Until you locate where they come from. Till dawn, if necessary."

He posted the others around the monastery and gave them the same assignment. "I'll take the corral. You two take the north and south sides of the hill. There's got to be another way in here. My hunch is, it's an underground passageway. It's imperative that we find it."

"Bats, Jesus," Giorgos Tembelos said.

DRAWING HIS GUN, Patronas crept toward the dark figure on the far side of the corral. The goats were restive, and he could hear them milling around inside, their hooves clattering softly against the gravelly soil. He had been chasing bats in and out of the corral all night, hoping the animals would lead him to the secret entrance to the monastery—the one he was convinced existed. He had ordered Evangelos Demos and Giorgos Tembelos to do the same.

"I've got my cellphone on," he'd told them. "Call me if anyone approaches the monastery."

He wondered what had happened, why they hadn't called, how the intruder had gotten past them. The figure was encased entirely in black, gleaming faintly in darkness, exactly as Costas Stamnas and Papa Michalis had described. Its skull looked distorted and Patronas saw no eyes, no face. Whoever it was, hunched over at the back of the corral.

Raising his gun, Patronas moved closer. He didn't know what it was that alerted the intruder, but suddenly he lifted his face and looked directly at Patronas. Then he bolted out of the corral and was gone.

"Stop or I'll shoot!" It was then Patronas realized that it was his phone the man had seen, the phone he'd taken care to turn to vibrate and to stow in the front pocket of his shirt. His phone, which was all lit up and shining like a beacon.

Patronas fired twice and charged after the intruder, moving through the herd of goats as quickly as possible, shoving the animals roughly aside with his hands. They began to panic, bleating and climbing on top of one another, desperate to get away. Without the lantern, he couldn't see well and slipped over something. At first he thought it was another goat, but it wasn't. It was his assistant, Evangelos Demos, lying face down in the dirt.

Patronas knelt down and rolled him over. "Evangelos, Evangelos, can you hear me?" He raised the man up and cradled him in his arms. The back of his head was wet. Patronas looked around. There was no sign of Giorgos Tembelos or the dark shape that had been in the corral.

EVANGELOS DEMOS TOLD Patronas he heard a noise and had gone to explore. It was a clanging noise, he said, the sound of metal hitting rock. He'd been knee-deep in goats when he'd seen the figure. Hooded it had been, black. He'd pulled his gun and fired a shot, but the intruder had been too fast for him and hit him hard with something, knocking him down.

"Did you get a look at his face?" Patronas asked. They were in the emergency room of the hospital, his assistant on a stretcher beside him. He wished he could smoke. Doctors were walking around. The sight of them always increased his longing for cigarettes.

"No. It happened too fast."

His assistant had survived the assault, though he had required emergency surgery to close the gap in his skull. Aside from the Frankenstein-like stitches, Evangelos Demos appeared to be all right. *Probably it was the thickness of his skull that saved him*, Patronas thought uncharitably. He'd spent hours at his assistant's side and his initial concern had worn off. Though they'd discussed the incident repeatedly, Evangelos Demos had been unable to come up with a single scrap of useful information. His assistant was and remained what he'd always been—*stupid with a helmet on.*

The shot Demos had fired had not hit his attacker, but a goat, a goat that had bleated pathetically as it bled to death, shitting and writhing in agony, irreparably compromising the crime scene. The two shots Patronas had fired had also hit goats, bringing the total for the night to three dead goats and no suspect. They'd buried the goats on the hillside. Patronas had felt like a fool, watching his men carry away the dead animals. There'd been bits of bloody fur stuck to the brush of the corral and the place smelled like a charnel house.

Evangelos Demos' entire family turned up at the hospital after breakfast and crowded around, offering their opinions in shrill voices. Patronas had never met such people. Between Evangelos' wife and his mother-in-law—a fearsome old battle axe from Sparta—they made a hash of everything, interrupting continually and correcting Evangelos Demos when he tried to tell Patronas his story.

Patronas finally ordered them out of the emergency room. "Now start over and tell me what happened," he told his assistant.

First, he and Giorgos had gotten tired of wearing the night binoculars, Evangelos Demos said. They were heavy and made their heads hurt and so they'd discarded them. Then they'd gotten hungry and Giorgos Tembelos had gone back to the monastery to get a little snack for them. Apparently, the intruder had waited until his assistant was alone before making his move. He'd been on that hill somewhere, watching.

"I called you on your cellphone," Evangelos Demos said. "Last thing I did before I passed out."

When Patronas had searched the area, he'd found a bloody shovel in the brush behind the lean-to, but no footprints or disturbed ground of any kind, no discarded cigarette butts. How could the man have gotten up there without leaving a trace? He had ordered his staff to bag the shovel and send it to the laboratory in Athens on the next plane, but he doubted the forensic specialists there would find anything. He was ingenious, this killer. He'd found a way to make himself invisible. Patronas rubbed his eyes. He felt like Theseus trying to get out of the labyrinth, only he was on his own. He lacked the thread.

"I still don't understand how he got by us," Evangelos Demos was saying. "Neither of us heard a thing."

"The goats could have masked the sounds." Patronas got up from the chair and walked over to the window and looked out. "Evangelos, was there anything else, anything at all that you noticed about the man who hit you?"

Evangelos Demos frowned. "He smelled funny."

"What do you mean, 'funny'?"

"Like rubber."

"Shit. That's a great help, Evangelos. What, he smelled like tires?"

"No. Different."

AT THE PRESS conference that afternoon, Patronas told the reporters that Evangelos Demos was a brave protector of the people, struck down in the line of duty by an evil criminal. He called him 'courageous.' He might even have said 'noble'; he couldn't remember.

The Prefecture of Chios had insisted on the press conference. He'd told Patronas it was necessary to quell the rumors that were circulating and to reassure the people of Chios. They needed to believe the police were not *psychopathis*, the Prefecture had said, stalking bats and shooting up goats in the middle of the night. The people of Chios needed to believe they could rely on them.

And so Patronas had termed Evangelos Demos a 'hero.' *A man can risk his life and still be an idiot*, he told himself, like the soldiers in the "Charge of the Light Brigade," a poem he'd been forced to memorize in English class, riding into the valley of death. He could see Evangelos doing something like that. Riding into the valley of death with his saber drawn, his big thick head held high. When he spoke to the reporters, Patronas didn't mention the search for the bats or the dead goats. The Prefecture had been very specific on that point. Unkind even.

"How much longer do you think you'll be up at Profitis Ilias?" one of the reporters asked.

Patronas thought for a moment. "Until we apprehend the murderer or murderers of Eleni Argentis and Petros Athanassiou. Until we take them into custody."

CHAPTER 23

We know nothing. The truth is hidden at the bottom of a well.
—Greek proverb

STARTING UP THE Citroen, Patronas left the hospital in Vrontados and drove back to Profitis Ilias. He'd called Giorgos Tembelos after the press conference and told him he'd take over for him and that he could leave. He passed the police cruiser on the road to the monastery and Giorgos Tembelos circled around and gave chase, honking and waving, having fun, glad to be leaving. Calling Patronas on the police walkie talkie, he shouted, "Did you see that last turn? I was on your Citroen the whole way. I clung to you like a saddle burr."

"Yes, you did, Giorgos. Like the thorn in the side of Jesus."

The police car Tembelos was driving was relatively new. A large and expensive sedan imported from Germany, it wasn't meant to be driven like a race car. Tembelos, the size of a rhinoceros, bounced up and down in the front seat, the expensive Pirelli tires spewing gravel, the springs getting shot to hell. Patronas sighed. It didn't matter. He'd discuss Giorgos' behavior with the man another time—maybe suggest he lose some weight, re-read the pamphlet on the use of departmental vehicles. Tembelos was his best man, and if he had to sacrifice a car or two to keep him happy, so be it.

The goats were nearby, probably on the lower slopes; he could hear their bells jingling as he walked up the path. The shepherd must move them from hill to hill every few days in search of fresh pasture. He'd have to remember to check and find out who the man was and question him … also whoever was working the garden, though that would be harder to discover. One more task, one more useless task. He was beginning to think he would never find the killer. More than two weeks had passed and he knew no more than when he'd started. The wind had died down and the heat lay like a blanket on the still air. He could hear the chickens clucking inside the monastery. Before he went home, he'd feed them and water the garden.

The shepherd, a forty-year-old Albanian, turned up at the monastery later that evening. Patronas met him bringing his goats around to the place where the trenches were. The man had a cleft palate that had never been repaired and spoke poorly as a result. He'd probably taken on the work to get away from people, those who would tease him and mock his deformity. The goats nuzzled him with their heads while he and the man spoke; the Albanian had names for each of them and constantly stroked and petted them. Tall and well-built, the shepherd had the physical strength necessary for the assault on Papa Michalis, Patronas judged, but not the spirit. He seemed more child than man, cringing when Patronas reached for cigarette, hugging himself and cowering as if afraid of getting hit. His undershirt was dirty, his shoes were mended with duct tape, and his hair was cut so unevenly he had to have hacked it off himself, most probably with a knife. Patronas felt sure the shepherd was illiterate. He wouldn't know the value of a Minoan relic, nor how to go about selling it. This man was scared of his own shadow. An unsophisticated, feral creature, he'd be more at home in a stable than a house.

The man swore he hadn't been anywhere near the dig site the day Petros Athanassiou was killed. He liked to roam the hills and nap in the open air, he said. Uncomfortable with Patronas, he kept trying to shield his broken face with his hand, making him difficult to understand. On one point he was adamant, however: he'd seen and heard nothing. Although Patronas had threatened him with deportation, he hadn't budged, and the chief officer was forced to conclude he was telling the truth. The shepherd did say that he'd seen people on the hill, 'many people,' in the weeks before the attack. Three at least. But when Patronas asked who they were, he just shook his head. It was his garden, too, at the top of the hill. He'd begged Patronas to let him keep it. He was hungry. He had nothing. Patronas slipped him fifty Euros and told him to be on his way.

The shepherd stood where he was for a long time, looking down at the money in his hand as if he couldn't believe what he was seeing. He kept making a strange, wheezing sound as if something was caught in his throat. It took Patronas a moment to realize it was joy the man was communicating—that the strangled, tortured sound he was hearing was laughter.

⁂

AFTER LEAVING THE shepherd, Patronas reentered the monastery and checked the crypt under the chapel. It was as he'd left it. He could still see the button he'd pulled off his uniform and positioned beneath the metal door. Fingerprinting powder darkened the doorknobs and the windowsills of the other rooms in the monastery, making everything look soiled, unclean. Though the chalk was badly smudged, he could make out the outline of Papa Michalis' body one of his men had drawn on the pavement next to the well. How small the priest had been.

He fed the chickens then found a bucket in the kitchen and walked over to the well to get water for the garden. He attached the wooden bucket to the pulley and let it down, but it stopped abruptly after two meters. Something seemed to be obstructing it.

"What the devil!" Peering into the well, he dipped a hand in the water and swished it back and forth. The well clearly narrowed, a wall of some kind protruding into the shaft and blocking off a portion of it.

The interior of the well was paved with black and white cobblestones arranged in patterns—dolphins, anchors, boats, things he associated with the sea. Bands of larger stones divided the designs, radiating out from the well in a series of concentric circles. Perhaps Eleni had been onto something after all, he thought, remembering the divining rods and other water symbols on the Phaistos Disc, the spiraling pattern of the hieroglyphics. Water, yes. Perhaps water was the key.

He knelt and tried to pry off the metal facing of the well with his hands. He'd thought it would be heavy and was surprised to find how light it was. Set in a groove in the rock, it slid back easily, revealing a square opening. Thinking the well might be deeper than he'd originally thought—connected to the ancient cistern—he picked up a pebble and dropped it into the hole. There was no splash when it hit, no sound of water. Odd, that.

He peered in after it. The well had a false bottom. Below was empty space.

A smell rose up from the hole, the same deathly odor he'd smelled the night the priest had been attacked. He wished he had a flashlight, something powerful to light the space. It was already late. The sun was setting and it would be dark soon. Reluctantly, he replaced the metal panels and left the monastery, locking the doors behind him, thinking he'd bring his men back with him tomorrow. It would be better that way, more sensible than going it alone. He and his men would explore the opening thoroughly with propane lanterns. They could even break out the electric generators, if necessary, to illuminate the darkness. He told himself that this was only prudent, that to do it now would be foolhardy. He might hurt himself or destroy valuable evidence. But he knew the real reason: that hole scared him to death.

PATRONAS QUICKLY DROVE back to police headquarters. A modern two-story building, it faced the Plateia Vounaki, the central square of Chios. The tables in the patisseries were full of people and Patronas could hear children playing near the old mosque. Once again someone had spray-painted the bronze statue of Kanaris, the famous Greek captain who had rammed a Turkish warship with a burning boat and sunk it during the War of Independence. They'd stuck a spent cigarette butt in his mouth. Maybe the city should build a little fence around the statue, something with spikes that would keep the kids off. The air was so still, he could see the reflections of the boats on the golden surface of the harbor. A sailboat was casting off, part of a flotilla of tourists bound for another island.

He wanted to go sit by the water. Stay there until the stars came out. He was fearful of what lay ahead. That hole, the blackness at the bottom of the well. The prospect of meeting up with someone who could slice a woman to ribbons and throw what was left of her away, who could kill a child, assault a priest .... He'd begged Costas Stamnas and the other fisherman to accept police protection, but the fishermen had laughed him off.

"I'll take my boat out until you catch him," Stamnas had told him. "Fishing is good off Karpathos this time of year." Patronas had wanted to go with him, to throw his net in the water and feel the wind on his face. To be done with this miserable job.

He pushed the door of the police station open and went inside. Giorgos Tembelos was the only one there. He was sitting at his desk, smoking a cigarette and flipping through a magazine. Whether it was a sports or girly magazine, Patronas couldn't tell; that about covered the range of Giorgos' interests.

"Where's the evidence from Eleni Argentis' house?" he asked him. "I put everything I found in a cardboard box after I was done going through it. Where is it now?"

Tembelos didn't look up. Must be girly. "Evangelos put everything from her house on the shelf in the closet."

The chief officer rummaged through the box until he found the CDs. He was eager to look at them again, to compare Eleni Argentis' notes with what he now knew about the well. He called Athens and ordered additional crime lights, as the ones in Chios would never do the trick. "As soon as possible," he told the man at the Ministry. "Send them here on the next plane."

"I want you to call everyone and tell them to be at the monastery at first light," he ordered Tembelos.

"Everybody took the week off. You forgot? It's August Fifteenth, Monday."

"Oh, well. It'll just be the two of us then. I'll meet you there in the morning. And, Giorgos, I want you to be in charge of the equipment. We'll need lanterns, two generators, a string of electric lights, ropes and pick axes and grapples."

"Grapples? What happened?" Tembelos asked sleepily. "The bats fight back?"

CHAPTER 24

Unfading are the gardens of kindness.
—Greek proverb

PATRONAS SWERVED TO avoid a pedestrian as he drove through the old Turkish quarter. The deconsecrated mosque had once been a museum, but had been closed for over a decade in deference to Turkish religious sensitivities. The ancient busts and sarcophagi, most dating from the time of Caesar, still littered the courtyard. Dead leaves covered the pavement and collected in the rusting iron fence in front. The old baths were still there, too. Against the sky, he could see the silhouette of the burnished metal domes, an old Turkish cemetery behind them, the headstones shaped like phalluses, narrow with bulbous tops. As far as he knew, there were no headstones for women or children, and he'd often wondered where the Turks had buried them. Jutting out over the street were the large wooden rooms where the wives of the Ottomans had once been housed, watching the life in the street from their second-story windows. The quarter was one of the poorest on the island. The high wooden doorways of the buildings were in need of paint, and the limestone walls were covered with political slogans and ripped posters advertising cheap cellphones and local nightclub acts. The road forked at the end of the quarter. Taking the left fork, he drove toward Campos.

MARINA PAPOULIS WAS standing outside, watering the bougainvillea at the front of her home.

"Papa Michalis is coming from Athens today," Patronas told her. "I tried to reach you, but you must have been outside. They want me to meet his plane."

She let the hose drop and turned off the water. "Where's he going to stay?"

"I don't know. I can't take him back to Profitis Ilias. He's on crutches. He'd never make it up the path."

"How about bringing him here? He'll be more comfortable, and I can look after him. It's no trouble. We have plenty of room. While you pick him up, I can air out the guest room and put out clean towels. I've already cooked." She touched his arm. "We'll have a 'welcome home' party for him."

"Are you sure?"

He'd been worrying about where to put Papa Michalis ever since he'd received the call from KAT. When Patronas had called the Archdiocese, Bishop Gerasimos had suggested Psarra, saying Papa Michalis' fellow priests could look after him, but Patronas hadn't wanted to do that to the old man. He wanted him to be able to stay on Chios, near his friends and a hospital, and he was relieved when Marina Papoulis offered to take him in.

She nodded. "It will be my honor."

THE PASSENGERS FROM Athens were already disembarking by the time Patronas reached the airport. After everyone had exited, two flight attendants appeared at the door with Papa Michalis. He was standing on crutches, a tight expression on his face. He looked shrunken and old.

When he saw the chief officer, he raised one of his crutches in greeting. A pick-up truck was moving toward the plane, towing a wooden flatbed trailer. With great care, the two attendants helped Papa Michalis onto the flatbed and held him erect while they moved to the terminal. As always, Greeks had found a way to get the job done—to get a crippled man off a plane. Patronas watched the truck progress slowly toward him, Papa Michalis standing there on his crutches as if riding a float in a parade. Lacking modern equipment, the staff had improvised.

"Welcome home, Father," he said.

"Did you see that? They moved me like a suitcase." Papa Michalis grinned broadly at him. In addition to bandaging his head and putting a cast on his leg, the people at KAT had apparently fixed his teeth as well. The new teeth disturbed Patronas, who found the contrast between the man's eighty-two-year-old face and his sparkling new teeth unsettling. There also appeared to be a problem with the size. The priest obviously didn't think so, as he just kept smiling and smiling. *The poor man*, thought Patronas. *It was as if they'd filled his mouth with piano keys.*

"What's happening with the investigation? Have you got them yet?"

Patronas helped him into the car. "I'll tell you on the way to Marina's."

But, tired from the trip, the priest fell asleep almost immediately, his white hair sticking up in tufts against the seat of the car.

"AH, THERE YOU are." Marina Papoulis embraced Papa Michalis and kissed him on both cheeks. She'd invited her cousins to welcome the priest home and smiled at Patronas as she served the food, selecting the biggest piece of fish for him, the most perfect of the little potatoes. It was one of those unspoken rules that governed life: the guest always got the best of whatever was in the house. Marina ladled the sauce of olive oil, lemon, and oregano over the fish and handed the plate to him. She'd set up a long table outside, and her cousins were gathered around Papa Michalis. Her husband, Nikos, was pouring shots of home-made *raki* and insisting the priest drink one, patting him on the back and exclaiming how glad he was to have him back among them.

"After the Spartan regime at the hospital, this is too much," Papa Michalis whispered to Patronas. Sherlock Holmes never had to work his way through a bottle of *raki* and all this food. Nero Wolfe maybe could have managed, but then he weighed 300 lbs. and lived in his pajamas. He'd never make it. 'Give strong drink unto him that is ready to perish ....' Solomon had said this and he concurred. "If this revelry continues, I'll be dead in a week. My liver will give out. You'll have to carry me to the undertaker's in a truck and buy me an oversized casket."

When someone offered him another shot of *raki*, he shook his head. He didn't approve of all the eating and drinking, this light-hearted merriment three days before August Fifteenth, one of the most important days in the Orthodox calendar. This feast, which is also sometimes called the Assumption, commemorated the death, resurrection and glorification of Christ's mother Mary and was a time meant for fasting and reflection.

Margarita and her two brothers joined them for dinner, but had run off as soon as the meal was over. Marina's husband, Nikos, excused himself, too, saying he had to see to the livestock. One of his mules was sick. He smiled at his wife before he left and touched her arm.

Patronas had been watching them, noticing the way her eyes lingered on her husband's face, the affection in her voice when she spoke his name. Although it was his house, Nikos Papoulis had been a little shy during dinner and let Marina and the other guests do most of the talking. A stout man with a kindly face and callused hands, he'd deferred to his wife repeatedly during the evening. "I'm only a farmer," he told them, "what do I know? She's the one with the education." Marina and her husband reminded Patronas of his parents, who'd been happy together. *How rare*, he thought, *this simple thing.*

After they finished eating and the guests left, Patronas and Papa Michalis relaxed on the terrace. It was pleasant sitting outside at the table, the night-blooming flowers fragrant in the warm air, the fireflies flickering in the cypress trees that marked the end of the property. The streetlights had come on and the children were playing hide and seek in the trees. Patronas joined them for a few minutes, finding Margarita and racing her back to the house, while Papa Michalis applauded from the terrace. It felt good to get away from the case for a few moments, to laugh with children.

He was winded when he got back to his seat. Fetching the *raki*, he poured a glass for himself and the priest and told him what he'd discovered at Profitis Ilias. "Tell the truth, Father," he said. "You were mumbling about water when you were in the hospital. Did you know there was an opening under the well?"

"No, no. Of course not. But I did think there must be a tomb or old shrine nearby. It stood to reason. Eleni had found nothing of consequence, and yet, here comes Petros day after day, bringing these beautiful things. Also Profitis Ilias has an interesting history. It's considered a dark place by churchmen. I thought it might have been the scene of a massacre during 1822 like Nea Moni and Aghios Mena, but there was no ossuary there, and if something did occur, I could never find a record of it."

"What else do you know about it?"

"That it's the oldest inhabited place on Chios. You can find references to it as far back as the fourth century A.D. And it wasn't even new then. According to the records in the Archdiocese, it had been rebuilt countless times, so who knows how old it really is? I assumed it had been built on an ancient temple, like many old churches in Greece."

Patronas could hear the children playing in the distance. "You said it had been rebuilt? By whom?"

"Just about everyone would be my guess. The Byzantines, the Genovese. Perhaps even the Crusaders. Any of the marauding armies or bands of outlaws who passed through here over the years. Who knows? I never understood why they bothered. It's isolated. The icons are nothing special. Those are the original designs, mind you. They've been repainted over the centuries, but the designs themselves have never been altered. The land around it is too poor to sustain more than a handful of people. It's a forlorn place." The priest took a sip of his *raki*. "I've always loathed the icons there and that marble well … flames in a Christian shrine? Hellfire and damnation? More in keeping with the Protestant view, those images, the evangelicals across the sea, who believe the Apocalypse to be human destiny."

"You don't?"

"No." He repeated an old Greek saying: "*Other priests came; other gospels they brought.*"

"That was how I discovered the hole, you know. It's right under those flames on the side of the well …."

"Maybe the engravings were meant as a warning of some kind. To keep people away." The priest took another swallow. "They could even date from Minoan times, you never know. Maybe it was a picture of what they experienced, the Minoans—the volcano erupting, the death of their island. You know that tsunami in Asia last year? The people who live where it hit will be talking about it forever. The one on Thera was much worse, they say." He nodded toward the sea, glimmering faintly in the distance. "Can you imagine what it must have been like? The boiling water, the ocean sinking then rising up to consume you? Like something out of *Exodus*, the Minoans playing the part of the Egyptians." He began to chant: " 'And it shall rain fire and thunder unceasing and there shall be darkness over the land of Egypt. And a pillar of smoke shall lead them by day and by night a pillar of fire.' "

He shook his head. "Can you imagine? Casting off in one of those little wooden boats like they have in the museum, rowing with all your might, trying to escape the coming cataclysm? The sky black as pitch, fire raining down upon you. It must have been terrible."

"Not unlike Smyrna," said Patronas. "There were flames there, too, and death."

"Smyrna was inflicted by man. Thera is different. It's a question of scale, Chief Officer. The Turks might have burned us out and murdered everyone they could get their hands on, but they didn't erase us from the earth. They didn't sink our lands and drown our cities." Papa Michalis set his glass down. "What are you going to do?" His cheeks were red from the spirits.

"About the hole? I don't know. See where it leads."

"Have you told your men about it?"

"No. Only you."

"Don't worry. I won't say anything."

Patronas looked at him. No, he wouldn't. Not if you set his hair on fire or boiled his testicles in oil. Sometimes a person's innate stubbornness worked to your advantage. He'd wanted to use the priest as bait to draw out the killer, but sitting there with him on the terrace, he changed his mind. It was too risky. The old man wouldn't survive another attack. Perhaps the priest could help him in another way.

Patronas took a deep breath. "Father, how do you feel? Are you strong enough to do some investigating for me?"

"Yes, I think so. What is it you want me to do?"

"Go to Castro with Marina and talk to the neighbors of Petros Athanassiou. See what they tell you about Kleftis and Voula. You're a priest. People will tell you things they won't tell me." The chief officer tried not to look at the crutches he saw propped up against the wall, the frailty in the old man's face.

"Will I need to record them? I'm not very conversant with modern technology."

"No. Just talking should suffice." He pushed his chair back and got up. "It's late. I should go."

ஒ

DIMITRA HAD BEEN getting ready for bed when he got to the house. "Oh, Yiannis," she said when he came upstairs. "I wasn't expecting you. I thought you'd be staying up at Profitis Ilias." She had some white cream on her face and hastened to wipe it off. The television in the bedroom was on. She'd been watching the Greek movie, *Stella*. Dimitra would like it, he knew. Black and white and depressing, it was right up her alley. The cheap woman got punished and no one lived happily ever after.

He took his badge off and set it on the dresser. "Sorry I'm late. I had to pick up Papa Michalis."

They chatted amiably for a few minutes until he mentioned his trip to Marina Papoulis' house and how he'd stayed and eaten dinner there. After that, Dimitra's eyes had filled with tears and she'd stopped talking.

"She drank from the nonspeaking water," Patronas said out loud. The saying had been one of his father's favorites. "Watch out when a woman goes quiet," his father had always said. "Watch out for those nonspeaking waters."

After putting on his pajamas, Patronas got into bed and turned out the light. "Good night," he added.

There was no answer. No sound from the other side of the bed.

Remembering the warmth of Marina's house, the noise and commotion, he felt suddenly bereft. He looked over at the blanketed form of his wife. Perhaps if they'd had children.

ஒ

AS SHE POURED the coffee at breakfast, Dimitra inquired about what Marina had served for dinner. She asked this so nonchalantly, Patronas had thought he was safe and volunteered more than he should have. "She made an excellent *rizogalo*. Tasted just like my mother's."

"Oh, so now she cooks better than me, too."

After that, the conversation had deteriorated into a shouting match and he'd left the house without finishing his breakfast. Dimitra had been nearly thirty-seven when they'd married and so grateful to him for not breaking their engagement after he'd learned she was penniless, she'd cried on their wedding night and kissed the ring on his finger, as if she were a penitent and he were a priest. He'd been embarrassed and the night hadn't gone well. A pattern they'd repeated over and over again in their marriage.

Starting the car, he wondered what had become of the woman who'd kissed his ring that night. For the first two or three years of their marriage, she'd treated him like a pasha and did all he bade her to do without question, and he thought perhaps he'd made a good choice. But then one day this other

Dimitra had emerged. The one with the cloven hooves and the pitchfork. Dimitra, the scold. Dimitra, the shrew.

Oh, she'd throw an arm across his shoulders at night in bed and insist that he kiss her when he left for work. He didn't understand why she bothered. He knew he didn't make her happy. Nothing made Dimitra happy. She seemed to thrive on disappointment, to rejoice when someone let her down. She'd asked for a leather handbag once when he'd gone to Athens and he'd spent days going up and down Ermou Street, inspecting the purses at Gucci and Hermes, looking for one he thought would please her. He'd finally settled on a brown calfskin bag with a silk lining and a shiny brass buckle at the center like a horse's bit. Made in England, it had cost a fortune. When he'd presented it to her, she'd twirled it on her arm nonchalantly. "I guess you didn't have much time to shop," she told him. Like the sharks that have to keep eating, who never feel full, nothing ever satisfied Dimitra, nothing ever brought her joy.

Why this sudden jealousy, this neurotic interest in Marina Papoulis? he wondered as he turned into the station. *Why this war?* As if she were Leonidas, the king of Sparta, and Marina the invading Persian army. This wasn't about love, for all Dimitra's big words. He knew it wasn't about love.

CHAPTER 25

Look after your clothes that you may keep
half of them.
—Greek proverb

PAPA MICHALIS GOT out and directed Marina as she maneuvered the car into a parking space behind the Villa Hotel. The chief officer had asked him to speak with the two archeologists as casually as possible, to see if either had something to add to what the police already knew. He'd told him that the American liked to swim laps in the hotel pool in the morning. Papa Michalis scanned the pool. Perhaps Alcott was there now, and he could hand him a towel, hear his confession.

He wasn't, but the British archeologist was. Sitting under an umbrella at the side of the pool, he was working doggedly, typing on his laptop.

Papa Michalis introduced himself. "Good morning. Perhaps you can help me. I'm assisting the police with their investigation into the murders at Profitis Ilias, and the chief officer asked me to speak to you. You were at the monastery that day, too, weren't you?" Taking a seat, he signaled the waiter and ordered an iced coffee.

Without looking up from his screen, the Englishman nodded.

What to say? Papa Michalis had never interviewed a suspect before. What would Sherlock Holmes do? He'd lie, of course, lie in the interest of justice. "I don't know if you've heard, but the police discovered the identity of the murderer. They're planning to send the fingerprints to Interpol for confirmation."

Devon McLean turned and looked at him. He had his attention now. "You mean they haven't done so already? I would have thought dusting and identifying fingerprints would have been de rigueur, especially in a capital crime. But then this is Chios, isn't it? Known since ancient times for the stupidity of its inhabitants. Greeks tell moron jokes about Chiots, don't they?

Or has your position been usurped by the Pontios?"

He was speaking Greek, so his words created quite a stir around the pool. Unfortunately what he was saying was true, the priest thought, especially in Athens. If you said you were from Chios, people automatically assumed you had trouble screwing in light bulbs.

He tried another lie. He felt like he was poking a stick at a snake. "You arrived on July twentieth, I believe, by way of Cyprus?"

"I never said July twentieth," the Englishman snapped. "I said July twenty-fifth! And for your information, I've been on this God-forsaken island twenty-one days now. That's an unacceptable length of time to be held like this. I've done nothing wrong, and yet the police forced me to surrender my passport. That's a violation of human rights anywhere in the world, in any country. There's only one place in the free world where they detain people like this and that is at Guantanamo. And, in answer to your other question, I didn't come here directly from Egypt. I came on Olympic Airlines by way of Athens. There were no direct flights from Cyprus to Chios, Father. You should know that. This island is hardly an international destination. It's not Majorca or Capri." McLean turned back to his computer and began scrolling down the page. "Now, if you'll excuse me, I've got work to do."

"One more question. Do you know when Alcott arrived in Chios?"

"No, I don't. You'll have to ask him."

Judging by the man's hostility, Papa Michalis concluded he'd gotten all he was going to get. He finished his coffee and reached for his crutches. "I appreciate your cooperation," he said softly.

The Englishman grabbed his arm. "What? No more questions? Are you sure? You don't want to know where I stowed the knife? What I did with my bloody clothes?"

The priest shook his head.

"Good, I'm glad. I was beginning to feel out of sorts with you. A little fed up with your feeble efforts to entrap me. Angry, like Henry the Second." He pulled him down closer. "You've heard of Henry the Second, haven't you, Father? He was the king who had that priest Thomas Becket killed. Thomas Becket, the Archbishop of Canterbury? The king told his men: 'Who's going to rid me of this meddlesome priest?' And they took care of it. Perhaps he was drawn and quartered. I don't remember. Anyway, suffice to say he meddled and he died."

Papa Michalis felt a chill. *What was that?* he wondered as he hobbled away. *A threat? Was he threatening me?*

⁂

"Are you sure you want to go on?" Marina Papoulis asked. She and Papa

Michalis were sitting in the car outside the hotel. "You look a little tired. We can go home now if you'd like. Start again tomorrow."

"No, it's only two blocks away. Let's finish."

The part of Castro where Petros Athanassiou's grandmother lived consisted of a cluster of small houses built by the Greek government in the 1920s for the refugees from Smyrna. The refugees had moved on, and the area was now occupied by immigrant workers and their families. Contractors had dumped debris from construction sites in the vacant lots, and the unpaved roads were lined with aging metal warehouses in addition to the public housing. Most of the residents worked in the tannery at the end of one of the streets. The smell was all-pervasive and had made the area one of the poorest on Chios. Maria parked the car and they got out. The wind was blowing, stirring the gritty yellow soil, the garbage that edged the street. A headless doll had been caught in a drain by the curb. Papa Michalis felt as if he was standing at the end of the world.

He started toward the makeshift church at the end of the road. "We'll start with the local priest. A place this small, he'll know the family."

The priest greeted them warmly. He spoke with an island accent and explained that this was his first posting after graduating from the Orthodox seminary in Athens. No older than thirty, he was a corpulent young man with a high-pitched voice. "I'm expecting to be reassigned any day. The neighborhood is full of Muslims now," he said by way of explanation.

"Did you know Petros Athanassiou, the boy who was killed?"

"No, but I know his grandmother. She's one of the most devout women in the parish. His mother had gone to Athens to live before I got here, but I heard a lot of rumors about her." The priest wiggled his heavy body like a belly dancer, making it clear what the nature of those rumors had been.

"Were she and Petros in touch?"

The priest nodded. "He was always writing her, begging her to come home. His grandmother discussed it with me. She didn't know what to do. She didn't want her back."

"How about Manos Kleftis? You know him?"

"Her lover?" His tone was contemptuous. Respectable women didn't have lovers. Lovers were for sluts and whores. "No, I'm afraid I haven't had the pleasure."

After leaving the priest, Papa Michalis and Marina Papoulis worked their way through the neighborhood. Most of the residents were from Pakistan and did not speak Greek, but the one or two who did volunteered that everyone would be glad when Petros' mother and her 'man' left. He apparently frightened them, though exactly why was hard to determine, given the language difference. A dog whose barking he'd objected to had disappeared.

A man who'd argued with him over a parking place, his *apothiki*—storage space—had caught fire. That sort of thing. A group of ragged children were playing in a weed-strewn field, kicking a soccer ball around and yelling. Any one of them could have taken the dog, the priest decided. It probably meant nothing.

"When did Manos Kleftis come here?" Marina asked a man who was selling foreign newspapers at the kiosk by the church.

The Pakistani hesitated, worried. "Why you ask?"

"Petros Athanassiou," the priest said.

"Yes, the dead boy," the man said. "Sad." Not looking up, he continued to sort the magazines and put them out on the rack at the front of his stand. "Mr. Manos, he came a month ago."

"Has anyone visited him here?"

"A man. Foreign, not Greek."

"What kind of foreign man?"

"I don't know. I only saw from far away. Mr. Manos, he wasn't home. Man, he went away."

"What did he look like?"

He waved his hand above his head. "Like cartoon."

"CARTOON? WHAT DO you suppose he meant by that?" Patronas asked when they reported back to him.

"Probably one of the archeologists. McLean maybe." Marina Papoulis was silent for a moment, lost in thought. "They still would have needed someone else, someone who knew Chios."

She turned and looked at him, her face serious. "I think they've been playing 'papas' with us," she said, referring to the famous Greek con game. A card shark would deal out three cards, one of which was always a king, and begin moving them around. He'd take bets as to which card was the king. No matter how many times someone played, they would never find the king. The card shark always won.

CHAPTER 26

Then came a flood of evils.
—Greek proverb

MARINA PAPOULIS LOOKED at her computer screen again, then printed out the pages and put them in the envelope with the rest. Yesterday, after she and Papa Michalis had returned home, they'd gone over everything again. She'd read her notes back to him and he'd added his own thoughts. Poor Father. He'd dozed off at one point and cried out in his sleep. "Father, wake up," she'd said, shaking him gently by the shoulder. "You're having a nightmare." He told her he'd been dreaming of the assault at Profitis Ilias, remembering the terrifying feeling of weightlessness as he plummeted to the ground.

At the travel agency that morning it had been quiet, and she'd used the time to type up her notes. She'd included her interpretation of what the Pakistani had told them. She'd even put in how the Englishman had threatened the priest. The pages she'd printed off the Internet were last. She turned off her computer and pushed her chair back. Tomorrow was August Fifteenth, a national holiday, and there would be feasting, followed by a festival with a live band and dancing in the streets. She needed to get home and start preparing the food. She was planning a surprise for Patronas, but it could wait. She'd drop it off on her way home from liturgy tomorrow.

PATRONAS HAD WANTED to get to Profitis Ilias early, to explore the hole when the sun was high in the sky, but a fatal traffic accident near the harbor had taken precedence. A young tourist from Germany on a rented motorbike had been run off the road and killed by a hit and run driver. The Coast Guard had legal jurisdiction over the harbor and surrounding area, and it had taken hours to establish who would supervise the case. He and his men had gathered testimonies from eyewitnesses. Fortunately, a cruise boat had just docked and there had been a lot of people in the street. By five p.m. they had cleared the case and made an arrest: an eighteen-year-old Romanian laborer who'd been driving a truck for the first time. Concentrating on maneuvering the truck, he hadn't seen the motorbike and panicked when he heard the crash. He was deeply sorry, he told Patronas in broken Greek. He hadn't meant for it to happen.

After making the arrest, Patronas had summoned a high school teacher he knew who spoke German and returned to the station to call the girl's parents and make arrangements.

The sun was down by the time he and Tembelos finally reached Profitis Ilias, the courtyard full of shadows. The hole beneath the well was even darker than Patronas remembered it.

"Do we have to do this tonight?" Tembelos asked. He was on his hands and knees with his head stuck in the hole, peering down into the dank space. "I can't see a thing."

Patronas cursed. Although they'd removed two more of the metal panels in an effort to see better, it had made no difference. The gloom under the well was all encompassing. He moved his police flashlight back and forth, trying to see what lay below. He could make out a battered stone staircase built into the wall closest to him, but that was it. Neither he nor Tembelos had acknowledged the presence of the staircase or made any move to see where it led.

Tembelos withdrew his head. "Easy to miss a step in the dark, hurt ourselves, if we do this now."

Patronas let himself be persuaded. Truth was, he could use a break. He'd been up since four a.m. working on the hit-and-run, and he was worn out. He and his men had been occupying Profitis Ilias for weeks now. Aside from the assault on Evangelos Demos, he had seen no trace of the killer. Whoever the man was, he was clever. He wouldn't be waiting for them tonight at the bottom of the hole.

Clicking off his flashlight, he stood up and dusted himself off. "Okay, Giorgos. We're done here."

Before they left Profitis Ilias, Patronas made sure the gate to the tunnel was bolted and that the lights were turned on in the courtyard and all the rooms. He ordered Tembelos to bring the police scanner up from his car and set it near the well. If the murderer was in the vicinity, he wanted him to think the police were still here, occupying the monastery.

"Turn it on high," he told him. "Make it loud."

When he'd finished, Patronas locked the metal doors behind them with the key Papa Michalis had given him and started down the path to the parking lot.

"Leave your police cruiser where it is," he told Tembelos when they got to the lot. "I'll give you a ride home in my Citroen."

After he backed out of the parking lot, he returned to barricade the entrance and string crime scene tape across the gravel path. It wasn't only the killer he wanted to keep away. He wanted to make sure Spiros Korres or his son weren't up here looking for buried treasure while he was away.

"How about I take the day off tomorrow?" Tembelos said as they drove out. "It's August Fifteenth. I'm entitled."

"Sure," Patronas said. "I'll stop by here at some point, keep watch on the place. We can explore the hole after the holiday."

THE NEXT MORNING Patronas drove to Profitis Ilias. All appeared to be as he'd left it. Both entrances were locked and he could hear the police scanner, faint above the wind. He left and returned to the center of town.

Strings of colored flags decorated the campanile of the cathedral, and a makeshift amusement park had been set up in a vacant lot next door. Patronas could hear the whine of the merry-go-round and children laughing.

He stopped by the police station, hoping to take advantage of the holiday and call England while the place was quiet. "I'll take the rest of the day off," he told himself. "The investigation's stalled. One day more or less won't make any difference."

The operator told him the museum where Devon McLean worked was being renovated and would be closed until September first. No one was available in the Archeology Department, either. She suggested he call back after August eighteenth, when the Director of the Institute of Archeology would return, having completed his summer studies in Sicily.

Patronas hung up the phone. *Vrasta.* Another day, then.

The files on Eleni Argentis and Petros Athanassiou were spread out on his desk. He'd set out a photo of Dimitra when he'd first taken over as Chief Officer. That was fifteen years ago. The photo had faded into nothingness and was now yellow and overexposed, sort of like their relationship. He had no desire to go home. Somehow the feast days hadn't been the same since his mother died. Oh, Dimitra did her best, but as they were both only children, it was often just the two of them and sometimes her mother, which was no cause for celebration. Maybe they could go to Pyrgi tonight and dance in the square. It had been a long time since he'd done that. He couldn't remember the last time he'd danced in Pyrgi.

Marina Papoulis turned onto the rutted lane that led to Profitis Ilias. Both sides of the road belonged to Spiro Korres. Most of his acreage lay fallow now, the red soil dry in the heat of summer. It was so quiet she could hear the cicadas buzzing in the cypress trees that marked the end of his property. She veered too far to the right, and the car scraped the prickly pears on the side of the road. Their thorns sounded like nails as they raked the fender. Eventually, the road leveled out and continued on. A crow was calling from one of the trees. The cawing echoed over the rocks. No one she knew lived out here.

Two plastic cones blocked the entrance to the parking lot. She got out of her car, moved them and drove in. She parked the car next to the police cruiser and rolled down the windows. The air was hot and still. There was another car parked there. She wondered who it belonged to. Stepping over the police tape, she started to climb up the path, thinking it would be a long trek in her straight skirt and new shoes. But it took her less than fifteen minutes to reach the monastery.

She was surprised to find no one there and the doors locked. "Chief Officer?" she yelled, banging on the door. "Yiannis?"

She walked around the monastery and tried the gate in the back. It, too, was locked. Puzzled, she called and called. She thought she heard something, a radio perhaps, and called again. "Yiannis, are you here?" But it was only dead leaves dragging across the stones in the wind. She walked down to the dig site but found no one there, either. It was getting hot. She thought she saw a man in the distance and waved to him. The sun was high in the sky. She'd have to leave soon.

She heard a faint tinkling in the distance and made her way toward it. A herd of goats stood together on a distant slope near where she'd seen the man.

"Chief Officer," she yelled. "Yiannis?" There was no answer.

Hearing a noise, she ventured closer and called out again, more hesitant this time. "Yiannis?"

CHAPTER 27

What the wind gathers, the devil scatters.
—Greek proverb

DIMITRA HAD BEEN at work in the garden. The honeysuckle was tied up with string alongside the house, and the roses were freshly watered, the path swept. He'd forgotten she'd invited his cousin to celebrate with them and was pleasantly surprised to see him standing on the front steps.

"The prodigal returns," his cousin said, clapping him on the back.

His cousin had brought a spring lamb with him, and the two of them spent the afternoon rigging up the spit and grilling it over an open fire. They passed a bottle of ouzo back and forth as they worked, laughing and eating snippets of meat.

That night the three of them went to Pyrgi to hear the music. The medieval town was decorated with lights and Patronas could hear the band warming up. The village was a special place, its walls covered by intricate black and white designs: triangles and circles, chevrons and flowers. The designs gave the village a playful, jaunty air that Patronas liked, a kind of fairytale atmosphere. The tables in the square had been removed, and people were forming circles and starting to dance. He grabbed Dimitra's hand and they joined the long line, dancing the *Kalamatiano*, a popular Greek dance. Children were forming their own lines and imitating the grown-ups. The noise was earsplitting—the amplified music, the crowd, the screaming of the dancers as they whirled around on the cobbled pavement.

It was so noisy that Patronas didn't hear his phone ringing until they returned to the car. Patronas answered, wondering who was calling at this hour. He looked at his watch—close to three a.m.

It was the dispatcher at the police station. "Chief Officer, you better get in here," the man said.

"Why? What's happened?"

There was a long silence on the other end of the phone. "Just come," the man said.

When Patronas reached the station, he was surprised to see his entire staff assembled outside his office. Tembelos was out of breath, his face flushed. "I just heard," he said.

"What's going on?" Patronas studied the faces of his staff. No one would meet his eye. "What the hell is going on?"

It was Evangelos Demos who finally told him. "It's Marina Papoulis. She never came home."

Something stirred deep inside him. "What do you mean?"

"Her husband called. They've been waiting for her for hours."

"Is Margarita there? The other children?"

"As far as I know."

Patronas quickly called Marina's house and spoke to her husband.

"She was in a big hurry when she left," the man told him. "She said she had information for you and that she had to find you."

"So she went to the station?"

"Or your house. All I know is, she was determined to find you."

"Are there any relatives she might have visited on the way?"

"I've checked and they all say no. I called everyone I could think of, Chief Officer." The man sounded close to tears. "No one's seen her."

"DIMITRA!" PATRONAS SCREAMED.

She was upstairs, hanging up her clothes. He could hear her humming one of the songs they'd danced to in Pyrgi. He stood watching her from the door of the bedroom. "Why didn't you tell me Marina Papoulis was here today?"

"I don't know. It slipped my mind." She resumed her singing, dancing around in her slip, happy from their evening out.

"When was she here?"

"After I got back from church, early afternoon." Her eyes clouded, the joy slowly leaving her face. "It's not enough that she talks to you at the laiki; now she's got to come here in her car, looking for you."

She padded down the stairs in her slippers and opened a cupboard in the kitchen. Pulling out a china dish, she set it down on the table. He recognized the pattern as Marina's. "Seems you were asking for *svingis*." Dimitra spoke as if from far away.

"What happened when she dropped them off?"

"I told her I'd be sure you got them and thanked her in an appropriate manner."

"What else did she tell you?"

"Something about the investigation. She had some papers for you. I told her to leave them here. But she said 'no'; she needed to explain them to you."

"Where did you tell her I was?" he asked, his voice tight.

"Profitis Ilias." Unconcerned, she studied the donuts for a moment, then picked one up and began to eat it.

"My God, Dimitra, what have you done?" They'd discussed it. She had to have known how dangerous it was.

She turned and looked at him, a little defiant. "I told her you were up at Profitis Ilias. Just like I said." Her face was greasy and she had a ring of sugar around her mouth.

"You bitch!" He knocked the donut out of her hand. "You saw your chance and you took it."

She made a move toward him, but he pushed her back. "Get away!" he yelled. "You stay away from me!"

He thought about what she'd done as he ran to his car. In the past, Dimitra's meanness had been small-minded, directed largely at those who were defenseless, people no one on Chios would defend ... an unwed mother, someone's homosexual son. It was well-hidden. Like the tentacles of a sea anemone, it only appeared occasionally, uncoiling and stinging the unwary victim, poisoning them with invective, a stream of malicious and hurtful words. She'd moved beyond that now. This time it wasn't tentacles she'd displayed. It was claws.

CHAPTER 28

He who lives on hope, dies of hunger.
—Greek proverb

WHILE GIORGOS TEMBELOS and the others searched the area around Marina Papoulis' house, Patronas raced to Profitis Ilias. She'd be all right. She'd have seen the barricade and turned back. She'd probably had car trouble. Yes, that was why she hadn't made it home. Swerving in and out of traffic, he drove like the car was on fire, passing on the right side, honking continually.

It was nearly five a.m. when he turned onto the dirt road that traversed the Korres' farm. Instead of driving in the direction of the monastery as he usually did, he drove toward the house. "Open up, Spiros," he yelled, banging on the door with his fist.

Korres took a long time answering. "What is it?" he asked, fastening up his pants. His eyes were red and he smelled of beer.

"Marina Papoulis has disappeared. Have you seen her?"

"No, but we were in church all morning and then we went on to Pyrgi." He rubbed his face with his hand, trying to wake up. "I'll saddle a horse for you. If she's not in the monastery, you'll need to search the hills." He walked to the barn, hurriedly brought out a horse, a bay, and helped him into the saddle. "Give her a kick. It'll be quicker than walking."

In the distance, Patronas could see Marina's car parked in the lot next to the police cruiser. "Marina!" he yelled. "Marina!"

There was no answer.

He urged the horse forward as fast as he dared. There was no moon, and it was hard to find his way in the darkness. He and the bay were both old and he didn't want to cause injury to either of them. His mount seemed to sense his panic and trotted up the hill at a fast pace, stumbling once or twice on the stones, snorting like a race horse. The gravel kept shifting and he clutched the saddle to keep from falling.

Both entrances to the monastery were locked. "Marina!"

He got down from his horse and searched the area around the citadel, then remounted and rode out to the dig site. The ground was rocky and the horse shied away from the trenches. He waved his flashlight around the site, but saw nothing. A part of the tent was flapping in the wind, the white canvas ghostlike in the darkness.

"Marina!"

Turning his horse around, he was about to head back to the monastery when he heard the plaintive cry of a goat in the distance. Other goats soon joined the chorus, their bleating unusually high-pitched and frantic, as if they sensed a predator.

Patronas galloped to the lean-to where the goats were housed and shone the flashlight into the corral. The goats backed away from the light, stepping on one another in their effort to get away, clearly fearful. He didn't know what to make of it. Animals acted like that around butcher shops. He'd seen them, heard their awful clamor. But here? It didn't make sense.

"Easy now. I won't hurt you."

His horse began to shy away, too, breathing heavily and showing the whites of her eyes, her flanks drenched in sweat. Suddenly she reared up and charged away, bucking Patronas off. He got to his feet and grabbed his flashlight, holding it in front of him as he walked back toward the corral, fearful of being caught unawares in the dark. He, too, was beginning to sense a predator.

"Marina!" He didn't know how long he stood there, slashing the air with his light. He played it back and forth on the flat table of rock at the rear wall of the corral. There'd been no rain, yet the ground appeared to be wet. Patronas bent down and ran his fingers through the shallow puddle. Even in the darkness, he could tell it was blood. "Mother of God," he whispered.

Splotches of blood darkened the entire side of the rock. It looked like something had been dragged through the dirt there, slaughtered. Patronas closed his eyes for a moment. He found Marina's purse close by. It was open, looked as if someone had pawed through it. A pair of goats eyed him for a moment then galloped away to join their fellows spread out in the distance, their bells tinkling faintly as they moved. A few of the goats remained in the lean-to, watching him steadily with their leaden eyes.

Patronas climbed up on top of the ledge and waved the lantern back and forth. "Marina," he called faintly. A round piece of metal caught the light. It was about the size of a manhole cover and looked to have been pried loose from the dirt. Beneath it was a hole. The ground was disturbed all around it, torn up and covered with blood. There was no way to tell who'd been there or how he'd come, if it were one man alone or an army. Patronas kicked the metal plate to one side and let himself down into the hole. Crude steps led deep into the earth. There was blood on the first few, and caking the sides of the passageway, Marina's dress, or what was left of it, a ragged patch of pink on the pavement.

Patronas thought he heard something and clambered deeper, not knowing how far the shaft penetrated the earth or what he'd find when he reached the bottom. His flashlight was losing power and he knew he was destroying evidence, but he stumbled on, praying she was still alive.

It was damp in the hole, the smell of decay overwhelming. The darkness was total, the fading light from his flashlight barely penetrating the gloom.

Patronas dug out his phone and called headquarters. "Bring floodlights and a stretcher," he ordered. "Hurry."

Slipping on his gloves, Patronas inched forward. He turned the flashlight off a few minutes later, wanting to preserve the battery. The darkness was beyond anything he'd ever experienced. It was like being blindfolded. Desperate, he fumbled to turn the flashlight back on, his hands shaking. He was four to five meters underground, standing at the entrance to an immense cave. But unlike other caves he'd been in, this one had no stalactites or standing pools of water. Its walls were smooth, the floor even. He moved his foot back and forth. It wasn't lava he was standing on, but a chunk of roughly hewn stone, a pavement of sorts.

Clay pots, each about two meters square, lined the wall closest to him, hundreds of them. He raised the lid of one. Inside was a skeleton, its knees tucked up against its chest. It was decorated with lapis and gold, its bony fingers adorned with rings. Its teeth, bared in a grimace, were a thing of terror in the darkness. He let the lid down and checked another. It, too, held a skeleton. So it had been death they'd been smelling. Ancient death. A cemetery.

Finding no trace of Marina Papoulis, Patronas pushed farther into the cave, edging deeper and deeper into the darkness. No light penetrated this space, the endless blackness at the far reaches of the cave. Patronas wondered how far it extended beneath the monastery and surrounding hills. He swung the flashlight back and forth, as if the gloom were a cobweb he could sweep away at will. He couldn't see beyond the circle of light and dropped to his hands and knees. He was afraid of falling, losing his way in this world of night.

He didn't know how long he'd been crawling when he came to the chiseled opening in the rock. The blocks fit seamlessly together and ventilation shafts were cut into the rock overhead; he could feel cool air pouring in all around him. Holding his flashlight tightly, Patronas inched forward. After a few minutes, he stood up. He was looking out on a small city.

CHAPTER 29

The devil takes half.
—Greek proverb

HE COULD SEE streets lined with houses, the polished ceiling of the cave forming a protective arch above them. The houses were small, built one on top of the other like seats in a stadium, and wound down to the floor of the cave, lost somewhere in the darkness. They looked to have been made of mud brick and were nearly identical in their construction to houses he'd seen on Thera and Mykonos.

"Marina!" he bellowed. He stumbled through the ancient village, carefully inspecting the ground underfoot, seeking some trace of her. A thin layer of grayish dust covered every surface and muted his steps as he went. The pine beams that had once held the roofs in place had all rotted away, creating an intricate labyrinth, a maze of walls and alleyways, terrifying in the gloom.

Playing his flashlight over the interior of one of the houses, he was surprised to see the walls were painted with a delicate tableau of plants and gazelles. Four thousand years old and he could still see the colors, the ochres and greens, gleaming faintly in the weak light. He continued on to the second house, and the third, hurriedly making his way through the abandoned city, this Minoan ghost town. He saw clay figurines spread out on the floor—tiny chariots and cooking pots, farm animals, toys, he guessed, and an ivory game board with pieces still in place. He could smell cigarette smoke in the air and saw signs of digging everywhere, holes where something had been removed, places where the walls had been breached. He tried to measure the intruder's footprints against his own, seeking to determine if they belonged to a man or a woman, but it was too difficult, balancing on one foot, juggling the flashlight in the dark. "Later," he told himself. "I'll get forensics up here and we'll turn this place inside out."

He found a small statue lying next to one of the ancient coffins and pocketed it carefully, hoping for fingerprints. Unlike Eleni Argentis' orderly excavation, whoever had been working here had done so in haste. Some of the ditches were barely a foot deep, as if someone had probed the earth, found nothing and quickly moved on. He saw little piles of signet seals by a doorway, *galapetras*. He scooped up as many as he could and began going through them in the palm of his gloved hand. They were like jewels and incised with Minoan motifs, a bull or waving palms, the omnipresent snake goddess. The seals would be easy to transport and bring a fortune on the black market. Whoever was looting the site knew what they were doing.

Something stirred in the deep recesses of the cave.

Patronas paused, his heart pounding.

A cloud of bats came streaming by him, careening wildly as they returned to the shelter of the cave. An immense twitching mass, there must have been over five thousand of them. Their whispery fluttering terrified him, and he put his hands over his head and ducked down, willing them away.

Deeply traumatized, he resumed his search a few minutes later, spying a faint trail of blood on the ground, tricklings of it, still sticky, in the grit. The graveyard smell was back. Stronger, it seemed to fill the air around him. He gagged when he came upon a scattering of loose bones on the floor of the cave, brittle and yellow with age. The thin rill of blood led to a row of massive amphorae. The lid of one was slightly askew. A woman's shoe lay nearby. Black patent leather, it looked as if it had never been worn.

Whimpering softly, he pushed the lid aside. Inside was Marina's naked body, her arms crossed over her chest, her head lowered as if asleep. She'd been beaten and slashed with a knife. The cuts weren't deep, but there were a lot of them. Whoever had done this had taken their time. She was wearing a heavy amber necklace and a pair of gold bracelets. The jewelry looked to be ancient, and Patronas guessed it had once adorned the bones that now littered the ground at his feet. Someone had dumped the skeleton out of the sarcophagus, stripped it, and placed Marina's body inside, dressed it with the jewelry, and closed it up again. Blood caked the beads of the amber necklace, which meant that whoever had done this had done it while she was still alive, while she was dying. Her neck had been cut nearly in half and a small plate left in her lap to collect the blood. Human sacrifice, or a close approximation.

He staggered back. He was sure he must be somewhere under Profitis Ilias. He waved his flashlight around and caught sight of a square of burnished metal gleaming faintly above him. He searched for the staircase he knew must be there, found it and started up as fast as he dared. When he reached the top, he crawled through the hole and lay there, rocking back and forth, sobbing quietly. As he'd anticipated, he was in the courtyard of the monastery. All the lights were on, just as he had left them. The smell of death was strong in the night air.

Patronas looked up at the sky. He could see Orion and Mars, the Milky Way a great swath of white gauze. They could have his job, he thought. He didn't want to go back down into the cave. He no longer feared being entombed under the well or encountering the ghost of the Minotaur or its dead masters. No, he admitted to himself. It was meeting up with the man who had done this he was afraid of, the monster who had destroyed Marina, cut her up like chum on a beach.

AFTER RADIOING FOR help, Patronas finally returned to the cave. He removed his shirt and covered Marina Papoulis' body with it. He'd found a bloody envelope near her body. Inside were pages of notes, so soaked with blood as to be nearly illegible. Airplane schedules for June and July.

"Ach, Marina, to die for this."

He sat as close to her body as he dared without disturbing the crime scene. In the silence of the cave, he thought for a terrifying moment that he could hear her blood dripping onto the plate but then realized it must be the water in the well above, splashing against the stones in the courtyard. Beetles were at work in the dust, spiders, too, and he killed as many as could, grinding them into the dirt with the heel of his shoe. He kept clicking the flashlight on and off, fearful he would lose his mind if it went out and he was shut up here in the darkness. Finally, he began to weep again, crying for Marina, for her husband and her children. He even found himself praying—long, rambling, incoherent prayers—begging God to keep the shadows at bay, the evil he'd stumbled across from overwhelming him.

He couldn't bear to think of Marina's last moments on earth. He touched the clay pot that held her body, wishing he'd never gotten her involved, wishing many things.

PATRONAS GUESSED IT was close to dawn when he heard the first car. He had a sense of increased light, of growing warmth in the dank interior of the cave. "Bring a crime kit," he'd told Tembelos on the phone. He planned to process the scene himself. Judging by the people shouting, the thundering of equipment being unloaded, he and the others must be here. Not wanting them to find him lying there, groggy with fatigue, he brushed himself off and climbed out of the cave to meet them. "Go over the corral for fingerprints," he told Tembelos. "You'll need to take an impression of the footprints, too. Be mindful of the spatter. It's on the flat rock there."

Tembelos nodded, thinking Patronas wasn't himself, all business and strangely unemotional, as if the murder of Marina Papoulis was a routine occurrence. His own mother, a woman from Sparta, had been like that. When his father had died, killed in a car accident, she'd shed no tears, not one. Stone-faced, she'd identified the body, fingering the bloody stains in the front of his shirt, all without a sound. Crying would have lessened her pain and she hadn't wanted that, she'd told him. She wanted to keep the suffering alive, the agony of her loss fresh. It was as if doing so, in some small measure, would preserve her loved one as well. His boss, Patronas, he was the same. He would feel right at home in Sparta.

The policemen waited silently above ground while Patronas removed Marina Papoulis' body from its clay tomb, gently loaded it on a gurney and signaled for them to raise it, working the ropes he'd rigged around it like a pulley. He ordered his men to stay away from the cave, claiming it was too dangerous, that the roof was weak and might collapse, making a show of shaking the beetles out his hair and wiping the blood off his gloves. He didn't tell them about the city, the wealth of Minoan artifacts beneath their feet. They were poor men with families. They might be tempted, as Petros Athanassiou had been, to pilfer the ruins. If word got out, half of Chios would show up, people eager to lay claim in a sort of Minoan gold rush, and he wanted to trap the murderer before that happened.

After the darkness of the cave, the sunshine was blinding, and he was surprised to see Spiros Korres standing there, talking to the shepherd on the other side of the corral. The farmer'd caught the scent of riches and was not to be put off. Patronas ordered Tembelos to escort both men away from the monastery and make sure they stayed away. There was a path now, leading from the monastery to the corral, the brush beaten down by his men travelling back and forth. The goats had been driven off, housed in a makeshift pen on the far side of the hill. He could hear them bleating plaintively in the distance.

Thirsty, he went to the kitchen to get a drink of water. Papa Michalis, sitting at the table, greeted him sadly. Where had the priest come from? Patronas wondered. Had he hobbled up here on his crutches? Patronas got himself water, then opened a cupboard and rummaged around, looking for something to eat. He found a heel of stale bread, picked up a knife to cut it, then put the knife down again, overcome, remembering Marina's wounds. Without a word, Papa Michalis got up, limped over and took the knife from his hand. He motioned for Patronas to sit down while he cut the bread. Patronas ate half a slice then pushed it away and lit a cigarette, his hand trembling as he worked the lighter.

The priest watched him smoke.

"What's that you say in church?" Patronas could feel his face start to crumple, to come apart like a flooded riverbank. "It's on that list of things we pray for … 'a peaceful end to our days without pain, suffering or shame.' Marina had pain. The forensic man said she was still alive when he cut her. She had suffering and she had shame." He put his hands over his face and started to sob.

Papa Michalis got out a bottle of brandy, poured Patronas a glass and pushed it toward him across the table. "One day it will be easier," he said. "One day you will be able to bear it."

Chapter 30

A drowning man grips his own hair.
—Greek proverb

After overseeing the removal of the body to headquarters, Patronas and Papa Michalis drove to Campos to tell Nikos Papoulis the news. He was alone in the house and said he'd sent the children to stay with their grandmother the night Marina went missing.

Patronas took a deep breath. "She's dead, Nikos, I'm sorry. We found her body."

"But how?"

"Someone killed her."

"Killed Marina?!"

He started to scream and kept screaming, "No! No!"

Patronas turned away, unable to look at him. Every crime victim he'd ever interviewed had sounded the same, gasping and shrieking, their pain so visceral it was if they'd lost the power of human speech. He never knew what to say, and he didn't know now. "I'm sorry," he said again.

Gradually Nikos Papoulis collected himself, his major concern for his children. "I'll tell them in a day or so. Let them think she's still alive a little longer." He went on talking, oblivious to the tears running down his face.

They were sitting on overstuffed Victorian chairs in the parlor. There was a photograph of Marina and her husband on their wedding day on the table next to a drawing Margarita had made of a horse. A window was open and a faint hint of honeysuckle from the garden drifted in the air.

"My wife, Dimitra, said Marina stopped by the house," Patronas said. "She said Marina had something for me."

"*Svingi.* Yes, that's right." Papoulis gave him a wan smile. "She and

Margarita wanted to surprise you. They were planning it for days, giggling with *yiayia* about it in the kitchen."

"My wife said Marina had something else." Patronas fought to keep his voice level, to stay in control, professional. "Some information. Do you have any idea what it was?"

Nikos Papoulis shook his head. A few minutes later, he started to cry again, silently at first, and then with great, gulping sobs. Rocking back and forth, he pounded the arms of his chair, calling his wife's name.

"THE RUINS RUN under the entire place," Patronas told Papa Michalis. "Probably even beyond. They're at least as big as Knossos and in much better condition. Save for a couple of ditches the murderer dug in the back, it hasn't been touched in centuries. This will put Chios on the map. It will be like Pompeii."

"Why do you suppose they built inside a cave?"

"I don't know. My guess is, Eleni Argentis got it wrong. Whatever is up there isn't a palace. It looks more like a refugee camp. These people must have come after the volcano on Thera erupted and their homes got washed away."

"And they wanted someplace high," said the priest, nodding, "someplace safe. I remember you asked me about the Phaistos Disc."

"It was no use as a map, but it did get me started. I studied the drawings on it and then, when I was up at Profitis Ilias, I noticed the cobblestones were set in similar pattern. The Disc has a lot of symbols pertaining to water, fish mainly, and that drew me to the well. I don't think the Disc has anything to do with Chios, though. This place I found, it was an outpost, Father. A footnote. It's not the main act."

Patronas lit a cigarette. He and the priest were sitting in a taverna. At the priest's suggestion, they'd stopped to eat after leaving Nikos Papoulis. Although neither was hungry, they'd ordered steaks and drank three carafes of wine between them.

"I've ordered my men to stay out of the cave. I told them the walls were unstable and might come down at any time. The truth is, I was afraid if they got in there, they'd loot it, same as Petros did. You're the only person I've told."

Patronas emptied the carafe into his glass and held it up, signaling the waiter for more. "You know that poem, 'Ithaki?' "

Papa Michalis nodded. "Cavafy."

> And if you find her poor, Ithaka has not defrauded you, for at last you will understand what the search for Ithaka means.

"The point being, it's the journey and what you learn. But, tell me, Father, what is there to learn here?"

"Yiannis ..." The priest didn't like the desperate, keening note he kept hearing in Patronas' voice. The chief officer had been working for nearly forty-eight hours straight, and he had suggested they eat together as a way of making him take a break. He now thought this might have been a mistake.

As in the previous two murders, in spite of their best efforts, neither Patronas nor the forensics experts from Athens had found anything that would identify the murderer—no fingerprints, no usable footprints, nothing. Whoever this man was, his skills more than equaled those of the Greek police. The Ministry of Justice in Athens had gotten involved, and now there was talk of bringing in Interpol or the American FBI. Papa Michalis doubted Patronas would be able to keep his job much longer.

"I stayed up all night thinking about it," Patronas went on. "There has to be something I can take away from this. Some message. But what? Marina stopped by my house as an act of kindness and Dimitra sent her off to be killed."

"Yiannis, listen to me. She was killed by a madman. Dimitra didn't do it." His wife's culpability had been the theme for much of the conversation that afternoon, that and all Patronas' misspent years with her. Such talk wouldn't catch Marina's killer and the priest was sick of listening to it.

"Oh, she sent her there all right." Patronas drained his glass and set it down carefully. He was quite drunk. "The bitch." Patronas raised the carafe again. "Do you know, the priest blessed the two of us when we got married? Can you believe it? He said that we, the newly betrothed, were incomplete, that only together would we be 'made perfect.' Yet Dimitra and I weren't made perfect. We were anything but perfect." Impatiently, he looked around for the waiter. "We were nothing together."

As soon as the waiter returned with a new carafe, Patronas refilled his glass and drank it down. "I suppose I could have been kinder. Such a simple thing, kindness, and yet I wasn't kind." He was slurring his words now. "You should never take another human being for granted, Father. All of us deserve to be loved. And if we can't provide that simple service to someone, we should get out of their way and give them a chance to seek it elsewhere."

His eyes filmed with tears. "Anyway, who cares about Dimitra? What about Marina? You're a priest. Explain it to me. Why did this have to happen?" An edge had come into Patronas' voice. "You're a man of God. You know all the answers."

"Not to this. I have no answer to this." Papa Michalis wanted to hit him.

"From what Dimitra said, I just missed her. If I'd only stayed up at Profitis Ilias a little longer, I would have seen her. Fifteen minutes more, that's all it would have taken. Fifteen minutes and everything would have turned out differently."

This grieved him, the priest thought, the fifteen minutes. Patronas had talked of little else since the night he'd found the body.

"During the war, people spoke like you," the priest told him. "Soldiers. One man gets killed, another doesn't. Fifteen minutes more, fifteen minutes less. The arbitrariness of a bullet, a bomb … the randomness of death. You can't think like that. It doesn't do you any good." He shook his head. "Faith helps, but from what you've said, you have none."

"Oh, but I do. I believe in evil, Father. I have total faith in it. It's relentless, relentless and everlasting. And it always wins. You can count on it. Evil always wins."

Patronas emptied his glass and set it down. "My question is, does it exist on its own like bacteria or do we create it? I don't know about God, but I'm sure Satan exists. Yes, indeed. He walks among us, Satan does. He's everywhere."

Like a drunk in a bar who thinks he's discovered the meaning of life. The priest moved the carafe out of his reach. Patronas had had enough.

"Come on, Yiannis, pull yourself together. You've got work to do."

Patronas raised his head. "Marina's dead," he mumbled. "In no small part because of me. She died naked and alone after someone cut her up, cut her up …. Just think of that, Father. What exactly would you have me do?"

"To start with? I'd have you arrest the whole lot of them. As for the rest of this *saxlamara* you've been going on about, this blasphemous claptrap, it can wait for another day. If you didn't answer those questions when you were eighteen, Yiannis, you're not going to answer them now."

❧

PATRONAS THOUGHT ABOUT Dimitra as he drove to his mother-in-law's house. He wasn't looking forward to seeing her again, nor hearing her voice. He doubted that he'd ever look forward to anything connected with Dimitra again.

A row of abandoned windmills marked the beginning of Vrontados, and he could see the lights of the village up ahead. To the east was the promontory of *Dhaskalopetra*. It held a coarsely carved stone where Homer was said to have lectured. Chiots claimed Homer had been born on the island, but there was no proof, save the eroded rock and the legends that surrounded it.

His wife was outside, threading metal skewers with chunks of pork and laying them out on a grill. She was wearing an apron and her face was beaded with sweat. Intent on her work, she barely acknowledged him.

"The day she came, did Marina say anything about the papers she had for me?" Patronas said.

"You came here to ask me that?"

"I tried calling, but you didn't answer."

Setting the skewer down, she turned to face him. "We've already been over this, Yiannis. No, Marina Papoulis did not discuss what was in the envelope, nor did she leave any papers for you. All she left were *svingis*." She spat the word.

"Are you sure?"

"Yes, I'm sure."

"Did she say anything about what she'd discovered? Why she had to find me?"

"I already told you. She said something about 'playing the priest.' " And then it came, the flicker of malice. "What do you think? I'd invite her in and tell her my life story? We had nothing in common, the two of us. All we had in common was you."

He fought to control himself. "She's dead because of you."

"So you keep telling me." She turned back to the grill and began fanning the coals with a folded newspaper. Cinders and bits of ash flew in the air.

"Dead," he shouted. "You hear me? Dead!"

She was crying now. "Go away, Yiannis."

CHAPTER 31

He who is hungry, dreams of bread.
—Greek proverb

THE SERVICE FOR Marina Papoulis was a simple one. The church in Campos kept a coffin on hand, a plain wooden box that was used for funerals. After the bishop chanted the liturgy, the mourners followed him to the cemetery where her body was to be laid to rest. Patronas and Nikos Papoulis had conferred and decided that, in deference to Marina's wounds, they would wrap her in the linen shroud early, before people started arriving at the church, and not at the graveside as was the usual custom. Neither wanted to mar the dignity of her burial with a public display. After being disinterred from the communal coffin, she would be buried in the enclosed area that housed her father and her paternal grandparents, her mother's family having been too poor for the luxury of a stone tomb.

A large photograph of Marina on her wedding day was on display on a wooden stand provided by the undertaker. In recognition of her many years of service at Profitis Ilias, the bishop had ordered her bier covered with flowers, to which Patronas now added a small handful of his own—roses and jasmine, purchased from the florist across the street. The cemetery was crowded. Patronas had expected only family members to stay for the burial, but it looked as if most of Chios had turned up. He saw little Margarita, standing between her two brothers, her face pinched and white. She was wearing a black dress with a white collar and shiny new shoes with straps; her legs and arms impossibly thin. All worn out with crying, she didn't look like the child he'd played hide and seek with. He was surprised to see the grandmother of Petros Athanassiou standing behind Marina's family, grim-faced and isolated from the others. Why was she here? he wondered. *Come to pay her respects to a fellow victim?* Curious now, he scanned the crowd. *A sto diablo*, even

Antonis Argentis and his mother were there. Apparently Marina's funeral was a historic event on the island, an affair that would be talked about for years, not to be missed.

A group of elderly women from her village spoke to him of her goodness and generosity, how she'd sponsored their Easters and Christmases for years, leaving food for the feast on their doorsteps. Anonymously, of course, though one of them had seen her and told the others, so they'd all known it was Marina who'd been responsible. Another talked of how she'd single-handedly shamed the rich into providing dowries for the poor girls of the parish and fed the poor children in the neighborhood, seating them at the table with her own family.

"She wouldn't take no for an answer," the woman said.

No, she wouldn't, Patronas thought sadly, remembering what her husband had said about her. They'd been discussing why she hadn't turned around at the barricade and come home. Why she'd continued on to Profitis Ilias. "You mustn't blame yourself, Chief Officer," Papoulis had told him. "If she wanted to do something, she'd do it. There would be no way to stop her."

She'd been like that even when they were children. Once she'd wanted to steal figs from a neighbor's tree. He himself had been afraid and tried to talk her out of it. The man would catch him; the tree branches were too high; they'd fall. But Marina had insisted. She'd ended up standing on his shoulders, holding onto the trunk of the tree for support, while he held her ankles. She'd stripped the tree bare, raining figs down on him, laughing the whole time. Her husband was right: once Marina got an idea in her head, that was it. You couldn't tell her 'No' or 'It's impossible.' Just like Muhammad Ali, the American boxer, whose words had been plastered all over Greece during the Olympics. He'd said, 'Impossible is not a fact; it's an opinion. Impossible is not a declaration; it's a dare.' Nikos Papoulis had told him Marina had loved that quote and had copied it and put it up on the bulletin board in her daughter's room. 'Impossible' and Marina, they were incompatible.

Nikos Papoulis took the children away before they finished the service, leaving Marina's mother at the graveside. She began to cry, reaching out toward her daughter's grave with her hands and calling her name. The bishop signaled Papa Michalis, who gently led her away and found her a chair in the shade.

After Marina had been laid to rest, her relatives offered coffee and brandy to the mourners in the small building at the back of the cemetery. Papa Michalis stayed near Marina's mother throughout the burial and its aftermath.

If I take anything with me from these hours, Patronas thought, *it will be the image of those two old people dressed entirely in black—one crippled, the other wracked with grief—leaning against each other, struggling to stay upright.*

He kept thinking of the day he'd met Marina for the first time, of the young girl she'd been. Her mother had bought a new dress for her, a white sundress with a smocked top embroidered with tiny yellow sunflowers, and she was wearing white leather shoes, shined so recently he could still smell the polish. Remembering her like that—the way she'd smiled at him that first afternoon, her eyes full of mischief—he wanted to scream. To eat ashes and tear out his hair like the ancients had done.

Chapter 32

He grasps even the naked sword.
—Greek proverb

The travel Agency was located on a side street near the harbor, handwritten schedules for the boats to Athens taped to its front door. The owner rose from her desk to greet Patronas. "Chief Officer, what can I do for you?"

"I need to go through Marina's things."

"But your men were here already." He could see her calculating how much his presence, sitting at the front of her office, was going to cost her in tourist walk-ins. "They came two days ago."

"I need to do it again." He didn't tell her the papers he'd found in the cave were too bloody to read and that he'd had to send them to Athens to be transcribed by the forensic people.

Reluctantly, she led him over to an empty desk. Family photographs were pinned to the wall behind it, and there was a pair of worn slippers lying under the chair.

Patronas turned on the computer, thinking it wouldn't be hard to retrace her steps in cyberspace, just find the sites she'd accessed and follow them. She'd emailed Olympic Airlines and two or three shipping lines the morning before she died, and he called the airlines to see if anyone remembered the query. It took some time, but he found a woman who did. Marina had wanted to know if they'd had anyone flying to Chios from Cyprus by way of Athens on July twenty-fourth. "I told her no," the woman said. "She said she needed me to check a bunch of other dates, too, and asked for the names of all the passengers who'd flown here from the United States. It was a lot of work, but I got her everything she asked for."

"Did you keep a record of this?"

"Sure. She told me it was for a police investigation and might be used as evidence, so I made a copy and gave it to my supervisor. If you want, I can fax it to you. What's your number?"

A few minutes later, he had the list. Jonathan Alcott had arrived when he said he had, on July twenty-fifth—Olympic Airlines from New York to Athens and then on to Chios. Manos and Voula were listed as passengers on an Olympic flight from Athens to Chios on July twenty-sixth. He checked his notes; that was also the day they'd told him they'd arrived. Devon McLean and Titina Argentis, contrary to what they'd told him, had arrived together three days earlier.

He called the woman back. "Can you check and see when McLean arrived in Greece from Cyprus? Not Chios, Greece. Also Titina Argentis from London."

"He didn't," the woman told him when she called back. "There's no record of Devon McLean on any carrier from Cyprus in the month of July."

"Is there any way to check and see if he came by boat?"

"Not really. I can try. Maybe with all this commotion about terrorists, the cruise ships and ferry boats are keeping the passenger rosters, but I doubt it."

When she didn't find anything, he asked her to recheck the airplane manifests for June, also May. "Check for the others as well," he said.

Both Manos Kleftis and Devon McLean were listed—McLean on a flight from Cyprus to Athens on May thirty-first—but there was nothing indicating he'd taken a connecting flight to Chios at any point after. Kleftis had travelled from Athens to Chios on June first, accompanied by Voula Athanassiou, who was listed as a passenger on the same flight. They'd left again a week later only to return when they said they had on the twenty-sixth.

"Check again for McLean," he instructed the woman.

"Nothing. I'm sorry."

Patronas leaned back in his chair. "Playing the priest," he said aloud. When they played the priest, card sharks always dealt out three cards, kings usually, which meant Marina had been talking about three men. He was pretty sure McLean and Kleftis were involved. They'd both lied to him. Titina Argentis and McLean had travelled together on the same flight. But who was the third? Marina had told Papa Michalis the two had needed a local, someone who knew Chios. That ruled out Alcott. Could it have been Antonis Argentis? Or was the third person a woman? Voula or Titina perhaps? And what was that nonsense about the 'cartoon'?

"Did she discuss the case on the phone while she was here?" he asked the owner of the travel agency. He could petition OTE, the Greek communications agency, for the phone records of the travel agency, but that would take forever, time he didn't have.

She thought for moment. "She did call someone in Volissos a day before she went missing. I remember because she asked me if I had the number before she called. She said she wanted to check if there was a boat registered."

"In whose name? Do you remember?"

"No, Chief Officer. I'm sorry."

So Marina and he had been trying to establish the same thing … the date of McLean's arrival by boat.

The chief officer began to go through her files, reading every scrap of paper. Afterward, he got down on his hands and knees and checked the floor underneath her desk in case she'd dropped something. He picked up her battered cloth slippers and tenderly moved them aside. He pictured her kicking off her good shoes and putting them on, padding around the office in them. Tears welled in his eyes and he choked back a sob.

❧

The Pakistani drew back when Patronas walked up to his kiosk, his face wary. The chief officer had made a point of driving the Citroen, not a squad car, to Castro, but the man apparently knew both him and his car on sight. "Yes," he stammered.

"A couple of days ago, Papa Michalis and Marina Papoulis were here. I understand they spoke with you."

"That's right," the man said, relief visible in his face. Patronas was sure he was illegal, he and his family both. Let the authorities in Athens worry about it. The right wing politicians. He didn't care what part of the world people came from or how long they stayed. Borders weren't his problem.

"What did you tell them?"

"About Mr. Manos. Man who visit him. Company, *parea*."

"What did you say about the man?"

"Woman, she wants to know how he looks." He reached into the kiosk and pulled out two comic books. "I say, like this." He tapped the cover of the top one. "Like cartoon."

Patronas reached for the comics. "May I have them?"

"Sure. Take."

They were French comics, reprints of the original series featuring Tintin. Patronas scanned the first, *L'Affaire Tournesol*, while he sat in his car. Although his French was rudimentary, he could follow the storyline. It featured a Professor Calculus, who'd been kidnapped, and an obnoxious tourist, Jolyona Wagg, who wore shorts and got in the way. Tintin himself had red hair. *Okay*, thought Patronas, *which one is it?* Devon McLean had red hair, but was dissimilar to Tintin in every other respect. Wagg, the American from the Rock Bottom Insurance Agency, reminded Patronas a bit of Alcott, not in physical appearance so much as in dress and attitude. The other comic, *The Castafiore Emerald*, included a woman, Bianca Castafiore, who sang opera, wore a mink coat, and appeared slightly ridiculous. Titina Argentis?

It would be a stretch, but maybe. He'd have to check with the Pakistani again. But when he returned to the kiosk, the man was gone.

Frustrated, he drove back to the police station. Tembelos and the others were still up at the monastery, so the place was quiet. He got out his notebook and wrote down what the Pakistani had told him. When he finished, he read back through everything. What did he have? He'd verified that three of the suspects had come to Chios long before they said they had and that two had come together. A coincidence? He didn't think so. Manos Kleftis and Voula Athanassiou had both come in June and returned again in July, as had Devon McLean. He leafed through the comics again. It had to be Tintin the Pakistani had been talking about, Tintin with his orange-red hair. Which meant the 'cartoon' man was McLean. Based on the Englishman's appearance, his fair skin and womanish body, Patronas had dismissed him as a suspect. He'd assumed he was harmless, a rabbit. Apparently he was something else. Not a murderer perhaps, but someone who would pick through the leavings of one. A jackal, a crow.

CHAPTER 33

Even at the fountain, he finds no water.
—Greek proverb

A THOUGHT OCCURRED TO Patronas as he read through his notes, something he'd missed and needed to ask the shepherd about. He thought he was beginning to catch a glimpse of what had transpired prior to the murders, the people involved. He could be completely wrong. It might have been Antonis Argentis working with his mother, the two of them after Eleni's inheritance. But then why kill Petros and Marina? No, it had to be the discovery of the Minoan city beneath Profitis Ilias that had set the whole thing in motion.

The shepherd had proven to be an elusive quarry. No one had seen him on the hill since Marina's death, yet it was evident someone was tending the goats, freshening their water and seeing to it that the animals had food. It even looked like the new pen had been raked out, straw scattered on the ground.

Patronas rubbed his eyes. He had stayed up all night waiting for the shepherd, who he assumed came out while the others slept. It was a few minutes before dawn and he could see the hills around Profitis Ilias slowly taking shape in the pale light. He heard a rooster crowing in the village below. The wind was blowing, and it stirred the thistles, the dust in the abandoned corral.

The shepherd appeared a little while later, coming up over the rocks from the direction of Korres' farm. He was carrying a bale of hay, moving quickly and calling to the goats in his strange lisping speech. The goats began moving around the pen, restless, bleating plaintively in response.

"Kale mera," Patronas called to him. "Good day."

Perhaps remembering the fifty Euros, the man smiled and moved to shake the chief officer's hand. He was wearing the same tattered clothes and taped-up shoes, and his hair was even filthier than Patronas remembered, the grimy ringlets forming a matted halo around his face.

Patronas offered to share his breakfast with him, and the man seized the bread greedily and shoved it into his mouth, then reached for a piece of the feta cheese. He didn't want coffee, but cooed when he saw the figs, cradling them in his hand and eating them slowly, one by one. He smiled at him as he ate. Patronas tried not to look at him; his split lip was caked with seeds and juice.

No murderer this, he thought. *No, this is an innocent. Put him in animal skins and he could pass for John the Baptist or a prophet in the Old Testament, one of those who lived on snakes and nettles and didn't bathe.*

"As you know, a woman was killed here four days ago," he said. "August fifteenth it was. It happened here in the corral or close by. After she was murdered, she was dragged down the stairs and into the cave."

Still eating, the shepherd nodded. "I hear of this."

"Did you see who did it? Were you here when it happened?"

"No. I am far away. I only hear." He wiped his mouth with his hand and led Patronas to an outcropping of rock near the bottom of the hill, demonstrating how he'd crouched down in the shadows. "After Petros die, I am afraid. I hide when people come. I no show myself."

"You said 'people.' " Patronas wanted to get this clarified, as there was a language difference and the word in Greek frequently caused foreigners trouble. "How many came?"

"The day lady scream, two."

"What did they look like?"

"I no see." Uncomfortable, he moved his foot back and forth in the dirt. "I am away."

"Other times, did people come?"

"Two, always same. Come at night."

"Did you see either of them?"

The man shook his head.

"Did you ever see anyone else up here?"

"Once. Different person."

"What do you mean different?"

"Little."

Petros Athanassiou. It had to be. Patronas tapped the bale of hay. "Where'd you get the hay?"

"Spiros give it to me. He knows me. I stay in house on his land. Is good, has water pipe, electricity." He stumbled over the words, excited. "Heating that plugs in wall." As if this unused outbuilding, this shed Korres was letting him use, was something. Things must be pretty bleak in Albania.

"What do you do for food?"

"He and his wife give me. Cigarettes, too, sometimes. I even drive his tractor once."

Patronas gave him his sleeping bag and another fifty Euros. "Be careful," he warned. "Steer clear of this place."

Intent on counting the money, the shepherd waved him off.

∽

Patronas stopped off at the farm to talk to Spiros Korres before heading back to the police station. He was troubled by his conversation with the shepherd. He'd missed something, not followed up when he should have. Perhaps Korres could help him. He found the farmer behind his barn, repairing a loose board with a hammer.

Korres nodded when he saw him. "Afternoon, Chief Officer. What can I do for you?"

"I just interviewed the man who tends the goats up by Profitis Ilias. He said he lives here on your farm in the winter."

"The harelip?" Korres made a slicing gesture across his upper lip with a dirty fingernail. "Yeah, I let him stay in a shed out back. Best hold your nose if you're going there. He's downwind of the pigs."

The pigs were huge, chocolate-colored beasts, housed in a filthy, mud-slicked pen. The ground was littered with waste, orange peels and watermelon rinds, excrement, and the air was alive with flies, the odor so rank, it made Patronas' eyes water. He located the shed where the shepherd was staying a little farther down. Inside was a cot with a blanket and a chest of drawers. There was even a window overlooking some trees in the back. Inside one of the drawers, he found a small gilt brooch. It was shaped like a quail, with tiny rhinestone eyes.

Slipping on a pair of gloves, he put the brooch in an evidence bag and walked back to where Korres was working. He emptied the evidence bag out in the palm of his hand and asked the farmer if he could identify the pin or knew where the shepherd had found it.

"Harelip found it the day Marina died. Cast off in the bushes behind the goats, he said. My wife looks after him and he wanted to give it to her. I told him it wasn't his and to put it back where he found it, let you people deal with it. But he said he was afraid."

"Afraid of what?"

"Didn't say. Police would be my guess. I don't know where he came from, but he's scared of the authorities. Truth is, he's scared of everything. Like a horse that's never been broke."

"What else did he say?"

"Only that there was a lot of blood."

So the shepherd's footprints were probably mixed up with the killer's, ditto with the fingerprints and trace elements the forensic specialists had collected in the lean-to. He'd have to have the shepherd printed, Korres and his son, Vassilis also.

"You should have passed the pin on to me," he said. "Get it dusted for prints."

"Been pointless. Harelip had been carrying it around all day." He shrugged. "I figured what the hell, let him keep it. It was nothing, just cheap costume jewelry. You can see where it's chipped, there, the metal underneath. Should have heard him though, the way he was snorting and carrying on, you could tell old harelip thought he'd found himself the crown jewels."

"Did he find anything else up there?"

"He might have. He's always secreting things away. Food mostly. Stockpiles cans and crap under that shed of his. He's a funny one, gets upset when you try and take things away from him. Doesn't really understand the concept of ownership. Thinks that if he finds something, it belongs to him."

"It's good of you to let him stay here."

Korres waved him off, unwilling to accept the compliment. "Hell, someone has to keep the pigs company."

~

BEFORE LEAVING THE farm, Patronas made another turn around the shed, checking the crawl space for Minoan artifacts or anything else that might have bearing on the case. He found his fifty Euros zipped up in a soiled child's pencil case along with a used lottery ticket and a handful of coins, drachmas mostly, no longer in circulation. There was also a random assortment of cans: tomatoes, sardines, evaporated milk. Food, just as Korres had said. A blanket had been secreted under the shed as well. Folded up inside it, he found a rusted toy motorcar and half of a German paperback novel. He tucked more money in the pencil case, thinking that once he'd caught the killer, he'd do something for the harelipped man.

He looked down at the brooch in his hand, wondering what to do with it. He was sure Korres' assessment was correct, that the pin was worthless, gold plated at best, but what if it had belonged to Voula, not Marina, and been pulled off during the murder? Or Titina Argentis? That would place her at the scene. He sighed. He'd have to go to Campos and show it to Nikos Papoulis, see if he could identify it. If not, he'd speak to the others.

The road to Campos was empty. He parked in front of Marina's house and got out. A pair of red-throated swallows, glossy and black, were sitting on the wires in front of the house. No children were playing in the yard and all the toys had been taken in. He stood on the steps for a moment, collecting his thoughts, before knocking on the door.

As was the custom on Chios, Nikos Papoulis was wearing a black armband in mourning for his wife. His eyes were red, his face tired. "Chief Officer," he said, opening the door a little wider. "Come in, come in."

Patronas stayed outside. "I'm sorry to bother you," he said, "but a new piece of evidence has come to my attention." He handed him the plastic envelope. "You recognize this? Someone found it near the crime scene."

Papoulis opened the envelope and ran his finger over the brooch. "No. I've never seen it before."

"Are you sure? Could it have been Marina's?"

"I don't think so."

Patronas put the brooch back in his pocket. "Is Margarita here? I need you to ask her something." He thought the girl might be more comfortable speaking with her father. "I want to know if she remembers anything her mother said that day, the day she disappeared. She can read, can't she, Margarita?"

He nodded.

"Ask her if she saw the papers her mother had for me. What they said."

The man returned a few minutes later. His daughter had nothing new to add, he said. The papers had been in an envelope; she hadn't seen them. Their mother had trusted her with the *svingis* and she'd been holding the plate on her lap. She'd been worrying about getting the syrup on her good dress, concentrating on that. She was sorry, that's all she knew. "She started to cry." He looked on the verge of tears himself.

"What about the brooch?"

"She never saw any brooch."

CHAPTER 34

He shows honey. He mixes poison.
—Greek proverb

BOATMEN WERE YELLING out their destinations, seeking tourists for day trips to nearby islands, and there was a long line of trucks waiting to board the morning ferry to Athens. Patronas had chosen this hour on purpose, hoping to catch the people on his list before rumors of the Minoan city started to circulate. He would have to move quickly or he'd catch half of Chios in his net.

A row of rented sailboats were tied up on the quay in front of the hotel, and he could hear people talking on a few, English most of them, judging by the accents. He'd been foolish, trying to link McLean to a specific boat in July with all the transient traffic to and from the island. McLean could have used any one of these boats in partnership with one of the English owners, and no one would have been the wiser. And this was just the main harbor. There must be fifty quays where a person could moor a boat, and that was just the formal ones with breakwaters and supervision, not the hundreds of empty coves and inlets where a man could safely drop anchor and get ashore.

He crossed the lobby and spoke to the hostess in the dining room. She checked her list. "They haven't come down for breakfast. They must still be in their rooms."

The chief officer thought he'd start with Devon McLean and took the elevator up to the fourth floor. The inside of the elevator was mirrored and he frowned when he caught a glimpse of himself. Had he forgotten to shave this morning? Peering at himself, he ran an exploratory hand across his chin. Sure enough. Whiskers everywhere. His eyebrows seemed bigger than he remembered, too, sticking out like the tufts of fur on a lynx. He wetted a finger and smoothed them down. It didn't matter. McLean was English. He'd think he was an aborigine no matter how he looked.

The archeologist was the embodiment of graciousness, ordering breakfast for the two of them from room service. He even consoled him after a fashion about Marina's death, assuring him no one expected him to mount a proper investigation.

"I mean, frankly, Chief Officer, no matter how hard you try, you're going to miss things. What experience have you had with serial killers?" His tone was arch and patronizing.

Patronas frowned. *Vrasta.* Boil him. Taking a deep breath, he got out his notebook. "Last time we spoke about the excavation that Eleni Argentis was conducting at Profitis Ilias, you told me what she'd uncovered was virtually worthless. Suppose she found something more valuable than those shards? Something unexpected up there?"

"Like what?" The Englishman's voice was mocking. "The Elgin Marbles? Come, come, Chief Officer, you and I both know she'd found nothing of value. You've seen those trenches. There was nothing there. Nothing."

"It has come to my attention that she might have discovered evidence of a Minoan settlement." Bait the hook. "Perhaps even of human sacrifice."

"Really. Now that would be interesting. Who told you that?"

"Someone she'd contacted about it. An authority in Athens."

McLean sat back, making a tent with his long fingers. "Well, now. What was it she found? A temple felled by an earthquake like the one in Crete? Where the boy was being bled out? The skeleton of a giant bull with human femurs in its pen? What?"

"I don't know exactly. Among her things were photos of a site that appeared to be untouched. It was full of bones, thousands of bones. I don't know if that means anything. I'm just a layman." He thought the secret would be safe with the Englishman. Though McLean's Greek was good, he didn't strike Patronas as a man who would befriend a native. No, the Englishman's contacts would be limited to the waiters and maids in the hotel. Staff, in other words. People who were there to serve him, who knew their place.

"Perhaps the photos were from someplace else. Crete perhaps."

"No. They were taken on Chios. We recognized the location."

"Where was it?"

"A hill near Profitis Ilias."

"If that's true and not some police trick, it would be an astounding discovery. Minoan skeletons from the time of Thera are extremely rare. None have been found at *Akrotiri*. The feeling among archeologists is that the people there must have fled. No one knew where to, though. It's long been a mystery. The consensus is, they must have been consumed in the ensuing cataclysm."

Patronas regarded him intently. "Maybe not. Maybe they made it here."

“I suppose anything is possible.” The archeologist was unwilling to concede the point.

“We plan to turn the site over to a team from Athens on Monday.”

“Good idea. They’ll sort it out.”

“One last question: did Alcott discuss the murders with you?”

“Yes. He was as horrified as I was. The sheer brutality of it. Petros, especially. You told me he held him down and cut his throat.” Interesting, he hadn’t told him that. Not exactly.

“Do you have any idea why someone would do that?”

“You mean like a sacrificial lamb?” McLean said this casually. “I think it was protective camouflage, Chief Officer, a stage set designed to mislead you.”

“Is that why the killer mutilated Eleni Argentis?” He described what the two fishermen had found at the beach.

“I don’t know. Perhaps the killer was just trying to scare her and it got out of hand.” Realizing his poor choice of words, McLean covered his mouth, his eyes wide. He’d been naughty and it amused him. He looked over to see if Patronas had noticed.

“Out of hand.” Patronas had noticed all right. “Yes, I suppose it did.”

THE BRITISH TUTOR at Oxford had been reluctant to speak to him. “Ah, yes, Devon McLean.” There had been a lengthy silence. “You said you’re with the police?” His voice held no surprise.

“Yes.” Patronas had gone back to the police department to make the call. He had his English-Greek dictionary open on his lap, his pad and pencil ready. “We’ve had a number of homicides on the island and are trying to eliminate suspects. It would help us greatly if we could determine what kind of man he is.”

“He’s extremely intelligent. By far the most brilliant young man I tutored in my thirty years here.”

Not quite the answer he was seeking. He flipped through the pages of the dictionary, seeking the word he wanted. “What about his character?”

Another long silence. “I always thought he might have been happier in business,” the professor finally said. “Something competitive, perhaps involving money.”

“Really? Not archeology?”

The man sighed. “There is little glory in this field, little fame to be had. Take the Institute of Archeology at Oxford, for example. It is far newer than the rest of the university and was originally housed not in one of the colleges, not in Balliol or Christ Church, but in rooms on Beaumont Street. Have you ever been to Oxford, Chief Officer?”

"No."

"Well, Beaumont Street is not one of the more august addresses in town. Of course, this has all changed. The Institute has expanded and we now have wonderful facilities. Computers. All the modern accoutrements. However, though we are scientists, we are not biologists or chemists or physicists. No one wins Nobel Prizes in archeology. As for the nature of the field itself, I fear, Indiana Jones to the contrary, the time of Sir Harold Carter and Robert Evans and Schliemann—the time of incredible discoveries by individual men—has come and gone. Archeology is far more painstaking today, and consequently a great deal more collaborative. Devon McLean was always frustrated by that. He wanted to be a star, as it were. To stand alone and be applauded on a bigger and far more lucrative stage."

"So money was important to him?"

"Undoubtedly. Prestige even more so. He was obsessed with it. He was like an American in that respect. Money and fame. Hollywood's key to a happy life. If I had to summarize, I'd say they were the key to Devon McLean as well." Hardly obtuse now. The professor hadn't liked his student much.

Another moment with the dictionary. "Would you say he is unscrupulous?"

"Let me say he was persistent. Determined. Resourceful. And occasionally more enterprising than was warranted."

What did this doubletalk mean, 'more enterprising than was warranted'? Patronas took a chance. "Dishonest? You mean he was dishonest?"

"Not necessarily. Self-aggrandizing would be a more accurate description. He would always, and I do mean *always*, put forth the most grandiose interpretation of any work he was involved in. It was never a simple dig with him. It was always 'historic findings of unparalleled consequence.' He'd never find a skeleton, for example. Left to his own devices, it would be the skull of Plato. He was rather like Schliemann in this respect, though Schliemann can be forgiven. As a nineteenth century amateur, he really didn't know any better. Devon McLean certainly did and yet he persisted."

The chief officer tried again. "Are you saying he's dishonest?"

"Free and easy with the truth if it would further his reputation. Jealous of his colleagues. A man you would be unwise to turn your back on professionally."

"A man who would do anything?"

There was a long pause. "Yes."

"A dangerous man?"

Another long wait. "Possibly."

"He said he was working off the coast of Cyprus. What do you know of this?"

"Only that it was an ill-advised project, grandstanding of the first order. It has been going on for at least three years with very little to show for it. We would not support it here at Oxford. He had to appeal to the United States, to some little school in the Midwest to get academic sponsorship and to buy a boat for him."

"What kind of a boat?" Patronas kept his voice steady.

"A fast one. Fast and expensive." The professor was warming up to his subject, his antipathy to both McLean and people who funded him becoming more and more apparent. "Apparently, he found himself a private benefactor, an American or Japanese industrialist—I don't remember which—willing to underwrite the whole sad endeavor. The consensus among his colleagues here at Oxford is that Devon—please excuse my use of the vernacular—was 'milking him dry.' He has a group of Americans working for him, Elderhostel volunteers and the like, personnel from third and fourth class museums, scouts more like it from places which aren't too careful about the provenance of the items they exhibit in their display cases. It's second rate, the whole affair. Exceedingly second rate."

"McLean's kind of people, in other words."

"One would say."

"What was his relationship with Jonathan Alcott?"

"The American? He did not have a relationship with Jonathan Alcott. Jonathan Alcott loathed him."

"Perhaps Mr. McLean wanted to be—how shall I put this?—Professor Alcott's 'special friend.' Maybe he was looking for …." He hesitated. What word? What word to use? "Affection from him."

"I don't know what you are implying, Chief Officer, but if you continue, I am done here. No matter what I may think of Devon McLean's character or his worth as an archeologist, I will not speculate with you or anyone else about his sexuality, his emotional investment in men. I will not participate in a sexual witch hunt. Do you understand?"

Patronas apologized, afraid he'd lost him.

"I must say," the scholar went on, "I am very disappointed that a law enforcement official in this day and age would resort to sexual innuendo and character assassination under the guise of investigating a homicide. Maybe in the time of Oscar Wilde, it was permissible for a policeman to discuss who was or wasn't a homosexual with a potential witness, but no longer. Now if you will excuse me …."

"I am sorry, the English, it is hard for me." He thickened his accent, thinking the man, an Oxford don, would feel superior to him and let his guard down. He'd often found playing the fool to be useful in police work. With certain types of people, he'd say something he knew to be false and they'd rush to correct him, to fill in the blanks. They couldn't help it, and he'd learn something he hadn't known before. He didn't think it would work here, as the man already had his back up, but it was worth a try. "Mr. McLean says he was Alcott's assistant on a project here—"

"He most certainly was not. He was there as part of a consortium. Now if you will excuse me—"

"One last thing. Do you know who the people were from Chios that he worked with when he was here as part of the consortium?"

"I was Devon's tutor, not his keeper, Chief Officer. My job was to educate him, not keep track of his friends."

Patronas hung up the phone and leaned back in his chair. "Well, now."

Chapter 35

He who becomes a sheep is eaten by the wolf.
—Greek proverb

"Professor Alcott?" The door was open and Patronas made his way into the room. The suite was a pigsty, dirty clothes and room service trays on the floor. Patronas kicked an empty beer bottle aside. *Must be hard on the maid, vacuuming around this mess.* "Professor Alcott," he called again.

"Out here."

Alcott was outside on the balcony, sunning himself on a chaise lounge. A row of beer bottles was lined up against the wall behind him. He made an effort to rise, but only got halfway up before sinking back down again. The balcony overlooked the harbor, and Patronas could see water on all sides from where he stood, cruise ships lying at anchor below. It was like standing on the prow of a boat.

"How about a beer?" Alcott asked.

Patronas shook his head. "This isn't your first trip to Chios, is it?" He got out his notebook and pen. "You and McLean, you've been here before."

Alcott nodded. "Three times for me. Twice for him. I supervised an excavation not too far from here a couple of years ago. Didn't come to much. The site had been occupied a long time, and it was hard to unscramble it. What we archeologists call 'a pile-up.'" He took care with his speech, enunciating each word carefully or at least trying to.

Drunk, Patronas concluded. *It's eleven o'clock in the morning and he's drunk.*

"Saracens, Genovese, Romans, Dorians," Alcott went on. "There was even evidence of a Jewish settlement on Chios during the Middle Ages. Probably Sephardic Jews from Spain fleeing the Inquisition." Alcott's skin was ashy and damp, and his hand trembled slightly as he raised the beer bottle to his lips. The American had been drunk for days.

"When was this?"

"About eighteen months ago."

"Was Devon McLean involved?"

"Yes. A number of universities participated, Oxford being one of them. I don't remember how long Devon stayed. I know my graduate students participated. They'd work a couple of weeks and then another group would come and replace them. I wanted everyone to learn how to assess, excavate and evaluate the finds from potential archeological sites." He sounded alive for the first time. "Kids need practical experience before you turn them loose in the field. They need to get their hands dirty, but under careful supervision. It's so easy to destroy the past when you come upon it, to muck it up forever."

"Who helped you with the dig? Did you have laborers?" Patronas was after a local relationship, some tie in with Chios.

"Not as such. Spiros Korres furnished our supplies and drove us around in his truck that summer. He seemed to think we would find buried treasure. He had archeologists confused with pirates. He never really mastered the concept."

Add Spiros to the list. "Did you visit Profitis Ilias on that trip?"

"Yes. We joined the locals up there on July twentieth, the feast day of the saint, I believe it was. Our crew invited us, said we'd enjoy it, and so we went. They were grilling lamb in the courtyard and wanted us to stay and eat." He finished his beer and set the bottle down. "I demurred. Eleni and Devon might have stayed. I'm not sure. It was a long time ago."

"Was there anything different about the monastery then?"

"Back off, Chief Officer. I know where you're going. You think Devon and I 'cased the joint' then came back a year later and killed her."

"That's not why I'm here, Professor. Eleni was right. There is a Minoan settlement there. We just discovered it. Those boxes of shards were the least of it. We think she might have stumbled on something as important as *Akrotiri*. She might even have found evidence that the Minoans practiced human sacrifice."

"You don't say?" he said bitterly. "I'm sure the news will make her very happy."

"This will be big, won't it? I was told archeologists have been debating whether or not the Minoans practiced human sacrifice for years."

"Not the Greek ones. They don't want to hear about it. According to them, your ancestors were wise men discoursing on philosophy in the agora. Not people who sacrificed cows and goats and daughters."

"Do you think the killer was trying to reproduce Minoan rituals? Could that be the reason he cut off her leg and hand?" He hadn't shared this information with Alcott previously and was watching him carefully, trying to gauge his reaction.

Alcott refused to be drawn in. "Human sacrifice? No, Chief Officer, I don't think Eleni was mutilated as part of some ancient religious rite. I think whoever did it, did it to hurt her. Was she alive when they cut her up or was it done post mortem? My guess is it was post mortem, and the reason was practical: disposing of the body to get rid of the evidence. Though the taking of a limb as punishment has a long history in human society. In Saudi Arabia, they cut off the hands of thieves, in other places, the feet of runaway slaves. As recently as the late nineteenth century, the colonial government in the Belgian Congo *paid* for human hands. Did you know that? Native hands, African hands. Bought them by the sack full. No one knows to this day if anyone bothered to apply a tourniquet or if the victims simply bled to death—"

Ever the expert. Patronas cut him off. "How important would a find like this be to an archeologist?"

"It would make him immortal the way King Tut made Howard Carter immortal, Knossos did Sir Robert Evans, Machu Picchu and Hiram Bingham. As long as the field of archeology existed, he would be remembered."

"Do you think someone would be willing to kill for it?"

"I assume you are talking about Devon McLean or perhaps me. I don't know, Chief Officer. That's the truth. It does seem death and archeology have a natural affinity for each other. Take Devon, for example. He's been plumbing the depths of the sea, trolling for the bones of sailors who drowned in a Dorian shipwreck. Trying to resurrect their last meal, what clothes they had on when their boat sank, what they were ferrying from Cyprus to Egypt. If their wretched bones could talk, he'd be interviewing them. If that's not grave robbing, I don't know what is. I'm resigning when I get back to the United States. I'm done with archeology. Done with graves. Done with death."

Patronas flipped through his notebook. "But you said when last we spoke, and I quote, 'Someone should go through the dig site. That bull you showed me, the one that was mixed in with the shards, it might well be the only one in existence. Perhaps if we resumed the excavation, we could find more.' You weren't done then."

"I just wanted to keep Devon McLean away from the site. That's another thing archeologists are, Chief Officer. They're thieves, poachers. In addition to stealing from the dead, they steal from each other."

"Well, if you still want to take a look at the shards, you can. I'm moving the investigation out of Profitis Ilias. I've already notified the Archeology Department of the University of Athens. I plan to turn the site over to them on Monday."

They talked for a few more minutes, Patronas switching back and forth between Greek and English. Listening to his answers, the chief officer was sure Alcott could never have mounted a criminal conspiracy in Greece. His grasp of the language was too poor. One mistake after another. He confused the Greek word for Englishman, *agglos*, with the one for angels, *aggelos*, and called a colleague a *kathiki*, shit pot, instead of *kathighiti*, professor. Patronas switched back to English. "I've also decided to release you and Devon McLean. As of today, you are free to go."

"So I'm no longer a suspect," Alcott said. "I guess that's something. However, if it's all the same to you, I would like to stay and see this through."

"Will you please inform Devon McLean that he may reclaim his passport today? I neglected to tell him when I saw him earlier in the day."

"Sure, I'll tell him."

PETROS' GRANDMOTHER WAS outside, working in the garden on the side of her house in Castro. On her hands and knees, she was digging up greens with a small spade. She got up when she saw him, dropping a handful of *horta*, wild dandelion greens, in a plastic bag, and wiped her hands on her skirt. "Not much good now." She waved at the patchy soil with her spade. "Too dry." She was dressed all in black, her apron and stockings smeared with dirt. Out in the open away from her house, she seemed diminished, more vulnerable.

Patronas nodded. "Only tomatoes thrive in August."

"Come, I've got some in the back. I'll give them to you." Stooped and arthritic, she walked slowly around the house. Her garden was small but well-kept, with even rows of vegetables interspersed with marigolds and sunflowers. The majority of space was given over to tomatoes, neatly tied to long, slender pieces of graying wood. She had chickens in a wire enclosure behind the garden and a wooden cage filled with rabbits. Everything was tidy, but worn; the garden hose had been taped up, the chicken wire patched in places. She emptied the *horta* out onto the ground and began to fill the plastic bag with tomatoes. Something was wrong with her hands, the knuckles of her fingers swollen and twisted. *Arthritis*, Patronas thought with pity.

"Have you found out who killed him?" she asked.

"Not yet, Kyria Athanassiou. But we're making progress. We're moving out of Profitis Ilias and down into Chora, where we'll continue the investigation." He looked toward the house. "Is your daughter here?"

She raised her head and studied him, her eyes narrow against the sun. "What do you want with her?"

"I think I know why your grandson was killed."

She began to cry silently, tears running down her wrinkled face. "Tell *me* why," she said, wiping her eyes with the back of her gnarled hand. "She doesn't care. He was nothing to her. Tell *me* why my *engonaki*, my little grandson, was killed."

"I have no proof, but I think your grandson found a Minoan settlement near where he and Eleni Argentis had been digging."

Hearing their voices, her daughter, Voula, came out of the house. She was dressed in white capris and a black top that hugged her breasts. The cork heels on her sandals were so high she tottered like a geisha. Her make-up, too, was geisha-like, the pale foundation clearly painted on, her red lipstick too dark for the hour of the day.

"What's going on?" she asked.

"He came about Petros," the old woman said. "He knows why they killed him."

The daughter touched Patronas' arm. "Why?"

"He found a Minoan city."

Her eyes widened. "Manos," she called. "Manos, you'd better get out here."

Her boyfriend appeared a moment later. He was dressed as before, in a loose cotton shirt, khaki shorts and plastic flip-flops. "Chief Officer," he said in the same lazy manner. "I don't know … these women. Treating a guest this way. May I offer you a seat? Something to drink? A beer? Ouzo perhaps?"

"No, nothing."

"Yiayia, go get us something."

Wiping her eyes, the grandmother dutifully went back into the house, leaving the door open, and the chief officer could hear her putting together food and drinks in the kitchen. He wondered what the man's hold on her was. What was that in her black eyes? Fear? Hate? Or was she simply the relic of another time, one of those women raised to do a man's bidding, taught since birth to serve? They didn't bind women's feet in the old days, but they might as well have. Or was her servitude something more?

Studying Voula and her lover in turn, he recounted the discovery of the settlement up at the monastery and his decision to turn it all over to the university in five days time. Like the archeologists, they'd keep quiet about it. They'd be banking on getting a piece of whatever there was, and they wouldn't want to share. "The university people are better equipped to sort it out than we are," he said. "They'll post guards at the entrances and go through it slowly. We don't have the manpower to protect and evaluate it properly."

Manos and Voula exchanged glances. "Does the government pay for a discovery like that?" the man asked. "Was there any reward Petros could claim?"

"No. The law is very clear. All archeological finds belong to Greece and to Greece alone, not to the individual whose land they are found on, nor to the individual who finds them. Everything must be turned over to the government immediately. It's to prevent smuggling."

The man's interest seemed to flag. "Okay, then," he said. "No money." He leaned against the back of the house and lit a cigarette.

Patronas pulled out the brooch and handed it to Voula. "This yours?" he asked.

She took it, looked at it for a moment and returned it to him. "No."

"Are you sure?"

Something passed between her and her boyfriend. "It isn't mine," she said, not meeting his eyes.

Patronas put the brooch back in his pocket. "We are pretty sure someone was moving the artifacts out of the site and selling them. Whether they were working with Eleni and Petros, we don't know. But we are pretty sure whoever was doing the smuggling was the same person who killed them."

The old woman came out with a tray and set it on the table. She handed each of them a china plate with a spoon sweet on it, a tiny nectarine in syrup. Then she stood there as if bewildered, as if she didn't know where to go or what to do. Patronas could hear her chanting the name of her grandson over and over like someone reciting the rosary.

The daughter finally put her arm around her mother and took her back inside the house. Manos Kleftis ate his sweet, drank his water and wiped his mouth. When he was finished, he picked up the plastic bag the old woman had dropped on the ground and handed it to Patronas.

"Enjoy your tomatoes, Inspector," he said.

Chapter 36

Where you hear of many cherries, bring a small basket.
—Greek proverb

PATRONAS LIFTED THE brass doorknocker and let it fall. Ironically, it was shaped like a hand.

In spite of what Alcott had said, he doubted anyone would kill three people to get his name in archeology journals. He still thought Titina Argentis was involved. It stood to reason: she'd argued repeatedly with the grandmother of Petros Athanassiou and expressed hostility toward her stepdaughter both times he'd interviewed her. She'd flown to Chios with McLean. Her son was weak. He'd do her bidding. Yes, it would work. He'd have to check on their finances when he got back to the office. They acted rich, but then so did a lot of people. Dimitra and her mother for instance, and look where that had gotten him.

He could see tables set out in the garden of the Campos estate and gaily colored Japanese lanterns strung up in the trees. Either Titina Argentis had entertained recently or she was planning to. Not exactly the behavior of a murderess, but then one never knew. He'd read about killers, Americans mostly, who attended the funerals of their victims, even going so far as to console their grieving widows and children. Human behavior was an uncharted wilderness as far as he was concerned. Perhaps Papa Michalis was right, and it was a woman. One shouldn't let sexual stereotyping cloud one's judgment. No, with respect to murderers, it was best to keep an open mind.

The same maid answered the door and ushered him into the house. The stepmother was on the second floor and slowly made her way down the stairs to meet him. Again, he was struck by her regal posture, her impeccable grooming.

"Sorry to trouble you again. I was looking to speak with Antonis."

"Whatever for?"

"It's about his sister."

"Stepsister." She smiled to take the chill off the word. "He isn't here. I believe he's down at the harbor awaiting one of our freighters. He's signed a contract with a firm in China, and this will be the first of what we are assuming will be a steady flow of containers. He's hoping to dominate the traffic between Greece and China, to corner the Asian trade in this part of the Mediterranean."

"Profitable, I would imagine." The chief officer offered her a cigarette, which she declined, and took one himself. "Oh, by the way, Eleni apparently found a Minoan site up at Profitis Ilias. My guess is it will turn out to rival Knossos and Troy one day. It was an entire city, virtually untouched, an unbelievable find. She'll go down in history as one of the great archeologists, like Harold Carter or Schliemann."

"Really? Do you think that was why she was killed?" From the level of interest in her voice, he might as well have been a garage mechanic talking about an oil change for the car.

"Undoubtedly." He told her, too, about leaving the dig site on Monday. "My investigation up there is over. I might as well let the archeologists get started on the place." Like McLean, she wouldn't conspire with a local man or woman, and for the same reason. As Greeks said, *She's so high, she wears a toupee.* In other words, a snob.

She turned and walked down the long hallway into the study. "Have you discovered who killed her?" she called over her shoulder. Returning a moment later with an ashtray, she pointedly set it down on the table next to him.

"Yes, we are closing in on our murderer." He ignored the ashtray, letting the ash from his cigarette fall where it may. Hopefully it would set fire to the exquisite Persian rug underfoot and damage the parquet floor. He was sorry it was only a cigarette. He wished it was an acetylene torch.

"Oh, by the way, is this yours?" He showed her the plastic envelope with the brooch.

She examined it carefully before returning it to him. "No."

"Could it have been Eleni's?"

"I doubt it. She never wore costume jewelry." A little sneer in the way she said 'costume jewelry.' As if he should have known better, that only a fool would wear costume jewelry and he should not have troubled her with such an absurd inquiry.

She pushed the ashtray closer to him. "Antonis will be pleased to hear that. He's been most disturbed by this dreadful business." Antonis, he noted, not her. "When do you think you will be making an arrest?"

"Any day now. We are closing in on him."

"So Eleni has been vindicated," she said thoughtfully. "All her theories, her thrashing around on that hill. It turns out she was right, after all."

"Indeed she was."

"Too bad she didn't live to enjoy it." Was it his imagination or was there just a hint of malice in her words, a touch of a smile?

⁂

"WHAT'S THE STATE of Titina Argentis' fortune?" Patronas asked the accountant who handled her accounts.

The man smiled indulgently. "Fortune?"

"That's right. How much money does she have?"

Getting up, the accountant made a show of closing the door to his office. He then spoke in a hushed voice about the need for privacy and confidentiality, about not betraying his client's trust. It was all bullshit and they both knew it. After five minutes and a few idle threats, Patronas got what he'd come for: Antonis and his mother were living far beyond their means, and they had, in spite of his—the accountant's—frequent warnings, been doing so for years. They had yet to pay off the contractors for the house and had grave difficulties meeting their payroll at the shipyard.

"So she's broke."

"Not 'broke' in the usual sense, but they do have a very serious problem. It is my understanding that she and her son still possess a number of valuable assets in England: real estate, an art collection. I don't remember exactly. I've never seen any of this, but my superior in London told me he checked it out and it exists, at least some of it. Her son is trying to salvage Argentis Shipping and make it profitable again, which is probably a good move from a financial point of view. His mother, Titina, doesn't understand the need to guard one's principal, to live off one's profits and leave the rest alone. They've fought about it more than once."

"What about Eleni?"

"I don't know the state of her fortune. She inherited the bulk of her father's estate, so it's probably quite substantial. They might have put it in escrow after she died. You'll have to speak to her lawyer."

⁂

PATRONAS SAT IN his car, reviewing what the accountant had told him. Titina Argentis had married a rich man twice her age and fought with Petros Athanassiou's grandmother over a big box of nothing. If you could test a person's DNA for such things, you'd find greed all over hers. It was one of her defining characteristics.

Patronas had once assumed rich people led idyllic lives and never coveted what others had, that only poor people were greedy. But later, as a policeman, he'd changed his mind. Greed had nothing to do with what people had or didn't have. It was another thing entirely. Those who suffered from it, be they rich or poor, were perpetually uneasy, victims of a kind of cancerous, insatiable yearning that no purchase could long satisfy. Greedy people, they hungered. As simple as that. No matter what they had, it wasn't enough, they wanted more, and Titina Argentis was such a person.

But was she a murderer?

He wished he knew. He longed to arrest her, knock her off her high horse and drag her down the street in handcuffs, squealing like a pig, dirty her up a little with a fingerprinting kit.

CHAPTER 37

Making the same mistake twice does not indicate a wise person.
—Greek proverb

PATRONAS TOOK THE tomatoes Petros' grandmother had given him home. He thought he'd eat lunch before heading up to Profitis Ilias to organize the stake-out. "Dimitra," he yelled as he unlocked the door. As always, the house was orderly and impeccably clean. His clothes washed and put away, the garbage emptied. In the refrigerator, he found a fresh *pasticcio*—a kind of Greek lasagna—a bowl of eggplant spread and half a watermelon. Dimitra must have come and gone. He ate the *pasticcio* cold, standing in front of the open refrigerator, and drank two beers, dribbling some on his uniform. He wiped it off with his hand.

After he finished eating, he took a shower, remembering how he'd looked at the Villa Hotel—as if he were the desperado in an American western, the criminal the posse was after, not the proud sheriff leading them. Then he gathered up some bedding and food and headed out to the car. He tried his wife's cellphone as he drove.

She picked up on the first ring. "Speak," she said.

"Dimitra, it's me. I'm heading back to Profitis Ilias. I told all 'persons of interest' that I'm turning the site over to the authorities on Monday, which gives me five days to catch him. Hopefully that'll be enough."

"Did you find Marina's papers?" Her voice was guarded.

"Yes, but they were too bloodstained to be of any use." When he dialed her number, he hadn't meant to punish her, but as soon as he heard her voice, there it was. God help them if they stayed together. "Apparently Marina tried to hide them as she was dying. Remember how she told you 'they were playing the priest with us'?"

"Yes. She thought three people were involved. McLean and two others."

"Did Marina tell you McLean was involved?"

"No, I just guessed it was him."

He had to give it to her. It had taken him nearly a week to figure out that 'playing the priest' meant three people acting in tandem and that Mclean might be one of them. Dimitra had already put it together and hadn't thought to share it with him.

"I'm not convinced McLean is involved," he said, more sharply than he intended. "It might have been Titina Argentis. She and her son could have met McLean in England, planned the whole thing there."

"Titina Argentis would never kill someone with a knife, Yiannis." She spoke like a teacher addressing the dumb kid in the class.

"Why not?"

"Knives generate blood. She'd ruin her clothes."

"So now you're a detective, Dimitra?" Her skepticism made him furious. "When did that happen? When you were doing the dishes?"

"I'm sure Marina didn't count Titina as one of the three."

"We'll never know now, will we, Dimitra? She's dead. Fodder for worms. We can't ask her what she meant. We can't talk it over with her." He went on for a few more minutes, berating her for her role in Marina's death. After he'd finished, he told her of his preparations for the days ahead—how he had taken the blankets in the closet and the food in the refrigerator.

He waited for her to tell him to be careful, that the night air would be cold up on the mountain. The usual. It took him a minute or two to realize she'd hung up on him.

ELENI ARGENTIS' LAWYER was based in London and, when Patronas finally reached him, the man spoke in the same long-winded English the Oxford don had used, the kind that required a lot of patience and a dictionary. However, he was clear on one point: if Eleni Argentis died, according to the terms of her will, neither her half-brother nor her stepmother stood to inherit 'a tuppence.' She'd updated the will a year ago and left specific instructions as to how the money was to be used. She had instructed the law firm to establish a scholarship at Harvard University in her father's name for ten Greek students who wished to study abroad there and to endow a chair in the archeology department—also in her father's name.

Patronas sighed as he hung up the phone. He'd thought, before he'd talked to the accountant, that he'd solved the case. It stood to reason: Titina Argentis and her son were broke. They'd killed Eleni for the money and Petros had been in the way. Antonis Argentis, the hooded man in the corral with Evangelos Demos, the one who'd pushed Papa Michalis over the balcony. Patronas had even gone so far as to recheck their alibis and had discovered a discrepancy. Antonis had said he'd been with a woman, but if so, she was not the one he'd told them, whom Patronas had interviewed. Perhaps his lady friend had been married and he'd wanted to spare her grief. Perhaps his company was male and he wanted to spare himself gossip and scandal, shame. It didn't matter now anyway. He had opportunity, maybe, but his motive had just gone up in smoke.

"I've got nothing." As his mother used to say, his *treasure was coal.*

WORRIED ABOUT THE old man, Patronas called Papa Michalis that night and invited him for dinner. It was no good, him staying on at Marina's house, sleeping in that house of grief. Once he solved the case, he'd find a better place for him to stay. Him and the harelip both.

They drove to a fish taverna by the sea and parked on the sand. A full moon was rising, and he and the priest sat outside and talked while they waited for their dinner, watching the light play across the water.

"Last time I saw a moon like this I was up at Profitis Ilias," the priest commented. "I remember looking down at the well and seeing the moon's reflection in the water. The light was dancing everywhere, bright like sequins." He paused for a moment. "Four weeks ago that was, the night I was attacked."

"You tried to grab him, right?"

"That's right. But I couldn't get a grip. He was as slippery as oil."

"Rubbery?"

"I never thought of it that way. Yes, maybe."

Patronas nodded. He was almost there. He was sure this time. "I've been looking at this *anapoda,* backwards. It was Petros, little Petros Athanassiou, who set the whole thing in motion."

The waiter brought their order and set it on the table. Papa Michalis picked up his fork and transferred three of the fish to his plate. "No wine?" he asked Patronas.

"No, I have to get back to Profitis Ilias. The coroner, he talked too much about what happened. Got everybody nervous. Now Tembelos and the others, they stay inside the monastery with the doors locked. If this were a movie, this would be the time they'd break out the crucifixes and pitchforks. Just yesterday one of them told me, 'Something dark and bloodthirsty lives on this hill. It was no man who attacked her. It was a demon.' And this is a policeman talking, mind you."

The priest began to fillet his barbounia. Although he did his best to hide it, he was amused by what Patronas was telling him. "Your man thinks it was a vampire?"

"Who knows what he thinks? All I know is, it's hard to stay focused when cops bring up the supernatural, when they start acting like it's goblins they're chasing, not criminals. My men are saying it wasn't human the way he got by them, the night he assaulted Evangelos Demos—how he didn't make a sound. Even Giorgos Tembelos is spooked, and he's the best man I've got. He said we should close the cave back up and leave it. He called it the 'lair of the devil.' "

Still chuckling, Papa Michalis ate his fish. Shifting the bones to one side of his plate, he took two more. "Sounds like *The Hound of the Baskervilles*. Terrified a whole community, the murderer did, with nothing more than a tin of phosphorous. It was ridiculously complicated, that case. But Holmes solved it. Went out on the moors alone, he did, and watched for him. As simple as that."

The priest apparently had committed long portions of the book to memory, and without being asked, recited them to Patronas:

> A hound it was, an enormous, coal-black hound, but not such a hound as mortal eyes have ever seen. Fire burst from its open mouth, its eyes glowed with a smouldering glare, its muzzle and hackles and dewlap were outlined in flickering flame.

Patronas fought down the urge to throttle him. "Always dogs. Dogs not barking, dogs with dewlaps, dogs aflame."

In addition to monopolizing the conversation, the priest was eating more than his share of fish, a great deal more. He'd be lucky if he got two mouthfuls. Still, he was glad he'd invited him. That talk of Holmes and the dog had given him an idea, a plan.

Forking yet another fish onto his plate, Papa Michalis nattered on, oblivious. "You see, Chief Officer, it was just a dog in *The Hound of the Baskervilles*, a painted dog, but because people were scared, they attributed supernatural attributes to it. Holmes never lost sight of the criminal hiding there, just as you mustn't. Stay with it, Chief Officer. Don't let your men leave Profitis Ilias. There's no demon stalking that hill. It's a man you're after."

Chapter 38

The eyes of the hare are one thing, those of the owl another.
—Greek proverb

Spiros Korres' red pick-up truck was gone, but Patronas found his wife hanging up clothes in the backyard. She was a short, dumpy woman, dressed in a mended gray housedress. Her white hair was pulled back in an untidy bun and her deep-set black eyes were wary. She continued to work while he spoke to her, picking up wet clothes from her basket and pinning them to the line.

"Kyria Korres, would you give Spiros a message? Tell him we're leaving Profitis Ilias and moving our investigation back to police headquarters."

The old woman eyed him suspiciously. "What does that have to do with us?"

"The killer is still around. You and your husband need to be careful."

She tugged another shirt loose from the pile. "Very well, I'll tell him."

"Where's the Albanian? I need to talk to him."

"The harelip?" She nodded in the direction of the pigs.

Taking a deep breath, Patronas walked quickly past the sty. He stepped over the small stream that trickled through the bottom of the ravine and started back up the other side toward the shed. The end of summer, the river bed was nearly dry, the grass on the banks ratty and clogged with filth. There was a dead rat floating in a fetid pool, its eyes and tufts of skin missing where birds had pecked. The stench of the pigs was omnipresent.

The shepherd was sitting outside. He got up when he saw Patronas and greeted him warmly, kissing him on both cheeks and asking after his health as was the custom. "Come in, come in," he said.

Unlatching the door of the shed, he cleared a space on the cot and motioned for Patronas to sit down, then went to the dresser and got out a crumpled bag of cookies. He smelled nearly as bad as the pigs.

Patronas pushed the bag away. It made him feel bad, this hospitality. "I'm sorry I took the brooch without your permission," he told him. "I'll bring it back to you after the investigation is over." He made a ring with his fingers and held it up as if pinning it to his jacket, worried the man might not understand the Greek. "The bird pin, the little quail."

The shepherd nodded.

"The last time we spoke, you said there were two people."

"Yes. Two."

"Big? Small?"

"Big. Men."

Patronas thought for a moment. "You said you'd seen someone else."

"Yes."

"Was this before or after Petros was killed?"

"Both."

"Was it a man or a woman?"

"I don't know. Is small. Woman maybe."

Voula. "Just as I thought," Patronas said to himself. *Two donkeys fighting in a third one's stall.*

THE GROUP AT Profitis Ilias was much diminished. The army reserves from Marina's village had been ordered back to their base, and the locals had gotten bored waiting for something to happen, or perhaps grown frightened that it would. One by one they had slipped away, save for Spiros Korres. The farmer still came by every day, ostensibly to check on his goats, though Patronas had twice caught him trying to sneak down into the cave.

Hoping to pocket something valuable, was Patronas' guess. Korres would pilfer. A peasant to the core, he'd steal you blind if you let him. But he was also an old-time Greek, which meant he wouldn't kill a woman or slit the throat of a child. Patronas had checked on Korres' son, Vassilis, too; he'd been away when Marina was killed, visiting a girl on Mytelene his mother disapproved of. The wife of Giorgos Tembelos had supplied this last bit of information. While waiting in line to pay their electric bills at DEH, the two women had gotten into a discussion. The murderer had to be someone else, Patronas told himself, one of the *xenios*. He had him in his sights now, just at the periphery of his vision. All he had to do was bring him into focus.

It was a hot day, and Tembelos and the others had stripped off their uniforms and were sitting in the refectory in their undershirts, watching the World Cup on a portable television someone had brought from home. After letting him in, they padlocked the door and Patronas was dismayed to see that

Tembelos had his gun out, lying within easy reach on the stone table. *They were probably using the buddy system when they took a piss, the idiots.* As far as he knew, no one had ventured into the cave or disturbed the crypt under the chapel. Too afraid.

Korres was braver. Given half the chance, he'd get into that cave. Patronas nodded. Yes, he'd have to work quickly.

Whenever the Greek team scored, the men jumped up and yelled, alerting anyone within a mile of their presence on the hill, in complete defiance of his most explicit orders. "Stealth," he'd told them. "This mission requires stealth." He might as well have been talking to the wind. He'd assigned two other policemen to the lean-to. He had no doubt they were listening to the game, too, on the police radio. Not the bravest, most disciplined group, the Chios Police Force. Not exactly the FBI.

THE POLICEMEN GATHERED around and listened in stunned silence. "You want us to leave?" one of them asked.

"That's right," Patronas said. "You, Tembelos, go to the Villa Hotel and make a big show. Tell everybody what an ass I am, how I left Profitis Ilias in the middle of a murder investigation and ordered you to do the same. Return the passports to the two archeologists. Make it clear to them that as of today the monastery will be unprotected."

"I thought you wanted us here."

"Not anymore."

He pointed to the man standing next to Tembelos. "Haris, you go find Voula Athanassiou. Pretend that you need her to sign something, a form to release Petros' things. Complain while you're there. Make a point of telling Voula *and* her boyfriend, Manos—I can't stress that enough—that Profitis Ilias has been abandoned. That there's no one up here now."

Patronas was getting hoarse. He was shorter than his men and he always shouted when he gave orders, as if generating noise would generate stature. Standing there in the refectory of Profitis Ilias, he wished he had a bullhorn.

Unwilling to dismiss the two Argentises as suspects, he had decided at the last minute to include them in the dragnet. Maybe it wasn't money. Maybe, on the stepmother's part, it was hate.

"Michalis, your cousin works at Argentis Shipping, right? Use that as a pretext to visit. Make sure Antonis Argentis is informed as well. Lefteris, you talk to Titina Argentis. She's smart, so be careful or she'll see right through you. Tell her you are releasing what's left of Eleni for burial and ask her where she wants us to send it. Have her sign something, too. Make it look official-like. I'll talk to Spiros Korres and his son."

He continued loudly, "When you walk down to your cars, go in a group and make as much noise as you can. Stay close together. If our killer is watching, I don't want him to know I'm not with you. Tembelos, you drive my Citroen. Stay low and park it in front of my house. Have someone pick you up there. As soon as I call you, come back with a squad car."

"Why a squad car? Why not your Citroen?"

"The Citroen is for my personal use. I wouldn't want to sully it with criminals." Who the criminal was or how he planned to catch him, he didn't say. He was the boss. He didn't have to explain. It was dangerous, the mission he was embarking on, which is why he was sending them away. Leaders took risks. It was what made them who they were.

He watched his men leave from inside the monastery, taking care not to show himself. He noted with satisfaction that they stayed close together as they walked down the path. He wasn't much of a speaker. Often, when addressing them, he felt tongue-tied and awkward. He and his men had even joked about it. *The workshop wants a lame master.* But today had been different. Today he'd been eloquent, forceful. Demosthenes.

CHAPTER 39

The fox has many tricks. The porcupine has but one and better.
—Greek proverb

PICKING UP THE blankets and his lantern, Patronas slowly made his way down into the cave. He lifted the yellow tape that marked the place where Marina's body had been found and moved deeper into the shadows. He hated being here. The place reeked of death, death and defeat.

After his men left, he'd moved the things out of the crypt under the chapel and back down into the cave. 'Salting the site,' archeologists called it. With any luck, he'd catch the murderer tonight and turn the site over to the archeologists tomorrow. There'd be no need for anyone to learn of Papa Michalis' involvement.

He spread the blankets out on the ground inside one of the houses and sat down, checking first to make sure he couldn't be seen. The room was filled with amphorae, which made good back rests, the clay surfaces smooth and round. Fingering a pot, he wondered what had become of the people who'd made it and why they'd come here, seeking sanctuary. Did their descendents still live in Greece? On Chios? Or had they died out like the deer that had once roamed the plains of Attica? Sometimes he'd see a shopkeeper with the face of a statue and think, 'We haven't changed; we are the same as our ancestors.' Other times, he wasn't so sure. Greece had been invaded too many times, known too much trouble. And now it was full of tourists. His cousin's daughter had married a French man. They'd both been on holiday on Mykonos and she'd gone home with him, never to return. Other men he knew had married foreign women and now had blond children, Swedish mother-in-laws. In the past it had been easier. You knew who you were and how to live. You were a man like your father had been and you lived as he had. Now it was all mixed up. You weren't even Greek anymore. You were European.

He set his lantern down and turned it on. It was one of the old fashioned kind—glass with long metal handles on either side, kerosene in the bottom. He remembered when railroad conductors had used them, swinging them back and forth on trains at night. He'd taken it instead of a propane one, fearing the hissing of the propane would alert the killer to his presence. Squirming around, he made himself as comfortable as he could on the stony ground. The air inside the cave was colder than he'd anticipated.

He checked his watch. It was almost eight. As quietly as he could, he got up and stretched, then resumed his watch. He could hear the goats moving around in the corral high above him, their hooves clattering softly, almost like rain.

❧

The bats woke him. Flying around in a dense, black mass, they were so close Patronas could see their teeth, touch their bony wings. He ducked down and covered his head with hands, fearful one would get caught in his hair. A few minutes later they disappeared, exiting the cave all at once as if the wind had carried them off.

The bats returned a few hours later, swooping low and darting around him, their shadows huge against the light of the lantern. He had thought bats were silent creatures and was surprised by how much noise they made, chittering and chirping as they jockeyed for position. Gradually, they settled down and peace returned to the cave.

He dozed off again and slept until morning. When he awoke, he was stiff and sore. He got up and walked around, then unpacked his breakfast and began to eat.

As the air warmed, huge beetles began to emerge from under the amphorae, the ground alive with them. The bugs fell on the remnants of his meal like piranhas. Their thorny legs working, they tore at the chunks of bread, dismembering each other in their hunger. They terrified Patronas, and he stayed well away from them.

Later that day, he gathered fistfuls of gravel from the floor of the cave and laid them out on both sets of stairs. He didn't want the killer taking him by surprise. If he dozed off again during the night, the crunching of the gravel would serve as an alarm and wake him up. He wished he'd thought to bring coffee.

That evening, the wind came up and found its way into the cave, whistling and crying in the darkness. Patronas wrapped himself up in the blankets and hunkered down in his hiding place. He wondered how long he'd have to stay here, how many more nights.

~

PATRONAS HAD BEEN down in the cave forty-eight hours when he heard someone moving around in the courtyard overhead. At first he thought it was the wind, but then he heard the footsteps, so faint he had to strain to make them out. They continued for a few minutes. Whoever it was, was cautious, starting and stopping as they walked across the cobblestones, shuffling almost imperceptibly as they made their way forward. Patronas turned off the lantern and moved it aside, not wanting to trip over it in the dark. He stayed absolutely still.

A few minutes later he heard a soft clang. Someone was shifting the metal panels of the well. The intruder then crawled into the hole and entered the cave. There was no crunch of gravel on the steps, which puzzled Patronas. He strained to hear, sensing movement in the room where he'd found Marina's body. Whoever it was appeared familiar with the layout of the cave and whistled as they made their way toward the ruins. The whistling disturbed Patronas. Toneless and shrill, it didn't sound human.

A few minutes later a shrouded figure entered the Minoan city. The cave was so dark it was hard to see, but Patronas could make out a shadowy form coming toward him, encased entirely in black—the same faintly gleaming material Patronas had caught sight of the night Evangelos Demos was attacked. Head, feet, hands, all were covered. The covering muted the shape of the body, the physique, and made it impossible to tell if this were a man or woman, human. The face also was obscured. Some kind of a mask, Patronas guessed. Large and greenish, it covered the upper half of the head and had square, opaque openings where he judged a person's eyes would be. The figure was panting heavily, its breath rough in the stillness. Patronas fought to keep from panicking. He silently repeated what the priest had said: 'There's no demon stalking that hill. It's a man you're after.'

He could see a pinpoint of light playing across the leaden floor of the cave and for a moment was afraid the intruder had seen him. He held his breath.

The figure stopped and waited for a moment, then started again. Patronas could hear the sound of counting. *Steps?* he wondered. *A kind of spell?*

The counting continued for another minute or two, then the figure knelt down and removed something from its ankle and began to probe the ground with it … a knife. Patronas could hear the rasp of metal against the stone. Quickly unearthing two ivory statuettes, it raised first one then the other, inspecting them carefully with the tiny light before resuming digging. Patronas could see a nylon pouch like a spear fisherman's wrapped around its waist and a second knife strapped to its forearm. Whoever this was must have found the statues earlier and reburied them, waiting for this night.

The intruder continued to work, amassing a growing pile of treasure: a gold diadem of oak leaves and acorns, bracelets, rings. He played the flashlight over each item before moving on.

Patronas began to inch forward with his gun, praying the scraping of the knife would cover his ragged breathing. When he was about two meters away, he raised his gun and pointed it at the kneeling form. "Police!" he shouted. "Put your hands in the air!"

The figure turned slowly toward him, its green mask glinting eerily in the half-light. It continued to whistle the same flat song, a little louder now.

Mindful of the knife, Patronas kept well back. He wanted it gone before proceeding, before this monster could cut him with it. The intruder clicked off the flashlight. The darkness was total, an impenetrable wall of night.

Suddenly, the intruder grabbed him and hurled him through space. Patronas was struggling to get up when the shrouded figure came at him a second time, bearing down on him and smashing him into the amphorae. Patronas hit the pots so hard they shattered, the broken edges slicing into his arms and legs as he fell, the blood warm on his flesh.

He heard the knife slicing the air above him and ducked his head, but he was too slow and it nicked him. Blood began seeping down his neck and wetting the collar of his shirt. He touched the wound with his hand. He felt light-headed and feared he would die here.

The figure tackled him again, knocking him flat against the ground. Kicking him over with a foot, it then sat down and top of him, straddling his torso like a horseback rider. It made a passing motion at Patronas' eye with the knife and howled with laughter when he cried out.

It *was* a man, Patronas realized then. That easy laughter. He recognized the sound but couldn't place it.

Keeping him pinned to the ground, the man began cutting off Patronas' uniform. He started with the crotch of his pants, whistling louder and louder as he ripped through the fabric with his knife. He was so close Patronas could feel his breath on his face.

"No!" Patronas screamed. "No!" Wild with fear, he fought to throw him off, writhing and bucking like an animal.

His screams seemed to excite his assailant, who raked the inside of Patronas' exposed thighs with his knife, slicing the flesh in places and drawing blood. Taking his time, he moved the knife a little higher each time he cut.

Patronas began to sob, tears and mucus running down his face. The man continued to torture him with the knife, cutting deeper and deeper until Patronas' thighs were slick with blood. When he moved the knife higher still, Patronas nearly passed out from the pain.

"Stop," he cried. "For the love of God."

Groping the broken clay beneath him, he grabbed a handful and flung it. The clay bounced harmlessly off the mask, but the noise startled the man and he drew back, losing his balance and giving Patronas the edge he needed. He pushed himself out from under him and rolled quickly out of reach. He felt around for something he could use as a weapon and brushed up against his lantern wedged between the pots and the wall. Tugging it free, he twisted the cap off, swung it over his head and sent it crashing down on his assailant. The smell of kerosene filled the air as the glass broke apart. The man staggered back, momentarily stunned. Patronas reached into the pocket of his blood-soaked pants, found his lighter and flicked it on.

The man began backing away, holding his hands in the air.

Patronas threw the lighter at him and stepped away as the kerosene exploded.

The burst of heat nearly overcame him. He let the man burn for a moment or two, then grabbed the blankets and beat the fire out. The acrid smell of burning rubber filled the cave. The thick smoke pouring off the masked figure made it difficult to breathe.

With a groan, the man fell to the ground. Patronas wrapped him up in the blankets and rocked him back and forth, dousing the last of the flames. The black shroud was nothing more than a wetsuit, melted now in the places the fire had touched; the green headgear, a fancy kind of night binoculars, more elaborate and sophisticated than any he'd seen.

Patronas reached behind him, unhooked the handcuffs from his belt, and clapped them on the man's wrists. Taking a deep breath, he pulled off the mask.

"You," he whispered.

Manos Kleftis spat at him.

Kleftis was as black as his wetsuit. Patronas gingerly touched his face, thinking the skin had been charred in the fire, and was surprised when the color came off on his finger. Camouflage. Kleftis had painted himself up like a frogman. There were two or three burn marks on his chin, but the rest of his face was intact. The kerosene must not have reached that high.

Patronas removed the blankets and assessed the burns on the rest of Kleftis' body, worried he would need to have him airlifted to Athens. The wetsuit was covered with small fist-sized holes marking the places where the flames had penetrated, but the skin underneath was only a little red—first, maybe second degree burns at the most. His feet were more damaged, the soles blistered where the kerosene had pooled around them and melted the rubber. They'd heal in a week or two. Kleftis had been lucky. His disguise had saved his life.

"Manos Kleftis," he said again. Even now he had trouble believing it. Manos Kleftis, a son of Greece.

Kleftis just lay there, watching him, his eyes alive in the darkness.

Patronas found Kleftis' flashlight and clicked it on. The cave was so full of smoke he could barely see. It stank of rubber and his throat burned every time he took a breath. He dug his crime kit out from under the amphorae and bagged the two knives. They were heavy, the blades honed on both sides, and looked to be army-issue. His hand shook as he examined them. A few steps beyond he discovered his gun, half-buried in the soil.

He raised it and pointed it at Kleftis. He'd never been sorrier to be a policeman, to have to obey the law, the demands of the justice system. "Give me one good reason not shoot you."

Kleftis said nothing, his bloodshot eyes tracking his movements. His behavior unnerved Patronas, who checked the cuffs again to make sure they were secure. Removing a second set of cuffs from his crime kit, he cuffed Kleftis' ankles as well. He placed the knives inside the crime kit and zipped it up. Shouldering the bag, he started up the stairs.

He shivered. Kleftis had begun to whistle again.

PATRONAS FELT SICK to his stomach and kept gulping air as he limped across the corral, trying to steady himself. His thighs ached. The slightest movement caused them to bleed again. He probed the cut on his neck. It didn't feel deep enough to require stitches. Most of the blood had already dried.

The night air felt good on his face. The goats were crowded together at the far end of the corral, a shifting, moving horde. Wearily, he stumbled over to the ledge at the back and stretched out on the rock. There was no moon and the stars were bright in the sky. Surprised by their presence, that nothing had changed while he'd been in the cave with Kleftis, Patronas studied them for a moment. He picked out the *megali arkouda* and other constellations he knew.

On the distant shore there was suddenly a burst of light, so far away it was little more than a flicker on the horizon. Fireworks. Someone was getting married in Turkey. Patronas' grandmother had told him about the weddings she'd witnessed there: musicians playing for days on end, the bride journeying to meet the groom on a white horse, people raining sugared almonds and gold coins upon on her as she rode to her new home, a home she had to crawl into under the legs of her mother-in-law, held aloft by her husband and his brothers. The fireworks continued for a long time, lighting up the night like meteorites. Patronas wished them well, whoever they were, the unknown bride and groom across the water. He thought of Marina Papoulis and the way she'd looked at her husband, also of his parents and the comfort they'd taken in one another's presence. He'd never known that, but perhaps this couple would. "*Na zisete,*" he said softly. "Congratulations."

Chapter 40

When the devil's idle, he rapes his children.
—Greek proverb

THE SUN WAS rising when Patronas finally climbed down from the rock. He could see nearly all of Chios from where he stood, the rooftops of the old villages and the shaggy grandeur of the eucalyptus trees along the roads. Even Volissos and the black lava beaches to the north. A donkey was tethered to a tree in a field, bundles of wheat stacked beside it. It was ready for the day's work, the ancient task of separating the grain from the chaff. And surrounding it all was the sea, the open Aegean, surging like a thing alive. For a moment, he imagined he could feel the waves moving beneath him, as if the island itself were afloat, riding on the immense breadth of blue water.

At least a third of the island looked uninhabited, parched brown valleys beneath spurs of gray rock. Rows of cypress trees marked the boundaries between the empty fields, the abandoned farms. Perhaps there was room for the tourists after all.

Patronas wanted to stay here, feel the sun on his back, and watch the sea turn silver in the growing light, the hills to bronze. "I'll come back," he told himself, "when all this is over and I'm done with the case. I'll bring my lunch and spend the day up here."

Manos Kleftis was lying where he'd left him, breathing peacefully with his eyes closed. Looking down at him, Patronas wished that Greece had a death penalty. He wanted to hurt Kleftis in unspeakable ways, abandon him there in the cave, let the beetles chew their way into his intestines and feast on his heart.

Kleftis screamed when yanked to his feet. "Hurts, does it?" Patronas kneed him in the groin, then left him and went back outside to call the police station.

"Send Tembelos here in the old Ford," he told the dispatcher, referring to the squad car with the wire mesh between the backseat and the driver. It was used for exuberant drunks and, though the barrier was flimsy, would serve to keep Kleftis away from him.

After he finished the call, he returned to the cave. He got his gun out and kept it on Kleftis as he undid the handcuffs on his legs. He motioned for him to move toward the stairs, keeping well behind him. Kleftis cried out as he walked, trying not to step down on his blistered feet, like a child on hot pavement. It took them a long time to reach the parking lot.

~

TEMBELOS WAS WAITING for them next to the squad car. His eyes widened when he saw Patronas. *"Panagia,* what happened to you?"

Patronas looked down at himself. His pants were shredded, blood-soaked and filthy, and there was blood everywhere, caking his arms and legs, his hair and neck stiff with it.

Without saying a word, Tembelos got the first aid kit out of the glove compartment and began dabbing iodine on Patronas' wounded neck. "You should see a doctor," he told him.

"Later. We've got to process him first."

Patronas was uneasy on the ride back to the station. He felt as if Kleftis' presence contaminated the air in the car, as if he gave off toxins and could cause things to die. Patronas was surprised at his reaction, embarrassed, but no matter. If he'd had a crucifix, he would have held it up.

Apparently Tembelos felt the same way. He kept sneaking glances at Kleftis through the rearview mirror and crossing himself. They drove without speaking and parked behind the station, then dragged Kleftis through the station and locked him in the cell. Neither proposed removing his wetsuit or taking off the cuffs.

Patronas worried about keeping him in the cell. Chios didn't have much of a jail, only a single high-ceilinged room at the back of the station with dingy cement walls, a drain in the floor. The bars on the windows and door were thin and worked fine for the ouzo-soaked tourists, but they weren't strong enough to contain a battering ram like Kleftis. No one had ever stayed in the jail for more than three days, and Patronas didn't know what they'd do if they had to give him a shower. There were no facilities, and he doubted any of the local hotels would welcome such a visitor.

Kleftis was sprawled on one of the bunks, whistling the same flat melody Patronas had heard in the cave. He was still in his wetsuit and covered with black paint, which made the whites of his eyes stand out, his teeth seem enormous. Patronas remembered Eichmann, how the world had tried to reconcile the image of that little bespectacled man with all those dead people.

With Kleftis, it wasn't so difficult. He was evil and looked it. You could smell sulfur in his wake.

༄

"I can't believe he's Greek," Tembelos said.

"Yup. Born and raised in Athens." His associate would take comfort in that, Patronas knew. He would have been happier if the killer had been a foreigner, one of the *xenios*, but in a pinch Tembelos would settle for an Athenian. One of the new species of Greeks who'd come into being during the Papandreau years. The kind who didn't get up and give a priest his seat on the bus, who valued BMWs and Rolexes over family, who went to dance clubs and rock concerts but never was seen in church.

Afraid he might lose consciousness and wreck the Citroen, Patronas asked Tembelos to drive him home and wait for him while he took a shower and bandaged his legs. He'd been overcome by waves of dizziness since leaving the cave but didn't want to waste the time in the emergency room. Downing a handful of aspirin, he limped back out to the squad car.

"Even cleaned up, you don't look so good," Tembelos said, opening the car door for him.

"You're saying I'm not handsome?"

"If raw is your flavor ...."

Patronas winced as he got in the car. He could feel the blood seeping into the makeshift bandages.

Tembelos started the car. "What do you want me to do when we get back to the station?"

"Get a doctor and see that Kleftis' burns are tended to. We'll get in trouble if we don't go by the books. It's early but you can probably find somebody at the hospital. Be careful when you remove his wet suit. Take another man in with you and keep your gun on him the whole time. Kleftis is a maniac. *He'd kill a flea for jumping.*"

"What do I do with the wetsuit?"

"Send it to Athens. Same as the knives. Have them go over them for hair, prints, blood." He hesitated. "Semen."

Patronas examined the wetsuit again before Tembelos sent it off. The fabric was unlike any he'd ever seen, as heavy as rubber, yet pliant, flexible. He was sure that it, like the knives and the strange goggles, was military issue. Some new kind of neoprene, self-extinguishing. No wonder it hadn't burned.

They interrogated Kleftis later that morning. Dressed in prison garb, he looked smaller than he had in the cave. His feet were heavily bandaged and he moved as if they hurt him.

Patronas chained him to the floor and read him his rights. He had never questioned a suspect in a homicide before. At Papa Michalis' behest, he'd begun watching detective shows on television, thinking to hone his skills, and he had even gone so far as to take notes once or twice during the more pertinent parts. They knew what they were doing, those big city policemen on TV, and he was relying on them to guide him through this moment. The detectives were laconic for the most part, making statements in an unemotional manner, which was what Patronas did now, listing the crimes Kleftis would be charged with and asking him who else was involved.

Kleftis smirked. "Accomplice? What do I need an accomplice for?"

In Scotland Yard, they played verbal chess with suspects. Americans smacked them around. Looking at Kleftis across the table, Patronas fervently wished he was American. "We know you murdered Eleni Argentis, Petros Athanassiou, and Marina Papoulis."

He feigned surprised. "Is that what this is about? Those murders up at the monastery?"

"Yes. This is a serious matter, Kleftis. It will go better for you if you cooperate with us." He opened his notebook and made a show of reviewing what was written there. "Was Voula Athanassiou helping you loot the site?"

"No. She never went up there. The only thing Voula likes to do is fuck."

After three hours of questioning, he finally admitted he'd been working with Devon McLean. Kleftis referred to the Englishman, not by name but by expletives, 'cunt' being the kindest. The other expressions shocked Patronas. They described the act itself and he'd never heard them used before to identify a homosexual.

"He sold what I gave him. Being a poor, native born Greek, I lacked the contacts necessary to sell our nation's heritage. The *poustis*, he knew people who would buy what we found and not ask questions."

"How did you recruit him?"

"I didn't. He was helping Petros. I inherited him."

"Why did you kill Petros?"

"Who says I did? You found me in the cave. There was no corpse in there with me. No blood, no body parts." He drew out the last two words, keeping his eyes on Patronas.

"You're a dangerous man, Kleftis. You nearly cut my head off."

"Wish that I had," Kleftis said in a low voice. "Wish I had cut your head off and drank your fucking blood."

In spite of himself, Patronas felt a twinge of fear. He wished he'd asked Tembelos to sit in on the interrogation with him. He fought to keep his voice steady. "You're guilty, Kleftis. Don't pretend you're not."

"Is that why you set me on fire? Because you thought I was guilty? You held your own little trial there in the cave and decided to execute me? Seems a strange kind of law enforcement. One the Ministry of Justice might be interested in, not to mention the newspapers." He chuckled. He knew he had him. "Throwing that lantern at me was hardly due process."

"Shut up."

"You're no cop. You're a one-man lynch mob."

Patronas continued to question him, but Kleftis proved to be a shrewd and manipulative opponent, far more intelligent than he had originally assumed. He deftly refuted every allegation, knew his rights and could quote the law verbatim. He'd have a field day in court.

His story was an old one: the son of an illiterate workman from Epirus and a prostitute from Asia Minor, he'd been born in the slums of Athens and sent to live with his grandmother in a village so small 'it wasn't on the map.' She couldn't control him and when he was fifteen, he'd run away. He'd served as a mercenary in Sudan for five years, his specialty being night raids and hand-to-hand combat. Patronas wondered if that was where it had all begun—Kleftis' taste for blood, the sophisticated equipment, the knives.

"Who'd you work for in Africa?" he asked.

"Anyone who'd pay me. If I was fighting for one group of rebels and another offered me more, I switched sides. Didn't matter to me." He said he'd bummed around Greece after his return, 'living off women mostly.'

Patronas would have been convinced he was what he said he was, one of those Greek males who see every woman as an opportunity, save for the chilling way he turned himself off and on, the gleeful way he described his role in Burundi and Mozambique. He has a strange sort of charisma, Patronas thought, a way of seducing you. Kleftis could charm the birds from the trees if he wanted to, birds both feathered and human. But then, so could Charlie Manson.

"THAT'S WHAT THEY do, psychopaths," he told Tembelos. "They charm you. Then bite your head off."

"You think he's a psychopath?" Tembelos asked.

Patronas nodded.

"How did it go this morning when you questioned him?"

"*He threw ashes in my eyes*. He isn't going to confess, that's for sure, and without a confession, we've got nothing tying him to Marina and the other two—no witnesses, no fingerprints, nothing."

"What about the knives?"

"I'm sure the only blood on them will be mine. He's a cool one, our Mr. Kleftis. Served time and knows the drill. Being locked up doesn't bother him."

"Shit. He cut you up pretty bad. Can't you charge him with that?"

"I'd lose my job if it went to trial and the press heard what went on in the cave. No, Giorgos. That part's done. Kleftis and me? We're even."

He took a sip of his soup, chicken *avgolemono*. His mother's remedy, it always made him feel better. "The only thing we've got is the smuggling. Kleftis claims he just 'stumbled across the artifacts' when I 'encountered him in the cave.' He could claim he was planning to donate them to the National Archeological Museum and get away with it. Tell the judge I manhandled him, tried to burn him alive."

"What are you going to do?"

"Come at him from a different direction. He implicated the Englishman. Said he fenced the stuff he gave him. I'll lean on McLean, see what he has to say and confront Kleftis with it."

"How long can we hold him?"

"I don't know. As you know, this is my first homicide."

"Shit," Tembelos said again.

CHAPTER 41

"I'll eat the others first," the Cyclops told Ulysses,
"and save you for last."
—*The Odyssey*

PATRONAS AND HIS men were leaning against the fender of the squad car, watching Devon McLean and eating gyros.

The Englishman was across the street, drinking wine at one of the better tavernas. He was outfitted like a college student in jeans and a Rolling Stones t-shirt, Mick Jagger's leering face stretched tight across his paunch.

Like Kleftis, McLean did not go quietly.

"Get your hands off of me!" he yelled, scuffling when Patronas and Tembelos seized him. "I'm English. You have no authority over me!"

They drove him to an army base at the northern part of the island, thinking he'd be safer there. "We arrested Manos Kleftis last night and charged him with murder," Patronas said. "You're the only witness to his crimes and he knows it. If we put you in jail with him, he'll kill you. He likes to kill people, Kleftis does, but then you know that."

The parking lot in front of the stockade was edged with whitewashed rocks. *Ah, the military,* thought Patronas, remembering how he'd painted rocks as an enlisted man. His commander had been crazy for them. It had been peace time and shellacking them had kept everyone busy. As soon as they finished one coat, he'd order them to do another. It had been almost existential, that rock painting.

Patronas put McLean in a cell and locked himself in with him. He'd noticed how the Englishman had quieted down at the mention of Kleftis' name, and he thought he could probably use it as leverage if he refused to talk. "How did it start?"

At first the Englishman was hostile and demanded to speak to a lawyer. "I'm a foreign national. You can't treat me this way."

When he continued, Patronas exploded. "*What do you want, man with ringworm? A pearl cap?* If you don't talk, I'm going to have to turn Kleftis loose tomorrow. He's a dangerous man, Kleftis. Might even be a serial killer. It won't matter where you go, he'll find you. He won't rest until you're dead."

McLean walked over to the window and stood there for a long time, looking through the bars at the sleeping army base. The street lights cast a yellow glow over the room.

"Petros Athanassiou brought me in," he said quietly, all his bravado gone. "He was helping his grandmother at my hotel during my last trip to Chios. She was working in room service and brought the boy along and we got to know each other. He was a bright lad, interested in the dig I was involved with. He turned up three or four times that summer with shards he'd found. I paid him handsomely for them. Far more than they were worth and I suppose he never forgot it. When I left, I gave him my address and told him if he ever was in England to look me up, that sort of thing, the nonsense people always say when they leave a place, not meaning a word of it. I'd completely forgotten about him, to tell the truth, when I received a letter in which he described this site he'd found. Minoan, he said, a secret town. He called it the 'city of ghosts.' "

"When was this?"

"May, I believe." With a sigh, he turned away from the window.

"What happened then?"

"I was planning to return to Cyprus anyway, so I thought to myself, *Why not a trip to Chios?* But when I arrived here, Petros refused to show me the site. He was very cautious. We met in an empty lot near his grandmother's house. He bicycled there with the relics wrapped up in a towel, if you can believe it, and laid them out on the ground. As soon as I saw them, I knew. They were simply amazing, Minoan, no doubt about it, and judging by the workmanship, from the apex of their civilization. Fourteen hundred BC or thereabouts, give or take fifty years. An altogether extraordinary find. I pressed Petros to bring me more, thinking I'd start to catalogue them, to claim the site as mine as an archeologist, but he wanted money, a lot of money. With the advent of the Internet, he'd been able to look things up, and he knew what he had." McLean's tone was regretful.

"Go on," Patronas said.

"I knew a collector who might be willing to purchase the artifacts if they were fine enough and who would prefer to do so 'under the table,' so to speak. We agreed on the asking price for the lot. I persuaded Petros to let me set up a bank account and he, the collector, transferred the money there. As soon as I received it, I gave Petros his share in cash. Our customer was happy with the arrangement. He avoided difficulties inherent in removing antiquities from Greece, the paperwork and customs duties, not to mention the time consuming task of proving actual provenance."

"You didn't take a cut?"

"Yes. A small one."

"How much?"

"I don't remember. Shouldn't you wait until I secure a lawyer before you interrogate me? Don't I have the right to counsel?"

"Not in a capital crime."

"A capital crime?"

Patronas held up three fingers. "Actually three. Three capital crimes."

"I didn't kill anyone."

"If you cooperate, I'll recommend you be charged separately. Otherwise, you and Kleftis will go down together."

"How did you know I was involved?" McLean asked.

"Your boat. You anchored it at Volissos, didn't you?"

Something seemed to go out of him. "Yes. About a week after the smuggling started. I thought it would be easier to offload the artifacts at sea and then move them out of the country. Some of the amphorae were quite large. I didn't want to risk storing them in the hotel or a rental car. I stayed well away from the crowds. Figured I'd be safer if I anchored on the other side of the island."

"People saw a woman on your boat. Who was it? Voula?"

"The boy's misbegotten mother? No. It was Petros' grandmother. I don't even know her name. Sad little woman, hunched over, always dressed in black. Came to collect the money for him. I thought I'd be safer if it was a woman. Greeks were apt to talk if a sixteen-year-old boy came calling on an older man. Couldn't have that now, could we?" His voice was arch and self-mocking.

"Later we moved our operation to the parking lot below Profitis Ilias. It made it easier to transport the heavier items. We'd meet at night. Petros would show me what he had and I'd go over it with him and log everything in so that we could divide the money properly after I'd completed the sale; then I'd pack the lot up and, when it was safe, move it out to the boat. Everything was going swimmingly until Kleftis arrived."

"When was this?"

"Early July, I think. I don't remember, exactly. Petros had gone home with two little gold bulls. He didn't want to sell them. He wanted to keep them, play with them, I suppose. In many ways, he was still a child. He left one out on the table and Kleftis saw it. He slapped Petros around until the boy told him what was going on. Kleftis took half the money Petros had collected, then came after me. We had no choice but to let him in as a partner."

"What about Voula, Petros' mother? Where was she when Kleftis was beating the boy up?"

"Probably putting on make-up. She never interfered with Kleftis."

"Surely the boy's grandmother—"

"She tried to stop him. Kleftis broke two of her fingers."

Patronas remembered the woman's gnarled hands, the swollen knuckles on her fingers. He'd assumed it was arthritis that had crippled her and hadn't thought to ask. "How did the smuggling work?"

"Exactly as before, only with Kleftis overseeing the logging in of the artifacts and the dividing up of the subsequent payments."

"Did Voula get involved?"

"No. It was just Petros, Kleftis, and I. An unholy alliance if ever there was one. Grandma no longer came to the boat, no longer acted as courier. Kleftis didn't like her, said she was clever, someone you had to keep an eye on." A petulant note had entered his voice. "Whenever we were together, he'd torment me. Make sexual overtures to me in front of the boy, crude ones, grotesque. Or flick that knife of his into the ground at my feet and laugh like a hyena when I jumped."

"You came to Chios on the same plane as Titina Argentis. Why?"

McLean raised his eyebrows. "I underestimated you, Chief Officer."

"Yes, you did." He waited a beat. He hadn't felt this good in days. "You sneered and patronized me. You assumed because I was from Chora, not London, I was second rate, a backward peasant from a backwater town."

"It's a failing of the English, that. We hear an accent and assume the person we are speaking with is at best ignorant, at worst, a fool."

"Back to Titina Argentis. Why were you on the plane with her?"

"She wanted to sell her husband's collection of artifacts and someone gave her my name. We arranged to meet in Athens and go over what she had. I wondered why she wanted to do it there. It didn't make sense. After all, I was going to be in Chios a week later. I remember asking her about the provenance of some of the items, testing to see if the collection was really hers. Most of it was Minoan, and given Eleni's interest, I was sure her father would have left it to her in his will. Mrs. Argentis was evasive and I backed off. My guess is, she was trying to sell the things out from under Eleni."

"Did you have any further contact with her?"

"Titina? No. When she didn't get what she wanted, she became hostile and refused to talk to me. Made the trip here a little awkward, as we were sitting side by side on the plane."

"What happened on July twenty-sixth? Did Eleni Argentis catch you and Kleftis up on the hill?"

"No. She had no idea what was going on. Not that day, not ever." He looked down at his hands again. "I fear, Commissioner, that it was I who started it all."

"How?"

"Petros had accumulated an impressive collection of *galapetras*, seal stones. Astounding ones, larger and more exquisite than any I'd seen in any museum in the world. I counted them out when entering each one in the ledger—the kind of stone, the type of carving, estimates of age and worth, that sort of thing—and there were fifty. I was sure of this. I counted them twice just to make sure, so there was no doubt in my mind. Aquamarine, carnelian, agate, even a few emeralds mixed in. They'd be easy to sell, I thought, worth a small fortune. When I got to my boat that night, I wanted to see them again and opened the box I'd put them in. There were only twelve. I called Kleftis and asked if he had them and he said no. Petros swore he hadn't touched them either, but Kleftis didn't believe him and beat him half to death. What I didn't realize was that Kleftis had been haunting the site. Not the cave. Neither of us knew about the cave at that point. Petros insisted that we stay in the car when he was up there. I think he was afraid Kleftis would kill him if he found out where he was digging. Petros didn't trust us and would check up on us periodically, always coming from a different direction. Long nights, those were, Chief Officer, sitting alone in the car with Manos Kleftis."

"So what site was it that Kleftis was haunting?"

"The legitimate one, the trenches where Eleni Argentis was excavating. I assume he wanted to find the place where Petros was digging and take it over—squatter's rights, so to speak. Erase the boy from the equation, at least financially. After the seal stones disappeared, Kleftis got it in his head that Petros was stealing from us and that Eleni was somehow involved, and he confronted them at the excavation the next morning."

He hesitated for a moment. "Petros and Eleni had been examining one of the seal stones when Kleftis and I showed up. Terrible timing, that. Given Kleftis' suspicions, it couldn't have been worse. She was down in the trench and tried to hide it, to protect him, but Kleftis saw them and accused her of stealing from him. She was baffled. She kept looking at Petros. 'What is this?' she asked. 'What is he talking about?' Petros just hung his head and wouldn't answer. Shamed, I suppose."

"Then what happened?"

"Kleftis got out his knife." McLean raised his manacled hands, covered his face with them. He stayed like that for a few minutes. When he spoke again, his voice was hoarse. "I thought at first he was just going to threaten her with it," he said. "But he cut a deep gash on her forearm. Petros thought he was going to kill her and came after him, screaming, 'No, no!' Kleftis is a fast man with a knife and he grabbed him around the neck and slit his throat. And then, of course, he had to kill her, too. He took a great deal of pleasure in it, or so it seemed to me. He kept asking her where she'd hidden the rest of the stones. She didn't know what he was talking about and when she said this, he'd cut her some more. I never realized how much blood there was in a human body until that day. I don't know why he had to cut her hand off. A souvenir, maybe. A way to keep me in line. Who knows? After that, it went quickly. She bled out in a matter of minutes. I left it up to him to dispose of her. Rented a Zodiac for him in Izmir. Towed it over here with my boat. We sank it after he was done with it. I paid for it out of funds provided for me by the Americans. Figured you'd never find the trail that way. A bit frightened by that point. Not just of Kleftis, but of being caught and charged as an accessory to murder."

"Did you ever find the stones?"

"No. A couple of other things also went missing, but I never told Kleftis. Not after Eleni. I was too afraid. You should have seen him, Chief Officer. Wiping his knife on her clothes, whistling a little song while he worked."

"Was Kleftis the one who attacked Papa Michalis?"

"Yes. He wanted him gone from the monastery. Killed his rooster, too, tried to write obscenities with its blood in the dirt. Didn't work that way, though. Drew you people to Profitis Ilias like flies."

"Was that your wetsuit he was wearing?"

"No. He had his own, a special one. He claimed it would prevent him from leaving physical evidence."

And so it had.

"What about the other woman?"

"The lady in the cave?"

Patronas nodded.

"In the weeks after Petros and Eleni died, Kleftis and I explored the hills around Profitis Ilias, mostly at night, and eventually we found the cave. You didn't have enough police to protect the place and it was easy to get by them. He still needed me to sell the artifacts for him and we were hard at work there, carrying things out and boxing them up, the plan being that we'd move them down to the boat after it got dark. It was a holiday, so we thought we'd be safe, that everyone would be away, but then in she comes like Little Miss Muffet, calling for you. Saw us. Tried to get away, but of course, we couldn't let her. Again, Kleftis took his time about it. Enjoying it, luxuriating in it."

He shook his head. "She was praying and calling to God to save her. I finally got tired of her screaming and told him to end it or I would. He wouldn't, so I grabbed the knife and had a go. A mercy killing it was at that point. An act of kindness. Otherwise, he'd still be up there, torturing her like a boy with a magnifying glass, setting fire to ants."

"There were two areas of blood spatter, bloody footprints at both entrances."

"She broke free and ran through the cave, found the second set of stairs and tried to climb them, to get away. Manos pulled her down. Cut her some more."

Patronas had to leave the room. He knew she'd been raped, but he couldn't bear to listen to the details. Finally, he had Tembelos do it.

"Yes, that, too," Devon McLean said. "Repeatedly." He had foregone that pleasure, his taste lying elsewhere, but he'd watched while Kleftis 'ravaged her.' And ravage it had been. "If I hadn't been a homosexual before," he said, "that scene in the cave would have made me one."

ALTHOUGH IT WAS early, Petros' grandmother met him at the door in her apron. "It was Kleftis," Patronas said, "Kleftis who killed him."

Balling her fist, she pushed it against her mouth as he described the death of her grandson. How his mother's lover had killed him. "McLean told me it went fast," he said. "The boy didn't suffer."

"Fast," she repeated.

"Yes, McLean said he died in a matter of seconds."

She didn't cry, which surprised him. He'd expected her to keen, to fall to her knees and have to be helped up, to chant *miralogia* like the women in the Peloponnese whose funeral dirges were said to predate Homer. But she did none of those things. All she did was say Kleftis' name and spit. Then she bade him 'good day,' went back inside her house, and shut the door.

Patronas sat in his car for a few minutes watching the house, expecting some drama, for Petros' grandmother to reemerge, sobbing hysterically, for a host of grim-faced relatives to arrive to bear witness, but there was nothing. Just the sound of the wind, stirring the trash in the street.

Chapter 42

An uninvited in-law finds no place to sit.
—Greek proverb

A shutter had come loose and was banging against the window in the front. "Dimitra," Patronas called as he unlocked the door. The house was quiet. "Dimitra!" he shouted again. He didn't want to be alone, not after last night, not after what McLean had told him.

Quiet, too, was the refrigerator. Unplugged. Its metal shelves stripped bare. All his little treasures, the foods he cherished—the sausages and fish packed in oil, the smoked octopus and *pastourma* … gone. There were no sheets on the bed either, no clean socks in the drawer. He felt like he'd walked into the wrong house. He returned to the kitchen and started going through it again, sweeping his hands back and forth across the shelves in the pantry, the space where he kept his wine under the sink. But like Mother Hubbard, his cupboard was bare. There was no bone for the dog.

This was no warning shot. Dimitra had declared war.

He went in the bathroom and splashed water on his face. Perhaps he should change his clothes. No. Let Dimitra see the vomit, the trail of blood the doctor had left. After taking a shower, he combed his hair in such a way that the stitches stood out and practiced limping in front of the mirror.

Marriage and work, they were like playing backgammon, he thought. One had to dominate the board in order to win, to move from a position of strength. With wives, criminals … it didn't matter. It was the same. Never show your hand or let them know what you're thinking. He patted his pockets for cigarettes. Two packs. It would take at least that before he set things straight and got the matter of the unplugged refrigerator settled. This breaching of the dike of marital expectations.

His mother-in-law met him at the door. Without saying a word, she ushered him in. Dimitra was sitting on the sofa with her purse in her lap. She too had dressed with care. She looked as if she'd been preparing to go to church and was wearing stockings, high-heeled shoes, and a spotted black crepe dress she was especially fond of. She'd curled her hair—too tight as always—and put on fresh lipstick. She didn't greet him. She just sat there.

He sat down on one of her mother's overstuffed chairs. "What happened, Dimitra?" he asked in a neutral tone. "Why'd you unplug the refrigerator?" He didn't really want to know. What he wanted was breakfast. But it was a way of showing interest without conceding anything.

Noting the slight souring of his wife's expression, Patronas realized this had been the wrong thing to say. He should have greeted her first and asked after her health and the health of her mother. But he was hungry. He couldn't help himself. Although he fought against it, his voice took on a plaintive note.

"All the food's gone. You threw away all the food."

She smoothed down her skirt with her hand. "I didn't know when you'd be coming home and I didn't want it to spoil."

"What do you mean 'you didn't want it to spoil'? That's why people have refrigerators, Dimitra, to keep the food cold so it won't spoil." Even to himself, he sounded a little possessed, like a mad dog. A mad dog without a bone.

When she sat up a little straighter, he realized that this, too, had been a blunder. This was not just about food. Her trip to her mother's had been a protest, a complaint against him. Not a serious one. She'd never divorce him. In Chios, to be divorced would be to make oneself into a pariah, a woman others would shun, who would be the subject of talk, and Dimitra would never bring this upon herself. Complaining was allowed and complain she did.

"You haven't been home for more than two nights since July," she said. "I never know where you are or what you're doing. I call the station. They don't know. I call your cellphone, you don't answer."

He interrupted her. "I caught the killer. It was so dark I couldn't see and he came at me with a knife, tore me up pretty bad." He waited for his wife to chastise him, to comment on his bandaged head, to say he should have been more careful. His wife said nothing.

"It was Manos Kleftis, the boyfriend of the Petros Athanassiou's mother. He's the one who killed them." He stopped then, choking as he remembered what McLean had said about Marina's death and the rape and torture which had preceded it.

His wife opened her purse, handed him a tissue and watched coldly while he dabbed his eyes. "It's never going to end, is it, Yiannis?" she said. "This thing with Marina. It isn't enough you spend our entire married life hungering after her. Even dead she's got to ruin things for us."

"What are you talking about?"

"You think I don't see? You're crying, Yiannis. We haven't seen each other for weeks. You nearly get yourself killed and there you sit, crying over *her*, your precious Marina, your lost love." She got up and came over to where he was sitting, leaned down. "The sad thing is you thought I didn't know," she hissed. "I knew long before your mother said anything. I could hear it in your voice every time you said her name, 'Marina.'" She deepened her voice, imitating him, "'Marina.' You should have heard yourself."

Not today, Patronas said to himself. *Oh, please, Dimitra, not today.*

"I kept silent all these years, hoping you'd change. I thought if I tried a little harder, you'd get over it, maybe even come to appreciate me. But you didn't, did you? Not for a minute. I even talked to my mother about it. She said all men are alike. '*Andres einai.*' They're men. They can't help themselves. They take and take and take. 'That is the nature of men,' she said. I could live with that, with all that taking. But not this, not you living with me and loving her."

How like Dimitra, Patronas thought, *to think the best defense for sending Marina to her death was a good offense. To go on the attack.*

"Shut up," he said.

She began to cry then, her big hound dog eyes full of accusation and hurt.

"Do you know after Marina died, you called her name in your sleep?" she wailed. "Night after night you called her name. Tell me, Yiannis, if I die, will you call my name? Cry 'Dimitra' even once?"

"Marina's dead. In no small part because of you. Leave her out of this."

"This isn't about her, Yiannis. It's about us."

"Shut up, Dimitra. I swear if you don't stop right now, you'll regret it for the rest of your life."

"I spent the last twenty years of my life with a man who doesn't love me, who never loved me. What is there left to regret?"

Patronas had thought a long time about why Dimitra had done what she'd done. Being a wife was all she'd ever been, all she'd ever wanted to be. His relationship with Marina, no matter how innocent, had threatened this. It had violated Dimitra's most cherished belief about herself—that she was a respectable woman leading a respectable life. He knew she didn't love him. Marriage, it wasn't about love for Dimitra. Having a husband was like having a big car or Rolex watch, a way of showing off, of saying, 'Look at me. Look what I have.' And he had been what Dimitra had, God help him. Like food and water, a necessity. No cat is complete without its mouse.

She was like Medea, who'd burned her rival alive in a poisoned wedding dress and slaughtered her own children. More passive maybe, but the instinct was the same.

"What was it, Dimitra? Was it seeing her there on your doorstep with her daughter? Is that why you did it?"

"You think I sent her there because she had children and I didn't?" She turned and looked at him. "Good God, Yiannis. It's a wonder they don't fire you."

"Why then?"

"I wasn't thinking. I told you that."

"Dimitra, you've never done anything in your life without calculating the exact advantage or disadvantage to you. You wanted her gone. Maybe not dead, but out of your life, our lives. Isn't that true?"

"Don't give yourself credit, Yiannis," she said. "I would never hurt her or anyone else for you, to preserve what little we have."

CHAPTER 43

What happened to me has never been written.
—Greek proverb

PATRONAS DROVE BACK to his house and let himself in. He'd ended up shouting, "You bitch! You evil bitch! You want to kill me, too!" until Dimitra's mother had come in and asked him to leave, saying the windows were open and the neighbors would hear. He'd shouted at her too and backed his Citroen over her lilacs before he left. *Ah, sto diablo.* Why did his wife have to start in on him today? Why couldn't she have waited? He'd picked up a tray of tyropitas and three bottles of beer on his way home—Becks, a brand Dimitra never bought because it was too expensive.

He carried the tyropitas and beer upstairs and set them out on the bed. Fluffing up the pillows, he propped himself up and began to eat. He didn't bother taking his shoes off. No one to nag him now. No one to fuss about the mess he was making. Somehow this didn't make him as happy as he'd imagined it would over the years. With Dimitra gone, the house seemed too empty. Perhaps he should get a dog.

He didn't remember falling asleep. The last beer had tipped over before he finished it and he could smell it on the mattress and feel the wetness under him. The phone was ringing and he fumbled for the receiver, thinking it was probably Dimitra, that she'd repented. He'd be magnanimous when he took her back. Forgiving. He wouldn't mention this little episode.

"Chief Officer?" Papa Michalis' voice was tentative. "I heard you made an arrest."

"Yes, we did. Manos Kleftis and Devon McLean are both in custody. I'm going to talk to Kleftis later. Confront him with what McLean said and see how it goes."

Feeling sorry for himself, he then launched into what had transpired in the cave, how he'd been injured and come home like a knight errant from the crusades only to find his kitchen bereft of food and his wife gone. He tried to keep the hurt out of his voice as he described the scene at his mother-in-law's, the cavalier way his wife had dismissed his suffering, his need for food and water.

Papa Michalis offered no criticism. His job as a priest was to support the sacrament of marriage, not subvert it, but Patronas could tell from the old man's silence that he thought Dimitra had a point: Patronas had behaved badly with respect to Marina Papoulis. He was a *barka vouligameni*, a shipwreck of a husband, a pig.

Dimitra had been visiting the Papoulis family since the murder, the priest reported, bringing meals and helping out around the house. "She took Margarita shopping and bought her a new book bag for school and winter coats for the boys."

Patronas dusted the filo and bits of feta off the bed. He didn't want hear about Dimitra. "How are they doing, the children?"

"Not good." In dolorous tones, Papa Michalis described how the Papoulis children were struggling to deal with the horror of their mother's death. "I need to find another place to stay," he told him. "I'm in the way here. I'm too much of a stranger for them to be able to say what they need to say in front of me, to cry when they need to cry."

"What are you going to do?"

"I don't know. Maybe go to Psarra."

Who knew? Maybe it did all come down to kindness. "I have a better idea, Father. Why don't you come and live with me? I don't foresee my wife returning home in the near future, and there's plenty of room for us even if she does. We can restock the refrigerator and hire a woman to cook for us. You can have the bedroom on the first floor. It's plenty big and it will be easier for you than going upstairs with your crutches."

The priest would be better than a dog. Even with crutches, he could get himself to the bathroom. He wouldn't need to be walked.

CHAPTER 44

One shouldn't celebrate the beginning until the end.
—Greek proverb

A PHOTOGRAPHER FROM THE local newspaper was at the police station waiting to take Patronas' picture, and the dispatcher informed him there'd been a request from a television station in Athens for a live interview.

Evangelos Demos reported that both prisoners had spent the night quietly in their respective cells. "Well done, Chief Officer," he said. "I just finished transcribing the tape of your interview with McLean, and it was masterful."

Patronas spent the rest of the day fielding calls and finishing up the paperwork on the case. He toyed around with the idea of confronting Kleftis, but thought it best to let him stew. Perhaps, if he got bored enough, his mind would start to play tricks on him, his moribund conscience to stir. Tomorrow would be soon enough. His staff had taken to calling him Columbo. Truth be told, he felt like him.

Ach, TV. It's turning us all into Americans. Patronas remembered how he'd struck a pose with the photographer, striving to look like an American detective, one of the tough guys in raincoats who bit off their words. *To hell with that.* He rummaged around in his desk, looking for something to eat. He was Greek, a Greek detective, seeking to solve life's mysteries, to tame the demons that plague men's souls. He found a package of soda crackers and opened it. Chewing thoughtfully, he wondered whether someone like Kleftis even had a soul. He'd have to ask Papa Michalis. If he did, it was a feeble thing, Kleftis' soul. A dried out husk, papery, like the discarded skin of a snake.

Before he left, he assigned two men to watch over Kleftis at the station. "Do not let him out of here under any circumstances. If there's a fire, save the devil the trouble and let him burn."

Kleftis was dozing peacefully on the bottom bunk. "You may think you're the *diabolou kaltsa*, the devil's socks," Patronas muttered, watching him through the bars, "but I've got you, you son of a bitch." He banged on the metal until Kleftis woke up. Only the innocent were permitted to sleep like that. Not murderers. Never murderers.

PAPA MICHALIS WAS waiting for Patronas in front of the Papoulis' house. It was early evening and the air was fragrant with the smell of *vuxtaloulouda*, a flower that bloomed only at night. Patronas breathed deeply, savoring the smell. A dog was barking somewhere and the street lights had come on. There was no sign of Margarita or her brothers.

Patronas stowed Papa Michalis' things in the back of his Citroen, then helped him in and shut the door. He was surprised at how little the priest had: a worn leather satchel full of clothes, an icon of Aghios Markella—the patron saint of Chios—and two robes, neatly ironed and draped one on top of the other on a hanger.

"Where's the rest of your stuff?"

"In my profession, one is supposed to travel light," said Papa Michalis primly. "The instructions are very clear: 'Lay not up treasures upon earth. Lay up treasures in heaven.' After a period of self-doubt and reflection, I decided that passage referred not just to gold and silver, but to reclining chairs and television sets, so I donated mine to the hospital in Chora. They'll be moving them out any day now."

He moved his crutches to the side to give himself more room. "I spoke to His Eminence and he was not pleased when I told him I would be taking up residency in your house. He wanted me to go to the place the Church runs for elderly and infirm monks. I declined, of course. Who wants to live with a bunch of pious, incontinent old men in downtown Athens?"

"Did he say why he didn't want you to live with me?"

"He feared I would be contaminated by my association with a policeman, a man as worldly as you. He said, and I quote, that 'The police are about crime and punishment while I, as a priest, should be about forgiveness and redemption, the healing of lepers'—'lepers' being a biblical metaphor for social outcasts, criminals and the like. 'Jailing them is not the answer to their plight,' His Eminence said, 'salvation is.' He was quite adamant on this point. I found myself wondering what he'd make of Kleftis, whether he'd turn him loose if it had been him being cut to ribbons, not you, but I kept my own counsel. It's always best to keep silent when Bishop Gerasimos speaks. If you don't, off you go to the wilderness for forty years."

"How did you leave it?"

"I told him I would dwell in the house of the Lord all of my days, no matter where I stayed, be it your house or somewhere else."

Pulling over to the side of the road, Patronas got out his cellphone and called the Bishop.

After being connected, Patronas spoke for a few minutes, explaining that as Chief Officer he'd long noted the lack of spirituality on the part of his men and asked that Papa Michalis be released from his current duties and reassigned to the police department. The priest's responsibilities there would be threefold. First, he would provide moral guidance to the wayward members of the force. Second, he would counsel the public whenever necessary as a sort of ride-along social worker, and third, he would act as a religious adviser to ensure that canon and civil law co-existed in peace and harmony. It was all bullshit, of course, especially the last part, but Patronas thought the Bishop, who recognized no authority save his own, would like the sound of it, which was why he'd thrown it in.

Reluctantly the Bishop consented, after making it clear that these new duties on the part of Papa Michalis would be voluntary and that the Holy Mother Church would not be expected to pay him a salary while he did such a thing.

Patronas shut the cellphone. "It is official," he said. "You're working for me. You can help Evangelos Demos catch shoplifters."

"A policeman, eh?" The priest clapped his hands together.

"Well, sort of." What harm would it do? Miss Marple was eighty-two if she was a day. Why not let the old fellow have a little fun before he headed off into the sunset? Perhaps his presence would even improve things at headquarters. Get Tembelos to put away his girly magazines and the others to be more respectful in their speech and deportment.

Papa Michalis immediately launched into a lengthy discussion of how he would conduct his criminal investigation of the shoplifting at the harbor, starting with the installation of video cameras and the assigning of numerous plain-clothes men. Patronas let him natter on. The shoplifters were usually impoverished refugees passing through Greece and gone before daybreak. Catching them was like catching fish with one's hands. The priest's work would never come to much, but at least he'd have a sense of purpose, a badge. Like offering him a place to stay, it was an act of kindness.

IDLY, HE WONDERED what Dimitra was doing, what would happen to them. Technically the house was hers. Her parents had purchased it and she'd kept it in her name when they got married, and he assumed she could reclaim it if she wanted to and put him out on the street. He'd be homeless. Wandering the earth like a Jew. He'd always joked marriage wasn't for the faint of heart. But then neither was divorce.

He'd had a case once where a woman had thrown acid into the face of her rival. There was even a Greek expression for it: *vitroli.* He didn't think Dimitra would do something like that, but then he never thought she'd do what she did to Marina, and she had. And now this. Fighting with him at his moment of triumph, at the very apex of his career. He emptied his glass. *Ah, the perfidy of women.*

CHAPTER 45

An enemy's gift is no favor.
—Greek proverb

THE TWO POLICEMEN Patronas had left in charge had been playing poker, they said, when the old woman appeared. It was so slow they needed to do something, anything to stave off sleep.

"We didn't see her at first," one of the men told Patronas. "She was standing by the front desk, holding a plastic bag. She looked like she'd been crying and told us Kleftis was her son. She begged us to let her see him, said she'd come all the way from Athens. When we told her he wasn't allowed visitors, she didn't insist. She just handed us the bag and asked us to give it to him."

He said he'd pawed through the bag but hadn't seen anything, just a foil-wrapped package of rusks, *paximadia*. "She had bad arthritis. Her fingers were all twisted up."

The woman had specifically asked him to take the package in to Kleftis while she waited. "We didn't see the harm in it. Kleftis seemed happy to get the parcel and told us to thank 'his little mother.' Nothing out of the ordinary, Chief Officer. I swear. His mother thanked us when we came back out again and patted my cheek. Then she left."

Patronas looked down at Kleftis. The front of the man's shirt was coated with vomit and blood. Judging by the level of rigor mortis, he'd been dead for hours.

"The pain must have been excruciating as the glass moved through his bowels," the coroner said, kneeling by the body. "See here. His duodenum is torn to ribbons." A prissy man with thick glasses, the coroner had spent the better part of an hour performing the autopsy, weighing and re-weighing Kleftis' internal organs and dictating his findings.

Patronas looked away. Stretched out on the coroner's rubber sheet, Kleftis was clotted with blood that had leaked from every orifice. He had a large y-shaped incision on his chest, which the coroner was probing with a scalpel. The floor of the cell was stained with fluids he'd just as soon not think about. He made a mental note to get the room repainted.

"Wouldn't Kleftis have felt the glass?" he asked the coroner impatiently. Who cared about how many centimeters Kleftis' liver was or the length of his colon? Dead was dead.

The coroner had slipped his hand into Kleftis' body and was moving it around. "Oh, yes. He would have been in considerable pain."

Patronas reached for the bag of rusks, discarded on the floor. "How much glass does it take to kill you?" The rusks had been laced with glass, microscopic slivers of it, shiny like quartz. The policeman who'd been on duty said Kleftis had eaten at least two of them.

"A half teaspoon will do the trick. It's an old Ottoman trick. Women in the harem used it on their rivals. Stirred the glass into their victim's coffee; the grounds thick enough to disguise them. Your murderer used walnuts in much the same way. If Kleftis noticed anything, he would have thought it was a nut, when in fact it was a needle of glass. Usually it takes a long time to die like this as the wounds are very small and the glass has to be administered repeatedly."

Patronas got to his feet. "Did Kleftis complain of a stomachache?" he asked the two men who'd been on duty when he died.

They nodded. "Said his shit was all bloody."

"Why didn't you get a doctor for him?"

"We thought he was faking. The way he kept clutching his belly and moaning. It seemed sort of, I don't know, hysterical."

Patronas closed his eyes. Between Evangelos and these two, he now had a complete set: Larry, Curly and Moe. He turned back to the coroner. "So Kleftis bled to death?"

"I'm not sure. Usually it takes a lot longer, a couple of months, even a year after ingesting glass to die. No, I think your man was poisoned. Those rusks were soaked in something. You can find any number of poisonous agents in your garden if you know what you're looking for. Castor beans, pokeweed, rosary pea. She could have used any one of those or a combination. I'll bet money the poison was home-brewed, something she concocted herself. An agent or agents that worked in conjunction with the glass in his gut. Whatever it was, it gave him violent diarrhea, which in turn furthered the internal hemorrhaging, the shredding of his digestive organs. Whoever did this knew what they were doing."

"So he shat himself to death." Patronas had suspected as much. Kleftis had voided himself repeatedly during the night, the smell adding to the unholy stench in the cell.

Patronas turned back to the man who'd given the bag of rusks to Kleftis. "Would you recognize this woman if you saw her again?"

"I don't know, maybe. I could try."

"You could try?" Patronas bellowed. "You could try? You don't *try* to make an identification. Either you make it or you don't. Now I ask you again, would you recognize her or not?"

The man looked down. "Probably not."

The coroner had finished and was standing there, stripping off his bloody gloves, listening to the discussion. "Kleftis was an animal. I doubt he even had a mother."

"Of course he had a mother. What do you think? He was spawned by spiders?" Patronas sighed. *None of this was his fault. No reason to yell at him.*

"No," the coroner replied. "Scorpions. Scorpions would be my guess."

"There'll be hell to pay for this," Patronas told Tembelos. "I never should have left those two in charge. They're new to the force. They don't know what they're doing."

"You and me, we would have done the same had it been us on duty. Old lady shows up with cookies for her boy, you're going to tell her, 'Wait, I have to send them to lab, I have to go over them with my metal detector'?"

"Giorgos, he was shitting blood. They should have gotten him a doctor."

"The coroner said it wouldn't have made any difference. Kleftis was a dead man from the moment he took a bite. There was no way anyone could have found an antidote in time, no way to save him. Only question was the pace of his leaving. Anyway, I'm glad he's dead. The world is better off without him."

"That's not our decision to make," Patronas said. "That's never our decision to make."

He lit a cigarette, trying to steady himself. "I'm finished, Giorgos. Once the Prefecture hears I wasn't in the station, that I left two rookies in charge, I'm done."

"Me and the others, we'll talk to him."

"It won't matter. He'll haul me up for dereliction of duty."

Yesterday he'd come into work feeling triumphant like Jesus entering Jerusalem, expecting 'hosannas' from his superiors at the Ministry of Justice, the Prefecture waving palms. He'd get a call from Athens, of that he had no doubt, but now it would be a different one. And there'd be no palms in his future. *Me stravose.* They'll crucify me. No, when this was all over, his men would be gambling for his clothes.

Chapter 46

Though the wolf grows old and changes his hair, he
has not changed his disposition.
—Greek proverb

Patronas wanted to make the arrest quietly. She was an old woman, a grandmother. She was out in her garden when he pulled up in the Citroen, doctoring a sickly rose bush next to the chicken wire fence. She stood up when she heard the car and turned to face them, her hands caked with soil.

"Chief Officer," she said with a faint smile. She didn't look surprised. It was as if she'd been expecting him.

"Kyria Athanassiou."

"I need to wash my hands." She led him into the kitchen. After washing her hands, she dried them carefully on a worn hand towel, then turned and walked slowly through the house, running her crippled hands over the china knick-knacks and stroking the furniture, straightening the doilies on the arms of the chairs. The room was as Patronas remembered it: the cheap veneered tables, the machine-made Persian rug. The windows were closed against dust, the curtains against the sun. The foil-wrapped chocolates on display on the étagère hadn't been touched since his last visit. It was the salon of a poor person, but a poor person with certain aspirations. He thought she'd probably studied the rooms of the people she'd cleaned for and then copied them. The arrangement was stilted, artificial. Like the landscape in one of those paint-by-numbers sets.

"Where's Voula?"

"I sent her away yesterday. She's in Athens." The old woman slowly let herself down on the settee. "Leave her be. She had nothing to do with it. I'm the one who killed him." Again, the same thin smile. "Your men, they wouldn't let me into his cell. I wanted to watch him die." There was no trace of emotion in her voice. "I wanted to watch him die," she said again.

The hair that strayed from under her kerchief was greasy and there were lines of filth in the folds of her neck. He remembered her as a fastidious woman and asked her if she was all right, did she need something, a medic perhaps. When she shook her head no, he pulled out the tape recorder, set it down on the table and turned it on. They could do the whole thing here. She was willing to talk. There was no need to take her to the station house and interrogate her. "How did you kill him?"

"I boiled some oleander leaves and other things from the yard and ground the glass in the mortar the way you do when you make *skordalia*. Mixed it all up together. My grandmother was from Asia Minor," she added as if the poison was a legacy, a recipe handed down through the generations. "My father, he was from Tripoli."

Her head had been bowed, but now she raised it and looked at him, and Patronas noticed her eyes for the first time. Black and shiny, they were devoid of feeling, reptile eyes. He remembered what Kleftis had said about her: 'she was clever and not to be trusted.' There had been three, after all. "You were the one, weren't you?" he asked. "You were the one who started it all."

She gave a curt nod. "Petros told me about the cave the day he found it."

"How did he find it?"

"Chasing goats. He said he heard something clang underfoot. 'It was a disc,' he told me, 'a door.' 'Where does the door go?' I asked him. 'To a ghost town,' he told me." She smiled to herself, remembering.

"What happened after he found the cave?"

"I had Petros write to McLean in England. I knew he liked boys, McLean did. You could tell. I figured he'd pay more attention if he got a letter from Petros than one from me and it worked just like I planned. I wanted him to sell what we found, to take care of that part of it. I'd met him one summer, working at his hotel, and I knew he wouldn't ask too many questions. I thought we could make a lot of money; the cave would be a gold mine for us, if we were careful and played our cards right. String the man along a little. Petros gave me trouble about McLean. He was afraid that the woman would find out, think less of him. 'She doesn't care about you,' I told him. 'You're just a servant to her.' But oh, how he fretted. That's why he asked the priest to hold the stuff for him. He waited until the woman left every day before bringing the things down to me."

"You are talking about Eleni Argentis, the archeologist?"

"Yes. The one he worked for. The priest didn't know anything. He thought it was just Petros. He wanted him to give the money to me, his poor old Yiayia, instead of buying himself a motorcycle with it. He never realized we were in it together."

It was all becoming clear. "When did you lose your pin up there, the little quail?"

"After Petros died. I asked a neighbor to drive me to Profitis Ilias. I told her I wanted to see where it had happened, where he'd been killed. The place was empty. There was no one around and the doors were locked. I knew there was an entrance to the cave on the hill and I went there. I wanted to take more things from the cave. But when I got there, I heard people talking … men."

"What happened then?"

"I ran away. Something bad had happened. I could see blood on the rocks. The pin must have come loose then. I went back another time to look for it. Voula gave it to me and I was afraid that if you came around again, asking questions, she'd say it was mine. But I'm old. I don't see so good. I never found it."

"How many times did you go there?"

"Two, three. After I saw the blood, I stopped going."

"How did Kleftis get involved?"

"Petros wanted his mother back, and he wrote a letter to her after we sold the first batch of things. He told her she'd be rich if she came back to Chios, that he'd buy her diamond bracelets and a big Mercedes Benz. I didn't know about the letter. If I had, I would have torn it up, burnt it. But it was too late. Two weeks later they descended like hawks, Voula and Kleftis. I knew there'd be trouble the minute I saw him. Voula's father was a man like that. A man you had reason to fear."

She rubbed her gnarled hands over her arms as if trying to get warm. "That foolish boy, thinking Voula would ever be a mother to him. If only he'd done what I said and left her alone."

Patronas saw that her dress, too, was unclean, a line of grayish-white material across the knees as if she'd been kneeling in ash. "After Voula arrived, did she get involved?"

"No. Too lazy. Only knows how to do one thing, Voula, and she doesn't have to get up to do it. She didn't even get up when Kleftis hurt me." With a sigh, she held up her crippled fingers. "Wasn't her problem, she said. He threatened to kill Petros and me and it wasn't 'her problem.'"

"What was her relationship with Kleftis?"

"He was her pimp. That's why he came with her to Chios. To make sure no one got off with his property." She was watching him now. "What did you think? They were lovers?" She shook her head. "Only thing those two ever loved was money."

"What happened after they arrived?"

"Petros had found two bulls and wanted to keep them. I thought it'd be all right. I could sell them later, but he left one out by mistake and Kleftis saw it.

He beat him half to death, trying to find out where he'd gotten it. After that, we worked for Kleftis. He was in charge. I warned Petros. I told him to watch out. 'Never let him see where you're digging,' I said. 'He'll kill us if he finds out.' I was afraid for him. But we were already in the middle of it. We were trapped."

"Even though you were afraid, you continued, didn't you? You and Petros, stealing things on your own, away from Kleftis?"

She seemed surprised that he knew this. "Yes," she said. "We needed the money."

"How did it work?"

"Petros would hide things and bring them to me when Kleftis wasn't looking, little things he could slip in his pockets. Nothing like before, just some stones. I didn't trust McLean, so I sold them to a jeweler I knew in Chora. Never got close to what they were worth." A petulant note had entered her voice. She went on for a few more minutes, talking about how the man had cheated her, her lost wealth.

"What happened next?"

"Petros discovered more stones, handfuls of them like jewels, and I told him to bring some to me but be careful about it. But he was a boy, a silly boy, and he got caught. He was no match for Kleftis."

"What happened then? McLean noticed the stones were missing and asked Kleftis about them?"

"I don't know what happened up there." She wiped her eyes with the corner of her apron. "We had to go on, don't you see? Otherwise, we would have had nothing. Kleftis would have taken it all and left us with nothing."

"Papa Michalis told me Eleni Argentis gave your grandson a laptop computer, a Toshiba. What became of it? Did you sell it?"

"No, Kleftis smashed it. Smashed the computer on my hand the day he took over. Broke it. Broke my hand. I went to the Englishman after Kleftis hurt me and begged him to help us, but he was too scared. 'Just give him what he wants,' he said." She mimicked the man's high pitched voice. " 'Just give him what he wants.' "

"You knew Kleftis killed your grandson. Why did you wait till now to kill him?"

"I wanted you to prove it first. I was waiting for you. So everyone would know what he was … why."

"Why didn't you tell us, Kyria Athanassiou? We could have helped you."

"I've worked all my life cleaning up after people," she said softly. "Kleftis, he was part of my cleaning up. Where I come from, my people, we take care of these things ourselves."

Then as much to herself as to him, she said, "I was hoping that once he got enough money, he'd go away and, Petros and me, we'd be like before. I was praying for that. But instead he killed him. Killed my little Petros." She clutched herself and began rocking back and forth. "I should have known better. Men like that? They're locusts. They feed and feed until there's nothing left."

ꕥ

As the afternoon wore on, the old woman's conversation took an ominous turn. She began slipping in and out of the past, speaking to the dead as if they were there. The war featured prominently in her memories. At one point she sang songs she'd heard on the radio from that time and spoke of Walter Blume, a Nazi active in Greece during the war. A few minutes later, during the same conversation, she pointed to the window and said, "Look, there's my husband's freighter, the one he works on." She was quite adamant, insisting Patronas get up and go see it. He dutifully went to the window and looked out. All he saw was the chicken coop and her little garden, gone to weeds.

"I'm from Peloponnese—Kalavrita," she went on. "The Germans, they killed my brothers, my father. Shot them in the square along with the other men. My mother spent a week digging graves for them with her hands. For five years we had nothing but *horta*, grass, to eat. Nothing but rags to wear. My mother died of tuberculosis in 1944."

She was safe, Patronas thought. No matter what she'd done, no jury would convict her once they learned she was from Kalavrita. It had been one of the worst episodes of the war. After killing every male over ten, more than five hundred people, the Nazis had locked the women and children inside a schoolhouse and set it on fire. A German soldier had unlocked the door, allowing the women and children to escape. Yet there had been no escape. Starvation, tuberculosis, and death had awaited the survivors of Kalavrita. The suffering in Greece during the war had been terrible.

'Eine gewisse Brutalität, a certain brutality was necessary,' the German commander had said. And now the sons and daughters of the men who'd done those things came to Greece to get a tan. And the Greeks welcomed them, even in Kalavrita. *God help us all.*

Patronas wanted to stop the interview then. But she insisted on speaking. "After the war, I moved to Pireaus. Met a sailor from Chios and got married. Lived in Kastella. Oh, not in one of the grand houses, the ones by the sea. In a room over a garage. We moved to Chios when Voula was four. My husband was like Kleftis. He liked to hurt people. It gave him pleasure."

Patronas interrupted. "How did he die?"

She looked up at him sadly, disappointed he'd had to ask. "Car, Chief Officer. He was killed in a car accident. After he died, Voula started going with men. I worked in the hotel and people's houses. Every day of the week, I cleaned. She never did anything to help me. No one did."

She asked if they could eat together before he took her to jail. "Don't worry, Chief Officer," she said. "I won't poison you. I just want to cook dinner and eat at my table one more time before I go."

Although it violated police protocol, Patronas thought it would do no harm and agreed. He checked the kitchen before sitting down and waited until she took the first bite before serving himself. She noticed his behavior and gave him a wounded look.

The table she set was like her house: a machine-embroidered tablecloth, woven to look like damask, stainless steel flatware embossed like silver. The food was simple. She seemed proud as she put the roast on the table, meat still a cause for celebration.

Patronas didn't think he'd ever eaten a sadder meal, choking down the gristly meat, the stony potatoes, while she watched him from her end of the table.

She treated him to dessert liquors after, saying she'd steeped the fruit, the peaches and cherries, in the alcohol herself. "The sun is what does it," she explained. "You have to leave it out in the sun." She opened the doors of her cupboard and showed him the glass jars full of produce she'd put up herself, the white dishtowels she'd embroidered with flowers.

A person who'd been silent for too many years, she talked for over two hours. Patronas was reluctant to cut her off, struck by her need to speak. It pleased her that he was taping her, that she finally had a witness. She complained bitterly about her life, where she found herself in her old age. "Castro isn't like it used to be. It's full of Pakistanis now."

One last piece of the puzzle. "Why did you argue with Titina Argentis at the laiki?"

"Voula worked for them as a maid before she took off for Athens. She was only sixteen and pretty. Soft. Not like now. Husband cornered her, Voula told me. We were having coffee together, just the two of us, a couple of days after she got here. Had her in the garden, she said. I wanted Titina to pay damages for what he had done. I thought Argentis had been Voula's first, that Petros was his son and that's why she was the way she was." She pulled her sweater tighter around her. "After Titina refused, I went to the shipyard and spoke to her son. He didn't even ask me to sit down. He acted like I was dirty, like I would 'dirty his chairs.' "

"Was Petros indeed the son of Eleni's father?"

"No. Voula was a slut even then. When I told her, she thought it was funny, me going to Titina Argentis demanding money, claiming Argentis had 'besmirched her honor.' Voula laughed and laughed. Said, 'There've been so many, if they all paid I'd be a millionaire.' "

He could see her hands trembling in her lap.

"It is hard enough to be poor, Chief Officer. But to be the mother of a whore, to be poor without honor …."

Her voice rose. "You don't know what it is to struggle. To be walled in, forced to live in a tomb of a marriage with a man who beats you like it's his right, who shames you day after day after day. Knowing you were meant for better, that you deserve better. Diamantis wrote a story about it. I can see from your face you're surprised. What, you thought I didn't know how to read? I was unfamiliar with literature?" She smiled to herself. "I know more than you think. It's a good story. It was about an old woman who drowned baby girls in order to spare them from a life like hers, a life of hardship and pain, a life like mine. Diamantis got it wrong, though. She shouldn't have drowned the girls. She should have drowned the boys. You get nothing but pain from men. They ruin themselves and you in the bargain." She spat out the words. "Whether you love them or not, it's all the same. They ruin you."

Patronas had excused himself after dinner and gone outside to call her daughter in Athens from his cellphone. He'd suggested that she return to Chios to be with her mother, to help her now. Voula Athanassiou refused. "I can't, Chief Officer. Surely you understand. Seeing my mother in jail? It would be too hard on me."

He had hung up without saying good-bye. *Who would put flowers on the old woman's grave when the time came?* he wondered. Her situation filled him with pity. *What a life she'd had.*

"You said you kept some stones," he asked gently. "Where are they?"

She hobbled to the back door and opened it. "Out there," she said, pointing to the chicken coop. "Everything's in there. No one goes there but me. Too delicate, all of them. Too clean and fresh and sweet-smelling." There was spittle on her face. Her eyes were alive. Some spark alight now. When he'd started the interview, she'd been listless, whining and resentful. Proud, yes, but her pride had been misplaced. She anticipated humiliation. Saw it when it wasn't there. Apologized for her china, the poor quality of the coffee. "I am poor." Her statement thrown down like a gauntlet. Now she was different.

There were few things in the coop. A handful of *galapetras*, nothing more. Slipping on his gloves, Patronas turned on his flashlight and poked through them with a finger. Petros had been holding out on his grandmother. Even little Petros had betrayed her. Leaving the most valuable artifacts with the priest at Profitis Ilias instead of bringing them home. Probably McLean had been helping him, selling the jewelry and figurines for the boy and splitting the money with him. Or maybe he'd been holding them for a future time when he could salt an undiscovered site and claim it as his.

It smelled terrible inside the coop, the ammonia from the droppings so powerful it stung his eyes. The droppings clung to his shoes, covering them up to the laces. The dirt on the old woman's skirt had to have come from here. The chickens were wearing some sort of harness to keep them in place, their feathers worn away where the metal rubbed against their necks. *Prisoners*, Patronas thought. *Everywhere prisoners*. He stepped back outside.

The old woman was standing in her garden, waiting for him. "I couldn't wait," she said. "I'm too old. I wanted it settled." He realized she was talking about Kleftis. "I couldn't wait for justice."

PAPA MICHALIS WAS still up when Patronas got home, padding around the house in his bathrobe. "I couldn't sleep," he said. "Too much, all of this. Too much for an old man."

After pouring himself a drink, Patronas told him about the death of Kleftis, the role the grandmother had played in the whole affair. "I didn't take her in. I probably should have, but I didn't have the heart, at least not tonight."

"What did you do with her?"

"Left Tembelos with her at the house, told him to keep an eye on her. We'll jail her in the morning."

"What did she say about Kleftis?"

"She admitted killing him. 'He was a rabid dog,' she told me. 'You kill rabid dogs.' Very matter of fact, she was. No remorse, no tears, nothing."

He took a sip of his drink. "A real Spartan lady. She's not from Chios. She was born in the mountains of Peloponnese, Kalavrita."

"Was she there during the war?"

Patronas nodded. "A victim from the day she was born."

"What are you going to do with her?"

"Charge her with murder in the first degree. I don't care how old she is or what she went through. Nothing gives you a license to kill."

"Where she's from, it does. Kleftis killed her grandson and she avenged him. That's how they do things in those mountains. The people there, they don't need law enforcement. They settle things themselves. To her this is like the war, when we killed all the collaborators. No one cared what happened to them. No one bothered with due process. You just shot your enemies. The ones who'd sold you out to the Germans. That's what she did."

"She confessed," Patronas said. "I can't ignore it. It's not enough that my prisoner dies in custody. Now you want me to let a killer go? I can't. You know that. I'm sworn to uphold the constitution."

"Can't you find a legal way to absolve her?"

"Absolve her? That's your domain, Father, not mine."

Chapter 47

I am not yet dead, but they have lit my candles.
—Greek folk saying

The call from the Prefecture of Chios came the next morning. Patronas was relieved of his duties until further notice. His second in command, Evangelos Demos, was to take his place as Interim Chief Officer until a successor could be appointed by the Ministry of Justice in Athens.

The Prefecture had been quite specific about Patronas' inadequacies when he'd fired him: the poisoning of the suspect, Manos Kleftis, while under lock and key at the local jail, the failure to follow proper procedure with respect to Kleftis' murderer, the elderly widow, Calliope Athanassiou, who remained at home in spite of confessing to the crime, the lack of police oversight at Profitis Ilias on August fifteenth, which had resulted in the death of Marina Papoulis, the refusal to permit the suspect, Devon McLean, to use the bathroom in a timely fashion, resulting in a formal complaint filed against the Chios Police Department by the British Consul.

"Needless and wanton destruction of life and property under your administration," the Prefecture intoned. Patronas thought he probably could have survived had it not been for the British Consul's scathing letter, which had been sent to the Ministry of Justice in Athens. The Prefecture had read it out loud to him at the start of the phone call, his voice pained. To be shamed by a foreigner and to have your colleagues in Athens witness your shame. No wonder he'd been sacked.

"Your conduct throughout this investigation has been highly unprofessional," the Prefecture went on. "While Manos Kleftis was dying on the floor of his jail cell, you were seen drinking by countless witnesses at a taverna in Langhada. Evangelos Demos testified that you ordered him to chase *bats* at Profitis Ilias, *bats,* mind you, and this in spite of his most fervent objections, his legitimate fear that he might injure himself in their pursuit. He also stated that when he was assaulted there one night and the opportunity arose to seize Manos Kleftis, you gunned down, not Kleftis, but two goats, which subsequently died of their injuries."

"Testified? You had a trial."

"A hearing."

"Why wasn't I invited? Given a chance to defend myself?" To be tried and convicted, not by a jury of one's peers, but by Evangelos Demos.

"It wouldn't have mattered. Your dismissal was a foregone conclusion." The Prefecture instructed Patronas to clean out his desk by the end of the day and hung up without saying good-bye.

Patronas set the phone back on its cradle. He wanted to die, to run the Citroen in a closed garage until he was no more, drink hemlock like Socrates. Fired for incompetence. Fired for stupidity. *Ach, fired on the word of Evangelos Demos.*

He sat at his desk for a long time with his head in his hands. He ached all over. His wounds from the cave hadn't healed and now he had new ones. What was he going to do? Go home to Dimitra? He wished he'd let Kleftis kill him.

At the end of the day, he did as he was told. He gathered up his files and personal belongings and shoved them in cardboard boxes and carried them out to the car. His men stood around awkwardly.

"Prefecture's a fool," Tembelos said.

IRONIC HOW THINGS *work out.* At one point during the murder investigation, Patronas had wanted nothing more than to join the people in the *ouzerias* and coffee shops that lined the quay, to sit and watch the boats. Now that he had joined them, drinking endless Nescafé frappés among the hordes of German and Danish tourists, he hated it.

In the days immediately following his dismissal, Dimitra alone had called and pledged her support. Not her love, Patronas noted sourly. Her support.

Against his better judgment, he called her back.

"Hello, Yiannis," she said, speaking carefully, enunciating her words with just a hint of regret like a doctor about to give a patient the bad news. And bad news it was. "I've been thinking over what you said. You know, about my being jealous of Marina, the fact that she had children and I didn't."

"What about it?" Patronas asked impatiently.

"I never told you this, but after we were married and the children didn't come, I went to the doctor and got myself checked out. Took the plane to Athens. I told you I was going to see my cousin, but I wasn't. I was going to see a specialist there. A man who'd trained in England. It made me embarrassed the questions he asked. The doctor, he said I was all right, that it was you. Probably the mumps you had when you were a boy, the ones that messed up your ear. I didn't tell you. I thought, Yiannis, he's a man and men, they worry about making children, their man parts, so I kept silent. I let you go on thinking it was me, that I was one to blame, when all the time it was you."

My cup runneth over, Patronas thought to himself. *It isn't enough she made my life hell and sent Marina to her death. It isn't enough that I botched the case and lost my job. Now even my manhood is suspect.*

"Thank you for clarifying that, Dimitra." He slammed the phone down. What did she know? *Her word isn't worth the fart of a donkey.*

THE CITROEN QUIT in the rain that afternoon. Just stopped where it was and ceased to function. No amount of coaxing would get it to start. He kicked one of the tires. *All others with pebbles and thou with stones.* Fortunately, the car was light and he could roll it to the side of the road, out of harm's way. When he finished, he was thoroughly soaked. He fiddled with the heater, hoping to get warm, while he waited for the rain to stop. No luck there, either. The rain continued to pour down, rivers forming on either side of the road. A huge bolt of lightning split a cypress tree less than a mile away. The Citroen was elderly, arthritic in its elements, and Patronas knew he'd pushed it unmercifully over the last four months, driving back and forth to Profitis Ilias. Still, why did it have to choose today of all days to die? Why not give up the ghost when the sun was out, instead of in this cataclysm of water? The Citroen's canvas roof was worn in places and the rain quickly found its way in, trickling down his forehead and along the back of his neck. The heat failed completely a few minutes later. The windshield wipers proved to be worthless too, going back and forth every fifteen minutes and then only if the car was running. Patronas knew; he timed them.

"That's the way these old cars were designed," the mechanic told Patronas when he arrived with his tow truck. "The windshield wipers, they're linked like an umbilical cord to your engine."

"Can you fix it?" The mechanic studied the Citroen, listing beside the road, taking in its rusting fenders, dented in many places, the makeshift antenna Patronas had fashioned out of a metal clothes hanger after he lost the original, the front bumper held on with duct tape.

"I'd have to send to Athens for the parts. A geriatric model like this one, you'd be better off selling it to me for scrap and getting yourself a new car."

The mechanic gave Patronas a ride home in his tow truck. Patronas felt terrible, watching the man drive away, dragging the Citroen behind him, its taped-up bumper working its way loose as he rounded the corner. It had been his first and only car, a friend almost. He sighed. *This must be how people feel when a horse breaks its leg and they have to shoot it.* He had no money to replace the Citroen now. No money to eat.

TEMBELOS CALLED TWO days later and asked if they could get together. He made a point of calling Patronas 'Chief Officer' on the phone and treating him like he was still in charge. They agreed to meet at an ouzeria near the house when Tembelos got off work.

"How you doing?" Tembelos asked when he saw him. "On the mend? Wounds healing all right?"

Patronas didn't trust himself to answer. He just shrugged.

"How about the job? You okay with that?"

I tell him I'm a eunuch and he asks how many children I have, he thought. "Oh, yeah, Giorgio. I'm great. Having the time of my life."

"Things are moving apiece with the case," Tembelos offered, seeking to mollify him. "We arrested Petros' grandmother. Evangelos' orders, said we had to handcuff her and take her to jail. I don't know what the old dame thought, that we were Nazis probably, but she just went crazy. Me and the others, we just stood by. If Evangelos wants to arrest old ladies, he can do it by himself. He wrestles her into the car and about halfway to the station she starts complaining of chest pains, palpitations. So off to the hospital we go. Hospital staff took pictures of her injuries, black and blue marks on her arms where he'd manhandled her, the welt on her face where he'd elbowed her by mistake, wrestling to get the cuffs on."

From Tembelos' tone, it was obvious he considered Kyria Athanassiou a folk hero, a brave woman who'd righted a great wrong. He would have let the old woman go if it had been up to him.

"She's still in the hospital. There's going to be an internal investigation." Tembelos laughed out loud, unable to contain himself. "Her lawyer insisted on it. 'Undue force.' "

Patronas was gratified that Evangelos Demos had made a hash of his first assignment. Being Chief Officer wasn't as easy as he'd made it seem over the years. It was hard work. Thankless. Look at him. Twenty years on the job and what did he have to show for it?

"They ever talk about me, the men?"

"Some. You know how it is." Tembelos looked embarrassed. "Shame they took your pension away. What are you going to do?"

"I don't know. The priest wants to open up a detective agency. Cash in on my experience."

"Maybe you should. People might hire you. You never know."

As an endorsement, it was wanting.

"One thing I always wondered about," Tembelos said. "Why'd Marina go to Profitis Ilias that day? She must have known no one was there."

"She had some papers she wanted to give me. Travel schedules, dates I'd asked her to check on. I'd told her when people said they arrived on Chios and asked her to verify it. She discovered McLean arrived earlier than he'd said, as had Kleftis and Voula Athanassiou. She told Papa Michalis, 'They're playing the priest with us,' which meant she thought three people were involved—McLean and two others. I don't know who she thought the other two were. Kleftis and Voula would be my guess. I doubt she suspected the boy's grandmother, but she came pretty close to solving the case before she died."

"Why didn't she come to the station with it? Why go to Profitis Ilias?"

Patronas swallowed his ouzo and poured himself another. He'd kept silent about his wife's role in the death of Marina Papoulis. Even when the Prefecture had accused him of negligence with respect to sealing off the monastery, he hadn't said a word. Why, he wasn't sure. Perhaps to shield her, to keep what she'd done between them, within the family, so to speak. He was her husband, after all. He set his glass down hard. No reason to protect her now.

"My wife sent her there."

"Dimitra sent her to Profitis Ilias?"

"That's right. Knowing the risks, knowing there was a murderer loose on that hillside."

"What'd she have against Marina?"

"Marina was my childhood sweetheart. My wife was jealous."

Tembelos whistled. "Holy shit."

"We're separated now. She's staying at her mother's."

Let Tembelos think he'd thrown Dimitra out. Giorgos had big mouth. He'd tell everyone on the island that Dimitra and he were finished and why before the day was out. Patronas welcomed the gossip. Let people see Dimitra for what she really was: Medea made real.

"Must be hard," Tembelos said. Patronas could tell he was shocked, trying to work it through.

Patronas took another sip of ouzo. "What happened to the cave?"

"Archeologists arrived and took possession, cordoned off everything. You should go up there. You won't believe it. Looks like a stage set, way they rigged it up, huge lights and all. Bunch of Greeks and Americans. Alcott is in charge, working the dirt with a sieve the way my mother did the flour. Alcott said it'll take forty years to go through the site."

"Good luck to them. Remember you called the cave 'the lair of Satan'? You were right. Anyone who goes near it comes to grief."

"You went there. You survived."

Patronas studied the rheumy old men at the next table. Judging by their weather-beaten faces, they'd once been fishermen. He was like them now, a fisherman who no longer went to sea, his life's work but a memory.

He swallowed what was left of his ouzo. "That's a matter of opinion," he said.

CHAPTER 48

The jug comes to us in turn.
—Greek proverb

AFTER HE WAS fired, Patronas spent a lot of time on the hills behind Profitis Ilias, taking the bus and getting off by the Korres' farm. He explored the area where the corral had been and eventually found other entrances to the cave. The crag proved to be riddled with openings once he knew what to look for. The American archeologist, Alcott, told him the holes would have provided ample natural ventilation for the Minoans living in the space below. Many of the openings were covered with discs, the metal so corroded as to be almost unrecognizable. He assumed the bats left each night through the openings, though he never pinpointed which ones. Alcott suggested the Minoans hadn't built the network of holes themselves. They'd simply taken advantage of the porous quality of the rock and natural shafts left from some prehistoric eruption.

What had they had been so afraid of? Patronas wondered. *These Minoan people? Was it another tidal wave, a second onslaught of water? Or was it man? The Mycenaens perhaps, come to take what little the Minoans had salvaged from their ruined lives? Or had another, more malevolent group of men once haunted these shores?*

In the course of his walks, he'd come to know Alcott well. The American always stopped what he was doing when he saw him and came over to talk to him, pointing out the progress they'd made with the excavation, what they'd discovered and what it meant. They'd occasionally had a beer together and once or twice shared a meal. Patronas had revised his opinion of the American. Aside from his bothersome American heartiness and ridiculous Indiana Jones persona, he seemed to be a pretty good man. Hard working. Passionate. He was even trying to raise funds to build a museum on Chios for the relics he'd found in the cave. 'A tribute to Eleni Argentis,' he told Patronas. 'Something to remember her by.'

Patronas wished he could do the same for Marina. House her in a tomb like the Taj Mahal. He'd even talked it over with Papa Michalis. 'Her children will be her legacy,' the priest had said. 'If you want to honor her, help her husband look after them.'

Alcott had said the Minotaur might actually have existed. 'It wasn't a bull,' he told Patronas, 'but a man, a priest most probably dressed as one.' The acrobatic dancing depicted in the frescoes in Thera, the people riding the bull's horns, had not been a circus or any kind of play. It had been a rite of human sacrifice, ritual blood-letting. Patronas liked the idea. It reminded him of Kleftis, his black wetsuit and camouflage. Evil always had a human face.

⁂

"HOW'D YOU LIKE to come and work for me?" Alcott asked Patronas one evening in the middle of October. They were sitting in a taverna in Chora, drinking *retsina* and eating *mezedakia*.

Patronas speared a meatball. "Doing what?"

"Supervising the security of the site. There's a fortune buried on the hill and we've got twenty local people digging, in addition to the foreign archeologists on the team. You know the people here. You could make sure there's no pilfering from the site."

"That's a lot of responsibility. It's a pretty big place."

"I'll pay you well. Twice as much as you were making as a cop. There's a consortium of American and European universities participating in the excavation here, so I've got plenty of money. If that's not enough, write down your terms and I will try and meet them."

Patronas tried to keep a poker face. He'd never negotiated a salary before. It was like playing cards without the rules, without knowing if aces were high or low—which card to play, which one to hold. "I'd probably be working for you for years, from what you said about the site. Would I get a pension when I finished?" he asked. "I'm not a young man."

"I'm sure it could be arranged."

"What would be the nature of the work? Would I have to sleep there?" Just thinking about spending another night in the cave made Patronas' skin crawl.

"Of course not. I thought you could put a team of men together. Install some security devices. Work in shifts."

"When would you like me to start?"

Alcott smiled. "Tomorrow."

⁂

The priest was wearing an apron, stirring something on the stove, when Patronas returned to the house. At least it wasn't *trahana*. They'd been living on boiled strips of dough, *trahana*, for days now. Apparently the priest saw food not as a reward or expression of God's bounty, but as a penance. And suffer they did, eating one brackish mess after another, every bowlful the color of *mufti*. Patronas had heard the English ate something called 'mushy peas.' To his chagrin, he'd joined them, become a mushy pea eater.

"I'm making *briam*," the priest told him. "Eggplants were on sale at the laiki." He did all the shopping and had proven to be exceedingly cheap, recycling leftovers and adding water to make them go further. He reached for the salt shaker and shook it vigorously over the pan. The lid was loose and more went into the pot than he intended.

"Oops," he said.

Shit, Patronas thought. Tonight it wouldn't be fresh water for dinner, it'd be salt. He'd joked once about the priest's cooking, quoting the Bible, "*I will feed the wormwood and give them water of gall to drink*," but the old man had looked so hurt, he never did it again, eating whatever he put in front of him without complaining. Aside from the priest's limitations in the kitchen, he'd proven to be a good roommate and Patronas had grown fond of him. He cleaned up after himself, listened attentively when Patronas spoke. He'd even wept a little when Patronas described his wife's actions the day Marina was killed.

"You mean it didn't have to happen?" the priest had said, wiping his eyes. "It was an act of malice?"

"That's right. If Dimitra hadn't sent her there, Marina would still be alive."

Patronas still remembered how stricken Papa Michalis had looked. "May God forgive her."

"He's welcome to. I can't."

Patronas had expected the priest to argue with him, to blather about forgiveness and plead Dimitra's case, but he hadn't. He'd just sat there in the growing darkness, looking old and sad.

"I was shaped in iniquity, and in sin did my mother conceive me," he said softly. "The heart is deceitful above all things, and desperately wicked. Who can know it?"

A WEEK LATER DIMITRA returned home. She came in, carrying an armful of groceries, and set about making dinner as if nothing had happened. Patronas thought his new salary was what had drawn her, but Tembelos told him she'd become a pariah among the women on the island and was seeking to restore her good name.

"Wife said there was an incident at the hairdresser's. Women in curlers crowded around her, asking her if it was true, that she'd sent Marina Papoulis to her death. Dimitra says, 'Oh, no, she had nothing to do with it,' but the others, they didn't believe her. 'Why did your husband kick you out then?' one asks. There was a bit of shoving. Words were said. Must have been something. The old cows having at it."

They were making a circuit of the monastery, checking on the workmen. The excavation was like an anthill, alive with dust and noise, the clang of shovels. People were coming and going everywhere, some carrying bubble-wrapped pottery into the makeshift vault he'd created in the refectory, others pouring out buckets of dirt next to the entrance to the cave.

"Tell the truth," Tembelos went on, "nobody liked your wife. She used to lord it over people, bully them. She'd park wherever she wanted and demand store discounts she wasn't entitled to. Caused all kinds of trouble. She thought your job gave *her* special privileges. We used to discuss it, me and the others. Nobody wanted to tell you."

Patronas shook his head. "Hell's a picnic compared with Dimitra."

"You going to stay with her?"

"I don't know." He bent down and picked up a pebble, rolled it over in his hand. "I could divorce her, I guess, but then where would I go? By rights, the house is hers. *I spit high, I spit on my face. I spit low, I spit on my chin.* It will be all right. She'll hold her tongue with a priest there. She'll get the food on the table."

Neither the priest nor Patronas had welcomed Dimitra when she'd turned up the previous night. Patronas requested she sleep in one of the other bedrooms, saying he'd gotten used to sleeping alone at night and didn't want to change. His wife had taken sheets out of the closet and made up the bed without saying a word.

Papa Michalis had been more polite, addressing some of his remarks to her during the course of the evening. But then, he was a priest.

Patronas thought if she wanted to cook and clean for him, a man who despised her, who loathed the very ground she walked on, so be it. At least he wouldn't have to eat the priest's vegetarian slop anymore. No, if Dimitra had demonstrated anything over the years, it was that she was carnivorous.

CHAPTER 49

One swallow does not bring spring.
—Aristotle

PATRONAS LOOKED AROUND Profitis Ilias. He could hear Alcott shouting orders inside the cave. A row of amphorae were being crated up for shipment to Athens, each one being carefully painted with a pair of tiny white numbers by a graduate student. Alcott had been a good boss. He'd given him a lot of responsibility and made good on his pension. He'd even asked Patronas to ferry some of the more valuable jewelry from the cave to the National Museum in Athens. Cops had met Patronas' plane and escorted him across the city in a motorcade. Watching people's heads turn, Patronas had felt like the prime minister. Alcott always promoted Patronas as the one who'd actually found the ruins and arranged for the BBC to interview him about the discovery.

"What do I say?" Patronas had asked him. "The English, for me, it's a struggle."

"How did you feel when you first saw the city?"

"Astonished. I felt astonished. That place, it took my breath away."

"What else?"

"I felt like I could see the people."

"The Minoans?"

Patronas nodded. "I found some toys … a little wagon made out of clay. Some figurines I thought might be dolls. It was like the children were still there, hiding in the shadows."

"That's perfect," Alcott had told him. "That's all you've got to say."

And so Patronas had gone on television, talking about what the English reporter had termed 'the archeological discovery of the century.'

He liked being up on the hill, walking around in the open air with

Tembelos, discussing the finds with Alcott. And then, of course, there was the detective agency Papa Michalis was intent on establishing. Their work hadn't amounted to much so far, mostly accumulating evidence in divorce cases, but the priest had gotten business cards printed up with their names on them and was thinking of renting air time on the local radio station. "We'll call ourselves 'the eyes,' " he'd told Patronas. "Get it? Private eyes, all-seeing eyes." The old man would be crushed if Patronas pulled out now.

⁂

AS PATRONAS HAD predicted, an army of archeologists descended upon Chios from all over the world. A group of German scientists from Heidelberg had even come in their own plane, an ancient Convair, and there were now groups of foreign archeologists digging all over the island. A local resident was building an open air theater behind the cathedral in Chora, planning to stage a sound and light show reenacting Minoan life, and there were rumors of a new hotel going up on the Roussos farm, accommodations for the hundreds of tourists who now wanted to visit the site.

Alcott had divided up the cave. One area belonged to an American university in the Midwest, another to the Sorbonne, still another to the German archeologists from Heidelberg. It was like Berlin after the war, little flags marking each group's domain. Patronas now had a laptop and kept track of everyone allowed access to the site on something called a 'spreadsheet,' which Alcott had created for him. He'd check them in as they entered the cave, check them out again when they exited.

He had counted fifty people that morning when he was down in the cave, fifty people on their hands and knees, shifting soil back and forth, the way his mother had once done with flour. Some test results had come back, and Alcott informed him that the bones in the amphorae were far older than the rest of the artifacts.

"They're at least two hundred years older than anything else in the cave," he said, "according to all the tests we've run on them."

"What does that mean?" Patronas asked.

"If means when they fled Crete or Thera or wherever else they were, these people brought their dead with them."

And so we all do, Patronas thought. *We bring our dead with us wherever we travel, wherever we go. Their bones lay beside us as we sleep. Their eyes look up at us in the faces of our children. Their voices haunt our songs.*

He left the cave and stepped out into the wind. The fields below were barren, the grass of summer withered and gone.

⁂

PATRONAS OCCASIONALLY HAD dinner with Papa Michalis at a tavern by the harbor, inevitably footing the bill. The priest favored the most expensive varieties of fish, claiming they had fewer bones, and always prefaced his main course with five or six appetizers. Shrimp was a special favorite, the larger the better, as was *barbounia*, priced at sixty-four Euros a kilo. In spite of his age, he remained a prodigious eater and would tilt his head and down the smaller ones all in one gulp like a seal.

"Guess who just called me?" Patronas asked him late one night. It was too cold to sit outside and they were huddled at a table in the back near the kitchen. "Evangelos Demos."

Stunned, the priest put down his fork. "Whatever for?"

"To help him with a case."

"Tourist trouble?"

"No. Murder."

Like a dog hearing the sound of his master's voice, the elderly priest sat up a little straighter and leaned forward, his face intent. "Murder?"

He immediately launched into a long, convoluted discussion of the possible forensic techniques Patronas might employ to catch the killer, swabbing the fingernails of the corpse being a prominent one.

"Father," said Patronas gently. "The victim was a child, a seven-year-old boy."

The priest grew very still. "Where?" he finally asked.

"An island called Thanatos."

Greek Vocabulary

Aggelos: Angels
Agglos: Englishman
Aginares a la Polita: Artichokes in the style of Constantinople
Akrotiri: Ancient Minoan city on Santorini. 'The Greek Pompeii'
Anapoda: Backwards
Andreas einai: Literally, 'the men are.' Dismissive expression, as in 'what did you expect?'
Apolektikos: Apoplectic
Apothiki: A closet/storage space
A sto diablo: Go to the devil, equivalent of 'what the hell'
Bougatses: Dessert made of puff pastry and custard
Bourekakia: Appetizer made of eggplants stuffed with cheese and fried
Briam: A vegetable stew
Daskalopetra: Literally 'teacher's rock', a famous landmark on Chios
Dolmadakia: Stuffed vine leaves
Dolmates gemista: Stuffed tomatoes
Drakos: Vampire, monster
Eisai kala: Are you well?
Evlogeitos, H Kyrie: Words from the Orthodox memorial service. Literally, 'bless us, O Lord.'
Engonaki: Grandson
Gafa: Mistake
Galapetras: Literally 'milk stones,' ancient seals with intaglio inscriptions
Geliographia: Cartoons
Horta: Cooked wild greens
Kafenion: Old fashioned Greek coffee shop, patronized only by men
Kalamatino: Circle dance from Kalamata in Peloponnese, popular Greek folk dance
Kale mera: Good day
Kale spera: Good evening
Kamaki: Spearfisherman, a man who picks up women
Kathiki: Vulgar word for chamber pot
Kathighiti: Professor
Kokkoretsi: Grilled intestines, chittlins, offal
Kolopetsomeni: A person whose ass is made of leather

Kommotis: Hairdresser, beauty parlor
Kourabiedes: Special holiday cookies
Kouvetta: Sugared almonds used as favors at baptisms and weddings
Kyria/Kyrie: Mrs., a title of respect
Laderna: Portable musical organ operated by hand
Laiki: Open air market
Loucoumades: Fried dough covered with honey, walnuts and cinnamon
Malia pisgris: Literally 'cotton candy hair,' used to describe hair of the elderly
Meltemi: Wind from the Sahara
Meletzanasalata: Eggplant salad
Meletzanes: Eggplants
Me stravose: They crucified me
Mezes/mezedakia: Assorted appetizers
Miralogia: Rhymed funeral dirges sung by elderly women in rural Greece
Mouvgale to ladi: He/they squeezed the oil out of me
Na zisete: Congratulations
Nuxtaloulouda: Flowers that release their scent at night
Olympiakos: Soccer team of Athens
Ouzo: National drink of Greece, anise flavored and very strong
Paidi Mou: Term of endearment, literally 'my child'
Panageri: Celebration usually held at a church in conjunction with a saint's name day
Panagia Mou: Holy Mother of God, informal, equivalent of 'holy smokes'
Parea: Companionship, friends
Paximadia: Narrow hard-crusted sweetbreads, similar to Biscotti, rusks
Phaistos: Site of ancient Minoan settlement where the disc bearing its name was found
Poustis: Slang for homosexual, equivalent of 'faggot'
Psaria tou Morocco: Fish from Morocco
Psychopathis: Psychopath, psychopathic
Raki: Very powerful Cretan liquor
Refithia keftedes: Meatballs made from garbanzo beans
Retsina: Greek white wine flavored with the resin of pine trees
Rizogalo: Rice pudding
Skordalia: Sauce made of garlic, olive oil, and potatoes
Skylovrise: Nasty remark, literally a 'dog bite'
Smyrneiko: In the style of Smryna, a city in Asia Minor destroyed by the Turks
Striegla: Loud, shrewish woman
Styfado: Stew made of veal and pearl onions and flavored with cinnamon

Svingis: Donuts
Taramasalata: Spread made of fish roe and mashed potatoes
Theotokos: Formal term for the Virgin Mary, used only in church
Ti kaneis: How are you?
Trahana: A primitive pasta made of sourdough, usually cooked in broth
Trelli/Trellos: Derogatory term, 'crazy'
Trigono: Dainty sweets made of filo and nuts in the shape of triangles
Trikkala: Very small three-wheeled truck used in the Greek countryside
Tsipouro: Very powerful liquor from Crete
Varvarus: Barbarian
Vlachos: Moron, imbecile
Vrasta: Boil them!
Xontroulis: Fatso
Xenos/xenii/xenia: Foreigners, strangers
Yeia Sou: The equivalent of hello/greetings

THE DAUGHTER OF an itinerant scientist, **Leta Serafim** was born in Wisconsin and spent the first years of her life in San Diego. Her family moved to Washington, D.C., when NASA was created and her father went to work for that agency. A genuine rocket scientist, he served there for twenty-five years in many capacities—Director of Unmanned Space, Director of Astronomy, Associate Administrator and Chief Scientist—and supervised the American missions to Venus, Mars, Saturn, and Jupiter.

Leta attended Wells College in upstate New York for two years before transferring to George Washington University in Washington, D.C. She graduated with a degree in political science and Russian studies, with a focus on Dostoyevsky, Pasternak and Solzhenitsyn.

While in college, Leta worked at the *Washington Post*, writing obituaries and doing research for the national desk. She left to join the staff of the *Los Angeles Times* Washington Bureau. Following her marriage to a Greek national, Philip Serafim, Leta moved to Athens, where she taught art at home while raising her daughters, Amalia and Annie.

When Leta moved back to the United States seven years later, she wrote for the local papers and sporadically for the *Boston Globe*. Her mother began to lose her sight from glaucoma around this time, and disturbed by her plight, Leta went to work as Executive Director of the Massachusetts Society of Eye Physicians and Surgeons. Determined to educate the public about this disease, she designed and launched multiple media campaigns: posters on public transportation, billboards throughout the city, radio and television announcements, cable shows, etc. She received many awards for this program and served in a similar capacity as Public Health Director for the New England Ophthalmological Society, the oldest specialty organization in the United States.

Leta spends at least one month every year in Greece and has visited over twenty-five islands. She paints in both oils and acrylics, etches, cooks—she's mastered many native cuisines, but her main focus is Greek—and volunteers on a weekly basis as a tutor in an MIT-sponsored ESL program.

The Devil Takes Half is her first novel, and the first book in the Greek Islands Mystery series. Coffeetown Press will also be publishing her work of historical fiction, *To Look on Death No More*.

You can find her online at www.letaserafim.com.